WHISKEY RIVER

Also by Loren D. Estleman

BLOODY SEASON

PEEPER

WHISKEY RIVER

Loren D. Estleman

BANTAM BOOKS
NEW YORK • TORONTO • LONDON • SYDNEY • AUCKLAND

WHISKEY RIVER

A Bantam Book / October 1990

Design by Kathryn Parise.

LIBRARY OF CONGRESS CATALOGING-IN-PUBLICATION DATA
Estleman, Loren D.
Whiskey River / by Loren D. Estleman.
p. cm.
ISBN 0-553-07042-8
I. Title.
PS3555.S84W47 1990
813'.54—dc20 90-32895
CIP

Published simultaneously in the United States and Canada

Bantam Books are published by Bantam Books, a division of Bantam Doubleday Dell Publishing Group, Inc. Its trademark, consisting of the words "Bantam Books" and the portrayal of a rooster, is Registered in U.S. Patent and Trademark Office and in other countries. Marca Registrada. Bantam Books, 666 Fifth Avenue, New York, New York 10103.

PRINTED IN THE UNITED STATES OF AMERICA

To my father, Leauvett Estleman,
who told the stories

CAVEAT LECTOR

With notable exceptions—the killing of Jerry Buckley, the Collingwood Massacre, the recall of Mayor Charles Bowles and succeeding election of Frank Murphy, the McDonald murder-suicide, and the 1939 Ferguson-O'Hara grand jury investigation of the Detroit Police Department, as well as other incidents and people referred to but not seen—the characters and events depicted herein are fictional. There was no Jack Dance, no Joey Machine, no Sal Borneo, or Frankie Orr; saddest of all, there was no Connie Minor. But people like them existed in the city, and the situation in Detroit during the years 1919–1939 was as reported. All other characters and events except those suggested by figures and incidents in places other than Detroit are products of the author's imagination and any resemblance to actual persons living or dead is coincidental.

It is simply not possible to tell the truth about the past. My grandmother has become an angel; she couldn't possibly have been.

—EDWARD G. ROBINSON

The first day: September 25, 1939

The special prosecutor reminded him of Old Man Prohibition in the old cartoons, only younger: tall and gangling, longish black hair plastered back with water, a razor-slash of mouth in a narrow face with a lantern jaw and eyes set too close together. Only the stovepipe hat was missing. Trouble was he could never tell Old Man Prohibition from John Barleycorn as the cartoonists drew them. Maybe nobody could, and that was the source of the trouble.

He swore on the Bible, that anomalous ceremony wherein Church and State were wedded in perpetuity, and sat down in the box, experiencing anew that radical change of perceptions, as if he were looking down the wrong end of a telescope; and although there was no gallery, just the judge (one-man grand jury, to put the fine point on it, but a sworn judge notwithstanding and seated behind the high bench) and a paunchy old granite-eyed bailiff with a big revolver behind his hipbone and a young court recorder with a brush cut and freckles on the backs of his hands, he felt like a germ on a microscope slide. The judge had white hair with black sidewalls and wild hairs in his heavy eyebrows that swayed like feelers in the breeze from the electric fan on the railing.

"Please state your full name and occupation," said the special prosecutor.

"Connie Minor." He corrected himself: "Constantine Alexander Minor. I'm an advertising copywriter."

"You're a former journalist, is that correct?"

"Yes, I worked for the *Times* and the *Banner* and wrote a column for the Continental News Syndicate."

"Do you know why you received a subpoena to testify before this grand jury?"

"You're investigating allegations of misconduct in the police department. I assume you think I know something about the subject, but I don't."

"We're also looking into crimes perpetrated by certain well-known underworld figures in Detroit, some of whom have been mentioned several times in the course of these proceedings. I believe you're familiar with Salvatore Bornea, alias Sal Borneo, and Francis Xavier Oro, alias Frankie Orr?"

"Slightly. I met them both once."

"Your name was given to us by Miss Celestine Brown, Negro, who testified here last week. Do you know her?"

"I met her on two occasions."

"You knew her late Negro companion, Bass Springfield?"

"I did."

"You're aware of the circumstances of his death?"

"I am."

"You were acquainted with Springfield's associates, Charles Austin Camarillo, Andrew V. Kramm, and John Danzig, alias Jack Dance?"

They sounded like nothing more than people's names in the relentless prosecutorial mouth. It was a warm day for late September and the fan, oscillating to right and left like a reptile's head, looped cool air over the back of his neck once every forty seconds, drying the sweat that formed there in the intervals between.

"I knew all of them."

"You're aware of the circumstances of the deaths of Dance and Camarillo?"

"I was present when they were killed."

"Indeed? That isn't what you told the police. We have the report."

"There's a great deal I didn't tell the police."

"Why not?"

"You've been investigating them for five weeks. You should know the answer to that question."

"I see nothing to joke about, Mr. Minor. Official corruption is serious business."

"Also a high-paying one."

"Are you prepared to share your knowledge with the grand jury?"

"All of it?"

"Unless you have Fifth Amendment reasons for not doing so."

He glanced at the young recorder. "If I used them I'd sound like a thug."

"All citizens are protected by the Bill of Rights, Mr. Minor, not just thugs."

"You say that and I believe you, but what I see is a headline saying 'Minor Takes Fifth.' It would wash me up as a newspaperman in this town. I don't want to write ad copy forever."

"Our concern is truth. It should be yours as well. Now, are you or are you not refusing to share your knowledge at this time of crimes committed in Detroit during your career as a journalist under your Fifth Amendment rights guaranteeing you protection from self-incrimination?"

The motion of the special prosecutor's lips, or rather the edges of his mouth since he appeared to have no lips, fascinated him. It reminded him of the up-and-down chopping of the cutters that separated the long printed sheets into pages as they came off the presses.

"No, I guess not."

"Then tell us about your relationship with Jack Dance."

"The whole relationship?"

"If you would. As a matter of fact, I insist."

"I hope you brought your lunch, counselor."

PART ONE

1928–1930

The Black Bottom

We have the biggest of nearly everything: the tallest building, the biggest electric sign, the longest bridge, the most money . . .

—*Detroit City Directory*,
1925–26 edition

The "blind pig" conditions are worse in every way than in any other town I visited, and the liquor sold is of a ruinous quality.

—Ernest W. Mandeville,
"Detroit Sets a Bad Example,"
Outlook, April 1925

Chapter One

I saw Jack Dance the first time in Hattie Long's place on Vernor the night the bulls tipped it over. I guess he was going by John Danzig at the time.

Hattie hadn't been renting the place long. I remember my hack and I drove up and down the East Side for almost an hour looking for the stuffed rooster in the window. The rooster went everywhere Hattie went and it was how you could tell where she was set up on any particular night. For all the bulls cared most of the time, she could have advertised in the *Free Press*, but Hattie always had a keener sense of the proprieties than any of the auto-money hags in Grosse Pointe. Last I heard she was running a beergarden in Royal Oak or somewhere. I heard she lost her looks.

The rooster this time was in a window on the ground floor of a house with an undertaker's sign out front. She sublet it to the digger during the day and stored the liquor in coffins in back. The joke that made the rounds ran that you could get a bier in the daytime and a beer at night.

I sent the hack on his way and went in through the front. Although the side door was customary in those places, this one was five feet wide and meant for carrying out the stiffs, and not many cared to use it. We were superstitious in those days.

Hattie had about an hour between the time the mortuary closed and she opened for the night, but you'd have thought she had a week. The burgundy velvet curtain that separated the entryway from the slumber room had been pushed back, tables and chairs set in place, and a cherrywood bar with a brass footrail erected on the platform where in all probability a corpse had lain in state that afternoon. In place of the stand where visitors signed in stood two antique slot machines weighing two hundred pounds apiece. The bartender, whose name was Johnston, had on a white apron and a red bow tie on a shirt with garters. He parted his hair in the middle and waxed his handlebars like in pre-Prohibition days, but there wasn't anything affected about it because he'd been mixing drinks for forty years; his favorite boast was that he had once served a pink gin to Bat Masterson. Nobody ever called him on it, not with a faded sepia photograph of a young Johnston sparring with Jim Jeffries tacked to the wall behind the bar. The place smelled of needle beer and Lifebuoy soap from the cribs on the second floor and "Ramona" was playing on a wind-up Victrola by the big door. Hattie hated jazz.

This kid—I guessed he was twenty, but it turned out later he was barely eighteen—was leaning on the bar with his back to me, watching something. I noticed him because of his size and because the pants of the brown suit he had on were swinging a good three inches shy of his big wingtips. He was built like a lug and if I hadn't seen his face a minute later I'd have thought he was older still.

"How's the boy, Johnnie?" I asked Johnston, clearing a space for my elbows next to the kid. The bars were always crowded in places where there was no one to wait tables, with two full glasses in front of each beer drinker in case the kegs ran out.

"What'll it be?" Johnston wasn't much for the small talk.

I skidded a half-dollar across the bar and told him the usual. He poured two fingers of Old Log Cabin into a tumbler half full of Vernor's—Vernor's on Vernor, that's how I remember where the blind pig was.

The kid had turned around and looked at me when I said "Johnnie"—they were still calling him John then as I said—and that's when I found out he was a kid. He had some baby fat, and curly black hair that needed cutting. It would still need cutting years later when he had a Duesenberg and a tailor to make sure his cuffs came to his shoes. That night he looked like one of the big Polish line workers from Hamtramck that got tired of buying their boilermakers from a parked car in front of Dodge Main and came downtown. They were all youngsters.

He lost interest in me when he figured out I wasn't addressing him and returned his attention to the other end of the bar, where a shrimp in a cloth cap and a green tweed suit too heavy for the weather stood fishing in his pants pockets. He came up with a quarter and put it on the bar. Johnston filled a schooner with beer from the keg and set it down directly on top of the quarter. The shrimp put a hand on his cap, tipped down the beer in one easy installment, belched dramatically, set down the empty schooner, and put the coin back in his pocket. Then he went out past the velvet curtain. He was weaving a little.

"Who is that guy?" the kid asked Johnston.

"What guy?" The bartender swept the glass off the bar and plunged it into a washtub full of soapy water at his feet.

"The little guy. I been watching him for an hour. Every time he comes back from the toilet he slaps a two-bit piece on the bar, you draw him a beer, he drinks it, and puts away his money. I seen him drink six beers and you never took the two-bit piece once. Who's he, the mayor?"

"Jerry the Lobo." Johnston shook the suds off the schooner and wiped it dry with his towel.

"Lobo like in wolf? He looks more like a rat. I seen him try to pick a guy's pocket. He got his hand slapped."

"Not lobo like in wolf," I said. "Lobo like in lobotomy."

The kid looked at me with more interest this time. I tapped my forehead. "Croakers in Jackson cut a piece out of his brain. He was a first-class pickpocket when they sent him up the last time. They did it to relieve him of his criminous intentions. Didn't work. He's still a pickpocket; he's just not too good at it anymore."

"Bullshit."

"You can see the scar when he takes the cap off."

"They *do* that?"

"Only if you volunteer. They knocked time off his sentence for it. Anyway, that's why no bartender I know will take his quarter. They feel sorry for him."

"It's always the same quarter?"

"Far as I know."

"Hell, I'd do better than that. If I had a gun I'd put him out of his misery."

I never forgot that, what Jack Dance said about putting Jerry the Lobo out of his misery. Maybe I would have, except that time in Hattie's was the last time I saw Jerry. He disappeared soon after.

The kid stuck out a right hand the size of a bucket. "I'm John Danzig."

"Jew?"

"What if I am?" He drew back the hand.

"Don't get your balls in an uproar, junior. I'm Greek myself." I offered him mine. "Connie Minor."

"Connie?"

"Short for Constantine. Some civil jerk at Ellis Island changed the old man's name from Minos."

He took my hand then. His was softer than I'd expected. He wasn't using it to pull any levers at the Dodge plant. For all that I felt a crackle when we made contact. It was like petting a cat on a dry winter day. "You work here, Connie?"

"Just on this highball. I write for the *Times*."

"No kidding? Who owns this joint, Connie?"

"You thinking of buying it?" I was sore about the way he'd dismissed my profession with two words. Most people were curious about it. Radio was boring as hell then and people got most of their entertainment from movies and the tabloids.

"I'm looking for a job," he said.

"What do you do?"

"Right now I help out my old man in his shop. He repairs watches. My fingers are too big, though. Also I like to see. My old man's eyes started to go when he was thirty. He's almost blind, my old man."

I wanted to laugh. If he'd ever called his father "my old man" before that night, he'd probably gotten slapped silly. Except for his size he made me think of a squirt trying to talk his way in with the big kids.

"Well, you came to the right place," I said. "They don't fix watches here."

"Fresh transfusion, sport?" Johnston asked the kid.

He put a hand around his half-empty schooner, which he'd obviously forgotten about. "One's the limit."

"We sell drinks here. We don't rent glasses."

The kid dug around inside his pockets and came up with a handful of lint. I bounced a quarter off the bar. Johnston caught it and set a full glass next to the first one.

"Thanks," said the kid. "I really do stop at one."

"Johnston doesn't care if you drink it. His mother told him if he didn't use his bar space she'd give it to the Albanians."

"You didn't say who owns the place."

"Ask Hattie."

Hattie was coming our way from the back where they dressed and painted the stiffs. She was five-two but looked taller because she was so slender, and the drop-waisted flapper dresses she wore added to the impression of height. She was a strawberry blonde, bobbed and marcelled, with a broad forehead, a chin that came to a point, and a mouth that was a little too wide for the beestung lips that Mae Murray was making famous in the movies. Her eyebrows were big surprised circles of thin pencil. The gamblers at the *Times* were betting she traced them around Mason lids, but I'd seen her draw them on with only the aid of a mirror. Hattie and I went back a few. I remember how calm she looked that night, with all hell breaking loose upstairs and about to come barreling through the front door.

I was in the middle of introducing the kid to her when she put a hand on my arm. "Connie, I need to borrow you."

I gave the kid the high sign and walked off with her a few steps. She looped her arm through mine.

"They put strychnine in my best whiskey," she said. "I've got a dead justice of the peace upstairs and an Oklahoma oilman throwing up in the toilet."

"What brand?" I'd been swilling Old Log Cabin for ten minutes.

"Stop worrying about yourself. You don't think I serve this radiator juice to the guests upstairs."

"Who did it?"

"The Purples, the Little Jewish Navy, who cares? I've got to get these slot machines out of here before the bulls come and smash them to pieces. They're worth more than what's inside them."

"Did you call Joey?"

"It'll take Joey's people twenty minutes to get here. I need muscle now."

We were standing in front of one of the machines, a baroque nightmare in worked bronze with claw feet and a lever the size of a mop handle. I put my arms around it and heaved. The back legs came up an inch. I let it fall back with a crash. The record on the Victrola skipped a beat; one less fucking boop-boop-a-doo.

"You still need muscle," I said. "I haven't lifted anything heavier than a paragraph since I left the loading dock. What's wrong with Johnston?"

"He's got a hernia older than I am."

"This is your lucky night. That big kid at the bar's looking for work."

She glanced that way. The kid was glaring at Jerry the Lobo, who had just come back from the toilet and was playing the gag with the quarter again.

"Can we trust him?"

"Honey, you can't trust me. I came here looking for a story. One poisoned j.p. in a whorehouse could get me my own column."

"How you going to write it with ten broken fingers?"

I watched her. Hattie never smiled. If she ever told a joke no one knew it. "Even Joey Machine wouldn't touch a member of the press."

"How long you know Joey?" she said. "What's the kid's name?"

"John something. He's a sheeny."

"Well, he don't look like a Purple. Let's go talk to him."

That was how Jack Dance got in with the Machine mob, although he didn't know it at the time. Joey Machine had a part interest in most of the better blind pigs and hook shops on the East Side and owned Hattie Long's establishment outright. The kid listened to as much of the tale as Hattie told and said he'd be glad to help. He was smart enough not to impose conditions. All his life Jack Dance was a creature of instinct and it never let him down until the last.

"My brother can help," he said, and added: "He's a poet."

I didn't know what that had to do with anything, but we accompanied the kid to a table where a sandy-haired sheik in his twenties was talking with one of Hattie's girls over a bottle of gin with a Canadian label and a Dearborn ancestry. His suit was a better fit than his brother's but it was strictly Hudson's basement just the same. There was no family resemblance that I could see. He was built along slighter lines and his complexion was fair. I wondered if they were just close friends who considered themselves related, like the coloreds; but the kid introduced him as Tom Danzig.

"Your brother says you're a poet," Hattie said.

He played with his glass and never drank from it all the time we were there. The two had that in common at least. "I'm trying to be a writer. John thinks everyone who writes is a poet."

Hattie said, "All we need is a strong back. I don't care if you can rhyme."

He was slower to volunteer than his brother. On that short acquaintance I could see he was the thinker of the team, measuring everything against the consequences and what it meant to him. I don't know why that irritated me. With all the things Jack did later and everything he became I always liked him, and I never liked Tom. But then I gave up trying to figure myself out years ago.

Finally he agreed to lend a hand. Hattie told Johnston, who left the bar and trundled the big White truck they used for a moving van around to the side door, and with Hattie directing us to look out for the handles and gimcrackery the three of us carried out the slot machines. We got the truck doors closed just as the sirens came within hearing. Whoever had poisoned the whiskey had given the stuff time to take effect before placing his anonymous call to the bulls. It turned out to be just time enough for us. The Danzig brothers and I were sharing a table and a bottle inside with Hattie tending bar when Lieutenant Valery Kozlowski showed up with the walking sputum from the Detroit Prohibition Squad.

Chapter Two

A couple of years ago Chet Mooney, who held down the police beat at the *News*, wrote a book about the dry time in Detroit in which he claimed that Dusty Steinhauser had once offered a $1000 reward for the assassination of Valery Kozlowski. I asked Dusty about it in the tailor shop he ran after Repeal broke up his Little Jewish Navy. I couldn't use the one-word answer he gave me in the paper, but I did run his explanation: "If I had the grand to spare I'd of gave it to Kozlowski and then I wouldn't of had to offer no reward." Chet Mooney always was full of banana oil. The book, which carried a foreword by J. Edgar Hoover, sold out quickly.

I never minded Kozlowski. He was six feet and two hundred sixty pounds of hard fat in a fedora and a rubber raincoat, an ambulatory sneer with a cold stogie pegged into a corner of his mouth—just the kind of arrogant bull we liked to rag in the columns, only we didn't much in his case. It was an open secret in the newspaper community that the lieutenant was supporting a wife bedridden by polio, which gave him a better reason than most to rake off what he could. We didn't like him, but we understood him; and I at least was sorry when that psychotic bitch Janet McDonald took him down from beyond the grave.

There wasn't much original about the way he came into Hattie's that night. A uniform gnawed through the heavy door with a fire axe and Kozlowski stepped inside, kicking aside a splintered panel with one of his ridiculous Size Sixes; he always looked about to fall off his tiny feet.

The uniforms attacked the fixtures with axes and wrecking tools while he embroidered a graceful path through the scattering patrons up to the bar. A crowbar struck the center of the table the Danzigs and I were seated around and it fell apart in two halves. We got up.

"Where's Johnston?" Kozlowski asked Hattie.

"He's down with the influenza." She brought up the Dutch Masters box Johnston had been making change from all night and shoved it across the bar. Kozlowski pocketed the bills without counting them and left the coins. "Get the Victrola," he shouted over the noise. A moment later an axe split the turntable and Helen Morgan stopped singing with a shriek.

"I hear you're selling liquor with a boot in it tonight," Kozlowski said.

"We only sell the best."

"How many dead?"

"I don't run the funeral parlor," Hattie said. "Come back in the morning."

This went on for a little. The lieutenant had three plainclothesmen with him, two of whom were staving in the kegs behind the bar and letting the beer gush out in a yellow stream. Hattie let it foam around her shoes. The third detective, a sergeant named Wagner, stood watching the destruction with his hands in his pockets and a wide moronic grin on his narrow face. He was hatless, with his black hair brilliantined back Valentino style and a long loose jaw clustered with acne. Of all the subhumans on the Prohibition Squad, Wagner was the easiest to despise, a hophead who loved to watch things come apart without getting a smudge on his peaked lapels. Rumor had it he was into a Beaubien Street pusher for twice what the city paid him annually.

At length Hattie came around from behind the bar and squelched upstairs. Kozlowski told Wagner to keep an eye on things down there and followed her. I went that way. When the brothers started to accompany me I shook my head. They stayed behind. Jack was still taking advice then.

There were four bedrooms and a full bath on the second floor. The door to the bath stood open, and inside a big brick-colored Indian with his hair in a queue was kneeling in front of the toilet heaving. He was naked as a jaybird and hung like a horse.

The room stank of sweat and half-digested whiskey. After ten seconds I felt like joining him.

Kozlowski, lighting his stogie, chuckled. "Well, he won't need no stomach pump. What do they call you, Chief?" He flipped the match over the Indian's shoulder into the toilet. It hit the water with a spitting sound.

The sick man turned up a tragic face with unfocused eyes and a thread of vomit dangling from his chin. There was no room for comprehension there.

"He's from Oklahoma," Hattie said, apropos of nothing. "We don't ask them their names."

"Horseshit." Kozlowski produced a pair of handcuffs from his hip pocket, hooked one of the manacles around the Indian's left wrist braced on the edge of the bowl, and snapped the other around the pipe that ran up to the gravity tank. He patted the Indian's shoulder. "Stay put till we get back, Geronimo."

"What did he do?"

The lieutenant appeared to notice me for the first time. He had a mole at the bridge of his nose that looked like a third brown eye. "Who the hell are you?"

I showed him my police pass. His lips moved as he read it.

"The scribe from the *Times*. I remember now. You broke the story on the Rosenstein kidnapping, right?"

"Doug Keenan at the *Free Press* broke it. I was at the First Precinct when Rosenstein walked in free as lunch." I pointed at the Indian. "So far the only thing he's guilty of is tossing his jerky into a private facility. Why cuff him?"

"Just marking my place. Where's the cold stuff?" he asked Hattie.

She led the way to a door at the end of the hall and unlocked it. Up there the splintering and crashing below sounded remote, like a simulated sports broadcast on WXYZ. I wondered where Hattie's girls had gone. Their communications system was better than Detroit Bell's.

The room was a shoebox with a bed on a painted iron frame and a window looking out on a Pierce-Arrow sign. The dead man tangled in the sheets wore only a pair of boxer shorts gone gray from many washings. He lay half on his back with his scrawny legs twisted around each other and one hand clenching the mattress, yellow batting bulging out between the fingers. His eyes were half open and glittering, and all his teeth were exposed in a rictus wide enough to show they were false. He was bald with a white fringe. Someone had opened the window to vent the stench from his voided bowels, but the air was thick with it just the same.

"Strychnine," declared Kozlowski, chewing hard on his cigar. "It always makes them grin like Fairbanks. Anybody else?"

"Just him," Hattie said.

"Who was with him?"

"Lorraine. You need her?"

"Don't know yet." An empty glass and a bottle of Hiram Walker's stood on the nightstand. He lifted each and sniffed at it, then ran a finger down the inside of the glass and touched it to his tongue. He saw my expression and fashioned a rictus of his own.

"My grandmama used to dose my papa with strychnine when he went off his feed," he said. "Gives you an appetite if it don't croak you first. Also it's bitter as a drain crystal. This guy must of had tin tastebuds."

Hattie said, "The Indian spit his out."

"One lucky redskin."

The dead man's clothes, consisting of a black wool suit, a white shirt, and a knitted black tie, were draped neatly over the back of a wooden chair. Kozlowski found nothing in the coat and went through the pants. He drew out a battered brown leather billfold and opened it.

" 'Abel S. Turner, Justice of the Peace.' Looks like he found some." He glanced at the pictures in the other celluloid windows, then thumbed through the bills in the money compartment and put them in his pocket. Finally he returned the billfold to the pants and dropped them on the seat of the chair. "What was Oklahoma drinking?"

"Hiram's. I opened a fresh case tonight."

"Where'd you get it?"

"It was part of last week's shipment."

"The Roost?"

"Riopelle."

"Who handled it?"

"Couple of Joey's boys made the delivery. I knew them both. I don't know who was on the boat."

It was the kind of conversation I could never have written up in a way readers of the *Times* would have understood: a sworn officer of the law asking an East Side madam about her illegal liquor operation, the madam answering, and nobody getting arrested. If you want the real reason why the lid stayed on as long as it did, it was because nobody wanted to look like he'd just found out about it. Remember, it took a fresh kid to tell the emperor his ass was hanging out.

"Get rid of it and everything else that came that day," Kozlowski told Hattie. "Pour it down the sewer."

"Don't you want it for evidence?" I asked.

He looked at me with all three eyes. "Who am I talking to, you or your sheet?"

"Just me. I like my fingers the way they are."

"Evidence ain't worth shit if you don't make an arrest. For all I know the stuff was poisoned before it left Canada. You ever try talking to a Mountie?"

"If I did I'd remember."

"Well, for starters they wear Sam Browne belts with their pajamas."

Hattie said, "You know it was poisoned on this side."

He relit his stogie, which had gone out. I welcomed the reek of nickel tobacco in that room. "How's Joey getting on with the Sicilians?" he asked her.

"Okay. You know the Sicilians."

"That makes it the Jews. We'll do a sweep, stick 'em under the light. They'll get a tan and we'll kick them. It'll be like election time."

"Why bother?"

"It's no bother. I like to hear them kikes squeal when I shove my stick into their bellies."

"This is a homicide beef," I said. "Who called the Prohibition Squad?"

"On nights like this there ain't much difference."

Homicide never did get the Turner killing. It went into the jacket unsolved. The various police divisions in those days were like feudal fiefdoms, and unless it was a case nobody wanted—a nigger killing in the Black Bottom, say, or a little girl raped with a Coke bottle in the warehouse district—it went to whoever got there first. Pulling the file on an old case required a scavenger hunt throughout the Criminal Investigation Division.

"What about the Indian?" Hattie asked.

"I logged a raid. I need a body besides just personnel and the j.p. here."

"Take Connie. It wouldn't be the first time he ate on the county."

"I did my charity work tonight," I reminded her. "Besides, I've got four hours left in my shift."

She glared up at the lieutenant. "What did I buy downstairs? They rescinded the tipover order three years ago. You need a warrant."

"We was told there was lives in danger here. I could of called the county wagon, put bracelets on the clientele, get their names printed in the papers. How many you think would come back, with twenty thousand blind pigs in this city?"

A shot slammed below. The noises of destruction stopped.

Kozlowski said shit. "That bug Wagner. Last time he put a slug clear through a keg and hit my best man." He drew a stubby black revolver from his belt holster and hit the hallway running. We followed him.

It was hard to see at first on the ground floor. When the two-legged termites had finished with the fixtures and furniture they had started on the walls, and a cloud of yellow plaster filled the room. As it settled I saw John Danzig standing in the center of a circle of bulls. They had their guns out in the firing-range stance, pointing at his head. He looked like the hub of a spoked wheel. Sergeant Wagner lay on his back at the kid's feet with his knees drawn up, rocking from side to side and clasping the bottom half of his face with both hands. One of them held a revolver. Blood was sliding out between his fingers.

Tom Danzig stood outside the circle with his arms hanging loose. Jerry the Lobo slid a hand into Tom's pocket and was pushed away.

The lieutenant threw down his cigar. It extinguished itself immediately in the tide of beer washing back and forth across the floor. "What."

"This puke took a swing at Wagner." The speaker was a fat plainclothesman much softer than Kozlowski, in spectacles and a straw boater out of season.

"Looks like he connected. Who shot?"

"Wagner."

"Son of a bitch was waving it in my face." The kid had both fists clenched but looked peaceful otherwise. A lock of his dark curly hair had fallen over one eye. I think he was enjoying himself.

Kozlowski nudged Wagner roughly with his foot. "What'd you hit?"

"My nofe if bufted," Wagner said through his hands.

"It went into the ceiling," one of the uniforms said. "His piece went off when the kid poked him."

Kozlowski booted Wagner in the ribs hard. The sergeant whinnied, spraying blood. "You bastard, I was up there."

Fatso said, "The puke was acting smart, Lieutenant."

Kozlowski gnawed a cheek.

"Clear a space," he said. "Get away from him, for chrissake. He ain't Leopold and Loeb."

The bulls backed off, lowering their weapons. Kozlowski holstered his revolver, then put a hand inside the right slash pocket of his raincoat and drew it out as a fist. He took two steps and stood in front of the kid, who had half an inch on him. The brim of the lieutenant's hat was almost touching the kid's forehead. He slid his knuckles up and down the raincoat's lapel restlessly. "What's your name?"

"John Danzig."

"You a kike?"

"What?"

"A hebe. A yid. A sheeny. A goddamn pork-avoiding Christ-killer."

"What if I am?"

They were the same words he'd said to me, but the lieutenant wasn't having any. I didn't see his fist leave his lapel. The crack was as sharp and as loud as the pistol shot earlier. The kid staggered back into one of the bulls standing behind him, who shoved him away. He fell down on one knee, got up, and fell again, pitching forward from the toes. That was the end of it. I'd lost enough money on the fights to know they don't get up again once they go down on their face.

His brother didn't move then or later. He was the thinker as I said.

Lieutenant Kozlowski flipped the little sap he'd had hidden in his fist and returned it to his pocket. Then he unhooked a small key from the chain attached to his belt. "Run upstairs and cut loose the Indian, son," he said, handing it to me. "We got our body."

He was instructing someone to call it in from the box on the corner when I ascended out of earshot.

I didn't see Jack Dance again for two years. He was using his new name then and it was hard to believe he'd ever been off his feet.

and the war they had invented with Spain in 1898. Worse, he was a teetotaler. It did little for my journalistic pride to beat the *News*'s goddamn autogiro to the scene of some riverfront bloodbath only to see my account sandwiched between a gushing review of Marion Davies's latest costume epic and an editorial in favor of the Women's Christian Temperance Union. After three years at the same stand the soles of my feet were starting to crawl.

I was neglecting the free lunch at the House of All Nations for the butcher job a night editor had done on a piece of mine when a compact towhead in a neat gray double-breasted hung his overcoat and hat on the hook next to mine. It was January 1930, the room was overheated, and I could feel the cold wafting off the navy cashmere. He was smiling down at me when I glanced up from the newspaper.

"Connie Minor, isn't it?"

I looked quickly at his hands. He wasn't holding any papers, so I said it was Connie Minor all right.

"I'm Howard Wolfman."

"You're kidding."

"No," he said simply. "They told me at the *Times* you'd be here. Is it all right if I sit down?"

I flicked a hand toward the seat facing mine. It wasn't the trick name that threw me; I'd heard of Howard Wolfman. If I'd been expecting him I would have been looking for sweaty armpits, a beer gut, and gin on his breath. Someday maybe I'll learn not to write the story until I've met its subject. The man who sat down opposite me in the booth was a natty little albino with thin white hair combed down on his forehead and pink eyes like a rabbit's behind gold-rimmed glasses. I folded the newspaper and laid it aside.

"The *Times* told *you* where to find me?"

"I didn't exactly tell them who I was." He inclined his head toward the paper. "Good story on the Windsor Tunnel."

"It was before they got to it."

He caught the bartender's eye and made a circle with his forefinger. Two fresh beers were brought. Wolfman turned down the lunch. "Are you familiar with the *Banner*?"

"The stands are always out."

He turned, slid a rolled newspaper from the pocket of his dangling overcoat, and spread it out on the table facing me.

It was half the size of the broadsheet *Times* and printed on coarse

Chapter Three

Where to start.

Wide-Open Detroit was just yesterday, but so much has happened between then and now that it all seems like a half-pleasant dream that needs analyzing.

We had a jump on the rest of the country in the bootlegging department for two simple reasons: 1. Ontario, Canada, which was also dry but permitted the manufacture of liquor for export, was only three minutes away across the Detroit River; 2. Michigan went dry a full year before the Volstead Act prohibiting the sale and consumption of alcoholic beverages kicked in across the United States. By the time New York and Chicago got into the business, Detroit had rumrunning down to a science.

Not that there were many white coats involved. Although the practical Poles were mixing the stuff in their bathtubs in Hamtramck and selling it in Mason jars out of their car trunks on Joseph Campau, the main traffic was on the river. There the fastest boats in maritime history ran Coast Guard blockades to deliver crates of whiskey and barrels of beer to Cadillacs and Lincolns waiting on the docks in Ecorse—Robbers' Roost, the locals had christened that stretch along Jefferson Avenue—and at the foot of Riopelle Street in Detroit proper. The demand always exceeded the supply, and the supply was greater than in the days when it was legal. Everyone, it seemed, was in the liquor business. You could stand before an anonymous apartment house on Michigan Avenue or Gratiot and guess how many windows belonged to blind pigs, just like the suckers who lined up in front of J. L. Hudson's downtown to estimate how many marbles resided in the big jar in the display window and win a new Packard. Some experts said there were twenty thousand illegal drinking establishments in the city. Others said it was more like twenty-five thousand. There could have been a million. They didn't register at the Wayne County courthouse.

The city was growing fit to be tied, only you had to catch it first. America was on wheels and Detroit supplied the motors. Art deco buildings sprang up downtown like gothic toadstools; from 1923 to 1928 you couldn't walk a straight path across the Grand Circle in the heart of the business district without tripping over a hundred sawhorses. It was a red-bandanna town with white-collar dreams, and when a Sunday driver who wore coveralls during the week put-putted past the great pink-and-white marble mansions on Lake Shore Drive, instead of shaking his fist, he thought of the day when he'd occupy one just like them. Hadn't Henry Ford begun as a machinist's apprentice?

That placid certainty, that today was better than yesterday and tomorrow would be better still, stumbled in 1927, when Ford discontinued the Model T. That decision ended the beetle-black little chugchug's twenty-four-year reign, forced production cutbacks at the factory in Dearborn, and led to the layoff of thousands of foreigners, hillbillies, and coloreds, who had come swarming in like grease-stained bees toward the promise of five dollars a day and a company-owned home. It went down for the count on October 29, 1929—although most of us west of the New York Stock Exchange wouldn't get the message until the ripples from Black Tuesday reached us across Lake Erie a year later. Even then nobody thought things would get as bad as Lewis machine guns mounted atop the Rouge plant for the purpose of mowing down striking laborers.

Detroit was a night town then, trading overalls and work shoes for seersucker and black patent leather when the sun went down somewhere beyond Inkster. Dancing the Charleston and Detroit's own Black Bottom at the Arcadia Ballroom on Woodward, checking out Gloria Swanson and John Gilbert at the Oriole Terrace on East Grand, lapping up real nigger jazz, down and dirty, on Hastings Street, and drinking—always drinking, from hip flasks and coffee mugs, crystal flutes and clay pots, silver cups and the hollow handles of trick umbrellas. You could pass the pint around at Navin Field while watching Ty Cobb hit and Dutch Leonard pitch, or you could put on the dog and

sip champagne at the Polar Bear Cafe in Ecorse and hear Fran
Trumbauer and Bix Beiderbecke hotting up the band to cover
noise of Piejacki's Navy unloading Ontario's finest on the dock be
the dining room. There, and all along the riverfront they called Mi
gan's Barbary Coast, broken noses lined up with highbrows and
hard-eyed young killers who ran with the Purple Gang rubbed sh
ders with the sheiks who greased their hair down like Ramon Nova
and the hennaed shebas who tried to look like Theda Bara in pe
and fringe, not to forget the occasional city councilman. In 19
scribe at the New York *Times* wrote an article estimating the an
profits of Detroit's three top industries as follows: Automob
$2,000,000; Chemicals, $90,000,000; Liquor, $215,000,000. B
Blake sang it, and others joined in:

> When I start makin' money, she don't need to come around
> When I start makin' money, she don't need to come around
> 'Cause I don't want her now, Lord, I'm Detroit bound.

There were casualties, of course. The business belonged to the
vivors. In 1926 alone, three hundred and twenty-six Detroiters
from bullets, bomb blasts, and that faithful Sicilian export, the gar
compared to less than half that number in 1917, when you could
a beer in a public place without risking arrest. Little or no attemp
made to investigate these killings, most of which involved gang
and the odd citizen who violated the unwritten law against wal
into the crossfire. Oh, the dicks came around and made their
lines and smoked their cigars and had their pictures taken pointi
bulletholes, but the atrocities might have taken place in Turke
all the attention they got after a new one came along to shove the
the front page. I was present at a press conference in Mayor Cl
Bowles's office when he commented, "Perhaps it's just as well to le
scum kill each other off." The bulls were happy to agree, an
papers ran the murder count like box scores.

By then my days at the *Times* were numbered. The trouble
working for innovators like Mr. W. R. Hearst is they got all that in
ing out of their systems early, after which the ideas they came up
when they were bold enough to pop monocles and crack corset
assume the more depressing qualities of poured concrete. I
Hearst's case they were as old as his feud with the late Joseph Pu

gray pulp; I could feel the ends of the fibers when I turned the pages. The masthead, a simple block with no Old English flourishes, read *The Detroit Banner*. A grainy shot of two men lying on their faces on a splotched sidewalk filled the midget front page under the screamer:

BOWLES: "LET THEM DIE!"

Inside was an account of the mayor's press conference explaining his policy of noninvolvement concerning gang killings, side by side with a story about two unidentified men gunned down last night on the East Side.

"Nice," I said. "Only he didn't say, 'Let them die.' I was there."

"It made a better headline. What do you think of the picture?"

"It's okay. I didn't know any were taken."

"There weren't. My photo editor dressed two linotypists in hats and overcoats and had them lie down. What looks like blood is really just an oilstain."

"That's unethical," I said automatically.

He waggled a hand. "We wouldn't have done it if we'd been able to get a picture of the real thing. The timing was too good to let go. And we didn't actually say the picture is of the two men who were killed."

"I guess it sells papers." I was trying to imagine the *Times*'s photo editor showing that kind of initiative.

"Better than that. There's talk of a recall. The *Banner* can claim most of the credit."

"Jerry Buckley might not agree. He's been on Bowles's ass for weeks on WMBC."

"Radio's for housewives. People believe what they see in print." He tapped the newspaper. "This picture will be remembered long after Buckley's dead and his words are gone in the ether. Father Coughlin doesn't have that kind of power. Neither does Herbert Hoover."

Six months later, I remembered what he said about Buckley, and wondered if he'd had some kind of line.

"It's a good-looking paper," I said. "The writing could be better."

"It could be a lot better. That's why I'm here."

I sucked the foam off my beer. I knew what was coming next.

"How's Hearst to work for?" he asked.

"He signs the checks every other Friday."

"I mean from a journalist's standpoint. Are you happy at the *Times*?"

"Are you offering me a job, Mr. Wolfman?"

"Howard. I've got the newest equipment and the best photographers in the Midwest. I need good copy. I've read your stuff. What's Hearst paying you?"

"Seventy-five a week."

He smiled, blinking behind the spectacles. "Nearer sixty. I'll give you a hundred and fifty, plus a twenty-dollar bonus every time you scoop the rest of the city."

My hand was starting to shake. I clamped it around the handle of my mug. "I cover police and city government. And I get a byline."

"I already have a police reporter and a city government reporter. I'm offering you a column."

I let go of the mug and took his hand. "When do I start?"

"How soon can you clean out your desk?"

That's how I came to work for the tabloids. They're tamer now, and so much a part of the landscape that it's difficult to imagine the impact they made when they were new. Splattered with lurid photos (many of them dramatically doctored) and black headlines, they broke out in cities from the Canadian border to the Gulf of Mexico as suddenly as gang wars and swooped down on domestic murders, state executions, sex scandals, and anything else sufficiently scarlet to clear a newsstand in minutes. Little bullets of voyeuristic pleasure, they were portable enough to be read easily in cabs and streetcars and cheap enough, at two or three cents a pop, to be left behind. They obeyed few laws beyond supply and demand and sold in the millions. When a New York tabloid smuggled a photographer into Ruth Snyder's electrocution chamber and ran a picture of her snapped just as the switch was thrown—RUTH FRIES, the headline explained—the legitimate press lowered its flags in mourning, while scrambling behind the scenes to start tabloids of its own. The Fourth Estate would never be the same, and no one who moved around in the public eye would ever again be totally secure in his private life. The tabloids would force subtlety upon the corrupt and threaten heroes with extinction.

My new employer inhabited the fifth floor of the Parker Block, a Victorian wedge triangulated by Woodward, Michigan, and Gratiot avenues, with a cast-iron front housing Siegel's Department Store on the ground floor, dripping with cornices and scrollwork—a dotty old aunt of a building, and a strange home for a brat like the *Banner*. The office I shared with the cartoon editor was eleven feet square with an arched window looking out on Gratiot and the J. L. Hudson building across the street. The cartoon editor, whose name was Jensen, a woodsy-looking number with craggy features and a pipe he couldn't keep burning to pay the rent, never cracked a smile when I was around to see it and gave no indication when I told a joke that he understood English, but the cartoons he bought were the funniest I've ever seen. You figure it out.

I've forgotten the subject of the first column I wrote once I'd gotten past the novelty of a Remington typewriter with an entire working alphabet and no keys that stuck. I'm not alone, because it garnered no letters to the editor and Howard didn't stop by the office to congratulate me, something he made a point of doing later whenever I scored. The second was an obituary.

Two nights earlier, a driver named Little Augie Bustamente had plunged through the ice on Lake Erie at the wheel of a Stutz Blackhawk loaded to the roof with crates of Old Log Cabin. The car, part of a convoy, had driven too near the center of the lake where the current ran through. Little Augie was nobody's loss, being a known wife-abuser and convicted rapist, but the whiskey and particularly the car, which was a good ten years newer and several hundred dollars more valuable than the rusty flivvers the Machine mob usually sent out on the ice, would be missed. Rumor said Joey Machine had given it to his mistress for Christmas and that it had been pressed into service without his knowledge when a Model T touring car caught cold at the last minute. I believed the second part, but not the first. Joey was too cheap to keep a woman, let alone give one a bucket that cost twice as much as the Chevy he drove every day without benefit of chauffeur. In any case, I flatter myself that my piece was the first eulogy ever written for an automobile. It drew letters for a week and H. L. Mencken bought the rights to reprint it nationally. The morning after it appeared in the *Banner* I found a check for twenty dollars bearing Howard Wolfman's signature on my desk.

I was pondering whether to spend the twenty on a new suit or a battery for my Ford—the stock market was definitely out—when the telephone rang. It was on Jensen's desk; seniority. He took the receiver off the gallows, listened, and extended it to me without a word. I slung a ham onto the cartoon-cluttered desk and took it. "Minor."

"*Connie* Minor?" The voice in the tin cup was deep and slow, like a Victrola winding down. It sounded congested.

"There's only one I know of," I said.

"I thought you was a dame."

I made a mental note to have my picture taken for the top of the column. "Sorry to disappoint you, kiddo. What's your beef?"

"No beef." The owner of the voice cleared his throat with a gurgle. I guessed the condition was chronic. "If you got an hour this afternoon I want to talk to you about that story you wrote last night. My name's Joey Machine."

I took the time and place down on a cartoon. I don't remember if Jensen complained.

Chapter Four

"You know my real name ain't Machine," said Machine. "It's Maccino, Giuseppe Garibaldi Maccino. If I had it to do over I wouldn't make the change. Every damn scribe this side of the ocean can spell Joey Machine, and look at the mess it's got me in."

I looked politely, but the only mess he appeared to be in at present had to do with introducing a triple-decker meatball-and-liverwurst sandwich into a strictly single-decker mouth. He was eating a late lunch at a cheap yellow pine desk gouged all over and stained with the residue of other lunches past. The office was twice the size of mine and contained half the furniture, a big echoey room with windows in two adjacent walls and bare floorboards that buzzed whenever someone gunned a motor directly below. The Acme Garage on Griswold was Joey Machine's flagship. He and a partner, since deceased, had bought it in 1919 out of their salaries as fitters for the Michigan Stove Company, a small inheritance belonging to Joey's wife, and the income from a still the partners operated on Belle Isle. Everything else had come later, including the liquor concession for the entire East Side and a graveyard at the bottom of Lake St. Clair for those who lacked Joey's vision. Anyone could get a lube and an oil change in the garage, but chiefly the place served as the payoff point for every bull and city official on the Machine roll, or so the press suspected. Those parties serviced their private automobiles there with a regularity that defied any other explanation.

The St. Valentine's Day Massacre in Chicago the previous winter taught Joey the importance of defending a garage against armed siege. He had had the old wooden bay doors replaced with steel panels, installed bar locks on the back and side entrances, and rigged a warning buzzer that would sound in his office the moment someone tried to enter the building by force. A signal from his window to a lookout stationed on a neighboring roof, it was said, would bring a dozen men with machine guns to the scene in minutes.

I jumped at a noise from his desk, but it was just the telephone. He put the sandwich down with a sigh and barked his name—or rather his streamlined *nom de guerre*—into the mouthpiece. "Who's that? Yeah, what about him?" He listened, chewing. "What the fuck's he mean, it's got a bitter taste? Did I ask him for a fucking review? Remind him we got a contract. No, I don't care how you do it."

While he was talking I took inventory. He was smaller than his reputation, a dumpy five and a half feet and a hundred and fifty pounds in a twenty-dollar blue suit and a green tie with red dice on it on a dollar shirt. He had a large head, a pasty, pushed-in face with tiny eyes crowding a big nose, and reddish brown hair trained back without a part. He was pulling in fifty million a year by the most conservative estimate and looked like a salesman returned from an unsuccessful road trip. Where the money went was anybody's guess. I was betting on the mattress in his home in Rochester.

I was gratified to note that the office contained no doors beyond the conventional one through which I had entered. The *Free Press* had reported that Joey had bought the apartment house next-door and cut himself a secret escape route from his office into the adjoining structure, but I had doubted it, there being well-defined limits to the amount of money he would spend on his own safety. What he had done was hire a bodyguard. I'd been ushered into the inner sanctum by a doorway-ducker who had fought professionally for twenty years under the name Dom Polacki, and whose dented face and bitten-off left ear were the last things some would-be hellraisers had seen in a number of Machine-owned blind pigs before being pitched out into the alley. As he took his station in front of the door, the pistol under his pinstriped suit stood out like a swollen gland.

Joey hung up the earpiece. "I don't have enough problems before, now I got a customer moonlighting as a beer critic."

"You admit you're a bootlegger?" I had my notebook out.

"Why the hell not? Even the coppers don't tip a joint over unless there's something going on there besides liquor. Nobody ever screwed a shotgun into a guy's ribs and made him take a drink, for chrissake."

"Can I quote you on that?"

He made an expansive gesture and picked up his sandwich. "That was a hell of a story you wrote about Little Augie."

"Did you know him well?"

"I just paid him. He was a good driver up to the last five minutes. Ha-ha." He took a bite and washed it down with milk from a tall glass.

"What about the Stutz?"

"It was his, I guess. I don't notice cars much. I'm happy with my old can. Anybody pays more than six hundred for a fucking car, he's a sucker."

I wrote it down, editing out "fucking." I tapped my pencil on the edge of the pad. "Was it because of my column you invited me here for this interview?"

"Well, I was hoping you'd be a dame. Ha-ha. But the real reason you're here is Hattie."

"Hattie Long?" I hadn't seen her in months. She and the rooster had set up shop in River Rouge by then.

"I was with her when the paper came out with your piece. She said you was the scribe that sat on the story when that j.p. croaked on Vernor a couple of years back. She didn't say you wasn't a dame. What kind of name's Connie, anyway?"

"She said something about my getting my fingers broken if I wrote it up."

"I don't work like that," he said, without conviction. "Well, that was one piss-poor night. It was a couple of them Purple Gang pukes done it, Harry Fleischman and somebody named Goldbloom or Kornstein, some kike name like that. I heard they took a boat ride."

The Ecorse Police had gaffed a pair of bobbing corpses identified as Harold Lewellyn Fleischman and Frank Kornblum downriver a week after the poisoning at Hattie's. Someone had tied a car battery around each man's neck, but the weight hadn't been enough to hold them down once they bloated. No arrests were made in the case. Naturally I wasn't writing any of this down.

Joey was still talking. "So it was good to read the paper the next day and find out this guy, this justice of the peace—whatsizname, Wheeler?"

"Turner."

"—this guy Turner had a coronary in his own bed. A guy gets himself poisoned in one of your joints and people catch on, it don't do much for business. That's why you're here. A scribe that can keep his lip buttoned is worth looking at."

"So this is a reward."

"Call it anything you want. I don't give out a whole hell of a lot of interviews. I ain't Capone."

I didn't believe it. The Machine largesse was restricted to those who could do him a favor, not those who had already done him one free of charge.

"Are you in the Mafia?" I asked.

He mugged over his half-eaten sandwich at Polacki, who grinned back with all six of his teeth. "No, you got to be Sicilian to join that club. My people was Calabrese. I can't hack the lingo. I was born in Manhattan."

"Do you cooperate with them?"

"Just write that Sal Borneo and I stay out of each other's pockets."

I did. Salvatore Borneo was the president of the local branch of the Unione Siciliana, which was what they were calling themselves then. "Who killed Phil Dardanello?"

"Nobody killed Phil. He was welding a patch on a gas tank when it blew up."

The explosion in the garage had literally torn Joey's partner to pieces; he had been positively identified from part of a finger retrieved from an exhaust manifold. There had been a careful investigation, because on the morning of the day of the accident Joey had removed a brand-new tow truck from the garage and parked it down the street. He'd said they needed the room. In the end the coroner had ruled death by misadventure. Dardanello's passing left Joey Machine alone in charge of the most profitable bootlegging operation east of Lake Michigan.

Something for the sports page. "Who's your favorite ballplayer?"

"Charlie Gehringer. I support the home team."

"Do you go to the games?"

"I got a box."

"Do you use it often?"

"I ain't used it yet. It'd be like painting a bull's-eye on my forehead for the kikes."

"What do you think of Herbert Hoover?"

"He's getting a raw deal. They're pinning this economy thing on him when they ought to be blaming Coolidge. Old Cal spent all his time sailing his fucking yacht up and down the Potomac, what do you expect?"

"Did you vote in the last election?"

"No. First time I voted was for Harding, and when I saw what we got I figured I didn't deserve to have the vote."

"Do you know Al Capone?"

"Know him. Don't like him."

In fact he had been quoted as saying that if that fat gorilla ever set foot in Detroit he'd send him back to Chicago in a boxcar. That didn't alter the fact that Capone was Joey's biggest customer for Old Log Cabin.

Already it seems strange, this eagerness to know what a cheap gangster had to say about sports and politics and the celebrity scene. I wouldn't ask such questions of the lunks you see pictures of today climbing the courthouse steps holding their hats in front of their faces. Teapot Dome had fed us our fill of shifty-eyed Democrats and chortling Republicans, against whom the frank braggadocio of the slum rats who in a few short years had gone from stolen Fords to armor-plated Cadillacs seemed honest by comparison. You sneered at the religious hypocrisy of an Aimee Semple McPherson, but a mug accustomed to front-and-profile shots who posed shaking hands with Jack Dempsey and John Barrymore was someone to listen to. I don't know that he wasn't, comes to that. What were the merchants who dumped British tea into Boston Harbor, if not hijackers and bootleggers?

The interview continued in that vein, punctuated at intervals by the racing of an occasional engine below and blue exhaust rising between the floorboards. After twenty minutes I had a dull headache. How Joey stood it day after day was one for Harry Sinclair. I decided his pasty complexion was not due to lack of sun so much as monoxide poisoning.

The telephone rang again. Joey speared it and leaned back with the earpiece and candlestick receiver in one hand. "Machine."

That was where I came in. I put away my notebook and pencil and stood up. "Thanks for your time, Mr. Machine," I whispered. "If I hurry I can make the evening edition."

He shook his head and pointed at the chair. I sat back down. I wasn't going anywhere with the Polish Corridor blocking the exit anyway.

Joey had finished his sandwich. When he was through on the telephone he emptied his glass in a long draught that left a skin of cream up the side. "What kind of dough are you getting at the *Banner*?"

I'd had this conversation before.

"I tried firing a tommy gun on the police range once, Mr. Machine," I said. "I blew out the ceiling light and they took it away from me. I'd make a lousy rumrunner."

"That ain't what I asked."

I told him what they were paying me. He looked at Polacki. "Same as you, Dom." The big man said nothing. "Dom didn't make it past the third grade. He sits around all day waiting for the shit to hit the fan. For that I pay him as much as you, and you got talent."

"You ought to pay him a lot more. Nobody's asking me to take a bullet with his name on it."

"That ain't the point. Who's your boss?"

"Howard Wolfman."

"For real?" I didn't answer and he stopped grinning. "What kind of car's he drive?"

"I'm not sure he drives."

"Well, how's he dress?"

"Cashmere and gabardine."

"I figured. A guy like that spends more on spats than he pays you. Wait a minute."

A black iron safe with a combination dial the size of a baseball squatted on the floor behind the desk. He bent over it, swiveled the dial, and removed a brick of currency from inside. It made a solid thump when he threw it on the desk. "Count it."

What the hell. I picked it up, wet my thumb, and riffled through the twenty-dollar bills. There were fifty.

"One now," he said, "and one the first day of every month. Go ahead, put it in your pocket."

I held on to it. "What am I selling?"

He sat back, drumming all his fingers. Beneath our feet a hydraulic lift let go with an asthmatic wheeze. "You used to work for the *Times*, right? You ever read it? I mean all of it?"

"Everything but fashion."

"I'll bet you another stack of bills just like that one you never read the reports from the Federal Reserve."

"You'd win. Only bankers pay attention to that stuff."

"What if I told you fifty thousand Detroiters read it every day, wouldn't miss it?"

"I wouldn't call you a liar with Dom standing there."

"Not all of it," he said. "Just the last three digits. You ever hear of the policy racket?"

"Oh, numbers. The African lottery. The coloreds in the Bottom pick three numbers from a dream book and blow streetcar fare on them. Is that how they pick the winner?"

"It's ironclad. They publish it daily and it can't be rigged. I know because I tried. You know what streetcar fare comes to times fifty thousand? Every day?"

"Jesus."

"That's just what that greaseball Borneo said when I laid it out, only he didn't want to go partners because he's happy with booze. He'll lose his ass when they vote out Prohibition."

"Think that'll happen?"

"Got to. We got a depression on our hands and the feds are going to want to tax something. Meanwhile I'm doing my part, getting money back into circulation with the policy business. That's how I want you to write it up."

"You want a press agent?" I was goggling.

"If that's what it's called. If that fat slob in Chicago can open up soup kitchens, Joey Machine can spread the wealth. It'll keep them reform biddies off my neck."

I put the sheaf of bills on the desk. "Thanks, Mr. Machine. I'm not your man."

"Honesty jag, eh?"

"Not hardly. I've got a living to make in this town and you might not always be here."

"Know something I don't?" He grinned and winked at Dom Polacki.

"It would be like you trying to pass off that yak sweat they stir up in Hamtramck as the real Canadian. Pretty soon nobody'd believe you even if you served the McCoy."

When he made no response, I took out my notebook and flipped it on top of the bills. "I guess that means no exclusive either. I'm sorry I wasted your time." I stood.

"Write up the piece."

I left the notebook where it was. "Strings?"

"Just one."

I waited.

"I got a guy working for me wants to be a newspaper writer. He begged me for this job but I wanted a pro. Okay, so I give him a chance. They ain't filled your old spot yet at the *Times*; I checked. I figure a letter of introduction from you will square it for him."

"You're overestimating my drag. They were plenty sore when I left."

"All the more reason to hire somebody you put up."

I rubbed my eyes. The atmosphere in the room was making them water. "You had this in mind all along, right? You never thought I'd take the job."

"I don't play games with dough. What about it?"

"What if the guy stinks? We're still talking about my reputation."

"What's it worth to you?"

"Not money." I leaned on my hands on the desk. Polacki didn't stir from the door. I didn't know if that was an honor or an insult.

"I want to go on your next run to Canada," I said. "No reporter has ever gone on one. I want to be the first."

He blinked. "You said you wasn't no rumrunner."

"I'm not. I won't use any names. I just want to see how it works and write about it."

"That's if you don't get shot first. Or fall through the ice like Augie."

"I can't believe you're worried about that."

"I am, though. They'd say I had you croaked, like Capone did Jake Lingle."

"I'll be careful."

A big truck coughed and started in the garage below, making the desk vibrate and drowning out any further discussion. Joey put the bills in the safe, locked it, and spun the dial. The motor died. He sat back.

"I'll call you."

Thirty minutes later, he did.

Chapter Five

On the day of the Canada run, I got into the office early, knocked out a column based on an interview with Colonel H. W. Alden of the Rapid Transit Commission about a rumor that Henry Ford and Walter P. Chrysler were conspiring to squeeze out the city's streetcar system, and went home at noon to sleep. I was to hook up with the motorcade in front of the Acme Garage at 11:00 P.M.

My alarm jangled at 9:00. By then I'd been awake for some time, listening to cars swishing through the slush on John R and trying to talk myself out of the growing conviction that I'd made a mistake. Even Joey Machine paid combat wages to border parties, and here I was waiting to join one for the same yard and a half I made taking notes in some bureaucrat's heated office in the County Building. Falling through the ice was the least of my worries. Hijackers didn't hold their fire to check for noncombatants. In a kind of demi-dream I saw my riddled body turning in the gray current, covered with hoarfrost.

At length I rose, showered, and dressed in long flannels, two pairs of thick socks, canvas work pants, a heavy blue turtleneck pullover, navy pea-jacket, watchcap, and galoshes. I felt like Valentino preparing for a bullfight in *Blood and Sand*. From my top bureau drawer I took a hammered silver flask, filled it with rye from a pinch bottle I'd been saving since Christmas, and slid it into a slash pocket. Finally I pulled on a pair of fleece-lined gloves and went out. The cold made me gasp. The thermometer was crowding zero and there was only a thin sheeting of cloud between the earth and frozen outer space.

The ten-minute walk to the garage on Griswold might as well have taken an hour. Stiff winds slapped me around on street corners and, as I trudged along with my chin tucked into my collar, the air prickled in my nostrils. My face was a numb mask. I tried not to think about what it would be like out on the lake.

Eight cars were parked against the curb in front of the garage, big square antiquated sedans and ragtops with chains on their tires and toolboxes, spare tires, and gasoline cans lashed to the running boards. They looked black and grainy behind swarming bits of bitter snow blown up from the ground, like a newsreel I had once seen of an army convoy crossing Siberia. I had just stepped under the light of an electric sign when a man the size of Dom Polacki wearing a fur hat and a raccoon coat moved in front of me. He had both hands in his pockets.

"Go back the way you come, boss. You ain't got business here and we does."

He was an enormous Negro with flat features the color of anthracite. His nose was running but he didn't look chilled. The material across his shoulders tightened when I reached inside my coat for my wallet. I drew it out slowly and showed him my press card. "Connie Minor, the *Banner*. Mr. Machine invited me."

He stared at the card longer than he had to. It dawned on me he was illiterate.

"What's the story, Bass?"

We were joined by a bouncy bantamweight in a mackinaw and a cloth cap jammed down to the bridge of his nose by the band of a pair of red earmuffs. He was no larger than Howard Wolfman and almost as fair; a shrunken negative of big black Bass with bright blue eyes and a toothpaste smile.

"Man says his name's Connie."

The bright blue eyes flicked over me and came to rest on the card. "It's okay, Bass. Jack knows about it."

After a beat the big man took a .45 automatic pistol out of his right coat pocket and slid it off cock. It was a clumsy operation. Each of his hands was a gnarled mass of meat and bone that had been broken—no, pulverized—and knitted badly. The fingers were stiff and awkward, which I didn't think had anything to do with the cold. I noticed then that the automatic's trigger guard had been filed off. He would never have been able to get a finger inside it to pull the trigger.

"I'm Andy Kramm." The bantamweight grasped my gloved hand

with his small slender bare one. I could feel the taut cords through the glove. "This here's Bass Springfield. He used to play ball."

"The Biloxi Bullets," I said, looking at him. "I thought you looked familiar. You played left field."

"Sometimes center." The big man sounded a little less hostile. He had succeeded in applying the safety and returned the pistol to his pocket. "Not many white folks follow black ball."

"I broke in as a sportswriter. My first assignment was the Negro leagues. You were working on some kind of record when you dropped out."

"Hit safely in thirty-eight consecutive games," said Kramm. "Then the Klan got him."

Springfield nodded. "Tied me to a cottonwood and let fly at my hands with a table leg till I couldn't grip a bat no more." He looked at them, then put them in his pockets.

"Baseball's loss is our gain. Them Purples keep their distance when Bass is around." Kramm put a hand on my back. "Jack's in the lead car."

"Jack?"

"Jack Dance. He's barking the show. I'll introduce you."

Kramm and I started that way with Springfield following, providing a windbreak. The lead car was a six-year-old Hudson Model S four-door with its motor running, black over bottle green and shaped like a bus, with a plank mounted up front in place of a bumper. The front door on the passenger's side was open and the boy I had known as John Danzig sat on the seat at an angle, with one foot on the running board, pouring steaming liquid out of a thermos jug into a tin cup. He looked up, saw me, and grinned.

"Hey, Connie! Move any slot machines lately?"

If he hadn't mentioned the slots I might never have placed him. As it was it took me a minute to make the connection. He had lost the baby fat and looked big and hard in a black camel's hair topcoat over a brown pinstriped suit. He had a pearl-gray snapbrim on the back of his curly head and matching spats on tan wingtips that were better suited to the lobby of the Fisher Building than a windswept downtown street in late January. Then and later, always, he was overdressed for the occasion. He had worn his last twenty-dollar suit.

"You know each other?" Kramm was puzzled and, it seemed to me, annoyed. He'd been robbed of his introduction.

"We was in the moving business together. How the hell are you,

Connie?" He stood the thermos on the floor of the sedan and shook my hand. His was manicured, and as free of calluses as I remembered. My memory was working fine now.

"Freezing my balls off," I said. "Who's this Jack Dance?"

"Joey's idea. You know them wops, can't say a name that don't sound like that crap they eat. Hang a lip over this. It'll warm your belly." He held out the tin cup.

I accepted it, taking off my gloves first so I could feel the heat on my palms, and offered him the flask. He shook his head.

"Never touch it. Thins the blood. Go ahead, drink up."

I put away the flask and took a sip. "This isn't coffee."

"Didn't say it was. Chicken broth's better."

It tasted better than whiskey anyway. The fumes thawed out my sinuses. He watched me drain the cup.

"Joey says you're here to make us famous."

"I promised him I wouldn't use names."

"You can use mine. The bulls don't scare me."

"Not even Kozlowski?" He was still a lieutenant, still in charge of the Prohibition Squad. The department wasn't about to promote him and go begging for someone to take his place. Most bulls preferred a leper's sheet to the rubber raincoat.

"He worked me over with a lamp cord for a little, but nobody liked that bug Wagner. I heard he died of a bad needle."

"I hadn't."

"No?" His smile flared briefly, leaving behind a light phosphorescence, like a flashbulb. "Anyway, Joey sent down bail and gave me a job. Tom too."

"Where *is* your brother?"

"Waiting for your letter of introduction. He's all ready to start working for the *Times*."

"He's the one?" I remembered how carefully he had weighed the risks before agreeing to help Hattie with her slot machine problem. A poet, John—excuse me, Jack—had called him.

"Says he can't write no novels without getting experience first. I said he could have all he wanted if he stayed here, but he said that wasn't the kind he needed. He wasn't a lot of good anyway. He thinks too much. Thinks all the time." He worked his fingers into a pair of doeskin gloves. "That was some night at Hattie's. You remember that funny little guy, they cut a piece off of his brain?"

"Jerry the Lobo."

"That's him. Guy like that, he's better dead."

I knew then. It wasn't what he said exactly, or the way he said it. It wa that he even brought up Jerry the Lobo. The newsroom oddsmakers a the time, when they thought about Jerry at all, had decided that he hac wandered into a boxcar and was cadging his beers in Pensacola or someplace, thinking he was still in Detroit. I had never entered the discussion. Thinking about Jerry the Lobo made me sad.

"What's the radio say, Lon?"

Jack directed this at a skull-faced man in a greasy slouch hat and brown leather aviator's jacket, who had just come out of the garage.

"Overcast and flurries." He kept walking in the direction of the last car in line.

"Good." Jack smiled at me. "No place to hide on the lake when the moon's out."

"Who's Lon?"

"Oh, we just call him that on account of he looks like Lon Chaney in that picture, the one about the opera. His name's Camarillo."

That name I knew. He had shot down eight German planes with Eddie Rickenbacker's squadron during the war and had a medal pinned on his chest by Woodrow Wilson. That was the last good thing I had heard about him. "I thought he worked for Sal Borneo."

"He did. Now he don't."

"He's a killer. They're the only ones that can just up and quit like that."

"Mercy-go-run," Andy Kramm said. "Jack, you never told me I was keeping company with criminal trash."

Big Bass chuckled—a low, chilling sound, like wind whistling through holes in a steel drum.

"No-man's-land out there on the ice, Connie. You just joined the war." Jack took back the tin cup and corked the thermos. "Let's roll, kids."

I rode in back with Andy Kramm, who rested his feet on a long black metal toolbox on the floor. Jack drove and Bass sat on the passenger's side in front, blocking my half of the view through the windshield. The tire chains clanked and light from the streetlamps fluttered inside the

car. Behind us the headlamps of the other cars were strung out like mourners in a funeral procession.

We took Woodward down to Jefferson and turned left. "Lake Erie's the other way," I said.

Jack turned his head to grin at Bass. "We don't go *out* on the ice, Connie; we come *back* on it. There's no law against driving to Canada."

"Oh."

We crossed on the Ambassador Bridge. The Windsor Tunnel, which some Detroiters had already rechristened the Funnel for its potential as a conduit for alcohol, was still under construction. The river beneath our feet glistened like black oil.

The guard in the Customs booth had silver hair and rimless glasses under a fur cap. He looked over our ID's. "Reason for your visit?"

Jack said, "Pleasure."

He handed back the cards. "Enjoy your stay."

We drove on. Nobody else in the party was detained. Customs officials weren't dumber then than they are now, or any less honest. When eight cars of a uniform size and vintage crossed the border with chains on their tires, the man in the rimless glasses had to suspect their true purpose, along with the probable presence of a number of unlicensed weapons. Bootleggers brought money into Canada. Where they went with what they bought was strictly between them and their own country.

The distillery Joey Machine did business with was in Leamington, conveniently located near the point where a convoy loaded with contraband might push off for the trek across Lake Erie's frozen surface. On our way through the provincial village of Windsor I remembered why I was there and asked Andy Kramm how he had come to hook up with the Machine organization.

"I was a gunner with the Polar Bears. When I got home the war was over a year and there wasn't no work for a veteran. I guess that's how Lon wound up here too."

"What are the Polar Bears?"

"We stood behind to fight the Bolsheviks in Russia, but that war didn't go so good and they sent us home finally. I missed all the parades."

"You've been with Machine since 1919?"

"No, I bummed around some: Drove a truck for the Greeks, run with

the Little Jewish Navy, shot craps for Lefty Clark in Ecorse till my luck went west. Joey hired me off the floor the night Lefty canned me."

"As a croupier?"

"No. Hell, no. I never got back my luck for that. He wanted a gunner."

In Leamington, Jack pried the Hudson down a narrow brick-paved alley into a rutted lot and parked it at the end of a loading dock lit by a bare overhead bulb. The other cars arranged themselves around the dock, a ragtag cohort of Essexes, Lincolns, and Studebakers with missing fenders and rocker panels rusted through. Their exhaust pipes smoked thickly in the subzero air.

We got in. The wind off the lake had razors in it. Jack vaulted onto the dock, pounded on a door next to the closed bay, and went inside when it opened, tipping a brief L of yellow light from inside. The rest of us stood around with our hands in our pockets, stamping life into feet numbed by the inadequacy of old car heaters.

The lake was a great empty black hole spreading east to the blank sky and west to a lonely scattering of lights that was the city of Monroe, twenty miles south of Detroit. I felt the emptiness in the pit of my stomach. The cars seemed small and fragile compared to that bleak distance. I couldn't help thinking of Little Augie Bustamente, feeding the fish on the floor of the lake.

"Colder'n a witch's tit, all right," said Andy Kramm next to me. "I wouldn't turn down a pull on that flask of yours. Jack's chicken soup just makes me piss."

I got it out and handed it to him. I watched him tip it up. "Is it true he doesn't drink?"

"Nothing like the Creature to warm up the tubes. You buy good liquor." He wiped his mouth on the back of his hand and returned the flask. "Oh, he don't say no to a beer when he's thirsty. He ain't the only leg to steer away from harder stuff. Jack says it's what separates him from the suckers on the other end, but *I* say if it gets out he won't touch his own liquor, it won't be good for business."

"You mean Joey's liquor."

"Sure. Ain't that what I said?" He moved off, smiling.

Chapter Six

A chain rattled and the bay doors swung outward on parched hinges, pushed by Jack and a solid-looking fat man in an ear-flapped hunting cap and streaked overalls. The inside of the building was a cavern lit by a row of ceiling bulbs, stacked to the rafters with stenciled wooden crates and charred barrels and smelling heavily of sawdust and sour mash. It was a warm stink, like the interior of a stable, and took the edge off the bitter wind. I hadn't seen that much beer and whiskey stored in one place since the early days of Prohibition when the bulls were still gleefully smashing up the distilleries in the warehouse district for newsreel photographers. I could not conceive of its value on the 1930 market.

I had to scramble out of the way while the men in Jack's party, unbidden, formed three lines and began loading crates bucket-brigade fashion into the trunks and tonneaus of the cars parked at the dock. Jack, the hard fat man, and Bass Springfield brought out the crates and handed them down one by one to the first men in line, who followed suit. The cars filled with miraculous speed.

Nonparticipation is the reporter's hallmark, even when the event involves a perfectly legal transaction under Canadian law. In this case the efficiency of the system would only have suffered had I tried to take a hand. I had toured the River Rouge plant with Henry Ford and monitored the Detroit Police Department's twelve-week officer training course, and neither operation had worked more smoothly or with less waste. I stood out of the base path and conducted spot interviews.

Most of the loaders were in their twenties and younger, boys from poor neighborhoods whose heroes drove sixteen-cylinder Auburns and wore alpaca coats with tailored pockets for their revolvers. As they worked they leered at one another as if the common labor in which they were engaged—again, no laws had yet been broken—were somehow naughtier and less prosaic than stacking cartons in a market; as if they shared a practical and unprintably dirty joke. Asking them questions was not rewarding, unless sniggering and winking could be called good copy.

The oldest, a tall bareheaded bald man in his late forties named Hannion, was different. He had come to Detroit at the invitation of relatives after his release from the Oklahoma State Penitentiary at McAlester, where he had served nineteen years for the robbery of the Kansas, Texas, and Missouri Railroad in 1905. He had a road-gang complexion, sun-cracked and windburned, and a short cigarette smoldering in a groove in his lip that didn't move when he spoke, a characteristic of men accustomed to conversing in an environment where silence is enforced.

"You were a desperado?" I had grown up on a steady diet of Tom Mix and William S. Hart.

"Not as desperate as the ones that spent so much time chasing me." His rigid lips flattened his Southwestern drawl further. "There was quiet times."

"Quiet as this?"

He accepted a crate and passed it on. "Work like this here's the reason I went on the scout in the first place."

"So why are you doing it?"

"Trains run too fast these days."

Austin Camarillo—Lon to his fellow bootleggers—proved a disappointing interview. Stationed at the end of the line, the skull-faced former aviator socked crates into the back of a battered black Lincoln hard enough to rattle the bottles inside, wouldn't discuss his experiences in the war, and responded to questions about his current activities with monosyllabic snarls. So much for what Winchell wrote about the easy sociability of hired killers. I got a rise out of him just once, when I asked him how he came to know Joey Machine.

There was a lull while another stack was being carried from the depths of the warehouse. Camarillo fished papers and makings out of his shirt pocket and rolled a cigarette with a careless ease I would sooner have associated with Hannion, the Oklahoma bandit. He speared it between his meatless lips, struck a match on the seat of his pants, and paused with the flame shimmying an inch from the end of the cigarette.

"Influenza," he said, and lit the tobacco.

"Sorry?"

He blew smoke through his nostrils and shook out the match. "I came down with the influenza November ninth, nineteen-eighteen. We were short on planes, so somebody else flew my bus. Coming back from patrol the squadron ran into heavy Archie. Archie, that's anti-aircraft fire. A piece hit the fuel tank and my plane went up like a Catherine wheel with somebody else inside. Two days later I was strong enough to fly, but in the meantime the Kaiser signed the Armistice and I shipped home."

"So?"

"So if it wasn't for the influenza I wouldn't have come to know Joey."

The line started moving again and he went back to work. I thanked him and walked away.

Bass Springfield had been spelled early on the loading dock by Andy Kramm, who although he was half the colored man's size had two functional hands and worked just as fast. Springfield rested his bulk on an upended barrel with his mangled fingers spread on his knees. I wandered over there and leaned my elbows on the dock.

"Miss baseball a lot?"

"What you think?" He was watching the operation.

"Is this the only work you could get?"

He nodded. "I ain't any too good at it neither."

I asked him, after having asked Kramm, Hannion, and Camarillo, what I had come to think of as The Question.

"I don't know Mr. Machine nohow," he said. "I was hired by Mr. Jack."

"Where'd you meet him?"

"You should've seen it." Jack Dance came over to the edge of the dock, brushing sawdust off the front of his coat. "I was meeting a train at the station on Brush when I hear this banging coming from a freight on the siding, a real racket. The train's late, so I stroll over there and take a peek inside this boxcar where the noise is coming from. I see this big nigger walloping a white man's head against the side of the car. This other white man's laying on his face on the floor and you just got to figure he had the same.

"Well, it wasn't none of my business, except I'm a white man too, so I show the nigger the piece. He lets go and the guy just kind of slides into a pile on the floor. It was like his bones turned to piss."

"They was Pinkertons," contributed Springfield. "Come to put me off the train. They tried to grab my hands."

"I can see right off here's a nigger I can use if I don't have to shoot him, so I had him come down out of the car. I got him to tell me his name, which I don't know from Lenin's, not being a fan of colored ball like Andy there, and I asked him if he wanted a job. He didn't say no. Joey's train's coming in now, all the way from Atlantic City; I ain't worked for him so long I figure I can trot Bass up to the platform and ask can I keep him. I gave him a hundred to get cleaned up and buy some duds without nothing living in them but him and told him to come see me at the Book-Cadillac. I figure I bought him for the C-note if he don't show up, but he does, all decked out in yellow from hat to heels." He shook his head. "You should've seen it."

You should've seen it. I would come to recognize that as Jack's favorite phrase, a recurring declaration of his faith in the wonder of the world. I visited his grave recently in Hebrew Memorial Park and was disappointed to learn that no one had thought to inscribe it on his stone.

"What happened to the Pinkertons?" I asked.

Jack moved a shoulder. "I didn't read about them in the paper so I guess they must've come around finally. Either that or some hoboes stripped their carcasses and dumped them off along the rails somewhere between here and wherever that freight was headed." He raised his voice. "That's the load. Let's leave some room for passengers."

The lines broke up. Jack retired into the warehouse with the hard fat man, but not before I saw a thick packet of stiff new bills change hands.

Moments later, Springfield, Andy Kramm, and I were back inside the Hudson, Kramm resting his arm on a crate with a red maple leaf stenciled on it on the seat between us. Jack climbed under the wheel, uncorked his thermos, and helped himself to a swig of chicken broth. This time he didn't offer it to anyone else. He rammed the cork back in and reached inside his coat.

"Here, Connie." He stuck a Luger over the back of the seat with his hand wrapped around the barrel.

I stared at the brown checked grip. The sharp oil smell nipped my nostrils. "What's that for?"

"You flip back the little dingus on the side and pull the trigger. It goes bam. Take it. I got another."

"Thanks. I'm just an observer."

Springfield, staring out the window, muttered something about pulling weight. Jack told him to shut up. He took the Luger in both hands and studied it. His face in the light from the loading dock was childlike. "I filed down the trigger sear and converted it to full auto," he said. "You can empty a clip in two seconds."

"What's the good of that?" I asked.

"You don't always get time to aim. The other one's regular semi-auto for when you do. I only offered you this one because I don't know what kind of a shot you are. Hell, suit yourself." He put the pistol away and stamped the engine into life.

I heard a clank and watched Andy Kramm remove a disassembled Thompson submachine gun, glistening black with walnut handgrips, from the toolbox where he'd rested his feet on the way over. He rattled the buttstock into place, wound tight the lever on the pie-tin clip, and clamped it to the action. Finally he drew back the breech and slammed a cartridge into the chamber.

This was becoming real. I asked Jack if he thought guns would be necessary.

"Only for shooting." He let out the clutch. "Bon voyage, gents. We're in the wrong country."

We followed a confusion of side streets to an imperfectly paved road that paralleled railroad tracks for six blocks and then degenerated into gravel as we left the city limits. After a hundred yards of that we swung down an antique logging trail leading toward the lake, that blank expanse with the lights on the American side looking tiny and far away. The lamps of the other cars followed us and slowed when we slowed. We were barely moving as we crunched through spears of tall grass in the snow where the trail frayed out. The blades lisped along the running boards.

"This is the interesting part," Jack announced. "Sometimes it don't freeze all the way to the edge."

I said, "Shouldn't one of us get out and check?"

"Nah."

In decades past, the foot of the trail had provided a gentle grade for launching sleighs and barges loaded with logs bound for Detroit, Cleveland, and Buffalo; but the lake had receded since that time. Our front tires dropped from earth to ice with a sickening lurch, answered by a groan that seemed to issue from the depths of the lake and made my heart skip. But the ice held. After a moment Jack slipped the clutch again and the rear tires bumped down the bank and plunged with a jingling of bottles. The chains munched at the frozen surface. Behind us, the second car made a similar descent. The lamps of the third swayed, flickered, and then jolted into a frightening forty-five-degree angle, but righted themselves, and within minutes the entire procession had quit land. Anyone watching would have seen what looked like a ghost convoy rolling across the water, a Second Coming with backfires.

Papery flakes had been fluttering down when we left shore, but now a shrapnel moon glinted through an unpredicted hole in the clouds, causing the lake to glow under its layer of white, except in dark ominous patches.

"Fucking radio creeps," said Kramm. "Couldn't tell you it's raining if they was standing up to their ass in a puddle."

Jack was sanguine. "Don't get your balls in an uproar. Nobody knows we're out."

"What are those dark spots?" I asked.

"Shoals. Current flows over them and hollows out the ice on top. Little Augie drove smack across one and that's how come he's down there looking up." As Jack spoke he corrected his course to circle a patch larger than most.

After that I relaxed by degrees. We were in expert hands. Even the creaking and groaning of the ice, paralyzing at first, ceased to worry me as the others ignored it. The car was swaddled in black silence, heightened by the sight of the distant lights of Monroe beyond the windshield and the burbling of the engine under the cowl-shaped hood. The black box heater beneath the dashboard, little more than an extension of the manifold, didn't reach past the front seat, leaving the back cold and dank, but I felt safely cocooned, even drowsy. It was well past one.

Conversation—the first in many minutes—awakened me. The shore lights appeared much closer. I had done more than just doze.

"I didn't see nothing," Springfield was saying. "Maybe it was just your reflection."

Jack said, "Maybe not."

The Hudson was equipped with a police spotlight on the driver's side. Jack twisted it up by its chrome handle and switched it on. A hard white shaft rammed a hole through the darkness. I saw shapes of cars two hundred yards ahead, strung out in a horizontal line. Their lamps were dark.

Jack's eyes sought mine in the rearview mirror. "You tell anybody about this run?"

"Not a soul."

Something struck the post to the left of the windshield. Sparks sprayed. The report followed an instant later, a hollow plop.

"They're trying for the light!" Kramm cranked down his window hurriedly, letting in a blast of arctic air. He poked the machine gun's snout out the window.

Jack killed the spot and headlamps. Behind us the lamps of the other cars in our party broke formation in both directions and blinked out raggedly. I wondered how they could avoid the shoals without light. Then Jack hurled the Hudson into a skidding turn that barked my ribs against the crate of whiskey, and I wondered about *us*.

All the windows were down now except mine. Something buzzed past the car on the passenger's side, a hornet in January. Kramm nestled the Thompson's butt into his shoulder and squeezed the trigger. The pounding shook the car, spent shells bounced against the seat and floor, brimstone fouled the air.

I heard two spaced shots in reply, then I saw a spot of bright light flickering, the reports hammering behind the flashes like an out-of-sync soundtrack. My eyes were growing accustomed to the moonlight. The bursts came from the backseat of a long, light-colored sedan with dark fenders and running boards.

Something thudded against the side of the Hudson. I felt a hot wind on my face and my window disintegrated. I slumped down in the seat. For the next few moments I heard more than I saw.

Springfield leaned out his window and fired his .45 pistol, the shots pounding at a stately pace. I heard a burp that had to be Jack's goosed Luger disgorging the contents of its clip in a heartbeat. The other cars in our party joined the fight with automatic and single fire. A shotgun boomed. I hoped everyone knew where his friends were.

Jack said, "What color's that Packard?"

"If you're thinking of buying it, you better wait till the owner stops shooting at us." Kramm rattled the Thompson's breech. It had jammed.

"Don't Pete Rosenstein own a yellow-and-black Packard?"

"Black and tan." Kramm paused. "Holy shit, no wonder I couldn't do anything to it. That car's armor-plated."

"It must weigh three tons."

"Pete always did think with his prick."

"Next swing I make I want you to shoot at the ice under that Packard."

"It won't do nothing. It's froze two feet thick."

"Hang on. Don't fire till I say." Jack threw open the throttle.

I barely got upright when the Hudson swung into a sharp turn and I felt the wheels on my side leave the ice. They came back down with a bang and my head hit the roof. I snatched hold of the leather strap by my window. The lights of Monroe—or maybe they were the lights of Leamington; I had lost all bearings—went past in a streak. Our slipstream stiffened my face and numbed my ears.

We flashed past something metallic on my side. I hoped it was one of our cars, but I knew better. I heard shots, warped and curved like a train's whistle as it rackets past, saw muzzles flare. We executed a sliding turn, changed gears, and made another pass. As the other car swelled inside the frame of the windshield I recognized it as the two-toned sedan with the backseat gunner. A medieval-looking louvered visor covered the radiator.

"Now!"

Kramm had cleared the breech. Now he braced his foot against the hump in the floor over the driveshaft and stuck his entire torso through his window. I heard the clattering reports, the clinking of the spent shells striking the Hudson's roof. He fired two long bursts and pulled himself back inside.

"What the hell, everybody dies." Jack turned again. A spray of ice crystals coming off the tire chains caught the moonlight in an iridescent gusher.

I saw then what was happening. In his attempts to outmaneuver the lighter Hudson, the driver of the lumbering Packard had forgotten where he was. The armor-plated car's front tires, unchained, had locked and the car had slewed over the edge of a dark patch over a shoal. As we powered past within a hundred feet, drawing machine-gun fire which at that range was haphazard at best, Andy Kramm thrust himself half out of the Hudson again and hammered at the thin ice under the Packard.

At first there was no effect. The bullets vanished into darkness as if poured down a hole. Then a pattern of fine cracks starred the dark patch, etched white on black, spreading outward.

"Shit!"

Kramm fell back into the seat, the Thompson across his lap with its breech locked open. It was a bad time to run out of ammunition.

But bullets were still hitting the ice. As we sped away from the Packard, having veered too close to its gun for comfort, I watched the battered black Lincoln following our original path with Lon Camarillo standing on the running board, bracing himself with an arm hooked around the window post and pumping away with what looked like a Browning Automatic Rifle at the center of the network of cracks. His face in the moonlight with the buttstock against his cheek looked like the Grim Reaper's. At the wheel of the Lincoln, his bald head shining, sat Hannion, the train robber from Oklahoma.

"Son-of-a-bitch cowboys," growled Kramm.

The former aviator and his partner weren't the only ones who had caught on. The driver of the Packard was spinning his wheels in a white blur now, frantic to back away onto a better footing. His engine whined, but the car only subsided into a drunken tilt, spoiling the aim of the gunner in back and thrusting its armored prow farther out over the shoal.

A wheel broke through and the car stumbled, then went down on both knees as the ice collapsed under the other front wheel. White floes stood up in shards and slid under the black water. The Packard teetered, rear wheels turning in empty air, a scaled-down *Titanic* suspended on a cloud of exhaust.

We didn't stay for the rest. Jack threw on the headlamps and started in a long loop toward the Michigan shore. With their lead car foundering, the others in the hostile party had lost interest in the fight and sought to spread out to avoid a chain reaction. Bumpers and fenders tangled as more than one driver chose the same route. Friendly headlamps came on behind us.

"They'll try again in town," Kramm said.

"No, Pete's got a deal in Monroe." Jack's voice was pitched high, but not from fear. "How we doing, any fresh dead? Connie?"

"I'm okay." Actually I was. I had thought I'd wet myself in the excitement, then discovered that a bullet had pierced the crate at my elbow, smashing a bottle and drenching the seat in Old Log Cabin. "They'd go to all that trouble just for liquor?"

"This is a million-dollar load. He's got payments to make on that rolling hunk of boilerplate. Besides, he never did forgive Joey for kidnapping him that time. It made him look common."

"Wonder how the others come out." Of all of us, Bass Springfield seemed the least transported.

Jack said, "They know where to go when we get separated."

Kramm chuckled. "You see that lardbutt Packard go *down*? I never seen nothing like it, not even in Russia."

"Good thing Lon come along," said Springfield.

"I softened it up for him."

Jack wasn't listening. His eyes in the rearview mirror were bleak. "When I find out who stooled I'm fucking gonna pick his bones."

Chapter Seven

Minor's Majors

BY CONNIE MINOR

Bonaparte at Austerlitz had nothing on a local lieutenant of bootleggers, hardly more than a boy, who last night on the battlefield of icebound Lake Erie routed an army of hijackers with a few bursts from a submachine gun.

Historians tell us Napoleon destroyed the Russian Army in Prussia by directing his cannon at a chain of frozen lakes over which the enemy sought retreat, plunging horses and men into the icy waters and claiming victory. Although it's a fair bet this gang tactician has never read Von Clausewitz (or even Hans and Fritz) and knows nothing of the Napoleonic Wars . . .

And like that. It creaks a little now, but it read better when it was fresh. Well enough anyway to be picked up by the wires and land me my first Pulitzer nomination. I think I'd have had a shot at it, too, had not the deadline been months away; by which time, for reasons I'm about to set forth, the notion of gangsters as modern Robin Hoods was as dead as Franz Ferdinand.

The night the *Banner* with my Battle of Lake Erie column hit the streets, I celebrated. With a bonus practically in my pocket I started high, watching the Grosse Pointe suckers and getting suckered myself at roulette in the Aniwa Club on Van Dyke, then did Blossom Heath and floated from there to Doc Brady's and the Arcadia Ballroom, where Don Redman was blowing saxophone with McKinney's Cotton Pickers. At one point it occurred to me that some of the liquor I was drinking had probably come over in the load I had helped escort. Somewhere, although I don't recall stopping at her place, I collected Hattie Long, who had on a gold lamé shift under an ermine coat and one of those metal headpieces stuccoed with jewels like Marie Dressler wore in the movies, only on Hattie it looked less like the coronation of the Queen of the Dykes. I remember putting the arm on her for fifty when my pockets turned inside out over the blackjack table at the Green Lantern in Ecorse. My luck improved after that, but all told I figure that twenty I hadn't gotten yet cost me two weeks' pay.

Once—Jean Goldkette was directing the band, so it must have been in the dining room off the Graystone Ballroom—a liveried waiter brought a green bottle with gold foil on the neck to our table. When he pointed out the gentleman who had sent it, I looked at Jack Dance in black tie and black satin lapels raising a glass of beer to me at a table in the corner. The woman he was with was no flapper. She was wearing black velvet off the shoulders and pearls, and her hair was long and blonde in an old-fashioned sort of way, no curling irons or peroxide. She had a long straight nose like a Greek statue and when she turned my way her eyes went past me as if I were a fern growing there. Hattie told me later I waved back at Jack with an idiot grin, "like you were separated at birth and he saved your life and you were partners in a gold mine in Alaska or something." Women exaggerate.

The next morning, standing in the same clothes I had put on the morning before, I watched Hattie drawing on her eyebrows at the little French Empire vanity a Hupmobile vice president had given her when he went back to his wife. The bedroom of her apartment on Livernois was fussily decorated in a high school cheerleader's idea of Bourbon splendor, ruffled polka-dot bedspreads and flouncy curtains and gold fleurs-de-lis on pale blue wallpaper.

"Did I propose to you last night?" I asked.

"Not me." She did something with a brush that made her chin look less pointed. "It was the hatcheck girl at the Addison. Don't pretend you don't remember."

"I don't remember going to the Addison."

"If you can't hold your liquor, don't pick it up."

"So when are the nuptials?"

"She was already married to the bouncer." She exchanged the brush for a lipstick.

"I was wondering why my nose was so tender. I must've been drinking gin. Gin always makes me propose to hatcheck girls."

"All the more reason to take the pledge. Hatcheck girls always marry bouncers."

"If I were a sensible drunk I'd propose to you."

She painted on the beestung lips. "Don't joke about it."

In the streetcar later I said, "Whoops."

I'd been in the office ten minutes when Howard Wolfman woke me up by crumpling a twenty-dollar bill under my nose. He looked country-squirish in Harris tweeds and a red silk necktie that brought out the pink in his eyes behind the gold-rimmed cheaters.

"I got an angry call at home last night from an Agent McPeek with the Prohibition Navy," he said when I snatched the bill.

I couldn't read him. My eyes were still woolly from the night before and I didn't want to move my head too quickly for fear my brains would spring out like watchworks. I could read the twenty, though. I uncrossed my ankles on the desk, crossed them the other way, and stretched the bill in both hands. "What did the floating Keystone Kops want?"

"He said the Navy patrols that part of Erie with Model T's on skis and no battle like you described took place night before last or any other."

"The river was open that night. They were probably busy sinking some auto muckety's yacht off Belle Isle on the theory it belonged to Joey Machine. That's all they're good for, unless you want to run them in the funnies next to Happy Hooligan."

"Until that call came in I wasn't going to pay you a bonus. That Bonaparte stuff is a little heavy for readers of the *Banner*. You want to watch that."

"Columnists' disease. Every now and then I get the urge to prove I read a book."

"Fight it. This isn't the *Literary Digest.* What's in the hopper?" He inclined his white head toward the Remington on its slanty stand.

I cranked up the sheet. " 'Now is the time for all good men to jump over the lazy dog.' I'm stuck."

"Is it serious?"

"Critical. Happens every day about this time."

He hesitated a stroke. "Swayles is out today."

"Another binge so soon after the last one?" Swayles was the *Banner*'s police reporter. They didn't stay sober for long on that beat.

"No, he's really sick. Mumps. Can you run this down? I know it's not your department anymore, but it might turn into something." He handed me a sheet torn off a pad.

I recognized the telephone number. "Who's in the morgue?"

"That's the question. Two hours ago the police pried him out of the trunk of a stolen Chevy parked on Rivard."

"What makes him different from all the other John Does punched full of holes we run in the police blotter column?"

"Somebody took a needle and thread to this one and stitched his lips shut. It might not be anything. Maybe we can make it something."

"Is he white?"

When he screwed up his face like that he looked just like a rabbit. "If he weren't, they wouldn't have bothered to call it in."

"I don't know, I was counting on going home and catching a couple of hours' sleep. The column's not due till four."

"I was going to ask. You look worse than Swayles. Big night?"

"Chalk it up to research." I checked my watch. "Anderson should be on duty. I'll stop by the morgue on my way home."

Wolfman left and I got up to get my hat and coat from the rack by Jensen's desk.

"Need me?" Jensen relit his pipe for the eleventh time that morning.

I shook my head. Wolfman, who wouldn't blink at running a picture of a child cut in two by a streetcar, was strangely reticent about photographing corpses on slabs, and always had the cartoon editor do a sketch when he wanted to give readers an opportunity to identify a John Doe. Meanwhile the scribes at the *Times* kept a collar and tie in a file drawer at the morgue to put on the cadavers, and the boys in the darkroom airbrushed eyeballs onto their closed lids to make them look more lively.

Fred Ogilvie stopped me in the hallway to show me proofs of head shots for my column. A short pudge with thinning black hair and a strawberry mark on the lower half of his face, Ogilvie had been hired off the *Free Press* at twice his former salary to take over the *Banner*'s photography department. I was in a hurry, so I picked one of me chewing a pipe I'd borrowed from Jensen's desk—a mistake, as it turned out, because when the column went into syndication later, admirers started sending me tobacco and pipes. When I smoked at all I smoked Chesterfields.

Fred said, "I kind of like the one with the hat."

"So does Winchell. Use this one, starting tonight. I'm sick of getting mail addressed to 'Miss Minor.' "

"Yes, ma'am."

We were having a January thaw. The sidewalks were slushy and a wind was blowing up from Ohio that ought to have smelled of cherry blossoms. I walked the four blocks to the Coroner's Court Building at Brush and East Lafayette. The balmy air woke up several brain cells I'd given up for dead, and by the time I got there I was feeling a good deal better than most people when they enter the morgue.

It's a corner construction like the Parker Block where the *Banner* lived, built in 1925 to replace the old facility in the northwest corner of the County Building. It contains a private office for each of the two coroners, general offices, two courtrooms with chambers, a mortuary viewing room, a dissecting room, rooms for freezing, X-ray, and sterilizing, a wash room, and cold storage for one hundred and eighty-six bodies. The planners must have had an inkling of what Prohibition would continue to bring.

I showed a county employee in uniform my police pass and he let me into the dissecting room, where Paul Anderson had both gloved hands up to his elbows inside a naked male corpse dressed open on the steel table. The place smelled of fresh meat and ammonia and brine from the cooling system. Anderson was a big Swedish-born former linebacker with a curl of blonde hair on his pink scalp, meaty jowls, and forearms like Popeye; not at all the type you'd expect to see mucking around in a dead person's insides. He was first assistant medical examiner under W. D. Ryan, and liked his work. I never met a forensic pathologist who didn't. It isn't an occupation you drift into.

With him in the room was a pale attendant in his twenties wearing short sleeves and a rubber apron like his superior, a female police stenographer with an unmade face and her hair in a bun and long slim calves crossed on a straight wooden chair, and Lieutenant Valery Kozlowski.

Kozlowski was taller, fatter, and harder than I remembered. He had on a squashed fedora and his trademark rubber raincoat—a badge of the barrel-smashing Prohibition Squad—over a three-piece suit with creases in all the wrong places and a tie with a bullfighter painted on it.

He was chomping a stogie as usual but the stogie wasn't lit, in deference to the inflammable formaldehyde fumes swimming around the room. His mud-colored eyes flicked from the corpse's cavity to my face and back to the corpse without recognition. Well, we hadn't seen each other since the Turner poisoning.

"Read that back," Anderson told the stenographer. He withdrew his forearms, caked with blood, from the cavity and wiped his hands on a gory rag.

She paged back through the pad. " 'Body of a well-developed white male, aged twenty to twenty-five—' "

"Not that far back. Read what I just dictated."

She paged forward. " 'In the stomach, approximately a quart and a half of a pale liquid, the color and consistency of the gravy they serve biscuits in at the Star Diner in Flatrock.' "

"Better change that to 'a pale, watery liquid' and leave out the rest. Ryan's delicate," he added, winking at me. "Hello, Connie. Long time no see."

"Sooner or later we all come back to the morgue," I said. "Good morning, Lieutenant." I introduced myself all over again.

Kozlowski took the stogie out of his mouth, said, "Sure," and put it back. He never looked up from the corpse.

There was no need to ask if it was the stiff from Rivard. Someone who didn't know much about sewing had stitched the bloodless lips together with coarse black thread, making a jagged cross-hatch with the frayed ends dangling. The dead man was thin and gray-white, his dark hair matted. Two nights earlier it had been black and glossy, its owner flush from the cold and manic. He was one of the sniggering youths I'd interviewed among Jack Dance's crew in Leamington. His name was somewhere in my notebook.

"This a Prohibition beef?" I asked Kozlowski.

He worked the cigar to the other side of his mouth. "The guy that reported the Chevy stolen has a sheet for selling Hamtramck hootch in front of St. Stanislaus. When a beat cop spotted it we took the squeal. We think, maybe we got lucky. Maybe some puke had a joyride and never knew there was booze in back. That ain't the way it worked out. Know him?"

I said, "No. Shot?"

Anderson gestured to the pale attendant, who handed him a white enamel basin from an instrument stand on his side of the table. The medical examiner used a forceps to pick up a snarled bit of lead with copper fragments stuck to it.

"Copper-jacketed, either a thirty-eight or one of those foreign calibers. We don't have all the fragments yet, so it might be larger. That's for Ballistics. Read that part," he told the stenographer.

She took a moment to find it. " 'Bullet entered the left upper quadrant of the thorax, describing a thirty-degree oblique trajectory downward and to the right, shattering the fifth rib and fragmenting. The largest fragment ricocheted downward and to the rear sixty degrees, piercing the upper intestine at least twice before coming to rest between the tenth and eleventh dorsal vertebrae. Other fragments—' "

"He gets the idea," Anderson said. "There's another hole in the back of his neck with powder-burns. We'll have that slug when we get to the brain. That'd be the *coup de grâce*, delivered after the first shot put him down. A layman's opinion; I'm not a dick."

"Right," said Kozlowski.

"Why sew his mouth shut?" I asked.

"Maybe he used it once too often. That was a fresh touch. Usually they just shoot them in the mouth, or if they have time and they're Sicilian, lop off the poor bastard's penis and testicles and shove them down his throat. I like this guy's style. Tray." Returning the forceps and slug to the basin, he handed it back to the attendant, who set it down and held up a square tray with instruments arranged on it. Anderson snipped the thread in two places with a long pair of scissors, then used tweezers to tug the thread out of the holes. The dead man's lips remained tightly compressed. Freeing his hands, Anderson grasped the chin and forced the jaw open.

"What do you know?" he said. "It gets better."

It sounds screwy, but I knew what it would be, or at least what it would mean. Kozlowski didn't, of course, and it surprised him enough to make him take the stogie from between his teeth and forget to replace it.

After feeling around inside the dead man's mouth, Anderson withdrew an unused cartridge, shiny brass with a copper nose, of the type designed for use with the nine-millimeter Luger.

Chapter Eight

"Some kind of signature, I expect." Anderson held the cartridge up to the light. "Know anyone who owns a Luger, Lieutenant?"

"Shit, half the population of Michigan's German and the other half come back from the war with souvenirs. Who don't?" He remembered his cigar and pegged it into his favorite corner. "Anyway, if the sheeny turns out Purple, who done it won't matter. If it was up to the chief, the city'd pay him a bounty."

"What makes him a sheeny?" I asked.

He pointed. "They didn't shoot the end of his dick off. It was that way already."

I didn't pursue the point. In Lieutenant Kozlowski's simple world, the inhabitants were divided into two camps: Those who had been circumcised and those who hadn't.

He buttoned his raincoat. "When you finish digging that slug out of his noggin, run it over to Ballistics. We'll blow some taxpayers' money and pretend that Luger ain't on the bottom of the river by now. Then when we don't get noplace, we'll hand it to Homicide. No sense jamming up the files at Prohibition with another open case."

After Kozlowski went out, I asked Anderson if I could have the cartridge.

"Collecting souvenirs?" he asked.

"Sort of. You need it for evidence?"

"A bullet isn't evidence until it's fired." He gave it to me.

I put it in my ticket pocket, gave him the high sign, and left on the trot. I wanted to ask Kozlowski a question, but a pair of raised voices at the door at the end of the hall broke my concentration.

"Nobody in without a badge or a pass," the deputy at the door was saying.

"I keep telling you I haven't been issued a pass yet. I just started the job. Here's my press card."

"That ain't a police pass. Nobody in without a badge or a pass."

Kozlowski joined them. "Pipe down. You want to wake up the stiffs and fuck up all the paperwork?"

"Man don't have a pass, Lieutenant."

The civilian swung his attention to Kozlowski. "Tom Danzig, the *Times.* We met once. Is someone afraid I'll smuggle out a kidney in my pocket?"

"You think that don't happen?" The lieutenant struck a match on the doorframe, scratching the varnish, and lit his stogie. "Where was it we met?"

"You wouldn't remember. It was two years ago and I was working somewhere else."

I'd recognized him before he used his name. He hadn't changed as much as his brother. His jawline had hardened, making him appear more lean than slight, but his hair was the same sandy shade at the temples under a soft brown felt snapbrim and he was still fair where Jack was dark. He wore a tan double-breasted under a light topcoat, inconspicuously tailored, and the kind of necktie that didn't exist in Kozlowski's world, wine-colored silk that glistened softly under the harsh institutional light. If he was dressing like that on the sixty a week the *Times* had paid me, he wasn't eating or paying rent. I thought about the thousand dollars Joey Machine had thrown at me, along with the promise to repeat the performance the first day of every month if I wrote what he wanted.

"Don't ever tell a bull he don't remember," Kozlowski said. "It ain't every day somebody gets himself poisoned on my shift."

That was impressive, and I could see Tom knew it. The lieutenant had seen thousands of faces in two years and poisoning or not, the raid on Hattie's had been just one more obligatory tipover in a career awash in them. Just because a bull's bent doesn't mean he isn't a good detective. I watched Tom learn that, saw him file it away. That was the basic difference between the brothers. You could see Tom think, while everything Jack did came straight out of left field, as if some shadowy Muse had whispered a course of action into his ear just before he took it.

I saw something else too. I saw Kozlowski noting Tom's clothes, putting them together with his announcement that he worked for the *Times*, and, although he hid it well enough from anyone who wasn't looking for it, saw him relax. For all his professed amorality, a man who's been bought is always at a disadvantage with others until he sniffs a kindred soul. In less than a minute the pair had stamped and pigeonholed each other, and only I saw it. The deputy was too busy yawning.

"How's your brother?" asked the lieutenant. "Still running with the wops?"

"We don't stay in touch. Right now I'm investigating a murder."

"No kidding. So am I. If the chief don't trust you enough to give you a pass, why should we?"

"It's not a matter of trust. Can I help it if the killers in this town are more efficient than the bureaucracy?"

Kozlowski pointed over Tom's shoulder with the butt of his cigar. "That's your curtain line, bub. Take your bow."

I put in an oar. "He's the police reporter at the *Times* okay. I helped clear him for the job."

Tom hadn't taken notice of me before. Now he looked, made the connection. I had handed the letter of introduction directly to Joey, who had arranged things from there.

Kozlowski was looking at me too. My clothes didn't satisfy him the way Tom's had. "I didn't know the *Times* and the *Banner* was on speaking terms."

"You can call his editor if you want."

He sighed. "Let him by, Pike. He ain't Sacco and Vanzetti."

The deputy shrugged. I would see that shrug in many different places as the decade wore on: Representing, in the long hangover after the ten-year binge of the twenties, a contentment just to keep one's job.

The lieutenant left. I lingered. I'd forgotten what I was going to ask him anyway.

"Thanks," said Tom. "I could have talked my way in, but you saved me some time."

He couldn't talk his way onto a public street without help; I'd been doing some pigeonholing of my own. But I said nothing. After a moment he shook my hand and headed toward the dissecting room. No mention of the letter. He knew I'd been compensated.

I patted my ticket pocket. Well, it was as good a way as any. I called after him. He stopped and turned. Fishing out the unfired cartridge, I walked down the hall and extended it. He took it automatically. "What's this?"

"Give it to your brother next time you see him. Tell him he owes me."

He wasn't a full-fledged scribe yet. I left before he could ask any more questions.

I'm not clear even now on why I didn't volunteer the dead man's name, or speak up when Anderson made his discovery inside the silenced mouth. The stitched lips said as plain as anything that the man on the table had leaked information on the Canada run to someone in Pete Rosenstein's camp, and the stashed cartridge, compatible with Jack Dance's trademark Lugers, was as arrogant a boast as a killer could make, even if I was the only one who made the connection; Jack always assumed he and his works were better known than they were. True, I didn't owe anything to the bulls. When an entire legal system pledges its services to a small band of thugs and pirates, the duties of citizenship are suspended. But I never thought of my silence in terms of sticking it to the authorities. I'm not a rebel. It's tempting to think, because of what I said to Tom, that I was investing in a source of good copy, but that doesn't answer everything. Maybe I just liked Jack. In those days it was becoming increasingly hard to accept the simplest explanation as the truth, but sometimes it was.

Winter went, as winters will, even in Michigan. The investigation into the murder of Lewis Welker—for so the young man with the sealed lips had been identified when the bulls matched his fingerprints to a set on file at the Juvenile Detention Home—stayed alive on the front page of the *Banner* for a week, helped a little by Swayles when he shook off the mumps, then guttered out as the campaign to recall Mayor Bowles got too hot for the second leaders. (It wouldn't have lasted even that long but for the needlework.) Ballistics failed to find a match either in its files or those of the Justice Department for the striations on the nine-millimeter bullet taken from Welker's brain, after which the case went to Homicide, who pulled in every known member of the Purple Gang, the Little Jewish Navy, the Unione Siciliana, and the Machine mob—all except the gang chiefs, who were always out of town during a sweep. The bulls posed with them for newspaper photographers in their hats and coats at the Wayne County Jail and then cut them loose. I still have a group shot taken by Fred Ogilvie for the *Banner*, with Jack Dance at one end turning to say something with a smile to the man at his right, and every time I come across it the faces look younger. Hatless and dressed in varsity sweaters, they'd have passed muster in a high school yearbook, not a Dillinger in the bunch. If Repeal and the Depression have done nothing else, they've taken crime away from the kids and given it back to seasoned professionals.

I didn't do a column on Welker. I had brass then, but not *that* much brass. Instead I wrote a series on evangelists that didn't tell anyone anything he didn't already know or suspect and snared me no bonuses or nominations and only one letter, a scorcher from the chairman of the local chapter of the National Committee to Draft Billy Sunday for President.

As the spring floods receded, recall fever, inflamed by the *News*, the *Free Press*, and the *Banner*, and by Jerry Buckley on radio, mounted. In May, while Bowles was attending the Kentucky Derby, the *News* published a photograph of a bookie recording bets on the same race. This was not in itself newsworthy. What made it so was the fact that the photographer had been standing at a window in Bowles's office when he pushed the button. Inspired, Police Commissioner Harold H. Emmons took advantage of the mayor's absence to crack down on such handbook operations with a series of raids citywide. When Bowles returned, he fired Emmons. That action put the petition drive over the top, and the recall election was scheduled for July 22. If successful, it would make Detroit the first major city to recall its mayor. The eyes of the nation, to swipe a phrase from the newsreels, were on the Motor City.

Although neither the press nor even the demagogic Buckley would say it without evidence, it was clear to a blind deaf-mute that Bowles and his ring were in the pay of the men in sharp suits who smelled faintly of sour mash. When a Detroiter was in a hurry of an evening, he learned to detour around Riopelle and East Jefferson to avoid being delayed by a polite young man with a submachine gun while a cargo of liquor was being offloaded. "Where are the cops?" ran a close second to "Wanna buy a duck?" as the joke question of the decade. The terms "Vice Squad" and "Criminal Investigation Division" became double-entendres.

Thus unhampered by the watchdogs of justice, the gangs had little to look out for but one another, which kept them busy enough that year.

They shot it out on the river and in the streets, in apartments and from the running boards of Cadillacs and LaSalles. As the days rat-tat-tatted by, the Battle of Lake Erie—Connie Minor's battle, copyrighted and on file at the Library of Congress—became just one skirmish in an escalating war. Lewis Welker became part of a statistic that threatened to top the all-time high of 1926.

It's hard for a newspaper not to look good in that kind of climate, but the *Times* suffered. The distant Hearst's support of Prohibition was untenable, and a poorly planned series of articles about the policy racket's promise to make any poor Negro a Cinderella rang tinnily amid the clamor to rid the city of gambling and every other vice not served in glasses. Joey Machine's hand-picked boy Tom Danzig had a hand in that, but the decision to print the material was made higher up. I began to suspect that Joey's pockets ran deeper than I'd guessed. He'd limp ten blocks on a blister to save two bits on a new pair of shoes, but when it came to improving his business he could be as generous as Schweitzer.

It was still black out one balmy morning in May when the telephone rang in my apartment. I came awake with my head doubled under my arm stork fashion. The bell rang seven times before I got the kinks out of my neck and found any feeling in the arm below the elbow. I tipped the candlestick off the nightstand and caught the receiver.

"Connie?"

"I'm not sure." I turned on the lamp, looked at the alarm clock. "Jesus."

"Wrong. I'm the guy that owes you a favor."

I didn't need any more waking up after that. In time I'd learn that Jack never identified himself over the telephone. He'd heard that the feds had tapped into Capone's line and not being electronically gifted had come to the conclusion that they could eavesdrop on anyone's conversation anywhere simply by flipping a switch. It was the only thing he was ever cautious about.

"What's the deal?" I sat up.

"You know the Black Bottom?"

"I hope you didn't wake me up to ask me out dancing."

"Not the dance, shithead, the place. You know Crystal Street? Runs next to Hastings."

"I've been there."

"Bass Springfield's got a room there. He ain't got a phone. I need to get a message to him."

"So go see him."

"If I could do that, you think I'd call you? The war's on, Al. Andy and Lon and me are squirreled in here." He gave me an address on Howard. "The Purples got Baldy Hannion tonight. Gunned him in his car in the middle of Woodward."

That took a moment to sink in. Something had gone wrong with the natural order when an Oklahoma train robber was shot to death at the wheel of an automobile in downtown Detroit.

"When?"

"Hey, I'm not talking to your sheet."

"Sorry. What's the message?"

"That's it. Tell Bass what happened. Tell him to get his ass down here and cover it on the way. That son of a bitch Rosenstein's got a hard-on for the whole outfit."

"Why me? I'm not one of the boys."

"You answered your own question, chum. Pete's gorillas ain't looking to put one in you. You're the only one outside I can trust."

"What makes you think you can trust me?"

"Lew Welker."

I fumbled for my Chesterfields in the drawer of the nightstand. "Do you always repay a favor by asking for another favor?"

"He's got a woman there, Nadine or Francine, one of them nigger names. Bass might want to send her on vacation."

"I'll tell him." I got the address on Crystal and then the connection broke.

I'd been to the neighborhood many times, but never after two in the morning, which represented an unspoken curfew for whites in the Bottom. After that, if you were the wrong color and you were caught on the street, you stood a good chance of being bumped off a practically empty sidewalk and, if you still didn't take the hint, the bulls might find you after daylight sitting in a weedy lot with your guts in your lap. I cranked up the Ford and prayed the moon would stay hidden.

The house was a two-story saltbox, whitewashed clapboard with the wood wearing through under the streetlamp out front, but the windows were clean and the strip of grass between the foundation and the sidewalk had been cut recently. Things are changing now, but in those days, residents of the most rundown neighborhoods kept them neat, even the alleys. I left the motor running and climbed the stoop. There was a movement in the shadows and a lanky Negro I hadn't noticed in a cloth cap and a baggy suitcoat stopped leaning against a lightpole on the corner and passed under the streetlamp out of sight.

I rapped on the screen door. After a moment an old colored woman came to the screen without turning on a light inside. She had on a hairnet and a faded housecoat with gnawed elbows. Her face was a length of carved dark wood.

"Bass Springfield," I said.

Her eyes took the slow tour. "You *po*lice?"

"No, just a friend."

A long silence let me know what she thought of that. Finally she reached up and unhooked the screen door.

When I stepped inside she turned on a lamp. The parlor had a square of rug, threadbare but clean, two sofas with mismatched floral covers, and a crystal set on a painted pine table.

"Upstairs," she said.

I climbed the stairs. In the dark hallway I knocked on a door with light showing under it. Bessie Smith was singing on a phonograph inside. The light went out, but the music continued.

"Bass?" I said. "This is Connie Minor from the *Banner.* We met last January."

"What you want?" It was a young woman's voice.

"Jack Dance sent me. I've got a message for Bass."

"He ain't here. You can give it to me."

"It's personal."

"How I know you're who you says you are?"

I stooped and slid my press card—not the police pass—under the door. I hoped she was a better reader than Springfield. After a moment the card poked back out. I retrieved it.

"He at the Red Door," said the voice.

I knew where that was. I thanked her and left. There was no sign of the old woman in the parlor.

Three young colored men were gathered around the Ford with the hood folded up on one side and the motor still running. One of them was the man who had been holding up the lightpole before. I hesitated a beat, then walked between two of them and secured the hood. They smelled of sour whiskey and old lavender. The hairs on the back of my neck stood straight out.

The men stepped back when I nudged the car forward. The Red Door was just two blocks away but I wasn't going to walk them. The trio followed on foot down the center of the street.

Puddles stood on Hastings from a recent rain, reflecting green and purple from the neon lit saloons that lined the block on both sides; the street had been outlaw too long to observe the usual blind-pig proprieties. I parked in front of a brownstone at the end of the block. Stepping down, I saw an Auburn two-seater on the other side of the street with two men inside. Their features were in shadow, but the boat-tailed Speedster was worth noticing in that neighborhood at four in the morning, especially when it faced the wrong way. As I entered the brownstone, the glass in the door reflected the three Negroes walking around the corner onto Hastings.

Two flights up I knocked on a door painted red and told the black face behind the go-to-hell panel I was there to see Bass Springfield. The panel slid shut. I listened to a muted cornet on the other side. The door opened.

They had gutted two apartments, set up a bar and a platform at one end, and brought in tables and chairs from anywhere at all. Three colored couples shared a sofa and a brown cigarette near the door. The air was smeared with smoke, tobacco and marijuana. The cornetist on the platform was growling his way through "Potato Head Blues" with help from a banjo and bass fiddle.

Springfield sat flat-footed at the bar on a stool that would have left anyone else's feet dangling, with his crippled hands wrapped around a white china mug. Every eye in the place saw me put an elbow on the bar. The bartender, fat and bald in a pink shirt with garters, kept one hand out of sight under the taps.

"I remembers you," Springfield said when I spoke. He had a soft cap pulled down to his eyes and was watching his image in a mirror advertising Listerine's Halitosis Cure behind the bar.

"Jack sent me," I said. "They got Hannion."

He drained the mug two-handed. I smelled raw alcohol. "Celestine tell you where to find me?"

"Is that her name? You ought to send her away. Three men followed me from your house." I described them.

"I told them to watch the place."

"You knew about Hannion?"

"I expected Mr. Andy. He takes more chances. But I knowed it be one of us. Mr. Jack and them at the place on Howard?"

"He said to join them and watch your ass. By the way, there's an Auburn parked across the street. Those friends of yours too?"

"No. They followed me."

"What are you going to do?"

"Make 'em wait." He pushed his mug toward the bartender.

"They'll be there when you come out."

He said nothing. The musicians finished playing. In the silence between sets I heard a long tinkle of glass in the distance. I turned from the bar. Springfield grasped my arm. His grip was weak, but I hesitated. "My car's parked outside."

"It ain't your car."

More glass broke. I remembered the three Negroes. "They'll get shot."

"That's covered."

"You mean they're armed?"

Everyone in the room laughed. The bartender took his hand from under the bar and filled Springfield's mug from a bottle.

"What will they do to them?" I asked.

"Just rough 'em around some. They be walking home."

"That won't make Rosenstein any happier."

"They ain't from Rosenstein."

I tried to read his profile. "Jack said—"

"Mr. Jack always was full of horseshit," he said. "He knows they ain't Purples. Them boys works for Joey Machine."

PART TWO

May–November 1930

Bloody '30

I think the Prohibition laws can be successfully enforced against commercial operations. We propose to make these our objective and not to dissipate our energies in other fields. . . . We will exert a steady, unrelenting pressure against the outlaw liquor traffic until it is driven from the land, or our last drop of energy expended.

—Amos W. W. Woodcock,
Prohibition Administrator

Some of the wets talk as though they had several drinks and some of the drys talk as though they needed them.

—*The Detroit Free Press*

Chapter Nine

By July 1930—that terrible, blood-and-shit-splattered July in the City of Detroit—Jack Dance no longer had to pretend he was notorious. His name flew around the exclusive Detroit Club and opened the doors of blind pigs from Outer Drive to Cadillac Square, and his unruly curls and screw-you grin were as famous as Father Coughlin's voice of doom.

In May, while Jack was holed up in a rented house on Howard Street with Bass Springfield and little Andy Kramm and Austin Camarillo, the former air ace whose wasted features gave him an unlucky resemblance to the Phantom of the Opera, I "braved hails of lead" (my words, from the *Banner*) to interview the rebel chief in a room filled with pistols and rifles and enough hand grenades to open a hole in the Siegfried line. His name appeared in print for the first time and he coined a statement that's become part of the language. "We didn't start this fight," I quoted him, "but we're sure as shooting going to finish it."

The column contained three lies. The hails of lead presented no obstacle because there weren't any, the interview having taken place during one of the frequent lulls that occur in a protracted gang war; Jack said "sure as hell," not "sure as shooting;" and there was no fight until he started it. For some time Jack and his little band had been embezzling liquor from the Machine stock and selling it to neighborhood dealers who couldn't afford Joey's prices. In many cases the shipments never made it to the warehouse, one or two carloads having been diverted to a blockhouse Jack had arranged for the purpose with a caretaker at historic Fort Wayne. Off the record, the young gangster was astonishingly candid about the details. For the first time I understood Andy Kramm's slip in Leamington when he had referred to Joey's liquor as Jack's.

Joey, who knew every nickel he had ever earned or stolen by serial number and date and where it had gone, was not long in discovering the leak and who was responsible. He had sent Dom Polacki, his hulking bodyguard, around to Jack's room at the Book-Cadillac Hotel with a friendly warning to return the spoils by way of breaking Jack's kneecaps. But Jack was ready for him, and twenty-four hours later a private messenger service delivered Dom's oversize hat to the Acme Garage, along with a note demanding a thousand dollars for his safe return.

The word around was that Sal Borneo, in the interest of public relations, had restrained Joey from sending a convoy of gunners down Michigan Avenue where the hotel stood, and chipped in half the ransom from Unione Siciliana funds as a gesture of good faith. The money was left in a telephone booth in the Union Depot on Fort Street and Dom reported to the garage that afternoon, bareheaded but unharmed. Joey was quiet for a week. Then, as Baldy Hannion, a known Dance associate, was driving up Woodward Avenue, Detroit's main stem, to spend the night with his wife, a gunmetal-gray Pontiac sedan drew abreast of his Plymouth coupe and a man in the backseat poked a sawed-off shotgun through the open window and blew off the top of Hannion's head. His car sideswiped a Model T truck, spun completely around, bucked up over the sidewalk, and came to rest against the base of the marble steps leading up to the Detroit Public Library.

Joey had had his blood, but was enraged the next day by news that the two men he had sent to the Black Bottom to make a similar example of Bass Springfield had been severely beaten by Springfield's Negro associates. Jack's room at the Book-Cadillac was broken into and ransacked, but no evidence of his present whereabouts was found, and the storm abated. It was during that quiet spell that I conducted my interview.

"Just don't tell 'em where we are."

Jack, in vest and shirtsleeves, had one of his Lugers knocked down on top of a folding card table and was wiping the parts with an oily rag. He had rented the place furnished in loud Polish taste: corpulent lamps with beaded shades and mohair overstuffeds and red roosters on the curtains. A floor model Radiola was tuned low to the Casa Loma Orchestra.

I realized then that I had never seen Jack in repose; that he was always doing something, as if one quiet moment might cause the dynamo that charged him to shake itself apart. And I thought for the first time how exhausting it must have been just to be Jack Dance.

Camarillo—Lon—sat opposite him cheating himself at solitaire. He looked badly emaciated in a BVD undershirt and loose pinstriped trousers, like French prisoners in picture books about the Great War. The bones of his arms stood out like umbrella staves. Andy Kramm, small and neat in an argyle vest, white Oxford shirt, and black pegtops, leaned against the kitchen arch sipping a Coke. He looked too young with his bright blue eyes and close-cropped towhead to have served in the war. Springfield was asleep upstairs, having stood sentry duty the previous night. But for the heavy ordnance the three might have been grown brothers come home for a reunion.

I tried to get comfortable with a pad and pencil in a quagmire of cushions and antimacassars masquerading as a davenport. "Why'd you tell me Rosenstein had Hannion killed?"

"I wasn't sure you'd help if you knew it was Joey." Jack began reassembling the pistol.

"How deep are you into him?"

"I bought a brewery. You figure it out."

"Why a brewery, with Canada five minutes away?"

"Beer's where the money is, but it takes up too much space coming across. I bailed a guy out. He was making that legal three-two wolverine piss and going under, so I bought the works."

He was being uncharacteristically modest. By the time it was finished, Jack Dance's brewery would represent the largest single bootlegging investment in Detroit since the frantic six months following the passage of the Volstead Act. Pooling his chiseled profits with the resources of his handful of loyalists in return for venture shares, he had acquired the brewery and the warehouse that sheltered it and was at that moment engaged in retooling and in employing experts to improve upon the brewing techniques used by Machine in his less ambitious operation. With the help of an immigrant German brewmeister named Scherwein and three tank trucks purchased from a failed gas company in Toledo for deliveries to his commercial customers—the trucks painted to resemble Standard Oil tankers—he would threaten Machine's East Side monopoly with a superior product offered at competitive prices.

What Jack never mentioned, and what didn't come out until he and Joey were both dead and Sal Borneo was defending himself in court against charges of income tax evasion and interstate labor racketeering, was that Jack's major cash outlay involved bribing certain authorities to let his enterprise alone. For this he had borrowed heavily from loan sharks connected with the Unione Siciliana. It was an old underworld maxim that the Italians would sell a *paisan* into slavery for a greater share of the market, and here was one Jew willing to put it to the test. Meanwhile Borneo pocketed the proceeds and went on playing the disinterested mediator.

I took down as much as Jack was willing to share about the brewery, as well as the details of his posturing in the face of the Machine threat, which was in the process even then of being resolved through Unione efforts. When I got up to leave:

"Come back when this is over and cover my wedding." Jack dry-fired the Luger at a kewpie doll on a shelf, testing the action.

"Who threw the loop over you?"

His smile over the pistol was actually shy. "Her name's Vivian Deering. You saw her at the Graystone the night after the Erie run."

I remembered the woman with the Greek profile. "I know that name."

Andy said, "You should. She was Gus Woodbine's old lady."

"She ain't no old lady," Jack said testily.

It's funny how you forget things. In 1922, when Vivian Deering Woodbine was sixteen, she had sued Philip Howard Augustus Woodbine, General Motors' major stockholder, for divorce on grounds that he had mistreated her during their marriage of three months. The details of their relationship, including weekend visits to a nudist colony in Florida and the collection of feather dusters Woodbine maintained in the bedroom of their Grosse Pointe mansion, had kept the tabloids hugging themselves for weeks. They might have squeezed another month out of "Dearie and Daddy" had not Woodbine, despondent over the divorce and the fact that his own Woodbine motorcar never got off the drawing board because of the monopolistic practices of Henry Ford, shot himself to death with an elephant gun he had carried while on safari with Teddy Roosevelt in Africa. He left ten million dollars to

Vivian in his will, but attorneys for his grown son and daughter had stalled it in probate.

I sat back down. "Where'd you meet?"

"This ain't for print." He laid down the Luger and wiped gun oil from his hands, paying special attention to his manicure. "I was collecting for Joey last August at the Club Royale and when I come out of the office she was sitting at a table. She was with this stiff from Des Moines or someplace; he was here for his college reunion in Ann Arbor. He was three sheets to the wind, so I tipped a waiter to pour him into a cab and sat down to keep her company. You should've seen her." He drew a gold watch from a vest pocket and popped it open. Inside the lid was a photograph, tinted with oils, of the woman with the dark blonde hair and the classic nose. I knew then why I hadn't recognized her. In 1922 she had been slightly chubby and worn her hair bobbed. The new style was a lot less brassy.

"The watch is nice too. Gift?"

"That's nothing," Andy said. "You ought to see the cufflinks she gave him. Real diamonds."

Lon made an unpleasant kissing noise. Ignoring him, Jack put away the watch.

"Wedding's next month if we settle this other thing before then," he told me. "You're invited, but no announcement. It's private."

"Formal?"

"Soup and fish. I'm being fitted."

"Bride dressing?" Lon asked.

Jack snatched up the gun and leaped to his feet, upsetting the card table with a crash and scattering the solitaire game. Lon sat back, regarding him with dead eyes. I was trapped in the deep davenport. Andy froze with the Coke bottle lifted halfway to his lips.

The cover was off the dynamo now. The sparks from its charging wheels lit Jack's face.

Bass Springfield, barefoot and shirtless, appeared on the upstairs landing with his .45 automatic, crouching to peer under the overhang. His chest was blue-black and slabbed with muscle. "Something?"

That broke the spell. Lon breathed. "Forget I said anything," he said. "I haven't been outside for a week."

"Shit." Jack threw the pistol into a wingback chair and turned away, shoving his hands deep in his pockets. "Get out of here, Connie. This place is for shooters."

I didn't argue.

Jensen came into the office lighting his pipe an hour later just as I finished my column. I asked him if Andrea was around.

"Her door's open. You can request an audience."

Andrea St. Charles was the *Banner*'s gossip columnist and covered the woman's angle on major breaking stories those days when nothing fresh was forthcoming. She was a sob sister in the grand tradition, the warbling voice no one took seriously at press conferences who could dictate a story over the telephone five minutes before deadline that would make an iron girder weep rusty tears. I had been banging around newsrooms for nine years and had never known a better journalist or a more autocratic personality. I poked my head into her office and rapped on the open door.

"Why, good afternoon, Mr. Minor. What happy circumstance brings Mr. Wolfman's star columnist to Andrea's boudoir?"

It could have passed for one at that. Wolfman was priggish about men and women sharing workspace out of wedlock, and so had given Andrea her own private office, the only one on the floor besides his. She had had it repainted dusky rose, laid down a braided oval rug, and hung ruffled curtains and her framed certificate of membership in the D.A.R. Her desk was standard-issue scarred yellow oak, but she had added a vase with cut flowers that she freshened every day from the florist's shop down the street. She herself was a flower preserved from another era, the Edwardian: Thin and ethereally pale, her hair dyed black and pinned up under a hat like Robin Hood's, complete with feather; her bony frame covered by a smartly tailored powder-blue suit, white cotton gloves to the elbows. She looked forty, was probably past fifty. She finished erasing something from the sheet in her typewriter and blew away the shreds.

"Just passing by," I said. "What's on the griddle?"

"I just got off the telephone with Mrs. Lindbergh. Charming creature. They're celebrating their first anniversary next week, the darlings."

"That's the beat?"

"Heavens, no. She's in the family way. *That's* the beat."

"Just what the world needs. Another aviator."

"Or aviatrix. Oh, twaddle." She had discovered an ink smudge on the index finger of her right glove. Without hesitating she stripped off the pair, flipped them into her OUTGOING basket, and requisitioned a fresh pair from a drawer in her desk. I don't know how she did it. I couldn't type wearing my University of Detroit class ring.

I watched her smooth the gloves over her narrow angular hands. "I need an address, preferably with a phone number. If anyone has it or can get it, it's you."

"Darling boy, Andrea's no directory. Do you have something for her?"

I was prepared for that. "A wedding announcement. But you can't use it until the day they tie the knot."

"Pooh. Agreed. Whose address?"

"Vivian Deering's."

She clucked her tongue. "Be an angel and hand me that telephone."

It was within her reach on the desk, a white French job with gold trim, but I picked it up and held it out. She took it and dialed.

"Darling! Andrea. Aren't you sweet. Andrea needs a favor."

Three "darlings," two "dear boys," and a "precious" later, she hung up. I took the telephone from her and put it back on the desk.

"The Statler," she said. "Suite 714. The hotel switchboard will put you through."

I wrote it down. "Have I proposed to you lately?"

"You'll have to ask Mr. St. Charles to grant me that divorce. I think he's in Switzerland. Who's the lucky couple?"

"Vivian Deering and Jack Dance."

She wrinkled her nose. "Who is Jack Dance?"

"Read tonight's paper."

"My dear, ladies of my breeding wouldn't be caught dead reading a rag like the *Banner.*" She flicked her hands at me. "Shoo, now. It's quarter to four. Mrs. Lindbergh's baby turns into a pumpkin in fifteen minutes."

I blew her a kiss and got out. In January 1937, Andrea St. Charles was killed when the Ford Tri-Motor she was riding in on her way to Franklin Delano Roosevelt's second inaugural ball crashed outside Columbus. I miss her and all her fawning, twittering, indispensable tribe.

Chapter Ten

"I'm not sure why I agreed to see you. Maybe it was the picture at the top of your column. You didn't look anything at all like the weasels who pestered me eight years ago."

I said, "It's the pipe."

"I was impressed with your writing too," Vivian Deering said. "It's pulp, but it sounds like the truth. You wouldn't believe some of the things they wrote about Gus and me. I'm surprised anyone did."

"You have to admit it was a hell of a story. Excuse my language."

"All I wanted was a divorce. If I'd been married to a foreman at General Motors it would barely have made the legal notices."

"May I quote you?"

"No. You're not here to discuss my first marriage. Jack and I agreed on that. Do you take sugar?"

"Just black."

She handed me a cup. I had seen too many William Powell movies. I'd expected a penthouse at least, with a hostess in satin lounging pajamas and a maid named Colette to pour tea. Instead I had been met at the door of a quietly furnished suite by Miss Deering herself, who led me to a balcony with wicker furniture where she proved she could pour coffee from a silver-plated carafe without calling up the troops. She had on a navy cotton dress with a yellow yoke that brought out the highlights in her honey-colored hair. She was not a pretty woman but a handsome one, with frank eyes and a grave mouth and a profile that belonged in ivory.

On the way through the suite I had noticed the stack of *Banner*s I'd sent her on an end table, next to yesterday's *Times* with its Page One account of the truce between Joey Machine and Jack Dance, complete with head shots of the former combatants on either side of a grainy blow-up of Sal Borneo in a fedora, photographed at a funeral in 1928; he shunned cameras. Tom Danzig had stolen a beat on the rest of the city with his first bylined article, about Borneo's peacemaking coup. Just getting scooped didn't rankle me half as much as the knowledge that it had been my column about the gang war that had made Jack famous enough to warrant the front page in the first place.

I sipped coffee and admired the view. It was a picture-postcard day in late May and you could see clear to Belle Isle. The buildings on both sides of the river had razor edges. "Very nice. What do you do, Miss Deering?"

"Gus gave me a thousand shares of General Motors stock as a wedding present. This is what I do." She poured a cup for herself and added cream.

"You're a bit older than Jack, aren't you?"

"I'm twenty-four. He's twenty. It's not what you think."

"What do I think?"

"What I'd think, if I weren't me and Jack weren't Jack: That he's after my money. He proposed to me the night we met. I turned him down, of course. The point is he didn't know then who I was or how much I was worth. All he knew about me was my first name."

"He might have known all that going in."

"He might have, but he didn't. I'm a lot less naive than I was in 1922; I can smell a chiseler a mile off. Even when I told him who I was it didn't mean anything to him. There are still a few Americans who have never read a tabloid, Mr. Minor." She raised the cup to her lips, watching me.

"I was just fishing, Miss Deering. I know Jack. He'd swipe a nickel from a street peddler but he wouldn't marry Garbo to get his hands on a million dollars. He'd rather grab it running."

"I agree, except for the part about stealing from a peddler. He has ideas. He doesn't plan to spend his life as a common hoodlum."

"Is that why you're marrying him?"

She met my gaze. "I'm marrying him because it's right. His isn't the first proposal I've had since Gus. The right man had to ask."

That's the thing with smart women, and Vivian was no dummy.

When they manage to do something boneheaded it's usually over a pair of pants. Well, I sat through Jack's trial for the Sylvester Street killing later and heard more than a few women sigh when he sat down at the defense table. He was big and good-looking like Red Grange, and when he swung open that barn-door grin you could smell female heat all over the gallery. I guess if a slippery politico like Jimmy Walker could trip himself up over a sweet young thing like Betty Compton, women had the same privilege. That's what the suffragettes had been squawking about. I asked her if they'd set a date.

"The second Saturday in June. He called today. The reception will be at the Chesterfield Inn."

"He asked me not to announce it. I won't use any of this until after the ceremony, but I had to promise someone a scoop to get your address. Would it be all right if we ran an announcement that night? Chances are you'll be starting your honeymoon by then."

"I don't see why not."

"Where are you going, by the way?"

She smiled for the first time. "Atlantic City. Jack's never been there."

It was the logical choice. The local rackets had many friends in Jersey, where the New York bosses went to gamble and visit the whorehouses and trade their soiled bills for fresh Detroit green. Atlantic City would represent the exotic end of the universe to Jack Dance and his crowd, many of whom had never been farther from home than Ontario. There he could show off his elegant bride and impress potential backers with the ideas that made Vivian so proud.

The rest of the questions had to do with her life before and after Woodbine. Not much there, unless you were Andrea St. Charles: Born in Buffalo to a minor railroad baron and his society wife, raised in Southampton, educated in finishing schools, introduced to the auto magnate at a party on Long Island when she was sixteen, married to him six weeks later in Detroit with her parents' consent. The next three months were as well known to readers as Buster Brown's adventures in the funnies. After Woodbine's suicide and the reading of the will, his adolescent widow had gone back home to Southampton to live with her parents for a time, but the scribes followed her there and camped out on the patio, so she toured Europe for a year, took the waters, met Mussolini, and saw a bullfight or two before coming back to defend Woodbine's will from the first of many legal attempts on the part of his children to have it set aside. The press had covered the opening round perfunctorily, but probate was too Byzantine for short declarative headlines and it moved on to fresh scandals. Since then, with the exception of visits to Southampton and family, she had been living in town.

I drank a second cup of coffee, thanked her for the interview, offered congratulations, and left. Sitting on the story until after the wedding wasn't likely to raise my blood pressure. The bride-to-be was no moll, and shorn of Daddy and his feather dusters she was flatter copy than the Anti-Saloon League's candidate for President in 1932. Quality folk made poor press. It was one of the reasons I stayed around Detroit.

The event took place on schedule. Because Vivian was a Catholic who had nettled the Church with a noisy public petition for divorce and Jack hadn't been to Synagogue since he was ten, the couple was united in a brief ceremony in the County Building by a justice of the peace. What the nuptials lacked in pomp the reception at the Chesterfield made up for in volume, with a fourteen-piece dance band blasting out the latest from Chicago and New Orleans for what had to be the largest gathering of area characters this side of the last Prohibition sweep, cutting up the floor in monkey suits with janes in beads and satin who hadn't been off their backs for that many hours in succession since Coolidge. Jack looked as fit as Dempsey in white tie and tails, and Vivian, wearing green sequins and a diamond choker, stole the show from the wedding cake, which was as tall as Howard Wolfman and came courtesy of Sal Borneo. Borneo himself couldn't be there but sent someone in his place: A smooth dark Italian in his late twenties named Frankie Orr, who spent the evening nursing the same drink and memorizing faces. Also absent was Joey Machine, but a package with a card signed by him stood taller than all the other gifts on the table. Jack made a show of ducking when it was opened. It turned out to be a cut-glass vase for long-stemmed roses, imported from England.

"A dame must of picked it out," said Andy Kramm, who wasn't feeling much pain by then. "Joey wouldn't know crystal from his dago ass."

Jack was less ebullient. In his circle you never knew what was meant by a gift involving flowers.

Tom Danzig attended, looking more polished than his brother in evening clothes with a redhead on his arm, one of these hollow-cheeked ascetic types in a white gown who looked as if she read T. S. Eliot without being forced to. Tom shook my hand, said something with a reined-in smile that was lost in the "Black Bottom Stomp," and moved on.

Lon didn't drink and left early. Andy said he didn't like crowds or music. "Old Spooky didn't come back from France with all his checkers," he explained. I found out then that Lon was known as the Spook when he pulled the trigger for Borneo, not entirely because of his appearance. Alcohol was an aphrodisiac to Andy's natural love of gossip.

I was stag. I had asked Hattie to come with me, but the Elks were in town and she was busy directing traffic at her joint in River Rouge, where she'd been for a record six months. I introduced myself to another loner, a thin, trampled-looking old man with curly white hair and spectacles as thick as coasters. He wasn't much bigger than Andy and had on a black suit with dust in the creases. "You know my boy John?" he asked.

It took me a moment to realize he meant Jack. "You're Mr. Danzig?" He looked like the watch repairman he was. Jack and Tom must have gotten their size from their mother's family. We tried talking, but the music was loud and he indicated that his hearing was no better than his vision. We separated. When I looked for him later after the set was finished I learned he'd gone home.

At dusk Mrs. Dance threw her bouquet into the arms of a Charlotte Street professional, who squealed as if she were sixteen and unbroken, and the bride and groom left for the train station in Jack's new LaSalle. Truce or no truce, no chances were taken. They were escorted in two Buicks, front and rear, driven by kids from Jack's gang with Andy Kramm and Bass Springfield riding shotgun. It was the first I'd seen of Springfield that day. Negroes weren't allowed in the Chesterfield unless they wore aprons or carried musical instruments.

The reception was still going when the *Banner* hit the pavement. The lead item in Andrea St. Charles's "Lives of a Saint" column read:

> Motor City freebooter Handsome Jack Dance and Vivian "Dearie" Deering (and we *all* remember Daddy Woodbine, don't we, darlings?) joined destinies today in a civil ceremony downtown. It's not known yet whether the gay couple plans to raise Hades or a family.

Jack brought a Kodak to Atlantic City, and the Dances took each other's picture posing on the boardwalk and in front of the Ferris wheels and clowning in their swimsuits on the beach. A snapshot Vivian took of Jack, natty in seersucker and a Panama hat, squaring off with a rifle to knock down a tin duck, appeared in the *Free Press* the day after Sylvester Street; a reporter copped it from an album in the living room of the Dance home in St. Clair Shores while his partner kept Vivian busy in the front hall when Jack was in hiding. Because of the gun it's the one they use most often when his name comes up, just ahead of the picture that originally appeared on the *Banner*'s front page with my wedding story, of the couple slicing the cake with a big knife, on account of that Ripper tag the *News* hung on him. But I'm getting ahead of myself again, and I swore I wouldn't.

They took a day out to visit New York City, where they watched the Empire State Building crawling up its steel skeleton and caught Gertrude Lawrence and Leslie Howard in *Candlelight* on Broadway and Jack bought a painting in a gallery. Done in dark oils and framed in cheap amber Bakelite like crystallized honey, it showed a blonde girl praying in profile beneath a crucifix on a mustard wall, hands clasped under her slightly retiring chin. The typewritten card that contained its price identified it as *The Pious Heart*, by Arthur Rayburn Couzzens. It was a flagrantly Christian painting for so flagrant an agnostic Jew as Jack, executed unremarkably by an artist the world had forgotten long before he ended his life by drinking a glass of turpentine in 1921—the year, the curator reported, that *The Pious Heart* had entered the gallery—but it went wherever Jack went from then on. I would come to look for it the first time I visited him in a new place. He never explained why he liked it and I never asked him; it was that kind of picture, the girl's corn-fed face so vapid in its rapture it made you turn away in embarrassment, as from those likenesses of Jesus whose eyes open and shut depending on where you're standing. Vivian had tried to talk him out of buying it, which goes to show you how little she knew about her new husband. That anonymous girl prayed in more interesting places than Elmer Gantry.

While Jack was away, the truce fell apart. Joey was considering Borneo's suggestion that he cede a small portion of his holdings on the East Side to Jack in return for a cut of the profits from the new brewery, when someone hijacked a convoy of ten-ton trucks hauling beer from a brewery Joey did business with in Cleveland. The scout car for the convoy drove around a tree that had fallen across a country road ten miles from the Michigan border, and as the lead truck tried to do the same, a biplane that had been buzzing and farting around the sky a thousand feet up without attracting much attention suddenly went into a steep dive and the man in the rear seat slung a tommy gun over the side of the cockpit and tattooed a line of holes across the truck's radiator. A couple of hand grenades followed, one exploding under the scout car's rear axle and dumping the car over sideways. By the time the gunners scrambled out and returned fire, the aeroplane had climbed out of range. Then a small army led by a big Negro charged down a slope from a cluster of trees, firing machine guns and high-powered rifles. One of the men from the car was killed and two more wounded. The one remaining dropped his shotgun and threw up his hands. He was forced to lie down on the ground with his hands behind his head. Then the drivers were pulled from the trucks and told to join him while others took their places at the wheel. From start to finish the raid took twenty minutes.

There was no mystery involved. The pilot of the plane could only have been one person, and I had a pretty good idea who the airborne gunner was. The big Negro clinched it. As soon as word reached Detroit I headed straight for the house on Howard, which although Jack had moved out, had become the unofficial headquarters of the Dance mob.

Bass Springfield opened the door four inches, enough to show me his .45. When I convinced him I was alone he let me inside. Immediately my hand was seized by a manic Andy Kramm, who pumped it as if we hadn't seen each other in years and I had brought a bottle. As a matter of fact I had, but it was no orphan there. His face was flushed and his eyes were brighter than ever.

"Connie, Connie! Come in and take a load off."

"Where's Lon?"

"He's at the blockhouse. You hear about it?"

"Jesus Christ," Springfield muttered.

"You mean the hijack?"

"Hijack, hell! It was a major fucking offensive with air support. Sit down."

I took a seat at the card table this time and transferred the flat pint from my hip pocket to the table. I had wondered a little about the paradox of bringing booze to a bootlegger, but as it happened, he had just run dry. Jack's rule against drinking on the job had kept the stock low.

Within twenty minutes and half the bottle, I had a full account of the raid for publication minus names, including the name of my source. Springfield tried for a while to stand on Andy's tongue, but coloreds didn't tell whites what to do in that company or any other and he gave up. Off the record, I asked Andy if Jack was aware of what happened. His toothpaste grin was lopsided. "Hell, who you think planned it?"

"What's he got against peace?"

"Same thing he had against working for Joey, I guess. Not enough noise."

The evening my exclusive "interview with an insider" ran with the first public details of the Ohio hijacking, I accepted an invitation over the telephone to have lunch at the Detroit Club the next day with Lloyd Bundle, director of the regional bureau of the Continental News Syndicate. I had abalone for the first time in my life in a wood-paneled dining room that looked and smelled like the inside of a humidor. Bundle, chubby and pink-featured with a head of hair the color and thickness of lemon sherbet, might have passed for a Dutch Master in a Rembrandt get-up, but he had on a banker's blue suit instead and a Masonic ring on his left pinky. Over the baked Alaska he offered me syndication in two hundred newspapers and $8,500 annually plus ten percent of each new subscription, on top of my salary at the *Banner.*

I did some quick mental arithmetic. All told, not counting bonuses and subscription royalties, it came to $16,300. Governor Green made $15,000, not counting graft. If you placed any stock in people's names, Bundle was well placed.

"What about the *Banner*?" I asked.

"Wolfman gets a cut. We take care of home plate. You won't even have to change offices."

"That's not a point in your favor."

He chuckled. He knew he could afford to. I pretended to think it over. In the kitchen someone had the radio tuned to WMBC, and whenever the door swung open Jerry Buckley's slightly brassy voice came out gloating over his listener poll, which was running three to two in favor of recalling Mayor Bowles. Buckley said; which had a way of becoming truth once he said it. Between him and Father Coughlin it was even money which man had the firmer grip on his audience's testicles.

"Mr. Bundle, you've bought yourself a columnist."

He wiped ice cream off his chins and grasped my outstretched hand. "Any ideas on the subject of your first column?"

A waiter flapped through the swinging door, letting out a little more Buckley.

"One or two," I said.

Chapter Eleven

Three sainted adjectives became decanonized early in the thirties. Within a short span of years, we learned to measure a politician's crookedness by the number of times "Honest" appeared in front of his name; "rich," except when applied to certain foods and fabrics, became a term of proletarian contempt; and "crusading," most exalted of all, lost its power to uplift, coming to signify demagoguery and arrogance. But in July 1930, Gerald E. Buckley wore the first and third with Borgian pride and defined the second.

In looks and personality, he was an unlikely spellbinder. Despite a somewhat heavy-lipped, slope-browed resemblance to a trout, he had a reputation as a ladies' man, and his harsh voice and overly aggressive delivery at the microphone, instead of having the opposite effect, drew listeners to the Mutual network the way the *Banner*'s shrill headlines created mobs at newsstands. From his tiny studio on the mezzanine of the LaSalle Hotel at Adelaide and Woodward—Buckley's answer to Father Coughlin's electronic pulpit in the Shrine of the Little Flower—he exerted a derisive, brow-beating, tent-revival influence over numbers that would impress a senator.

For months, since before Bowles's now-infamous "Let 'em die" speech, Buckley had been beating the drum for recall. The big, amiable mayor with the thinning black hair and horn-rimmed glasses had, he said, created a climate in which crime was encouraged to prosper. When the police bothered to arrest a suspect in a gangland slaying and bring him to court, the judge or jury almost invariably freed him for his service to society. This, said Buckley, amounted to a mandate to go forth and commit more murders. By July the statistics were firmly on his side. Violent deaths averaged one per day. Detroit was marked up like a butcher's chart, each portion bearing the stamp of a different marauding band: the Machines, the Rosensteins, the Oakland Sugar House Gang, and the rivergoing Little Jewish Navy, with the Purple Gang claiming free range throughout the city and the communities downriver, forming and breaking alliances with the amoral license of post-Christian Vandals and hiring out their guns as far west as Chicago, where every little kid knew they had supplied the shooters for the St. Valentine's Day Massacre. In spite of numerous attempts by Sal Borneo's fraternal Unione Siciliana to maintain some semblance of peace through the assignment of sovereign duchies, splinter wars flared up sporadically along ethnic lines as old as Exodus, made more deadly by the prospect of financial reward and the presence of modern weaponry. It was Dodge City with choppers and V-8 Fords. All this Buckley laid at Charles Bowles's wide-open door.

Late on the night of the 22nd, the lights of every newspaper and radio station in the city were burning as results trickled in from the polling places, where a record number of voters had turned out to decide whether Detroit should be the first large American city to give its mayor his walking papers. The trickle became a torrent, and by midnight it was all over, including the shouting: The public had voted by a majority of 30,000 to dump Bowles.

The *Banner* beat out every other election extra in the city by minutes. Two front pages—"SO LONG, CHARLIE" and "ELECTION FRAUD!"—the former illustrated with a four-column blow-up pulled from the morgue of Bowles waving to reporters as he boarded the train on his way to the Kentucky Derby, had been prepared days earlier; and in less than ten minutes, with Ernie Swayles barking the numbers ward by ward into his ear through a receiver held by a copy boy, Walter DiVirgilio on the rewrite desk clattered out a twenty-inch story. Another boy tore each sheet out of the machine as it was finished and ran it down to typesetting. When the last one vanished, Walter lit up a cigar to celebrate, and by the time he had it half smoked the newsies were crying it in the street. Howard was there, the only man on the premises not in his shirtsleeves that sticky summer night, and shook everyone's hand at least once. The festive air was fouled only a little by the fact that while Walter was typing, Buckley was reading the final tally over the air on the radio in Howard's office. I don't think any of us caught the significance then. Did the dinosaurs observe the furry little mammals darting between their legs and think of anything but how to make a meal of them?

I was there just for the ride. My column, a lightweight thing comparing the recall system to the old Roman custom of hacking to pieces those leaders who had overstayed their welcome, was being reprinted from the regular evening edition. I stayed at my desk, out of the way, with a cup of coffee laced with bourbon, noodling around with my first piece for syndication. I had discarded my first opening as pompous and stilted:

> On paper, Jerry Buckley's broadcasts read like a page of notes from a high school civics lecture—broken, half-formed, puerile. What makes them sound like the Sermon on the Mount? When time stills the voice and the red-hot topics are fossils, will future generations read the transcripts and condemn us for gullible half-wits?

It was past two A.M. and I had taken an entirely different tack without liking it any better when Ernie Swayles leaned in through the office door. The knot of his tie was down around his knees, he had sweated through his tan poplin jacket, and his nose, potato-shaped and cocked off-center, registered a blood-alcohol level in the mauve range. I could smell the junipers on his breath from where I was sitting.

"Hell of a fine job, Ern."

"You hear?"

I misunderstood him. "Yeah, I'm here." He was drunker than I'd thought.

"Who told you?"

"I was standing by Walter's desk when you called him."

I still wasn't getting it. He looked more confused than I was. "I ain't talked to Walter since I dictated my story. My phone was ringing when I got in just now. What'd *you* hear?"

"Let's start over. What happened?"

"Buckley's dead. They gunned him in the lobby of the LaSalle."

"Who did?"

"The bulls don't know yet. That's who called me. I'm on my way down. Want to come?"

"No, I'll wait." The truth was I couldn't leave my chair. Ever since that night on the ice I had reacted to shock with paralysis. Courage is the first casualty of experience.

He shrugged and left. When I could move, I upended my much-kicked steel wastebasket and bent down from my chair to sort through the crumpled sheets until I found that original opening. You never know what you can use.

The story Swayles came back with, and that kept the linotypists and pressmen on duty for several hours more while the front page was redone and another extra was put together, had something for every-one, including a mysterious dame.

After finishing his broadcast, Jerry Buckley had shut down his mi-crophone in the LaSalle and descended the stairs from the mezzanine to the lobby, where he bought a copy of the *Times* election extra and sat down in one of the overstuffed leather chairs to read it. He had told someone at the studio that a woman had called him and asked him to meet her there. No name was mentioned. Since it was nothing unusual for him to make a late-night date, no one thought anything about it. Then, at 1:55 A.M. Wednesday, July 23rd, three men dressed as busi-nessmen entered the lobby. One hung back by the street door while his companions walked up to where Buckley was sitting and shot him eleven times in the head, chest, and stomach. He stood up, then fell forward. The three then walked out the way they had come. Buckley was dead when his face hit the floor.

Typically, Howard Wolfman had an idea for the front page of the extra-extra that exceeded the *Banner*'s abilities, and an immediate solution. Discovering that there was no headline type in the cases large enough for his purposes, he grabbed a young printer's devil who carved duck decoys in his spare time and put him to work with a knife and a block of soft pine. Then he used the telephone to get Jensen out of bed and commissioned a cartoon for the front page.

There was a little delay as Howard paced the halls waiting for Swayles to come back and write the story, Walter DiVirgilio having left to make the rounds of the blind pigs after finishing the election piece. Then the gears went back into motion. Just before dawn the first bundle hit the stands. The black legend DEAD! covered half the front page in letters eight inches high—a little crooked because the young woodcarver hadn't had time to make a neat job—with a recent smiling head shot of Buckley on the lower half next to Jensen's cartoon. This was an angry thing showing a broken-nosed silhouette in cap and turtleneck leering down with gun smoking at a corpse sprawled at its feet. On the other side of the corpse, also looking down, stood a female figure in a headscarf and dress with a blank face bearing a large question mark and a skeletal hand clutching its throat. There had been some grumbling about this choice of illustrations for Page One while a fresh shot taken and developed by Fred Ogilvie of Buckley's body itself, crumpled on the floor of the LaSalle lobby, went inside, but Howard argued that every other paper in town had had a photographer there as well and would be sure to run the same gory picture up front.

His instincts proved right. It was an old-fashioned front page, reminiscent of the war, and as such it stood apart from all the others on the rack. Readers were more interested in the mysterious woman whose call had lured Buckley to his death than in staring at yet another picture of cold meat, and the *Banner* sold out quickly. I never worked for a publisher who understood his readership better than Howard Wolfman. He'd have been a bigger tycoon than Hearst if the tabloid business hadn't suddenly gone bust a few years later.

The bulls had plenty of leads in the Buckley slaying, if they dared pursue them. Ex-Mayor Bowles might have hired it done, either as a parting shot or to remove the radio commentator as an obstacle to his re-election, for which he was automatically a candidate unless he withdrew his name from the ballot. Buckley had threatened repeatedly to expose the quiet men behind the Machines and Borneos who arranged deals with the city's political structure, and they might have had him killed to ensure his silence. Other, darker suspicions involved the victim's own alleged ties to the underworld and the possibility that he had double-crossed someone by supporting the recall. Then there were the romantics who suggested that the mystery woman was a scorned lover who had put him on the spot for revenge.

The investigation concentrated on the trigger men. Once again the streets were emptied of tramps, grifters, known gang members, and suspicious-looking strangers, and once again most of them were released because none of the witnesses had gotten a good enough look at the men in the lobby to pick them out of a line-up. The rest were held for carrying blackjacks or pistols without permits or whatever else the bulls could dig up or plant on them to gain time to work them over with lamp cords and rubber hoses in the basement of 1300 Beaubien. Police Commissioner Wilcox, sensitive to pressure from the newspapers and radio, not to mention the scrutiny of whoever might succeed Bowles, pushed for convictions in these lesser crimes when no confessions to the Buckley murder were forthcoming, as evidence of the new hard line. It didn't work; when Frank L. Murphy was elected mayor on a liberal reform ticket, Wilcox was one of the first of the old regime to go.

The heat kept up. Aided by reinforcements from Homicide and Vice, Lieutenant Valery Kozlowski and the Prohibition Squad tipped over several hundred blind pigs and whorehouses in a two-week binge, destroying the fixtures and inventory and arresting everybody who looked as if he belonged in the mug file. One of these raids, on a house on Charlotte Street, turned into a gun battle when three U.S. Treasury agents who were enjoying a night off thought the place was being robbed and opened fire on the plainclothes detectives. Kozlowski killed one and was suspended from duty pending an investigation. Until he was reinstated, he was a *cause célèbre* among reporters who a few weeks earlier would have rolled over on a source to see him brought up on charges, crippled wife or no.

Despite the push, nobody was ever arrested for the murder in the LaSalle Hotel. The mystery woman was never identified and a spokesman for the police department announced that they had abandoned that search. Buckley received short play as a martyr, then went down under a mudslide of speculation, encouraged by the scandalmongering public journals, that the radio celebrity was nothing more than a blackmailer who had tried to shake down the wrong party. After all this time I still don't know if he deserved that. Certainly there was no evidence to support it, other than a messy death at an inconvenient hour. As I said, remaining a hero had become twice as tough since the rise of the two-penny press.

Bowles's ouster, and the area-wide crackdown after the killing (following the lead of their neighbor upriver, the police in River Rouge had closed down Hattie Long's place, among others, ending her seven-month run of good luck and even confiscating her stuffed rooster) made it obvious that Detroit's wide-open days had come to an end. Getting a job became more important than having a drink, and although the liquor racket continued to prosper, as it will in times good and bad, people stopped buying papers to read about the latest death in the gutter and turned directly to the Help Wanted ads. Unemployment went up, hemlines came down. In a few years a new kind of crime, daylight bank robbery, would capture the consciousness of a nation facing foreclosure, interring the bootlegger forever in a tomb of yellowed newsprint and empty bottles.

But in the summer of 1930 Detroit was still thirsty. On the last day of July, Andrea St. Charles reported:

> Having returned from six weeks of newly wedded bliss in Atlantic City, Mr. and Mrs. Jack Dance wish to announce that they are At Home in their charming new cottage in St. Clair Shores—to everyone but you, Joey M.

Chapter Twelve

"What's the good word, Professor," said Howard, "and is it in Greek or Latin today?"

I had just handed him tomorrow's column, the second part of an interview with Ty Cobb, the first in depth since the former Tiger's retirement from baseball two years ago. The first part had just gone on sale. The mean-tempered son of a bitch had started the session in his hotel room by throwing a beer bottle at me. The bump on my forehead was still tender.

"I don't get you," I said.

Howard leaned back in his chair in his triangular office overlooking Michigan and Woodward. It was a sweltering day in late August and he had his heavy silk jacket on and every window closed. It struck me then that he didn't sweat. " 'Tyrus Raymond Cobb, who can barely read and write his own name, is a horsehide autodidact,' " he read from my column. "Define autodidact."

"Self-taught."

"At least you weren't bluffing. Why not just say self-taught? People are going to think he abuses himself with a fielder's glove."

"That's an adjective. I needed a noun. I don't think our readers are that stupid."

"I'll bet you my box at Navin Field not one in ten of them knows what 'autodidact' means. When a man comes home from the line at Ford's with the *Banner* under his arm, he wants to relax with it. He doesn't want to have to get up and hunt for the dictionary."

"This isn't just about my choice of words, is it?"

He swiveled right and left, white hands folded across his spare middle. "Last month when you were writing about the recall, you quoted from Gibbon. Edward, not Floyd. When Buckley got it you wrote ten inches on the ephemeral nature of oratory that would snare you a Ph.D. from Princeton. I got a letter from a woman in Royal Oak asking if this fellow Demosthenes was free to address her Tuesday afternoon tea social. And let's not forget that little lesson in Napoleonic tactics you gave us last January. I'm thinking of adding a poetry page and letting the newsboys go. A sheet this cerebral shouldn't be shouted in the street."

Lloyd Bundle had loved the Buckley thinkpiece, my first column for CNS; but I didn't mention it. When a property goes into syndication, the newspaper of origin loses much of its authority over the content. Howard wouldn't appreciate being reminded of the fact.

I said, "I got the idea from you. The day you hired me you said that phony picture in the Bowles press-conference issue would be remembered when Buckley was dead and his words were forgotten. When he was killed I thought maybe you knew something."

"It was just an example. And I didn't bring in the Greeks."

"I'll watch it."

He swiveled left and right. "How's your head?"

"Okay, if I hang my hat on my right ear." I touched the lump.

"The darn cracker laid out my photographer when I was with the *Plain Dealer.* It cost Hughie Jennings five hundred dollars to avoid a lawsuit. Nice to know the old boy still has his arm." He laid my column on top of his OUTGOING basket. "It won't kill them to learn a new word just this once. Are you free for a drink?"

"I've got a date."

"Hattie Long?"

I paused. "Who follows me, that little red-headed sneak from composition?"

"I was at the Oriole Terrace with my wife when you walked in with her one night back in April. We ran a spread on local bordellos in the first issue, when she was set up on Randolph. That's how I recognized her."

"Any objections?"

"Not as long as you don't leave any crabs on the toilet seat down the hall."

"You need a vacation, Howard. You're starting to talk like the *Banner*."

He smiled his measured smile. "Who do you think taught it to talk?"

The city was enjoying a quiet spell after the carnage of July. The Tigers were sliding out of the pennant race with a win-loss record of half and half for the season, and it looked as if it would be St. Louis and Philadelphia in the Series. Bowles was serving as mayor pro-tem until an election could be got up. It was summer in Detroit, and weekends the city reconvened on Belle Isle in the middle of the Detroit River to picnic, play softball, and watch the Prohibition Navy chasing rumrunners. The runners, long on capital and unhampered by bureaucracy, had the best boats and the most powerful engines—the fastest craft afloat anywhere in the world—and were almost never caught. When they were, nine times out of ten they dumped their cargo overboard with floats and bags of salt attached, then when the salt dissolved and the floats carried the crates to the surface, they came back under cover of darkness to reap the harvest. The less showy spurned boats entirely and hauled the stuff across the floor of the lake with winches concealed in service stations.

Early in the month, a green Nash sedan had cruised past the rented house on Howard Street and a man wearing overalls and a cloth cap had thrown an incendiary bomb through a window, blowing out the rest of the windows and unrolling orange streamers of flame out through the empty frames. A box of hand grenades stored inside exploded all at once and tore off the roof. Five engine companies spent the next several hours pouring water over the blaze and ducking small-arms fire as boxes of ammunition went up like strings of firecrackers. Casualties included a woman next door who had suffered a concussion when the grenade blast hurled her off her feet, and a milkhorse blown to bits while waiting for its master to finish his break in a blind pig in the basement of a house across the street. Neighbors told police they had seen the occupants of the demolished house throwing suitcases into a car early that morning. The owner was located and questioned about his tenants, but said he knew nothing about them beyond the fact that he was paid in cash the first day of every month by a big, good-looking, curly-haired young man who dressed like Rod La Rocque. The owner spoke only Polish and read a Polish-language newspaper. Shown a picture of Jack Dance, he nodded and said that was the man. Jack was arrested in St. Clair Shores for keeping dangerous explosives in a residential section and released the next day on $2,500 bail. But the explosion was the only big noise that month. The *Banner* suggested that Joey Machine peruse its classified ads and buy a second-hand aeroplane "if he expects to keep up with the Dances."

Over a sunset dinner at the Book-Cadillac—Jack's home until the trouble with Joey—I raised my Zippo to light the cigarette in Hattie's amber holder. She ignored it and struck a match. She was sitting with her back to a bright west window, but she was starting to show her age just the same, in hairline cracks around the eyes. I preferred the cracks to the black glop some women used to cover them. I had a few myself, courtesy of my thirty-sixth birthday.

I said, "You haven't seen the new apartment. I moved out of the place on John R."

"I'm getting a cold."

"Sorry to hear it. You know, I never actually met anyone with a summer cold before. My mother always said they were the worst."

I was babbling. I had spent most of the previous night parked in my Ford off East Jefferson on a tip that two Detroit police officers were making nightly withdrawals from a liquor warehouse there. The bulls never showed, and Fred Ogilvie, who had sat up with me with a camera in his lap, had called in sick that morning. I'd reported to work on two hours' sleep and was still running on ethyl ten hours later.

Hattie flicked ash into a glass tray and said nothing.

"New place open yet?" I asked.

"I haven't decided if it will. Joey and I lost a bundle in Rouge. They smashed the slot machines."

"Speaking of Bundles, Lloyd paid me today." I produced a roll from my pocket. "How much do you need to walk around on?"

She looked at the bills. "Changing professions?"

"Humor me. I've never been in a position to make a loan before."

"I can get all I need from Joey. Put it away before you get rolled."

"In here?"

"It's still Detroit, isn't it?"

I pocketed the roll. "What's wrong?"

"Nothing's wrong. You're who you are and there's no good trying to make you someone else. I don't know why I worry about it."

"Sorry about the slots."

"To hell with the slots and the rooster too. I was getting sick of schlepping them all over the East Side. I'm talking about you and me. Mostly you."

"What'd I do, forget a birthday?"

"Where were you last night?"

"Working. Did we have a date?"

"Where were you night before last?"

"Same thing. I had an interview up in Warren."

"What about all day today?"

Now I had a line on where this was going. "All right, I work a lot. I'm worth what they pay me. As I recall, you and I never made any deals about how much time we'd spend together. This is the first time we've been out in almost a month. I didn't even know where you were until last week."

"That's the way I wanted it."

"Oh." I sat back.

"Then when you tracked me down I thought, what the hell, we might as well talk. I'm thirty-nine, Connie. A thirty-nine-year-old whore and I'm running around with a newshawk who wears the same shirt three days without changing because he's never home."

"I changed today. If I thought my wardrobe meant so much to you—"

"Shit." She plucked the cigarette out of its holder and stabbed it out. "For a guy who makes his living from his powers of observation, you're as dull as a handle. You don't even know when a girl's proposing to you."

I felt the old paralysis. As I sorted through my vocabulary, the glitter in her eyes dimmed slowly, like the incandescence in a lightbulb after the power goes out. Finally she dropped the cigarette holder into her purse and snapped it shut.

"Yeah. Well, like the man said, if you don't ask. Can you give me a lift across town? I'm staying with one of the girls."

"I didn't say no," I said. "It isn't like you asked me out to the track."

"I can see how tough it is for you not to jump up and down."

"It's not a bad life. What makes you think I want to change it?"

"You don't have to. I'll catch a cab out front." She stood.

"Sit down, for Christ's sake. Since when don't we talk?"

She sat. The light hadn't gone out entirely. "You're a middle-aged man, Connie. You want to wind up banging a typewriter in a corner booth at seventy because if you retire you'll have nobody to stay home with?"

"And bang?" I grinned.

She lifted her lip like Gloria Swanson. "Honey, if you're still banging 'em at seventy, I'll still be getting banged at seventy-three. Hattie's learned some things staring at ceilings."

"Don't talk about yourself in the third person. You remind me of Andrea."

"She's seen some ceilings, I bet."

The waiter came with our bill and left with our dishes. "A lot's happened to me this year," I said. "Give me some time to sort it all out."

"I can give you a week. That's as long as I can expect Joey to wait to hear if I decide to reopen."

"I guess you won't starve."

"Starving's for suckers."

I put money on top of the bill. "Is this why you didn't go with me to Jack's reception?"

"I really did have the Elks convention. But I was pretty sore at you then. I was still stewing over that crack you made about being drunk enough to propose to me. I couldn't trust myself among all that wedded bliss. Not that those two belong in a storybook," she added. "Jack showed up at my place later."

"I thought they went straight to the station."

"No, I mean after the honeymoon."

"Your place was closed by then."

"It was July nineteenth. I know because it was the last Saturday before the bulls tipped me over."

"You're sure it was him?"

"I've known him as long as you have, remember? I ribbed him, asked if the little woman was waiting in the car. Why's it so important?"

We were standing now. The waiter reappeared and helped her on with her shawl, diaphanous violet silk embroidered with swastikas for good luck. I sometimes wonder what she did with it after Schickelgruber took over in Germany.

"Maybe it *isn't* important," I said when the car was brought around. "But Jack didn't come back officially until the thirty-first. Nine days after Jerry Buckley was killed." I tipped the attendant a quarter and we got in.

Chapter Thirteen

I had moved the stuff that counted out of the old apartment, sold the rest, and furnished a larger flat—I preferred to call this one a flat—on the sixth floor of a building with an elevator on Park. The change was dramatic. I had a bathroom all to myself, a good view of the trees and shrubbery that gave the street its name, and a Westinghouse refrigerator in the kitchen; no more balancing-act carrying a trayful of water from the icebox to the sink. But all I could think of when I was there was what a shame it was I hardly ever saw it.

On the Friday evening preceding the Labor Day weekend, I stood on the sidewalk in front of the building watching the traffic thicken. The cars were all packed with trunks and kids and red-and-yellow beach balls. It was a big time of year in Detroit, bigger than Christmas. Labor Day, arriving in the old-gold part of summer, was a reminder that the days of swimsuits and seersucker had numbers. Before long it would be overcoats and galoshes and the seven-month nightmare of winter on the Great Lakes. Everyone you saw at the wheel of a northbound car had that fixed grimace of someone determined to have a wonderful time even if it wiped out the family.

I had been standing there five minutes when a dream car, midnight blue with ivory side-panels and wire wheels, separated itself from the near lane and glided over to the curb. It was a Duesenberg, the J Club sedan, as long as a baseball diamond and loaded with horsepower. Jack Dance leaned over from the driver's seat and opened the door on my side. He was wearing a white linen suit with a straw boater tipped over his left eye.

"Dive in, Connie," he said. "There's room enough in here to play croquet."

I sank into the seat. The inside smelled like new leather and oiled wood. The door closed with a discreet snick. Bass Springfield, sitting in back in his cap and old suitcoat, grunted when I said hello.

"What happened to the LaSalle?" I asked.

"I figure I'll drive it this winter when the streets get slushy." Jack pried a hole in the traffic with his left front fender and wedged the rest of the car in after it. A horn blew. "Speedometer goes up to a hundred and sixteen, but I ain't tested it yet. Best I did so far is ninety-eight."

"The brewery must be doing well."

"We start shipping next week. I'm just on my way home from there now. Thanks for letting me pick you up. I'm on a short leash these days."

"Thanks for agreeing to talk to me. How you doing with that explosives beef?"

"Next month's the hearing. Nate says I'll get off with a fine."

"Nate?"

"Nathan Rabinowitz. Vivian's lawyer fixed me up with him. He's slicker'n snot on a doorknob, they say."

I'd heard of him. He'd served as president of the Detroit Public Lighting Commission and had run for Recorder's Court judge twice without success, but his reputation was as the mouthpiece who had won acquittal for six Purple Gang members accused of the shotgun murder of Michael P. "Mike Freak" Faryniak, boss of the eleventh ward and a known supporter of the Machine-Dardanello association, in 1926. Since then Rabinowitz had not lacked for clients among the local underworld.

I said, "That was lucky, Andy and Lon clearing out just before the bombing."

"Yeah, wasn't it." Jack tapped the horn button when the driver ahead didn't react to the green light. Four notes crooned from under the long hood in descending order. The offending car started forward.

"Who's your informant in the Machine set-up?"

He laughed. He had a pleasing tenor—people who had heard it said he'd have given a mick singer a run for his money—and his mirth was contagious. "I like you, Connie. You got chutzpah. There's some things

I don't even tell Bass, and if a nigger can't keep a secret from a white man, who can?"

Springfield, watching the scenery crawl past, said nothing. In Jack's vocabulary, "nigger" was an endearment. Springfield must have been aware of that, because when the big Negro was arrested for murder later and a bull called him a nigger, he almost beat the bull to death with his knees and elbows and had to be clubbed down by three other officers.

"How's life on the lake?" I asked.

"Damper'n frogs' drawers. The Lugers rust if I don't clean 'em every day."

"I meant how's married life."

"Everybody ought to be married. You take the drop yet?"

"Not yet."

"Who you waiting for, that Glenda Farrell dame?"

The whole country was talking about *Little Caesar*, a corker of a movie about a hood named Rico who rises out of and falls back into the gutter with the help of a smooth chum who throws him over for a nightclub dancer. Douglas Fairbanks's kid played the smoothie and Glenda Farrell played the dancer. There was a line in it that made audiences laugh across the continent. Says Rico, wounded in an attempt on his life: "Tell 'em the cops couldn't get me any other way, so they hired somebody to kill me." No one laughed in Detroit.

"How was the Atlantic Ocean?"

"Just like Lake Erie, except nobody was shooting at me, ha."

"I hear you came back early."

He didn't change expressions. "Where'd you hear it?"

"Who's your man in Machine's camp?"

"Ha. I get it."

We hit Jefferson and turned east. The traffic was lighter there and he accelerated, cutting in and out to avoid slow-moving vehicles. The engine burbled. The sunlight died orange on the scalloped surface of Lake St. Clair.

"Someone saw you," I said.

"Hard not to get seen in a Doozy."

"I mean at the LaSalle Hotel. The night Jerry Buckley bought the farm."

He laughed and looked up at Springfield in the rearview mirror. "You see why I like this guy?"

"You admit it?" I pressed.

"Bass, I'm gonna let you out."

"Okay."

Jack pulled over and Springfield got out onto a grassy strip between the pavement and the beach. "Pick you up in a little," Jack said. As we rolled away the big man started walking east along the shoulder, throwing a shadow as long as the Duesenberg.

"Who's asking," Jack wanted to know, "you or the *Banner*?"

"This one's off the books. If it turns into a story later I'll let you know. Either way this conversation never happened."

He took off the boater and laid it on the seat between us bottomside up. The red silk lining was soaked. It was the heat that made him sweat; for a guy with plenty of nerve, Jack had no nerves at all.

"Hattie told you I was at her place. Only two people knew I was in town, and you didn't talk to the other one. I didn't even tell Bass or Andy or Lon. Nobody saw me at the LaSalle, because I wasn't there. Not on foot."

I didn't say anything.

"Buckley was an asshole. He wasn't like you, Connie. He talked about anything he heard or thought he heard, on or off the books. He didn't know half what he said he did. Sometimes that's worse than knowing more than you should. What the hell, it was a quick three grand, and I could use the friend. I took the job."

It was starting already. My legs had gone dead. "Who's the friend?"

"Pete Rosenstein. He dumped fifteen G's on the anti-recall campaign. He had his boys out all day election day stuffing the boxes. He said the commissioner promised him the East Side if the recall fell through. The bulls'd bust up Joey's joints and leave his alone."

"But the recall didn't fall through."

"Didn't mean Bowles couldn't be re-elected. It was too late to rub out Buckley; a thing like that could've put the recall over the top if it wasn't already. Doing it *after*, in case Bowles lost, would take Buckley off his neck and give the whole schmeer time to blow off before the next election. Pete looks ahead. You got to give the son of a bitch that." We were gliding past the stately homes of Grosse Pointe now, where the Duesenberg was no more out of place than a diamond in a platinum setting. The acres of lawn in their wrought-iron cages were billiard-green, each equipped with its own black iron jockey.

"I thought you were enemies."

"Joey's enemy enough. Anyway, somebody's got to buy my beer."

"You said you weren't at the hotel that night."

"Not on foot's what I said. I was supposed to be there before Buckley finished his whatchacallit, broadcast, but I got hung up. I borrowed a car from Pete on account of I couldn't get to my LaSalle without letting too many people know I was in town. I was looking for a place to park when these three mugs came out putting heaters away under their coats. I knew then someone beat me to it, and I hauled my freight out of there."

"Rosenstein double-crossed you?"

"That's what I thought at first."

I waited, but he didn't elaborate. "Did you get a look at their faces?"

"There's a light in front of the hotel. Two of them I didn't know from Steamboat Willie. Well, maybe I'd hire out of town too, for a job like that. I knew the third one, though. He was at my wedding reception."

I'm Greek, and I wouldn't wish a journalist's life on a Turk. There are questions whose answers you know you'll wish you'd never been told, but you have to ask them anyway.

"So who was it?"

"That bird Frankie Orr. You know, the guinea Sal Borneo sent."

"I remember him. How sure are you it was him?"

"I seen him as clear as I see you."

"I thought Borneo was a peacemaker."

"Sal didn't get where he is shaking no tambourines. He's got as much stake in keeping the town open as Pete. More." He grinned. "It's kind of funny when you think about it, both of them hiring triggers to do the same guy on the same night. Old Jerry was dead twice and he never knew it."

"It's like Shakespeare."

"Now you sound like Tom. He was always one for reading that shit, even when we was kids. I guess that's okay for guys like him and you, but in my business I got to keep my head clean. I better go back and pick up Bass while I can still see him." He swung into a driveway with a grilled gate and turned around.

"Glad you come along," Springfield said when we had collected him and resumed our eastward journey. "I was scared I'd end up standing on some white man's lawn with a iron ring in my hand."

It was the first and last joke I ever heard him tell.

"We got a German cook," Jack told me. "She makes strudel like my mama never could. If you clean your plate good enough, she might give you some."

"I didn't mean to invite myself to dinner."

"Vivian's used to unexpected guests. We put up Lon and Andy when the place on Howard went up. Bass, he's got his own place and a woman, but she's working tonight."

St. Clair Shores was a brand new community, founded and built by rumrunners with families who didn't want their children gunned down on the streets of Detroit. The houses were large but not ostentatious, with lawns bare of shrubbery to deny cover to intruders and docks behind the houses with power boats moored to them for quick escape across the lake. The Dance home, described by Andrea St. Charles as a "charming cottage," had twelve rooms and an eight-foot stone wall enclosing the yard. A dog barked when we pulled into the driveway.

"Down, Devil!" Jack commanded, as we entered through the side door. The dog, a sixty-pound black-and-tan rottweiler, took its huge paws off Jack's shoulders and sat on its haunches, growling. Its square black head was as big as an oven.

Dinner was pot roast and boiled potatoes, with blueberry pie instead of the promised strudel, but just as welcome. The cook served. She was a small, dark-haired woman in her forties with rodentlike features and quick, jerky movements, not at all the large blonde dough-faced Hun I'd expected. Vivian, looking older than twenty-four in a starched white high-necked blouse with her hair pinned up, had greeted me coolly before we sat down. I got the impression she'd disapproved of my account of the wedding reception, with its inventory of the notorious characters present. But she was a good hostess and saw that my plate was well stocked and my glass kept full of a red bordeaux her father had put down before Prohibition.

"Bass isn't joining us?" I asked. He'd disappeared soon after we came into the house.

Jack said, "He likes to eat in the kitchen. I keep telling him Lincoln freed him, but he don't hardly believe it."

Jack's business never entered the conversation, which ranged broadly. Vivian warmed a little when I mentioned that I'd once interviewed Eddie Foy; he had entertained at a party at her parents' estate in Southampton in 1920. She knew a great deal about the theater. Her ambition to become an actress had ended when she married Woodbine.

Jack broke his silence of several minutes to declare that the only actor who wasn't queer was Edward G. Robinson.

All through dinner I'd had a question on my mind, another one of those I'd regret having answered. When Vivian went upstairs and Jack and I retired to a walnut-paneled living room with tufted leather furniture, I asked him another one entirely. "Does Vivian know why you left Atlantic City?"

"She don't ask me about my business." He turned on a tabletop radio and dialed through the squawks and squeals until he found Paul Whiteman. Music was all he ever listened to on the box. Springfield was standing on the grass outside the window with his back to us, smoking a cigarette. It was then that I realized he was performing as Jack's bodyguard.

I spotted *The Pious Heart* for the first time, hanging all alone on the wall opposite the dining room door. The cow-eyed girl kneeling beneath the crucifix wore her dark blonde hair in sausage curls tied with one of those big bows I hadn't seen since the war. Her clasped hands weren't fully developed, the fingers short and pudgy, and there was a babyish fullness to her cheeks that depending on your philosophy or how the day had treated you would make you want to tickle her under the chin or tear off her cotton underpants and take the devout look off her face. Jack told me then how he had bought the painting in a Houston Street gallery in Manhattan over Vivian's protests and of the artist's suicide in 1921. Cloying and simplistic, it clashed with everything I knew or thought I knew about its owner, but I didn't try for the obvious. Liking Jack involved a protocol all its own.

"Vivian doesn't strike me as the meek kind," I said, sitting down. "I mean about asking why you interrupted the honeymoon."

"I told her I had a problem with the brewery."

I asked it. "Why go to Hattie's if you didn't want anyone to know you were in town?"

He actually blushed. Nobody ever believes me when I say it, but Jack was shy about those things. "Guy gets horny when he's supposed to be on his honeymoon, Connie. You'll find out. I guess I forgot to tell Hattie to keep it a secret. Then when someone else did Buckley I didn't think it was worth telling her."

"What about the girl?"

"Which girl?"

"The girl you were with. Nobody goes to Hattie's to listen to her corny records."

He looked puzzled. "I was with Hattie."

I had just lit a Chesterfield. I paused, then snapped shut the lighter.

"Don't tell Vivian," he said.

Chapter Fourteen

James Aloysius Dolan, a/k/a Jimmy Dolan, Big Jim, Diamond Jim, Boss Dolan, and the Irish Pope, lived forgotten in a forgotten place once known as Corktown, an area of undefined boundaries on the near West Side where, in an era of paper collars and pomade, Detroit had drawn the majority of its bricklayers, ditch-diggers, motormen, prize-fighters, policemen, and petty politicians with names like Brennan, Sullivan, Rooney, O'Brien, and Flaherty. The house was a narrow brick saltbox with green trim on Porter, two blocks from Most Holy Trinity Church. In election years past, city councilmen in carnations and day-laborers in overalls had lined up on that street waiting for an audience with the master of the house, which now looked somewhat priggish in that declining neighborhood.

Dolan was an anachronism, a walking monument to a less sophisticated period in the history of American political corruption. From 1912 to 1926, although he himself never held any office higher than street railway commissioner, no government project was undertaken in the city and not so much as a screwdriver was sold to a municipal employee without his knowledge and approval. That approval carried a price, which varied widely depending upon whether you were contracting to excavate a sewer or requesting permission to operate a bawdy-house on East Grand River. He elected mayors, controlled the press so far as that bratty enterprise can ever be controlled, and arranged for the discreet disposal of those whose loyalty could not be obtained for money or fear. On the shiny side, he loaned vast sums without hesitation to ordinary citizens in trouble in return for their support at the polls and punished severely the grasping landlord and the arrogant city hack who forgot that his Tower of Babel was built on grass roots. At the peak of his popularity and fame, he could have been governor merely by agreeing to accept his party's nomination.

Then, in the autumn of the fourteenth year of his reign, after dining in his home with an associate, Dolan escorted his guest to a waiting cab just as four men stepped out of the doorway of the house next door carrying sawed-off shotguns. One of them held the driver at bay while his companions pumped between twelve and fifteen loads of double-ought buck into the two victims. Then the four climbed into a gray sedan that stopped in the middle of the block to pick them up and were whisked away.

The guest, Michael P. Faryniak—"Mike Freak" to his friends and constituents in the eleventh ward—died instantly when his head was blasted nearly off his shoulders. Dolan had been partially shielded by the open taxi door, but pellets had shattered his jaw and entered his chest, left arm, and abdomen. Doctors at St. Mary's Hospital, where he was taken after his wife called for an ambulance, didn't give him much of a chance to recover. He fooled them, but it was six weeks before he could stand up without help and two months before they unwired his jaw. Meanwhile, six men associated with the Purple Gang, two of whom were thought to have waited in the sedan while the others mounted the assault, were arrested and charged, although it was never established whether Dolan or Faryniak, who was friendly with Joey Machine and Phil Dardanello, was the actual target. A jury acquitted the six when both Dolan and the cab driver refused to identify them in court. Shortly afterward the Irish Pope, who had done a lot of thinking during his long recuperation, announced his retirement from politics. The supplicants stopped coming to Porter Street.

I was greeted at the door by a short stout woman of sixty or so, with gold-rimmed glasses attached to a gold chain around her neck and beautiful white hair combed in waves. She was wearing a print dress and brown leather walking shoes with thick soles. When I introduced myself she smiled with counterfeit teeth and said, with a brogue, that she was Charlotte Dolan. "Jimmy's downstairs in the shop. He said to show you right in to the study."

She hung up my gray felt hat, which I had broken out only that morning in honor of another Labor Day gone past, and led me down an immaculate hall lined with tasteful paintings of the saints into a small room containing a big desk. On the way I heard a child laugh somewhere deep in the house. I accepted Mrs. Dolan's offer of a cup of tea and she shut me in.

It was a man's room, done in leather and dark wood with no windows and a skin of dust on everything, in contrast to what I had seen of the rest of the house; Dolan belonged to a class and generation that didn't brook female invasions with feather dusters. It smelled of bootblack and tobacco. An oil portrait of the man himself, not too well executed, with his thumbs inside his vest pockets, leaned out from the wall behind the desk. On the one adjacent, a large crucifix carved from a single block of wood hung dwarfed by the nakedness of the wall around it. Rows of framed photographs with dust hammocked in the corners dangled crookedly from floor to ceiling on the facing wall. Many of them were autographed: John L. Sullivan, Henry Ford, James J. Corbett, Thomas Edison, Jim Jeffries, Father Coughlin, Jack Dempsey, Jess Willard, Bob Fitzsimmons, many others, some of whom I recognized, some I didn't. Most of them were Irish, many of them were prizefighters, and Jimmy Dolan was in all the pictures, pumping mitts and beaming like an overgrown leprechaun in his king-size three-piece suit with a Knights of Columbus pin on the lapel.

I heard heavy footsteps outside the door, and then it was opened by a large old man in a gray shawl-collared cardigan over a plaid shirt buttoned to the neck and old pinstriped suitpants sagging in the crotch, pushed down by a belly the size of a beer wagon. He had a huge red face, lemon-colored hair parted in the middle and smeared into curled wings on both sides of his brow, and white muttonchops. His feet were enormous in brown wingtips and he brought with him a woodshop scent of sawdust and varnish. His voice when he addressed me was a deep burr, the brogue very faint.

"Mr. Minor," he said, wrapping his great paw twice around my hand. "I've heard your name, but I don't read you. I am loyal to the good Democratic *Free Press*, don't you see."

"That's all right. Thanks for seeing me, Mr. Dolan."

"Jimmy, if you please. Mr. Dolan was my father, the teamster. Teehee."

It was a girlish giggle for such a big man. I extricated my hand diplomatically. "I like your study. It's like something out of *Babbitt*."

"It's a place to be. I don't spend much time in it anymore. These days I make furniture."

He moved behind the desk and sat down. This was an impressive piece of furniture in itself, as big as a dinner table, supporting a blotter stained many times over with "J. A. Dolan" in backward script with a turn-of-the-century flourish, an upright telephone with the black enamel worn down to dull metal where his big hand had gripped it, and a pipe rack, from which he selected a clay in the late stages of disintegration. I noticed, as he stuffed the bowl with black shag from a humidor with an Indian's head carved on the lid, that he held the pipe in his left hand, then leaned forward to take the stem between his teeth while he struck a match and ignited the tobacco with his right. Then when he got rid of the match he sat back and used his right hand to hold the pipe. It was obvious that he had never regained full use of his wounded left arm. Despite that, he appeared not to have Jensen's difficulty with keeping his tobacco burning. A smell like hot tar filled the room.

"You said on the phone you needed something," he said.

I remained standing. His was the only chair in the room. "Yes, sir. I need a line on a man named Frankie Orr. He works for Sal Borneo."

"Why?"

"I'm not at liberty to say."

He sucked on his pipe and said nothing. His eyes were glass-blue and not as warm as the red face and large soft frame made him seem. I backed off a notch.

"I got a tip he may be involved in a homicide. I'd use my contacts on the police force, but I don't want it to get out I'm interested. Not yet."

"Orr, you say?"

"It's probably not his real name. They're always shortening them."

"What is it you're thinking I can do? Most of the people I knew went out when Bowles came in."

"I heard you keep your hand in."

"You heard that, did you?"

"Yes, sir. The talk is Bowles would never have been recalled if you'd given him your support."

"That's the talk, is it?"

"Yes, sir."

He took the pipe out of his mouth, looked at it, and put it back. "And what if it's true? I don't remember the *Banner* ever doing a kindness for me and mine. I don't think it existed when I retired."

"Maybe it can do one for you now."

Someone tapped on the study door. Dolan said come in and his wife entered carrying a Dresden tea set on a tray. She set it down on a corner of the desk and put her hands on her hips. "Jimmy, why doesn't your guest have a chair?"

"He didn't ask for one."

She made a noise I have forever afterward regarded as wifelike, left the room, and returned with a straight kitchen chair, which I accepted. She asked me what I took in my tea and poured us each a cup. Without missing a beat she plucked the pipe from Dolan's mouth and carried it out with her, drawing the door shut. Her visit had diminished him a little.

"The damned doctors are determined to have me celebrate my hundredth birthday," he snarled. "Don't let the bastards sink their hooks into you whatever you do."

The brogue was more pronounced when he became agitated. I assured him I wouldn't and sipped from my cup. The tea was strong enough to float a car ferry.

He said, "I like this man Murphy."

"Which Murphy?" The new subject threw me.

"Frank Murphy, the Recorder's Court judge. The man's for jobs and against gangsters. They've had their run these past dozen years. Mothers won't let their children walk to school for fear they'll be trapped in the crossfire. What's your paper's position on Murphy for mayor?"

"I don't think we have one. The election's too far off."

"Well, I like him."

This was the new Dolan talking, the Dolan who had survived a gangland ambush at the cost of his career and part of the use of one arm. The old Dolan had done more than a little to create the climate he'd just described. Musing on that, I was a moment realizing he'd stated his terms.

"You've overestimated my influence, Mr. Dolan—Jimmy. I don't dictate policy at the *Banner*."

"Indeed. I've done some research on you since you called Saturday. Nearly a million people read your column. Who else on the staff can claim that?"

"It's available to that many. I doubt that many read it. Anyway, Howard Wolfman is his own man. If I told him who to endorse in the election he'd send me packing."

"To one of the other two hundred newspapers that subscribe to your wisdom."

"It wouldn't matter to him. I can't do it."

"You can write about Murphy."

I kept coming back to the same thing; first in Joey Machine's office, now here. "I don't endorse candidates."

"Never?"

"No reflection on you, Jimmy, but when you work for newspapers as long as I have you come into close contact with a lot of politicians. Too close to too many to ever want to support one. Besides, I have a national readership to think about now. Who's running for office in Detroit doesn't interest everyone."

"But a local murder does."

I shrugged over my cup. "I write for them. I don't try to explain them."

"What *do* you have to offer, Mr. Minor?"

"The name of the man who tried to have you killed four years ago."

"Tee-hee. I know that already. Pete Rosenstein. He was after Mike Freak."

"It wasn't Rosenstein. That's what the man wanted you to think; it's why he hired Purples to do it. And it wasn't Mike Freak he wanted. Mike was just there. You were the target."

"How is it you know this?"

"I had the first interview with Rosenstein after Joey Machine released him to the Purple Gang for ransom back in twenty-seven. He told me who ordered the shooters. Some of the scribes were saying Pete faked his own kidnapping to avoid arrest for the Freak killing. He wanted to set me straight."

"And you believed him."

"No reason not to. The shooters had been acquitted. If he sent them, they had nothing to gain by tipping the squeal on him. The bulls had no case."

"Why didn't you write about it?"

"It was off the record. He didn't want a reputation as a stool pigeon. He just wanted one scribe to believe him and not stir up rumors." I gave myself a tea transfusion. "It doesn't have to make sense. He'd just spent a week and a half in Machine's custody, and Joey isn't a gracious host. You don't think logically in a situation like that."

The room grew quiet. Dolan set his cup and saucer on the blotter, opened the file drawer of the desk, and lifted out a half-full quart bottle of White Mountain Irish Whiskey, from which he drew the cork and poured a jiggerful into each of our cups. The label said it had been bottled in 1909. He stood the bottle on the blotter and raised his cup.

"You've a Greek head, Mr. Minor. Are you of that race?"

"My father was."

"Then you are as well. The Jews say it's the mother passes it down, but then they've not had a country these three thousand years. To Premier Venizelos?"

"I don't keep up with the politics in Greece. But I like Irish." I lifted my cup and drank. The liquor gave the tea an amber flavor.

We drained our cups in silence. When I set mine down, he said: "Would you give me ten minutes, lad? The parlor is across the hall."

I got up. He had the receiver off the hook when I closed the door behind me.

The parlor was clean and comfortably shabby, with a worn horsehair sofa and chairs, and violets on the wallpaper. There was a crucifix, smaller than the one in the study, family pictures on the little fireplace mantel, a Philco radio, and a small bookcase containing a handsome leatherbound set of the works of St. Thomas More, arranged incongruously next to three bound volumes of *Boy's Life*. A window looked out on a sheltered porch where Charlotte Dolan was buckling a fair-haired boy of six or seven into a yellow slicker; it had started to rain. The boy had to be a grandchild. Most of the pictures on the mantel were of young men and women in caps and gowns and wedding livery and military uniforms, callow versions of the Porter Street Dolans. Outside, the raindrops made big fat circles when they struck the window.

After twelve minutes or so I went back across the hall and laid my knuckles on the door. I was invited in.

Dolan, holding the telephone in both hands, lifted an elbow to gesture toward the straight chair. I sat down.

"Chester, you always pitch them in," he told the mouthpiece. "How's that godchild of mine, by the way?" The brogue now was as thick as potatoes and cabbage.

The conversation, his end of it anyway, continued along those lines for two more minutes. Then he hung up and folded his big hands on the stained blotter. His eyes had flaked off a glacier. Once again his voice had lost its lilt.

"Francis Xavier Oro. Born Messina, Sicily, nineteen-oh-two. His parents took him with them to New York when he was eleven months old. In nineteen-eighteen he did a jot in the Elmira reformatory for setting fire to a coal wagon. In nineteen twenty-two he was convicted of violation of the Volstead Act and possession of an unlicensed firearm and served six months in Sing Sing. Three arrests for assault, in nineteen twenty-four, twenty-five, and twenty-seven, no convictions. In nineteen twenty-eight he stood trial for the murder of a man named Vincenzo 'Vinnie Cool' Cugglio. The jury was hung and the state elected not to try him again. He appears to have behaved himself these two years, although he was a known associate—I take that to mean bodyguard—of Lucky Luciano's before coming here. You know Luciano?"

"Never heard of him."

"Nor I. Apparently the thieving dagos set some store by him. How Orr came to be with Sal Borneo I can't guess. Perhaps it's like an exchange program. If so, I wonder who this Luciano got. In any case, Mr. Orr now resides at the Griswold House. Suite six-oh-one."

"Anything else?"

"Only this. Orr is a cold customer. Eyewitnesses to the murder of Vinnie Cool, whose memories failed them when the case came to trial, said in their statements to the police that Frankie tracked Vinnie through three crowded cars on the Third Avenue elevated railway and garroted him standing up in full view of a dozen passengers. Then he stood in front of the door until the train reached its next stop and stepped off. He passed two transit policemen coming in and never broke into a run."

I finished writing. "That's a lot of information in a few minutes."

"My source keeps records on all the new faces in town."

The White Mountain bottle remained on the desk. Significantly, he heeled the cork back in and sat back. It was my turn.

I said, "I hope you won't be disappointed."

"I know I won't be disappointed. Who wanted me dead?"

"Mike Freak."

"Ah." The exclamation meant nothing. I went on.

"They jumped the gun. So to speak. They weren't supposed to come out of that doorway until Mike's cab left with him in it."

His gaze slid involuntarily toward the crucifix in its lonely place on the bare wall. "Jesus, Son of Mary. The Slavic son of a bitch."

"I knew you'd be disappointed," I said.

Chapter Fifteen

That night I called Hattie. "I can't make it tonight," I said. "I'm working on something."

"I didn't know we had a date tonight," she said.

"Well, you gave me a week. It's a week today."

"You can say all I have to hear over the phone."

I was sitting by the window of my place on Park. I hadn't turned on a light. The window was open and the brimstone smell of rain on asphalt drifted in with the mist. I watched the last bus heading toward Woodward, its pistons drumrolling as it accelerated away from the stop. "Come on," I said. "How about lunch tomorrow?"

There was a pause. Then, "I'm with Joey tomorrow. We're going to talk about the new place."

"I thought you hadn't decided you were going to re-open."

"I just did. I'll see you, Connie." The connection broke.

I was still holding the receiver when the operator came on and asked me what number I wanted.

I became alert. "The Griswold House, please."

"Griswold House."

This was a male voice with a Franklin Pangborn accent. Its owner would have a pencil moustache.

"Let me speak to Frankie Orr," I said.

"We have no one registered by that name."

"Mr. Oro, then."

"There is no Mr. Oro here either."

"Have it your way. Tell him Connie Minor wants to talk to him about Mr. Buckley."

I left my number and hung up. Five seconds later the telephone rang.

"That was fast," I said, answering.

"Minor?"

I recognized the phlegmy baritone. It wasn't Orr's.

"Yes, Mr. Machine."

"I tried to get you at the paper. They gave me this number. I need to get in touch with your friend Dance."

"He's not a friend. Anyway, I think he's listed."

"I want you to do it. He won't trust it coming from me. This thing, this war thing between us, it's shit for the birds. We got to talk."

"Talk about what?"

"Last spring Sal said something about a trade. Ten of my joints on the East Side for twenty percent of Dance's brewery. I didn't like it then. I'm losing good men now and I like that less. Tell the Jew if he's interested, we'll talk turkey."

The plan was a simple one. The two men would meet in the middle of the Belle Isle Bridge. Two cars, no weapons. Each could have one companion. The meeting would take place on a weekday when they weren't likely to be interrupted. Joey would be standing alone in the middle of the bridge with his car parked on the island end; he would be visible from East Jefferson. Jack would leave his car and companion on the Jefferson end and meet Joey on foot in the middle. If Jack liked, he could send Lon Camarillo over in the aeroplane first to make sure everything was jake.

I wrote it all down. "I'll tell him."

"Think he'll go for it?"

"I don't second-guess people like Jack, Mr. Machine. Who else gets the story?"

"Just you."

"Last time peace came up Jack's brother got it."

"That was Sal's idea. The greasy fuck's got nothing to do with this one."

"I'll talk to Jack."

"Call me. I'm at the garage."

I spoke to the German cook first, who put Vivian on. "He's not here," she said.

"Is there a telephone in the brewery?"

"What brewery?"

Less than three months married and she was already acting like a moll. "Okay, have him call me at my apartment. He's got the number. It's important."

The telephone rang while I was listening to a ballgame. I turned off the radio and unhooked the receiver. "Jack?"

"This is Frankie Orr. Let me talk to Minor."

It was the first time I'd heard him speak. His voice was a sliding whisper. Whatever it owed to Little Italy had been repaid. I switched on a lamp. "This is Minor."

"I read your column. I think I see you at Jack Dance's wedding. What do you have to tell me about Buckley besides he died?"

"I heard you killed him."

"Who said?"

"What's your answer?"

He laughed softly. "Did you eat?"

"Not since noon."

"You'll like the dining room at the Griswold. I'll send a car."

"I can drive. What time?"

"Whenever you can come."

"I'm expecting a call," I said.

"I'll wait."

I didn't turn the game back on; baseball had lost its suspense.

Jack called ten minutes later. I told him Joey's plan.

"Tell him he can hang his fat guinea ass off the Ambassador Bridge for all I care," Jack said. "He cost me a house and a fine."

"He sounds on the level. I don't know what kind of trap he can lay that Lon couldn't see from the air. You've got family to look after. Vivian lost one husband. Besides, it's a good deal."

"What's he paying you?"

"Go fuck yourself."

Afterward I regretted hanging up on him. Talking to Jack, it was easy to forget what he was. I thought about Jerry the Lobo, buried somewhere in an empty lot probably, and Lewis Welker on the steel table in the Coroner's Court Building with his lips sewed shut and a brass cartridge in his mouth. When the bell rang again I snatched up the earpiece.

"You got such a hard-on to see me talk to Joey, you can come along," Jack said.

"Sure you don't want Andy or Bass?" The soles of my feet had gone dead already. If anyone violated the truce, I was convinced it would be Jack. Life in the crossfire was bright but short.

"You're better company. If you ain't there, I won't be."

I stamped my feet. "When do you want to do it?"

"Monday morning." I could hear him grinning when he said it. "It's his busiest time. He likes to stay in and count the policy receipts from the weekend. Friday's the day the suckers get their wages."

I called Joey.

"The kike bastard," he said. "Tell him eleven o'clock."

I passed the message on to Vivian and left the apartment.

The Griswold House was a little over a block and light years away from Joey Machine's Acme Garage. Its dining room catered to the sporting and theater crowd, where among the silver forks and white linen one might glimpse Sophie Tucker relaxing while on tour or wave to Barney Oldfield. I left my new Oldsmobile Viking V-8 at the curb and entered a large low-lit room where a string quartet was playing. A tall old maitre d' with a head of flowing white hair bowed slightly and took me past empty tables to a private room in back. There three men were seated at a long table draped in white with candles at both ends. The flames shook when the sliding doors were drawn shut.

"Good you could make it, Minor." Frankie Orr rose and grasped my hand. "We booked the place. Did you get your call?"

I said I had. He was in evening dress with a stiff collar, a dark slender young Latin with blue-black hair smoothed back and sleepy lids and a shadow of beard showing under his olive skin. His grip was strong. It would have to be to strangle a full-grown man in broad daylight on a train crowded with commuters.

The others were a man in his fifties, also in evening dress, with dark hair thinning on top and going iron-gray at the temples, a mealy complexion, and a prow of a nose that dipped down over a drooping moustache; and a man about my age who was running to fat and needed a haircut. He had on a blue business suit. It seemed a long table for just those three.

"You've met Salvatore Borneo?" asked Frankie.

I started. "No, I haven't. I'm pleased, sir."

The older man lifted himself an inch from his seat, took my hand in a moist palm, and released it quickly. I had never seen him except in rare photographs, none a good likeness of the Unione Siciliana president, who could have passed for a Sioux chief without the moustache. He said nothing.

"And this is Mr. Norman."

The fattish man made eye contact with me for an instant, then looked away. He didn't speak or shake hands.

"Since we're running late, I took the liberty of ordering for you," Frankie told me. "I hope you like London broil."

I said London broil would be fine. Frankie gestured toward the chair facing his and I sat down. I noticed then that only three places were set. There was no tableware in front of Borneo.

He rose and shook Frankie's hand. He was short for his reputation and stocky. "I'll let you get to business." His English was heavily accented.

"See you tomorrow, Sal." Frankie put a hand on his back and saw him to the door.

He took his seat. "Hell of an old man. You know his father fought with Garibaldi?"

"All their fathers fought with Garibaldi," I said; "to hear them tell it."

"Him I believe." He regarded me from under his lids. "I liked that piece you did about the Roman emperors when Bowles was recalled. I'm interested in the subject."

"My editor thought it went over readers' heads."

"Most of them, probably. I've got a room full of books on ancient Rome. Caesar's *Conquests* changed my life. Ah."

The doors opened and a waiter brought in our meals. Frankie had a rare filet, Mr. Norman a rack of lamb. My London broil was sliced paper-thin, swimming in champagne sauce, and garnished with fresh broccoli. The waiter poured purple wine into our glasses. When he turned to leave, Frankie got up, slipped the gold clip off a thick fold of paper currency, and laid several bills on his tray. "Divide that among the others and tell them to go home. I'll lock up."

"Yes, sir. Thank you, sir."

Frankie slid the doors together behind the waiter and shot the brass bolt. Then he sat back down and raised his glass. "*Salute.*"

I waited until he drank, then took a sip. I didn't think poison suited him. I was just careful about those things ever since Justice of the Peace Turner. Mr. Norman gulped down half of his. So far he hadn't said boo.

"Sal's an old customer here," Frankie explained. "I've got a thing about the serving staff eavesdropping and gossiping in the kitchen. We can talk in front of Mr. Norman. He collects the receipts for Sal in the Black Bottom. They've been off lately, haven't they, Mr. Norman?" He started cutting his meat with a knife with a serrated edge.

The fattish man forked in a mouthful of lamb. "Money's tight. President says we're in a depression. These niggers, they believe everything they hear on the radio."

"I never listen. Those announcers all sound like long-distance operators. Buckley, for instance."

I ate some beef. I had a hunch I wouldn't get the chance to clean my plate.

Frankie said, "I didn't like Buckley, so Minor thinks I killed him. What do you think of that, Mr. Norman?"

Mr. Norman chewed rapidly and took another gulp of wine. He still didn't look at me.

"I didn't say that," I said. "It's something I heard."

"Rumor's a dangerous thing. Look what it did to the stock market. Did you have anything invested, Minor?"

"I owned some Locomobile stock once. I guess I still do."

"It's just gambling. We do the same thing and they call us crooks. What about you, Mr. Norman? What do you do with your money?"

"I got a mortgage."

"You see, Minor? We're just people. I've never even seen a tommy gun close up."

I drank some wine. It had a smoky taste I didn't much care for. It's funny what you remember. "Just for the sake of argument, Mr. Orr, where were you the night Buckley was killed?"

"Same place I am every night at that time. In bed, asleep. I keep early hours."

"Was anyone with you?"

He touched his lips with his napkin and smiled. He had bad teeth, his only visible flaw.

"We're all gentlemen here. If I had to I could produce someone. So far I haven't heard why I'd have to. Maybe if you told me what you heard."

"I have a witness who claims he saw you leaving the LaSalle Hotel with two other men about the time Buckley hit the floor. You were putting away a gun."

"It's a he?"

"In journalism we always use he unless we're being specific."

"Why didn't this witness go to the police?"

"You're new here," I said. "Maybe you don't know our little town. We don't run to the bulls with anything as insignificant as murder."

"No town's that rotten."

"It isn't worth arguing about."

"Who's your witness?"

"You know better than that, Mr. Orr."

It happened faster than I could follow it, so I'm guessing. Frankie transferred his napkin to the table beside his plate. In almost the same motion, he picked up his steak knife and swept it backhanded across the top of Mr. Norman's collar. The ease and grace of what should have been an awkward maneuver distracted my thoughts from what happened next, leaving me with impressions only. It struck me that Frankie was double-jointed or a magician with stage experience. A bright orange arterial spurt arced past my head and thumped the door four feet behind me. The slash opened like a mouth without teeth, dyeing Mr. Norman's shirt, jacket, and tie deep scarlet. The blood covered his rack of lamb like thick marinade, welled over the edge of the plate, and fanned out across the tablecloth, making the white linen transparent as it advanced toward the corners. I stood, tipping my chair over. Mr. Norman tried to stand too, both hands reaching for his throat. Then he slid sideways and out of sight, although not out of earshot. His grunts had a yearning toward articulation. The knife had evidently torn through his voice box.

The doors rattled. Frankie laid the glistening steak knife on the table, covered it with his napkin—a grislily comical gesture in view of the fact that the place looked like a butcher's back room—and walked around the table, pausing to kick the grunting, thrashing man hard in the ribs. "When you get to hell, chiseler, tell them Sal gets what's his."

He slid back the bolt and pulled the doors apart four inches. A set of features appeared in the opening. "Any problems?"

"Oh, yeah, it looks like it, doesn't it?" said Frankie, irritated. "Everybody gone?"

"Yeah."

"Give them ten minutes to make sure nobody forgot his hat. Then grab Leo and come back and scrape up this sack of shit. He ought to be through kicking by then."

He turned toward me. For once I wasn't paralyzed. I was aware that I'd wet my pants.

"When you Greeks were writing poetry and buggering each other all over the Parthenon, we were out conquering the world," he said. "Some things don't change. Forget about Buckley or I'll feed you your fucking balls. Tell your witness the same thing. Tell him tonight." He threw the doors open wide.

Walking carefully in my soaked trousers, I went out. In a few days the smell of Mr. Norman's blood left my nostrils. In a few months I even forgot all about Jerry Buckley. After nine years, though, I still can't drive by the spot where the Griswold House stood without embarrassing myself physically.

Chapter Sixteen

We heard the plane before we saw it, a nasal whine that stopped and started in impertinent little surges, like an electric mixer with a loose plug. Then it grew out of a tiny smudge in an absolutely clear sky, widening and assuming detail as it approached, until we could see the box kite wings and the cigar-shaped fuselage and light shining through the wires and struts, the leather-helmeted head behind the windscreen. It passed over within a hundred feet, close enough to show the khaki patches on its olive-drab fabric and the way the wings bowed and flexed like a gull's. Then it turned its nose into the wind in a long climbing loop and headed in.

Belonging as it did to the air, the machine seemed reluctant to land. The carriage touched down twice, bounded back up, and struck with a bone-shattering bang, the wheels lurching over uneven ground until the tailskid dug in and scratched up a brown cloud that scudded over and settled in a fine layer on our shoes. The aeroplane swung into a slow turn and rolled to a stop. The motor sputtered and died. The propeller feathered, reversed, and drifted around in a half-dozen lazy circles before standing still. Quiet fell with a thud.

Jack and I stood by Jack's LaSalle in a field near St. Clair Shores. It was a blustery Monday morning in September, too windy for shirtsleeves, too warm for a topcoat, with the death-stench in the air that was fall in Southeastern Michigan. In half an hour Jack was due to meet Joey Machine on the Belle Isle Bridge.

Andy Kramm climbed down from the observer's seat behind the

wings, using the bottom wing as a step. Lon Camarillo bounded out of the cockpit straight to the ground and came our way behind Andy, unbuckling his helmet. The former ace was wearing his leather aviator's jacket and puttees, with an ivory silk scarf wound around his neck and tucked inside his collar. Andy had on his cloth cap and mackinaw. He blew on his hands.

"Jesus, it's cold up there," he said. "My balls shriveled up no bigger'n cantaloupes. Anybody got a bottle?"

I gave him my flask. Lon joined us, carrying his helmet and goggles. The lower half of his face was dark with smoke and oil. The white outline left by the goggles accentuated his skull-like features. "When do I get a new bus?" he demanded. "The only time that old Jenny's done better than sixty since the Big Show was when they brought it up on the truck."

Jack said, "When we can afford a better aeroplane, we won't need no aeroplane. What'd you see?"

"Ask Andy. I was too busy trying to keep us in the air."

"That's good hootch." Andy returned my flask. "Looks copacetic. Seen Joey's Chevy on the island and Joey standing on the bridge. No other cars or people close enough to do us a bother."

"Sure it was him?"

"Had on that cheap coat and that hat he wears, the one like Hoover's."

"Homburg," I said.

"That's the one. Say, you all right? You look like you could stand a pull yourself."

"I had a shock."

Jack said, "I don't like the coat."

"It's cold on the water," said Andy. "Anyway, Joey hires the hard stuff. He don't do it himself."

"Bass is in the Doozy." Jack flipped his head toward the dirt road that ran past the field, where the big car was parked. "You ride in back. Give us three or four blocks' start."

"My chopper there?"

"You'll have to load it. I never did figure out how to wind up that fucking drum."

"Joey said one car," I said.

"I stopped taking orders from Joey a while back." He was looking at me. "You sure you can do this? 'Cause if you can't, I won't. He can stand there till his dick rots and falls off."

"I'm jake."

"You better be. I don't trust guys that get sick or have to go take a dump just before the shooting starts."

"Lewis Welker," I reminded him.

"What about him?"

"Your memory's not that short."

He nodded.

I had checked with the hospitals and the morgue, but nobody answering Mr. Norman's description had showed up at any of them, and no complaint had been filed with the police department about a mess at the Griswold House. Frankie Orr's clean-up crew was worth whatever he paid them. I had called in sick at the *Banner* two days in succession. I had lost weight. Every time I thought of food I saw Mr. Norman's rack of lamb drenched biblically in blood. Actually, I was feeling a little better that morning, although Howard Wolfman and even Jensen the cartoon editor had remarked on my appearance. I'd told them I'd been fasting.

"I thought you were Greek Orthodox," Jensen had said, lighting his pipe.

Lon brought me back to the field. "I'll get the bird back in the hangar. It's throwing oil like a bitch."

Andy started for the Duesenberg and Jack and I returned to the LaSalle. He took his matched Lugers out of the glove compartment, the converted one sporting an extra long clip that extended three inches below the hollow handle, checked their loads, and put one in each side pocket of his suitcoat. I didn't say anything about the ban on weapons. He ground the motor into life, swung the car around, and bumped down the rutted path that led to the road.

On the way down Jefferson he turned on the radio. He never listened to the entertainment programs that were beginning to flood the dial, just dance music. Despite the name he took, I had never seen him dance with anyone, or tap his foot when a fast tune was playing, or heard him hum during a quiet moment. For all I knew he was tone deaf. He preferred things happening, and when they weren't he tried to create the illusion, and so the more frenetic the music the better he liked it. Jazz was a favorite, but he made no distinction between the corny trumpets and party whistles of Paul Whiteman and the smoky strains of Duke Ellington's Cotton Club Orchestra. I always thought it was a shame he didn't live to hear jitterbug. If he had, he might have had a better shot at dying of old age, but I doubt it. Whenever I think of him, there's a hot number playing in the background.

Nearing the Belle Isle Bridge, he pulled off onto the gravel apron, cut the motor, and coasted to a stop, blocking the end of the bridge. The Duesenberg glided over two blocks back and parked. Jack set the LaSalle's brake, cut the ignition. His window was open and I heard the water, the edged waves where the Detroit River broadened into Lake St. Clair slapping the seawall.

"Look at the son of a bitch," Jack said. "Thinks he's for Christ's sake Napoleon."

I noticed him then, leaning with his back to the railing halfway out to the island, a figure in a long black coat too heavy for the season although it was windy out there, the gusts molding the coat to the backs of his legs and pushing the hem out in front of him so that he looked like the letter *J*, his pale gray homburg held in place by his hand on the crown. The wind was kicking up little whitecaps on the water like paper sailboats.

"He looks on the square," I said.

"He'll be on the square when a priest shakes his stick in his face. Even then they'll have to screw him into the ground."

"What he said makes sense. This war isn't making anybody rich. Who was it said you could spit in Joey's face and steal his wife and he'd just laugh at you, but if you get in the way of a buck he'll rip your heart out?"

"Phil Dardanello. Just before Joey blew him to hell." He took out the Lugers again, checked the loads again, put them back in his pockets. Then he grabbed his door handle. "Anybody comes, get out and throw up the hood. Pretend you got engine trouble." He opened the door, put a foot on the running board. I laid a hand on his arm. I had never touched him before except to shake hands.

"Are you on the square?" I asked.

He showed me his teeth. "Hell, Connie, I never know what I'm going to do till I do it."

He left the door open, giving me an unobstructed view of the proceedings through a square frame, as if I were the only spectator in a movie house. I felt alone right away. Anyplace that Jack had been seemed twice as empty after he went. Out over the water, gulls swung like pendulums on the updrafts, their wings making lowercase *m*'s. That was the second letter that had occurred to me in a few minutes. I missed my typewriter. Hattie was right. I couldn't marry her until the *Banner* granted me a divorce.

Jack made his way out along the bridge, a tall, broad-shouldered young man—barely a man, just turned twenty-one—in blue gabardine and saddle shoes and a pearl fedora set at an arrogant angle, one hand touching the railing from time to time because in that wind it would seem to a landlubber that the bridge was swaying, although it was solid enough for truck traffic. He was alone out there with the creaking of the gulls and the loud raspberry of a speedboat heeling around the angle of the island. There were always speedboats.

I'm not sure which came first, Jack's slowing step or the movement of the man in the black coat and homburg, still fifty or sixty feet away from him. Maybe the two things were simultaneous, Jack getting close enough to see that it wasn't Joey Machine standing there, that Joey wasn't within a mile of that spot on that day, just as the coat came open and something that looked like a two-foot length of iron pipe swung up from underneath. There was something familiar about the movement, a wicked grace that reminded me of the private dining room at the Griswold House and a backhand sweep that severed Mr. Norman's jugular even as Mr. Norman was cutting the meat on his plate. And I knew who the man was in Joey's clothing.

Jack was fast for his size. I can still see him turning into the classic shooter's stance, sideways to his opponent and offering the narrowest possible target as his right hand came out of his pocket with a Luger in it and his arm straightened at shoulder level. Dirty gray smoke billowed from the end of the sawed-off and slid sideways in front of the wind. I saw Jack lurch without losing his footing. I couldn't see his gun because his body was in the way, but in the next instant I heard the round blooey of the shotgun and, just behind it, three rapid pops that had to belong to the smaller automatic, but not the one converted to full auto; Jack had gone with his best hand and single-fire for accuracy.

I didn't hear the next few reports. They were lost under the whine of the speedboat on the water, approaching the bridge now with its throttle wide open. As it neared the place where the two men stood it slowed down, the noise tailing off to a burble directly under the bridge. At that moment the man in the black coat went over the railing.

His hat and shotgun flew as he plunged feet first through air, arms rotating. Something else came loose on the way down, black and shield-shaped with dangling straps, falling slower than the man, planing on the air currents like an autumn leaf until, just after the man hit the water, it sliced the top off a series of waves, pulling a plume of white spray. Then it tipped up and stood tombstone fashion for a long moment before sliding under. It was a bulletproof vest, forty pounds of nickel steel with a black fabric covering. I had tried one on that disastrous day on the police range when I almost wiped out the force with a runaway Thompson and had decided I wasn't big enough to be a cop.

In the water, the man wriggled out of the overcoat, whose tails had spread like oil on the surface, and swam toward the bobbing boat, pulling himself along with an inexpert Australian crawl, head held up out of the water. Little white spurts erupted around him. I heard the pops and looked up at Jack supporting himself on the railing of the bridge with one hand and firing at the swimming man. The shots stopped just as the man reached the boat and was helped aboard by someone inside; Jack had emptied the magazine. Leaning awkwardly on his elbow on the railing, he switched weapons. I heard the burp of the doctored Luger, but by that time the boat was moving again, its bow lifting as the engine wound up. Long before it disappeared around the end of the island it had drawn out of range. Jack pushed himself away from the railing, still firing, and fell to his knees.

I had not moved since the first shot. Now the musical horn of the Duesenberg climbed my spine and I turned and saw Bass Springfield's face working behind the windshield, a hood's length away from the back of the LaSalle. He was gesturing wildly out his open window. I slid across the seat, pins and needles pricking my legs and feet as feeling returned below the belt, and stomped on the starter. It growled several times before I realized I hadn't switched on the ignition. I did that and the engine caught. I stalled it twice trying to work the clutch, but on the third try I hit a happy combination of gears and gas and drove the car away from the bridge. The Duesenberg's bumper clipped the LaSalle's taillight as it swung onto the planks. I got out and followed on foot, crunching over the broken tinted glass.

Springfield and Andy Kramm were both out of the car when I reached it, Andy clinging uselessly to his beloved machine gun. Jack was sitting on the planks with one leg doubled under him, trying to ram a fresh clip into one of the Lugers and missing. The entire left side of his suitcoat including the sleeve was slick with blood. It had slid out under the cuff and stained his hand and gun so that you couldn't tell where the flesh left off and the metal began. "Cocksucking wop," he was saying. "Too yellow to do his own double-cross."

"Mr. Jack, we gots to get you to a doctor." Springfield was trying to circle his arms under Jack's and smearing himself all over.

"It was Frankie Orr."

Jack didn't hear me. He was still trying to reload the Luger. "Wop cocksucker."

Andy said, "Get him in back. We'll use Teague. He don't report bullet wounds."

I told Jack again it was Frankie Orr. I don't know why it was so important at that moment. There was blood all over, although not as much as Mr. Norman had shed. Jack stopped playing with the pistol.

"How do you know?"

The question distracted Andy. He straightened, watching me. He was still holding the Thompson. Its black muzzle was broad, a single flaring nostril. "Jack said you're the one set up the meet."

"I didn't know."

"You didn't know, but you know it was Orr."

I couldn't think of a way to say it.

"Lay off that," Jack said. "He's gutty. He ain't stupid." Springfield had his arms around him now and was dragging him backwards in the direction of the Duesenberg. Jack's heels made smeary lines in the blood on the planks. "Drive the LaSalle back, Connie. Tell Vivian I won't be home. Don't say I got shot."

She guessed anyway, when I brought the car back without him. She was on her way out somewhere in a white lambswool belted topcoat and a cloche hat with a clamshell purse in her hand. I said someone would be in touch. She didn't say a lot, and what she did say I don't remember. I don't think it was, "Jack has ideas."

It was a near thing. I was told later that the edge of the pattern had ground up Jack's left upper arm as he turned, and pellets had lodged close to the heart. Too close anyway for Dunstan Teague, a former emergency room specialist at Detroit Receiving who had lost his license to practice medicine when he was caught removing drugs from a locked cabinet without authorization; he merely flushed out and stitched up those wounds and gave the patient a tetanus shot after plucking the lead out of the arm. Jack carried the remaining pellets to the grave. He had lost a deal of blood and burned up with fever, but it broke, and after ten days on a cot in Teague's spare room he returned home twenty pounds lighter with his arm in a sling and a dashing new white streak in his curly hair where it tumbled over his forehead. He gained back the weight and found the use of his arm, but he never lost the streak. It gave him a branded look, like a man I had read about in a rival tabloid who was struck by lightning and bore the mark of the bolt in a dead white line from the crown of his head to the ball of one foot for the rest of his days.

Something else had changed, too. The go-to-hell spirit was still there and always would be, but he didn't seem to enjoy himself as much. At times, when the world was turning around him, he would sit absent-mindedly rubbing the spot where the pellets had entered his chest, and the expression on his face would put me in mind of his more thoughtful brother.

When I visited him in St. Clair Shores the first time after his return, I was stopped and frisked in the front hall by a pair of young men I had never seen before. Vivian rescued me, explaining that they were reinforcements hired by Andy. They had Purple all over them. Jack greeted me in the parlor, looking more relaxed than I had ever seen him in slacks and an open-necked shirt. He kept taking his arm out of the sling to light cigarettes and twirl the knob on the radio, looking for the bouncy music he liked. I told him how I knew the man with the shotgun was Frankie Orr. It was the first and only time I mentioned the incident at the Griswold House to anyone.

"Clyde Norman." He rubbed his chest. "He carried the bag for Borneo in the Bottom when I was delivering there for Joey. I knew back then he was dipping."

"I wonder why Orr hooked up with Joey."

"Frankie's a whore. I guessed that the first time I seen him."

"Maybe it's not just him. Maybe Borneo's with Joey now. It makes sense when you think about it. That play at the bridge was too complicated for Joey."

"I thought he was a fucking ghost till I seen the metal shining through the holes I put in that vest. I tried for his head then but I guess I missed."

"He looked pretty healthy swimming away. What do you think, is it Machine and Borneo?"

"It don't matter. Joey's dead. He'll fall down when he gets the message."

In spite of what he said, the streets were quiet for a long time after the bridge fight. Meanwhile there was an election and Frank L. Murphy stepped into the mayor's office handily. The Belle Isle incident notwithstanding, it was an indication of how much progress the problem of economic depression had made beyond the problem of lawlessness that he was voted in on his promise to create more jobs. There were more people in bread lines than in blind pigs.

Jack's brother Tom was starting to get bylines in the *Times.* He wrote about everything but the policy racket, and it was evident that Joey Machine had abandoned his public relations strategy. I saw Tom at press conferences. He was getting better at asking questions, but I couldn't shake the conviction that he wasn't cut out for journalism. He was no plunger.

When I finally got around to calling Hattie again, a strange woman answered and told me she'd changed addresses. The woman didn't know where she was living now.

October leaves fell, November gales swept them into the gutters. On the Sunday morning after Thanksgiving—a big weekend for the numbers, when everyone bet on 620 in honor of the year the Pilgrims landed—Joey Machine, accompanied by his bodyguard, Dom Polacki, and his bookkeeper, a grave fat man known as "Presto" DiPesto, but whose birth name was Aaron Stahl, left a house on Sylvester Street where it was rumored the accounts were kept on every vice game on the East Side and started walking toward a coffee shop on the corner. A dark blue Duesenberg with ivory side-panels drew abreast of them and a young man with dark curly hair streaked white in front cranked down the back window on the curb side and fired at them sixteen times with a machine pistol. He missed all three of them but killed a fourteen-year-old girl on her way home from early Mass.

PART THREE

November 1930–May 1931

Indians

Is this city and this State to be ruled by the assassin or by the forces of organized government?

—*The Detroit Times*

There is more law in the end of a nightstick than in any court in the land.

—old Detroit policeman's saying

Chapter Seventeen

The murder of Mary Margaret Connor made the front page of every evening edition in the city and went out over the wires to both coasts. For days afterward, anyone who wasn't aware that she was an honor student at St. Benedictine, took piano lessons Thursday afternoons, wanted to be a nurse, and looked a little like Freddie Bartholomew with her page boy cut and parochial collar and dark solemn eyes, didn't read newspapers. If she had ever sat in a mud puddle in her Communion dress or kicked the milkman in the shin or stuck her tongue out at Sister's back or otherwise behaved as a normal healthy little girl, her teachers and her parents' neighbors didn't report it. Death's like that.

Based on eyewitness descriptions of the man in the Duesenberg, and of the car itself, there was little doubt concerning the identity of her killer. Joey Machine, who observed few laws but his own and often violated those, broke the old mob rule of silence when, pausing to address reporters waiting for him on the steps of Detroit Police Headquarters, where he had gone to make his statement, he said: "That kike's bugs. If the bulls don't put him down, somebody else will." He had on a new homburg and overcoat and a square of sticking-plaster on his right cheek where some of the skin had been scraped off when Dom Polacki body-checked him into a row of trash cans to take him out of the line of fire. A white and shaken DiPesto had made no public comment at all. A CPA who had never before been shot at and didn't own a gun, he had stood frozen in the middle of the sidewalk while the bullets sped around him. He left Joey's employ soon after and showed up later under his real name as a candidate for Roosevelt's Brain Trust until his past caught up with him and he was forced to withdraw his application.

A search of Jack's house by Detroit police and Wayne County sheriff's deputies turned only Vivian Dance, who said she hadn't seen Jack since Saturday night. She was brought in for further questioning—meaning she would be stripped by matrons and deloused to teach her a little humility and to demonstrate some results for the press—but Nathan Rabinowitz, Jack's lawyer, was waiting at headquarters with a writ of habeas corpus when they got there and she left with him. It would be years before an internal investigation revealed Rabinowitz's paid source of information in the department, by which time the lawyer had retired to a brick mansion on Mackinac Island.

The day after the shooting, the Duesenberg was found parked on East Larned a stone's throw from the spanking new Windsor Tunnel. This sparked wide speculation that the fugitive had fled to Canada until a U.S. Customs official blandly pointed out that a man walking through a vehicular tunnel would have drawn some attention. Nevertheless Jack Dance was seen riding a streetcar in Windsor. Others reported him ordering bacon and eggs in a diner on Kercheval, reading a newspaper at a bus stop in Monroe near the Ohio border, and wandering around the University of Michigan campus in Ann Arbor. When a service station on Fort Street was reported robbed by a man answering Jack's description Monday night, bulls flooded the place, but the attendant who called the police turned out to have a record of burglary convictions under another name and was arrested without fanfare.

In the midst of all this, Mayor Murphy announced a reshuffling in the police department. These things always start out nobly on paper, a major housecleaning and ventilation, but prove disappointing in practice. Commissioner Wilcox was out, replaced by a murky committee until a permanent substitute could be named. Casting about for a chief of detectives, the mayor's eye lit upon the impressive arrest record—including the first rap for John Danzig—of one Valery Kozlowski, lieutenant in charge of the Prohibition Squad. Thus the plainclothes division acquired a new leader, a large hard fat man with tiny feet, a stogie squashed between his molars, and an eleven-thousand-dollar annual mortgage on his horse ranch outside Kalamazoo that he presumably paid out of his forty-dollar-a-week salary as a civil servant. In turn—mainly from default, the position being a notorious dead end except when reform fever was in the air—the Prohibition unit went to a former sergeant named Hermann Gabriel.

Gabriel, a dish-chested tubercular with a long yellow face and ears that turned out under a Panama hat he wore in all seasons, should have been retired on a medical disability years earlier, but because the job he'd held for five years—investigating Negro murders in the Black Bottom—was an even more thankless one than enforcing the Eighteenth Amendment, personnel regulations concerning health and fitness and danger to the community had been waived. The glitch was that, through a chain of circumstances no one could have planned or predicted, for the first time in the squad's twelve-year history it had come under the supervision of a reasonably honest man. Gabriel had been broken down from motor patrolman to bunion duty back in 1920 for arresting the driver of a beer truck after the truck went through a stop sign on Jefferson. Although he had not repeated the mistake and had managed by doing his job and closing his eyes to the indiscretions of his superiors to be promoted to detective sergeant, he lived within the means dictated by his station and kept no flashy blondes or secret bank accounts, or at least none that could be traced; and they tried, once they learned what he was about. He would be heard from.

A special *Banner* Sunday edition on the Connor slaying was in the chase when Howard Wolfman entered the print shop pounding his palm with a rolled-up copy of the *News* and ordered the front page taken out and re-made. The new layout featured a six-column blow-up of Jack Dance holding the cake knife at his wedding reception under the eighteen-point head JACK THE RIPPER! Chet Mooney, covering the story for the *News*, had tossed off the moniker in his lead and Howard, who kept up on the competition the way a brilliant surgeon studies medical journals, had decided it was too good to waste on the broadsheet press. Ernie Swayles's account, written while the bulls were still counting the bullet holes, was as blaring as the new headline, but factual to the ground, a highwire act he pulled off as neatly drunk as he did sober. Six years later an equally balanced piece on Father Coughlin and the Francis Townsend presidential campaign had him primed to take over *Collier's* Midwest bureau when his liver got him first.

As the paper's resident expert on Jack Dance, I filed a noncommittal sidebar column on his marksmanship and cool nerve under pressure. Had I known where it would lead, I might have chosen another tack.

In command of the manhunt, Chief of Detectives Kozlowski fell back on the old Prohibition Squad formula and pulled in every thug and grifter not on speaking terms with an attorney in hopes of shaking loose the whereabouts of the killer and his associates. Lon Camarillo, making a run across the river at the time of the shooting and thus unaware of the excitement, landed his reconditioned JN-4 with a load of Old Log Cabin in front of the barn he used for a hangar in Oakland County and was arrested as soon as he stepped down. Andy Kramm, driving Jack's LaSalle, tried to ram a sheriff's blockade on Grand River west of Outer Drive, lost heart at the sight of the waiting Thompsons and shotguns, and surrendered. Both men received the Beaubien Basement Treatment but swore through bloody and swollen lips they didn't know where Jack was. Despite sound alibis they were charged with accessory to murder and jailed. Ironically, a square-jawed shot of a younger, less cadaverous Charles Austin Camarillo in dress uniform with Army Air Corps wings on his chest appeared in the newspapers next to an old front-and-profile mug of Andy Kramm from an early arrest for gambling.

The dragnet now concentrated on the gang's leader and Bass Springfield, who police believed had manned the wheel during the attempt on Joey Machine. Celestine Brown, 26, a colored file clerk employed by the Ford Motor Company, was arrested for questioning, and because no lawyer appeared with a writ, underwent stripping and spraying for cooties at the Detroit House of Correction. She admitted that she lived with Springfield but claimed ignorance of his current locality. She was booked for unlawful cohabitation. Tom Danzig presented himself at headquarters to state in the presence of the detective chief and a police stenographer that he hadn't seen or spoken to his brother in weeks. He was questioned hard, but without rubber truncheons, and allowed to leave once he'd signed his statement. Even a Turk like Kozlowski knew better than to turn a member of the press on the spit. As for me, when Tom's story got out, I believed him, if no one else did. I'd known distant cousins who were closer than these two sons of a Jewish watch repairman.

Meanwhile, Hermann Gabriel wasn't letting any dust settle on his new lieutenant's bars. On the Wednesday after Sylvester Street, he piloted a flying wedge of unmarked police vehicles led by a Mack truck through the steel-reinforced doors of a warehouse on Orleans and coughed lung-tissue into a borrowed handkerchief while his men handcuffed Ernst Adolf Scherwein, an eighty-year-old brewmeister late of Heidelberg, Germany, and nine of his assistants. Then they set to work staving in kegs and barrels and a wooden vat as big as Grand Circus Park with axes and sleeve bars and stood back to watch the green beer gush out, its fumes making the fixtures wobble and weave like an iron fire escape on a hot day.

The raid on Jack Dance's operation was the first on a local brewery since 1919. A blind pig was nothing. It could be tipped over, gutted and punched full of holes at midnight, and then re-open the next evening. Making beer required a huge investment, much of which went to officials whose business it then became to hold their noses against the stink of fermenting hops and find interest elsewhere when the trucks trundled out with their cargo. Gabriel was no ex-Commissioner Emmons, grandstanding in the morning and seeking new employment in the afternoon. He knew that in the climate surrounding the violent death of a fourteen-year-old girl, no bent wardheeler was about to draw attention to himself by complaining. It was as brilliant a payback for a ten-year-old demotion as the city had ever seen.

Every police-sanctioned scribe for miles around attended the press conference in Gabriel's office the morning after the raid. There, amid the chewing gum-and-tobacco mulch that only a parade of apathetic bulls could bring to a building barely seven years old, we jammed like lemmings into the glassed-in room with its institutional green desk and kicked-in file cabinets and interoffice correspondence going brown and curling on the corkboard while the lieutenant read from a prepared statement. In between sentences he hawked and expectorated into a succession of paper tissues which he plucked from a box on the desk, used, scrutinized, wadded, and tossed into a steel wastebasket. They were the first I'd ever seen; I was fascinated by how quickly they filled it to overflowing. His narrow grim jaundiced face brought back memories of Calvin Coolidge, and he had puffy eyes and chestnut-colored hair slicked back with Vaseline that showed a ridge where his Panama settled when he went outdoors. The statement ran: "After weeks of surveillance upon the warehouse building on Orleans Street, and upon obtaining a warrant as required by law . . ." I could have written it myself without leaving the office.

When it was finished, Gabriel fielded a handful of the dozens of questions, then got up from behind the desk and towed the reporters out into the squad room, where he turned them over to officers who would escort them to the property room and let the shutterbugs take pictures of the weapons confiscated in the raid. It was a staple, that shot of slab-faced detectives standing behind a table displaying handguns of various makes and calibers and boxes of ammunition and the inevitable Thompson, in this case recruited most likely from the department's own arsenal because simple brewers seldom armed themselves so fiercely. I was still in the office when the lieutenant returned. He raised his eyebrows, but went around and took his seat without pausing. "Minor, isn't it?" He had a thin, Georgia Cracker kind of voice, aged years beyond his late thirties.

I nodded. "What's shutting down Dance's brewery got to do with the Connor shooting?"

"It was in the statement. It's half of a two-pronged assault. While Chief Kozlowski's anti-racketeering task force concentrates on hunting Dance down, the Prohibition Squad will continue to carry out raids on his places of business. Did you see that picture *Dracula*?"

"I missed it."

"The book's better. Everybody's after this bum Count Dracula who bites women in the neck and sucks out their blood. He's got to stretch out in one of these coffins full of dirt from his backyard by sunup or he'll croak, so they find them and smash them up and scatter the dirt so he'll have to come out in the open. Jack Dance is no different. Staying underground takes dough. Cut off his sources of income and you flush him out."

"He doesn't have any other source except his wife," I said. "The brewery was it."

"So maybe it won't take so long."

"You wouldn't be taking advantage of the situation to dump over as many places as you can before the neckties upstairs cut you off at the ankles."

He chuckled. It turned into a coughing jag and he spat into a tissue and inspected it before flipping it onto the pile. "Great invention. You wouldn't believe my old laundry bill. If you want to write that I'm the only square man in a bad town, I won't stop you. It's better than making some kind of Robin Hood out of that crum Dance. That's part of how we got in this fix."

"Save it for the newsreels. I think you're just getting yours for all those footbaths you took when they stuck you back on the beat for doing your job. Would you care to comment on that?"

"It's a crock of shit. You can quote me."

"If it weren't for that crum Dance you wouldn't be behind that desk."

"I wasn't unhappy in the Bottom," he said. "One time this big buck, twelve hours out of the joint, came looking for his girl in a whorehouse on Hastings. Someone decided to make a fight and five niggers got stabbed to death, six with the girl. If you didn't hang onto something when you walked through later you could slip and fall on your ass in the blood. The boyfriend wasn't cut into so many pieces they couldn't be sewed back on, so we booked him and he got ninety-nine in Jackson. The fight got three lines next to the shipping reports. This puke gangster hits some little whitebread brat with a stray bullet and he's Public Enemy Number One on every front page in town."

"What's your point?"

"When the hand's poker you don't play pinochle. When it was Hastings nobody gave a shit, so we cut one out of the herd and fed him to the system. When it's Sylvester we do it with brass bands and bright lights."

"Dance had just the brewery. If you hit more places you'll be raiding the competition. Machine and Borneo, the Purples."

He shrugged. "After the shooting's over, who's going to go back and sort it all out? Meanwhile we do some good."

"And incidentally get the rest of them sore enough at Dance for bringing heat to do your job for you."

"Bowles was on the right track about letting the rats thin out their own ranks," he said. "He just didn't know how to use it."

"Thanks, Lieutenant."

When I was at the door, he snatched a fresh tissue out of the box and folded it. "This conversation is off the record, by the way. If you use it I'll have you banned from the building."

The hunt continued through December. Blind pigs were turned inside out and doors in hotels and private houses were kicked in all over the city, but finally even the police grew tired of saying they were "following promising leads," and the papers began to sneer all over again at official incompetence the way they had under Mayor Bowles. The *Banner* ran a Jensen cartoon showing a bunch of fat-assed Keystone

Kops tripping over their own flat feet and pointing guns at one another, "Doing the Jack Dance." One of them was labeled "Chief Kozlowski." Things got busy again after a group calling itself Citizens for a Safe Detroit, made up mostly of the wives of Ford and General Motors board members, offered a reward of $5,000 for information leading to the arrest of Mary Margaret Connor's killer, but only because the crackpots had had some time to rest since the initial flurry; one old woman in Corktown turned in her seventy-five-year-old landlord. Christmas came and went. It was generally believed that Jack had left the city.

About eleven o'clock Monday night, December the 29th, when Howard and Jensen had gone home to bed and I was wrestling with a column about life in the Black Bottom, my telephone rang. Getting my own line had been one of the perks of syndication.

"Minor, the *Banner*."

"Connie, this is Hattie."

I took my foot off the Remington. "How are you, Hattie?"

"I tried your apartment first. Are you alone?"

"Just me and the guy on the night desk."

"Can you get rid of him?"

"I guess."

"Do it, okay? And hang around."

"How long?" She'd hung up.

George Capstone, the night editor, had a new pregnant wife at home. He didn't argue when I told him I'd watch the desk. Forty-five minutes later I was sitting alone in the city room, the pool of light from the desk lamp the only illumination on that floor, when Bass Springfield came forward out of the shadows.

He moved with an unreal silence for his size, as if the darkness in the open door to the hallway had grown deep enough to have mass and animation. He was wearing his old cloth cap and the raccoon coat he had worn the night I met him. It gave him no small resemblance to a grizzly, or a mythical man-beast from my father's books on the old legends, with his lower features showing in the light shining up through the green glass shade. The light glistened on the big automatic in his right hand, the one with the trigger guard filed off to make room for his misshapen finger. He stood there without speaking for a hundred years. Then his head turned and I saw the angle of his jaw. It needed shaving.

"Clear, boss."

Jack made a lot more noise coming in. His camel's hair coat was open, swishing, and his rapid footsteps on the linoleum floor mocked his preference for automatic fire. Despite the display of nervous energy, he looked tired. The green light trapped under the brim of his hat found lines and hollows I'd never seen in his young face, a day's growth of whiskers. His smile was a self-conscious imitation of the broad grin I knew.

Before I could say anything, his hands came out of his coat pockets with the Lugers in them. I felt my limbs go dead. Then he laid both pistols on the desk.

"I'm bushed, Connie," he said. "Call the bulls and tell them to make a bed for me at County."

Chapter Eighteen

JACK DANCE SURRENDERS TO *BANNER* COLUMNIST

Too long.

JACK DANCE SURRENDERS TO *BANNER*

Too passive.

BANNER CAPTURES JACK THE RIPPER

Run it.

(Picture on the front page of Chief Kozlowski, Jack Dance, and Connie Minor, the columnist looking small and slight next to the two big men as posed by Fred Ogilvie.)

Inside:

Minor's Majors
BY CONNIE MINOR

A furtive and exhausted Jack Dance, hunted by the police in two countries for the murder last month of St. Benedictine honor student Mary Margaret Connor, walked into the *Banner* office early this morning and gave himself up to this writer, asking him to intercede with the police in his arrest.

Asked why he didn't surrender himself to the police directly, Dance, who refused to disclose where he had been hiding, said, "The papers stab you in the back. They don't shoot you in the head."

In fact he told me, off the record, that Hattie had put him up in a second-story room of her new place on Monroe east of Greektown, four blocks from police headquarters, almost in the epicenter of the largest manhunt since Nathan Leopold and Richard Loeb raped and killed the Frank boy. "No Man's Land, Connie. Safest place to piss on the sidewalk in town is right in front of Thirteen Hundred. The bulls look right at you, they don't see you because you can't be there."

"Accommodating of Hattie," I said, "considering she doesn't like to take chances with her business."

"Oh, she's the goods."

I let it go. It didn't mean anything anymore anyway. I was conscious of Springfield hovering behind me, the raccoon coat smelling of mothballs. "What happened on Sylvester?"

"Off the books?"

I nodded.

Jack bummed a Chesterfield and let me light it. He was straddling a chair backwards facing the desk with his arms folded on top of the backrest. "I had a clear shot. Bass took me close enough to bounce a baseball off the guinea son of a bitch's schmuck. Then that big Polack of his seen me and knocked him down like a fucking tenpin. I guess I should've used single-fire and took my time, but I had the full auto in my hand already. Then that girl ran right into it. I bet her old man promised her the strop if she was late, fast as she was running. I stopped and we got out of there, but she was down by then." He took a drag, coughed, and put the cigarette out in an old burn-hole on the desk. "Never did get the hang of these things. I don't know how I could've not hit nobody else. You should've seen that fatty—whatsizname, Pesto?"

"Presto DiPesto."

"Dumbass wop name. On account of he's so good with numbers, I guess. He was standing there like a fat fucking scarecrow. You should've seen it. I bet he dumped in his pants." He smiled his new weak smile. Then he stopped. "It's too bad about the girl. She shouldn't've ran in like that."

He did feel sorry about the girl. But it was a detached kind of sorrow, as if she'd been caught up in a natural disaster beyond anyone's control. Maybe she had, at that. He'd once told me he never knew what he was going to do until he did it.

For a man like Jack, jail and a sensational murder trial must have looked pretty good after a month cooped up with Bass Springfield in Hattie's spare bedroom, allowed to roam through the house only during the day when the girls were out, with all the curtains drawn. As for the girls, they must have wondered about the guests they never saw. Did the hiding men smell their perfume, the odor of Lifebuoy that permeated those places and that still gives me an involuntary erection whenever I come across it unexpectedly?

"I missed Vivian," Jack admitted.

I said she was okay.

"I figured. She can take care of herself."

Springfield said, "They let Celestine go yet?"

"I heard they did. The neighbors bought her a lawyer."

Jack rubbed his unshaven chin. His eggshell silk collar was dirty and his powder-blue suit needed pressing. "I ain't been taking care of my*self* so good. I don't guess there's nothing left of the brewery."

"You want to look out for that Lieutenant Gabriel. He's tougher than Kozlowski."

"They shouldn't've arrested Andy and Lon. They wasn't there. Speaking of Kozlowski." He nudged the telephone my way.

"Can I call my editor first? I'll be out on my ass if I don't get a picture."

"He take the pictures, does he?"

I compromised and got Fred Ogilvie out of bed without telling him why I wanted him and his camera. Then I called 1300 Beaubien. It was a dead heat between Kozlowski and the photographer.

The chief of detectives, who had learned something about life under the public lens since his promotion, was docile, allowing me to hand him Jack's guns while Jack stood between us looking tired but not unhappy in handcuffs, standing with me on either side of the prisoner with our hands on his shoulders like old friends, and—the pose Howard Wolfman chose for the front page—grasping Jack's arm while I touched Jack's other elbow like the father giving the bride away. Springfield was in two shots, but Howard rejected both of them. Jack smiled, Kozlowski looked big and uncomfortable, I wore the expression of someone who would rather be anyplace else, which was as close to the truth as that edition ever came. For someone who just wanted to cover the news, I had made a lasting reputation for being part of it.

I don't think the *Banner*'s competition ever forgave me that moment under the light. The *News* and *Free Press* reported merely that Jack had been apprehended in an office in the Parker block. The *Times* said that the police made the arrest on a tip by "an employee in the building." Howard made up for it by trumpeting my role in the drama for the next week, and got it into every story about Jack thereafter; and there were many of them from the time the doors closed on him at the Wayne County Jail until the judge delivered the verdict at his trial. Even now, on those rare occasions when my old colleagues find reason to mention me, they append "the reporter to whom Jack (The Ripper) Dance surrendered" to my name, effectively sealing me away in Jack's coffin. Now that Jack himself is part of regional history and his times a smoky dream of childhood, the old jealousies are suspended. To be made peace with is unassailable proof that one is finished.

Jack never said what happened to him after Kozlowski and a gang of very large bulls in crumpled fedoras and cheap coats took him away, but I heard that Bass Springfield, who sent a sergeant to Detroit Receiving with a broken nose and eleven cracked ribs for calling him a nigger, was beaten to the concrete floor in the basement of police headquarters and stripped and tied naked to a chair under a bare bulb and worked over with those eighteen-inch lengths of hard black rubber that are so much more effective than hoses and electric cords and leave all their bruises under the skin. Working in shifts, the bulls laid the truncheons along his ribs and belly and poked at his testicles with the ends and flicked hot cigar ashes into his lap for twelve hours and never asked a question. When he soiled himself and the stink got too bad they sluiced him down with buckets of ice water and waited until he came to and started in again. Then when he passed out and couldn't be revived they untied him and dragged him down to Holding and dumped him, still naked, into the cage. A three-page typewritten confession of his part in the Connor killing, with an X on the bottom said to be his mark, was offered into evidence at the trial. That, he said later, was the first time he'd seen it.

The morning after the arrest, Andy Kramm and Lon Camarillo were released. They'd been held for four weeks without arraignment or counsel.

I saw Nathan Rabinowitz for the first time at Jack's arraignment. He was short and pudgy in a gray wool double-breasted with a white handkerchief arranged in three points in the breast pocket, a bullet-headed man in his fifties who shaved his temples and combed his graying hair sideways across his scalp. The exact opposite of the braying mob mouthpiece of fable, he spoke quietly with a light Yiddish accent, so that you had to strain to hear him even inside the white Italian marble walls of Recorder's Court. Jack, standing beside him in front of the bench, was dressed conservatively for his taste in charcoal wool and a tiger-striped necktie. He kept his hands folded in front of him and said nothing. Judge Thomas A. Steelbarger, neckless in his pleated black taffeta gown, with coarse red features and thick black hair that started just above his eyebrows and went straight back, showing the marks of the comb, listened to Rabinowitz's motion for low bail—"My client is a well-known figure locally, a native of Detroit, with a wife and home in St. Clair Shores"—and Assistant County Prosecutor E. Wharton Clay's strident demand that the defendant be held without bail—"a community menace, a gangster, a crazed child-killer"—then set bail at thirty thousand dollars and cracked his gavel. Bass Springfield, also represented by Rabinowitz, received a fifteen-thousand-dollar judgment. Vivian, who attended the proceedings in a hat and veil and something tailored, arranged both amounts with a bailbondsman and the two were set free. The *Banner* that evening led off with a shot of Jack, old grin in place, firmly shaking Rabinowitz's hand. The attorney's smile was shy.

A funny thing happened in the courtroom when bail was set. The amount, which might as well have been thirty million for as close as the average Detroiter could ever hope to come to it in that first year of the Great Depression, was little more than walking-around money for the crowd Jack ran with those days, who tipped doormen with fifty-dollar bills and drove cars that cost more than houses and booked forty tables at an exclusive nightclub just to have privacy for a party of eight. Everyone had to know that the figure was as good as a pass out the front door. Yet they cheered. The store clerks and window washers and typists and bank tellers and firemen's wives and tailors and insurance underwriters who squeezed onto the mahogany benches and stood at the back of the room and jammed the big double doorway, who a month earlier had been calling for the hide of this maniac, this runaway Jew, this killer of Catholic schoolgirls, celebrated his freedom. It had to do with human nature, with a solid month of watching the guardians of justice turning over every manhole cover in the city and arresting whatever crawled out blinking into the sunlight, of being force-fed Mary Margaret Connor's academic record and piano virtuosity and angelic nature, of shaking their heads over their chipped coffee mugs in their drab kitchens at a handsome young man, sought in every corner of the land, who stepped out of darkness into a downtown building five minutes from police headquarters and laid down his guns, asking to be arrested and tried. It had to do with the limits of human patience, of disdain for the pious moralizing of a system which like a perpetual-motion machine generated only enough energy to keep its many parts moving, forget effectiveness. It had to do with Robin Hood and Jesse James and a society that called for individual sacrifice on Tuesday and taxed it on Friday. It had nothing to do with the death of a little girl. It didn't even have anything to do with Jack Dance. It was the bellow of the primitive from the depths of the caverns beneath his civilization.

Joey Machine, interviewed over the telephone at his home in Rochester by Doug Keenan of the *Free Press*, put it more succinctly. "This whole town's as bugs as that crazy kike."

The trial was scheduled for February. Meanwhile the old year played itself out the usual way, with horns and confetti, the gaiety even more forced than usual because it's supposed to be based on the belief that better things are coming. The automobile industry was faltering—everyone was patching up the old jalopy and making do—and lines of muffled men and women without jobs blocked the sidewalk in front of the Department of Public Welfare from before dawn to well past dark. The murder tally for 1930 topped out at 192, a four-year high. At those times you blew the horn extra loud to cover the sighs and doubled up on the confetti so you couldn't see the tears.

After half a dozen calls to his storefront office on Michigan, I got Nathan Rabinowitz to agree to meet me at the House of All Nations. The reputation of the place had been bad since the days when anarchists were all we thought we had to worry about, but it was convenient to both of us and I liked the way it smelled when the souvlaka and the boiled cabbage came together. Also I had a warm feeling for the establishment where Howard Wolfman had rescued me from the *Times*.

In a corner booth we had club sodas, as if the beat bull seated at the bar with his cap at his elbow wasn't blowing the foam off a tall cold one, and the attorney set fire to a cigar that didn't smell as if it came from the same hemisphere as the four-for-a-quarter stogies smoked by Chief Kozlowski. His three-piece suit, a little less conservative than his courtroom double-breasted, was blue with a faint orange windowpane check and the three symmetrical handkerchief points in his breast pocket looked like massed torpedoes. His eyes were light brown with gold flecks and warm-looking for a man of his reserve. I asked him what strategy he planned to use in the Dance case. The warm eyes crinkled, he shook out the match, and dropped it on the battered table; there were no ashtrays and damn few other heavy blunt instruments at the House of All Nations.

"Do you follow football?" he asked.

"I used to when I wrote sports. I'm a horsehide man by choice."

"They're not the same. Baseball is a soldier's game. Football is for generals. Would a football coach tell a reporter his Sunday game plan on Saturday?"

"Off the record, then. I'm broadening my base here. I haven't covered many trials."

"Jack says you can be trusted, but I'm not Jack. Fortunately for him."

I knew what he was thinking. "You can talk about him in front of me. I like him, but I wouldn't let him carry my wallet. With Jack, there's no link between thought and deed. They're the same thing. And he doesn't regret afterwards."

"We see him similarly," he said. I noticed there was almost no trace of an accent now. It was a courtroom tool, like the quiet suits and the soft speech that made you lean forward as if everything he had to say was manna from heaven. "I'll just say the state has no case. Nobody can place Jack on Sylvester Street at the time the Connor girl was killed."

"There were several eyewitnesses."

"Witnesses are not necessarily eyewitnesses."

"He was seen and recognized. So was the car. The police have his guns."

He rotated his cigar, pulled on it. I had the impression that line of questioning had been overruled; he had, after all, tried twice to be made a judge. I moved my freight to safe port.

"Because of cases like the Faryniak killing and this one, you have a reputation as a mouthpiece for gangsters. Do you think it's a fair description?"

He flicked ashes on top of the curled match. "I'm a criminal lawyer. My clients are people who have been accused of crimes. Gangsterism is the most visible crime in Detroit. If I practiced in Calcutta, where it's a capital offense to eat beef, I imagine I'd have a reputation as a mouthpiece for hamburger hounds. As long as you're good at what you do, it doesn't matter what you're called. Do you think tabloid scribbling is a fair description of what you do?"

"I'm not on the stand, Mr. Rabinowitz. So you're planning to stick with the not-guilty plea you entered at the arraignment?"

"As I said, the state has no case." He drained his glass and put a hand inside his coat.

"My treat," I said. "I'm grateful for your time."

"I wasn't reaching for my wallet." He withdrew a long fold of thick paper showing Gothic boldface over finer print and thrust it at me in a single practiced motion. I had my hand on it before I realized it.

"What's this?"

"A subpoena to testify for the defense in Jack Dance's trial. You've been served, Mr. Minor." He rose and took his hat and coat off the peg.

Chapter Nineteen

Danny Moskovitch, better known as Mouse because of his habit of scurrying out from between pillars at the County Building to tug at the sleeves of judges and county officials, was a sharp-featured midget in a boy's-size Sears Roebuck suit turned up at the cuffs and a bulky overcoat that he always seemed to be trying to run out of as he scampered along holding on to his porkpie hat with one hand. Depending upon your ethnic or political persuasion, he was either a noodge or a chooch or a professional lobbyist, and if he ever paused long enough to tote up the score he'd probably have found that he'd done more good for his clients than an army of lawyers. It was Mouse, catching his breath for a rare moment between buttonholes, who explained the troubles of the time for me in words I never forgot.

"Start with the Indians," he said. "Well, the limeys was a bitch before them, but they was easier to get along with at least until that tea thing. It took us almost three hunnert years, but we finally rounded up the bastards and stuck them away on reservations. Then it was the Kaiser. We done him pretty good, us and the limeys and the frogs. After the Kaiser it was anarchists, and after anarchists it was gangsters. Now it's commies. Next it'll be niggers. Point is, we should of never got rid of the Indians, 'cause all we been doing ever since is fighting them under different names."

In 1931, with talk of repealing the Eighteenth Amendment in the wind and the bootlegger off the front pages and stuck away on the entertainment reservation—*Underworld*, *Little Caesar*, *The Public Enemy*

—the Indian in Detroit had taken a new shape, a thickset one with its collar turned up and its hat pulled down, bludgeoning order out of chaos with brass knuckles and a blackjack in factory parking lots and on docks where ore carriers dropped anchor to unload thousands of tons of iron pellets at the Rouge plant. *Strikebreaking* was an unfamiliar new term to Detroiters, but as the months passed and the economic situation began to look less like a depression and more like a black bottomless pit, it would fall on their ears with the dull thud of a phrase heard so often it had lost its power to create emotion.

The people who keep track of such things point to December 10, 1936 as the beginning, when a woman working on the line at the Kelsey-Hayes Wheel Company faked a faint and Walter Reuther climbed on a box and delivered an oration in favor of the United Automobile Workers union. For me it started much earlier, in the middle of January 1931, three weeks before Jack Dance's trial and almost a year to the day since the night I had accompanied the Machine mob on the Canada run across the ice of Lake Erie. About midmorning, an anonymous call came in to the *Banner* reporting trouble on Wyoming Street in Dearborn. Ernie Swayles was out, so Howard dropped it in my lap.

You could drive down Wyoming every day on your way to and from work for years and never notice the little plant where a few hundred employees made hood latches for the DeSoto straight-eight Chrysler; it was a dumpy square block building set back from the street with only its address visible from the curb. As we pieced it together later, the trouble had started months before when the company began nickel-and-diming workers for replacing lost and broken tools and paying insurance premiums, deducting the amounts from paychecks so that in some extreme cases employees had gone home with less than a dollar for fifty hours' work. Workers were hired at one salary and paid another much lower, and when they complained, the brass told them nobody was forcing them to work there and if they cared to quit there were thousands of others willing to take their place. There had been a number of slowdowns and one walkout that fizzled when the majority failed to join the rebels, who were then barred from the plant.

On this particular morning, after a pregnant woman was fired because she could no longer stand at her drill press for ten hours, some thirty of her fellow employees shut down their machines and refused to go back to work or leave the premises until the woman was reinstated.

The plant brass, who had been anticipating a demonstration of the kind, had then called in strikebreakers to drag them out. A brawl had ensued, other workers joining in, and boiled out into the lot. That was when someone, possibly a striking employee, although more likely one of the timid ones who didn't take part, had called the *Banner.*

When I got there with Fred Ogilvie, the Dearborn police were filling the first of three panel trucks parked in front of the plant with men and women in handcuffs. A crowd of what looked like several hundred people fumed and bubbled on the slushy strip between the block building and the sidewalk, although when things calmed down and a tally could be made it would come out to less than fifty, not counting officers in uniform who moved among them wielding riot clubs equipped with perpendicular handgrips like those on submachine guns for ramming the ends into guts and kidneys, and big men in coats and hats who could have been detectives but weren't. As I alighted from my Viking V-8 on the edge of the crowd, one of the latter standing not ten feet from me swung his fist and sunlight glinted on brass just before he connected with a hatless man in shirtsleeves and overalls, whose head spun on his neck with a splat just before he dropped into a junkpile of unrelated limbs. Fred took a picture across the roof of the car, eternalizing the thug, faceless in the middle of his follow-through, and the stricken man falling, his arms out like a diver arching backwards off the high board. It was a Pulitzer shot, if only it had appeared.

He used his flash. There was a suspended moment after the burst, like the vacuum that follows a gunshot in a quiet room; then the man with the brass knuckles turned our way, blinking. I saw his flat nose, the black inverted U of his mouth like a trout's, the pink insides of the pouches under his tiny eyes, the burst purple capillaries in his cheeks that said he hadn't been observing Prohibition any more closely than the rest of us. Then he came straight at me, the easy mark, the one without an automobile between him and a new place to plant his brassbound fist. I clawed behind me for the handle of the driver's door. It wasn't where I needed it to be. I missed, and then he was on top of me, his ham hand cocked back and glinting. I smelled garlic.

"Stink!"

He halted his swing. He had thrown so much weight into it that stopping propelled the rest of him forward almost into my arms before his big thick-soled Oxfords dug into the slush and asphalt with a crunch like tires braking in gravel. He whirled halfway around, his fist still cocked. The man who had shouted was shouldering his way through the crowd, grasping an occasional body in two hands and shoving it aside. I could tell it was Jack before I ever got a clear look at him, by his gait and the way he went through rather than around the obstacles in his path. A blackjack swung from a strap around his wrist, its bulbous leaded head dangling like a phallus.

"He's jake," he told the man with the knuckles. "Can't you tell he ain't no striker?"

"One of 'em taken my pitcher." The words wheezed out as through a broken steampipe.

"Next time smile. C'mon, Connie." Jack closed a hand around my upper arm. He had a blue welt under his right eye that grew deeper as I looked at it.

"Where we going?"

"There's a place around the corner."

Fred was still standing on the running board on the other side of the car with his camera resting on the roof. I tossed my keys at him. He trapped them against his chest with both hands. "Get that picture back to the office. Tell Howard I'll call in my story."

It was a workingman's pig, the walls hung with rusty pictures of prizefighters and lit by a smoky shaft of sunlight canting in through the front window, the kind of place where all the bartender had to do all day long was walk up and down the bar filling the shot glasses from a bottle on one pass and scooping the beer mugs under the taps on the next. We were the only customers until two men Jack's size in coats and hats came in and sat down at a table near the door. They might as well have been wearing their shields.

"Right on time," Jack said, turning back to our table. The blackjack in his pocket made his coat hang crooked. "I ain't lonely these days."

The bartender, fat and beetle-browed with a faded "Remember the *Maine*" tattoo on his thick right wrist, set beers in front of us. Jack paid, then handed him another dollar. "Ask the gents by the door what they're drinking."

When he left us I said, "I thought you were keeping close to the ground until the trial."

"The work's legit. The Dearborn cops pay us to nail the lid on the Communists. I need the dough. Nate don't work on IOU's and I'm through putting the arm on Vivian. I ain't no pimp."

"They didn't look like Communists."

He grinned, lopsidedly because it hurt his eye. "What's one look like?"

"They have scruffy beards and slouch hats and carry big round black bombs with burning fuses. Those were just factory stiffs you were beating on."

"Thanks for the thanks. You know who that was I pulled off you? Stink Barberra."

"Whoever named him knew what he was doing. He must've had a whole head of garlic for breakfast."

"Far as I know he never eats it."

"I couldn't mistake that smell."

"It wasn't his breath you smelled it on," he said. "It was his fingers. He rubs the stuff on his bullets."

"What's it do?"

"It's supposed to give you blood poisoning in case the bullets don't kill you. Personally I don't believe it. It's just something you do when you ain't sure how good a shot you are. Someone put a round through Stink's windpipe in twenty-five and that's how he lost his voice. Maybe they didn't use garlic."

"What's a professional killer doing breaking heads for the bulls?"

"Same thing I am, making dough to eat. How you think they live from one job to the next? When Stink works, I mean *works*, he works for Joey. The rest of the time he sits around rubbing garlic on his bullets and hitting himself with an ugly stick."

"You're working with someone who works for Joey Machine?"

"The town ain't that big, Connie. Anyway, if he's working, he ain't *working*; get it?"

"Really like walking the edge, don't you?"

"Beats reading the wallpaper at Hattie's all to hell." He turned and raised his mug to the bulls by the door. One of them lifted his right back. The other ignored him. They'd surprised me by accepting the beers. I don't know why I should have been surprised. I counted it a good sign that I still could be, living there as long as I had.

I was starting to think of something to say to get loose from Jack—a new experience, rider to the hounds that I was, but I was there to cover a disturbance at the plant, not to discuss career opportunities in labor racketeering or whether garlic is any more deadly on a bullet than on someone else's breath—when my story walked into the blind pig. Stumbled in, rather, in the person of a square-built young man with short dark hair in disorder on his forehead and one strap of his overalls broken and hanging down. The loose flap of the bib reminded me somehow of a man's scalp I had seen dangling in front of his face at the scene of an accident I had covered my first year out of sports. That man had scalped himself bucking back through the hole he had punched through a windshield with his head when the Plymouth coupe he was riding in had struck a lamppost. There was less blood in the present case, a crust under the young man's nose and a spray that had dried on his shirt, but something about that broken strap and the way he came in spoke of a disaster hardly less devastating. His shirt was torn and his eyes had a disoriented cast. Even aside from the way he was dressed, I'd have known he had been involved in the brawl—no, the rout—around the corner.

He held up inside the door, made himself slow down. I saw him hesitate when he spotted the men seated at the table nearby; then when they returned their attention to their beers after a brief curious glance his way, he walked up to the bar and ordered whiskey. Suddenly we were all in a western movie.

"What happened, Al?" The bartender filled an ounce glass and collected his four bits.

Al gulped the top half of his drink, coughed. He was younger than his thick build made him seem, not much older than Jack. "The fuckers murdered us."

"Which fuckers, Al?"

"The fucking goons, which fuckers you think?"

The bartender paused in the midst of screwing the top back on the bottle. "You ain't hot, are you, Al?"

Either it was the bartender's glance in our direction, the first of four strangers who had just come into his place where he knew most of the clientele because they worked at the plant, or the nervous way he kept repeating the young man's name. Whichever it was, Al caught it and turned to look at us sitting at a table by the wall in a place not noticeable from the door. I could feel his fear and hostility like a shadow across my face. He was standing with his back to the bar now and his hands on it. The movie was *The Virginian.*

Meeting his gaze but talking to Jack, I said, "I'm working. See you later, okay?"

Jack was looking too. "You better bring your chair. I don't think you can take him barehanded."

"If you leave, maybe I won't have to. He just saw you beating on his friends."

"I think he's the one hit me."

"I don't think so. He's still alive."

Jack laughed. "Be seeing you, kiddo. I hope your head knows what your ass is up to."

He left. The two plainclothesmen took one last gulp of their beers and went out behind him. None of this was lost on the young man in overalls, who stood up straight as I approached him. He was shorter than I'd thought, although not short, and everything about him was square except his face, which was round like a boy's and wore a pouty expression he probably thought was defiant.

"Nothing in here, men." The bartender laid an ancient bulldog pistol on the bar with the blueing worn down to bare metal in places and a wad of duct tape wound around the grip.

I had my wallet out with the press card showing. "Connie Minor. I'm with the *Banner.*"

"I see your picture," the young man said, relaxing not at all. "You write about gangsters."

"Not all the time. I'd like to talk to you about what went on at the plant."

"Why, didn't your friend tell you? He was there."

"I'm paid to get all sides. I want to get yours."

"How do I know you're not spying for the plant?"

I smiled then. "What am I going to tell them, you're on strike?"

He appeared to take that in. He wasn't as dumb or as ignorant as he wanted me to think he was. I have some education myself, and it's easier to fake than not having any. In the end he proved to be more tired than he was suspicious. He picked up his drink and we went back to the table. I got the bartender's eye and made a circular motion with my index finger. He broke out a fresh mug and shot glass.

The young man's name was Albert Brock. He was an auto worker—*ex*-auto worker now, he reflected—by default, having had to give up employment as an independent steelhauler when the bank repossessed his rig. He was twenty-four and a native of Ecorse, a little town down-river from Rouge owned down to the doorknobs by the Purple Gang, so he was no stranger to rotten barrels. He had a good speaking voice and a controlled kind of anger that might have brought him a career in politics if he hadn't lived his whole life downwind of the local political situation. It was inevitable, working where he did, that he'd be chosen as a spokesman for unionization. In that very bar he had taken part in the kind of after-work discussions conducted in low voices that can so easily come to nothing unless converted into action by an event like the woman's firing that morning. Brock and a handful of others, some of whom, if captured, would almost certainly be singled out for special treatment—the boot in the stomach, the nightstick applied to the kidneys—had managed to escape after the strike deteriorated into a melee. The problem, he saw now clearly, was that they had acted too fast, in the first heat of their anger, without a proper plan. That wouldn't happen again.

"How are you going to lead any more strikes if you're out of work?" I asked.

"I don't know. I'm new at this like everyone else. But I'll learn."

I called the story in to Walter DiVirgilio on the rewrite desk. Howard Wolfman gave it four inches on page 16 without Fred's picture or the interview with Albert Brock. The facts weren't changed, exactly, just turned ass-backward with details acquired from a last-minute telephone call to the plant brass, like a sports story with the correct score, but with the teams switched. The headline read DEARBORN POLICE QUELL COMMUNIST RIOT. I understand Brock still has a clipping, tacked to a bulletin board in his office at the American Steelhaulers local. He was elected to head it last year, and he's no friend of the Detroit press.

Chapter Twenty

By the beginning of February, with Jack Dance's trial two weeks off, Joey Machine had other things on his mind. Shortly after the Connor killing in November, agents of the United States Treasury Department had invaded the house on Sylvester Street armed with sledgehammers and a warrant, punched through a plaster wall, and seized a stack of ledgers containing transactions relating to the East Side operation. They then began to construct a case, digit by digit, zero by zero, decimal point by decimal point, against Joey Machine; not for murder or extortion or bribery or gambling or violation of the Volstead Act, but because he hadn't paid his taxes for the years 1924 through 1930. Encouraged by similar proceedings involving Al Capone in Chicago, the agents paid a call on Joey at the Acme Garage and informed him he was under arrest for income tax evasion.

But there would be no jail for Joey. Not then, anyway. The federal men, explaining neatly that Mr. Machine had too many enemies in the Wayne County Jail while managing to imply that the turnkeys there might accidentally leave him alone in the booking room with the door open if he was of a mind to use it, which if you thought that you didn't know Joey, put him up at the Statler pending arraignment. I was among the scribes waiting in the hotel lobby on his morning in court when the accused came off the elevator towing four men whose pressed raincoats and hats all worn at the same conservative angle made him look like a hunky dressed up for a funeral. His bargain-basement coat and homburg, new since Frankie Orr had lost the originals off the Belle Isle

Bridge, already showed wear, and his short brown-and-yellow necktie flapped outside his vest, an untidy flag for that fleet made up for the most part of the sartorially bureaucratic faithful. In the rear, towering over everyone in a black wool topcoat and size twelve fedora, lumbered Dom Polacki, and Nathan Rabinowitz walked beside Joey in a soft hat and herringbone tweeds carrying a maroon leather briefcase.

Some reporters expressed surprise in print that Rabinowitz should represent both Joey Machine and Jack Dance in their respective travails, mortal enemies that they were. Those reporters were new to the underworld scene. In those days attorneys glided in and out among opposing camps like Homer's meddlesome gods, invisible when they had to be, vocal when required, and crucial to the outcome, in which their own stake, at most, was minimal. The role seemed dangerous but wasn't. Of all the mob rubouts of my personal knowledge and all those I had ever heard about in Detroit and other places, all the slain hoodlums, stool pigeons, bulls, bookkeepers, molls, reporters, radio commentators, clergymen, aldermen, doormen, wheel men, bag men, juice men, trigger men, men of distinction, tramps, sharps, sawbones, cookers, bookies, runners, waiters, hotel clerks, nurses, housewives, children, and other innocent bystanders—Christ, even one optometrist, that schlemiel Schwimmer who wandered into the Chicago garage massacre—of all of them buried in gangland state and family plots and potter's fields or holding down the bottoms of great bodies of water, I knew of not one lawyer in private practice who had lost his life. It was as if their briefcases deflected bullets, their framed diplomas composed in Latin and printed in German Gothic cast a halo over their heads that defied the shiv and the garrote. They were like those insects the scientists said would inherit the earth after the great global holocaust they'd been predicting since Genesis. It was depressing to think of a world populated only by cockroaches and their attorneys.

"How are you pleading, Mr. Machine?"

"What's jail food like at the Statler?"

"Who's minding the store?"

"Where are your handcuffs?"

"Why don't they just convene court in your suite?"

"When's the victory party?"

He wasn't as smooth with the press as some of his fellow public enemies. It would never occur to him to single out one or two reporters he recognized and call them by their first names like the President did, establishing a friendly atmosphere and sending them away to write that Mr. Machine appeared calm and confident, that bullshit, and he hadn't learned the art of throwing a glib line over his shoulder like a hunk of meat for the pack to claw one another over while he made his escape. Instead he stopped and considered for the better part of a minute. The federal men fidgeted. I think they really believed, these Washington policemen who pounded their beats with slide rules and adding machines, that his gang was going to barrel through the revolving doors any minute and try to bust him loose like Billy the Kid, but they were too well-mannered to lift him by his armpits and charge the exit. God knew what a Detroit bull would make of them.

"They say I owe three and a half million in tax," Joey said finally. "I don't see it, but I offered to pay them anyway. They turned me down. They'd rather blow half a million on a trial they can't win. I ask you, is that any way to run a government in a depression?"

They liked it. Pencils scratched.

"You gonna make 'em give you back your books, Joey?"

"How many times did the big guy order room service?"

"Who pays for the room, Uncle Sam or the policy suckers?"

I asked, "What do you hear from Frankie Orr?"

His head swung around, and just before our eyes met I saw another Joey Machine. Not the buffoon who couldn't keep his tie inside his vest or the harried businessman who bellyached about the fucking kikes who wanted to put holes in him, but the slum-bred little Italian stove fitter who blew up Phil Dardanello, kidnapped Pete Rosenstein out from under the murderous gaze of his own Purple Gang, and threw Harry Fleischman and Frank Kornblum into the Detroit River with heavy six-volt batteries tied around their necks because they'd spiked his best brand with strychnine; the president, chief comptroller, and chairman of the board of the most ruthlessly efficient criminal enterprise between Capone's South Side and Luciano's Harlem and the sole executive survivor of every beer war that had taken place in the nation's fourth largest city since 1919. It was the face he had made when, as his late dismembered partner had once put it, somebody tried to steal a goddamn dime from Joey.

Which was what somebody was doing, a lot of dimes. Anyone with his ear to the ground was aware that while Joey had been involved with planning his defense against the income tax beef, leaving the nuts and bolts of his rumrunning, saloon, and gambling operation to subordinates, someone else had been cutting himself in on the numbers racket in the Black Bottom and the handbook on the East Side. Two of Joey's collectors—gray men in green eyeshades who recorded the bets on little squares of rice paper suitable for swallowing in the event of a raid, changed the greasy coins into stacks of bills, and carried them in leather satchels to the Acme Garage—had vanished along with their satchels, and a third had announced his retirement, all within the ten days since the feds had gone public with their intention to indict Joey. The figures were still infinitesimal, but the East Side book was falling off. The rumbling in the pipes said the Conductor had set up shop in Machine territory, and if you knew how Frankie Orr had killed Vincenzo Cugglio aboard the New York elevated railway, you didn't have to ask who the Conductor was. The only question was whether he was acting independently of Sal Borneo or the Unione was behind the invasion.

All this paraded across Joey's doughlike face as his gaze swept the assembled reporters, looking for the one who had asked him about Frankie. It settled on me and his expression returned to normal. I don't know if he placed me. More than a year had passed since the interview in the blue monoxide air of his office over the garage, and except for one telephone conversation and a brief impromptu press conference among a yapping crowd of scribes and bulls on the steps of 1300 after the Sylvester Street shooting, we had had no personal contact in the time between. In the depths of his legal and business dilemma I was just a newshound who had asked an impertinent question.

"Never heard of him," he said, and resumed walking.

The men from the Justice Department, caught napping, lunged to close ranks around him and the party swept out of the lobby and into an Oldsmobile ragtop sedan parked in the loading zone in front of the hotel. We were left on the sidewalk watching it glide down the street escorted by a Detroit black-and-white fore and aft.

"Say one thing for you," said Chet Mooney, the *News*'s police reporter and a horse's ass of the first water in spats and a pearl stickpin, "you know how to break up the ball before it gets old."

I told him where to stick his pin.

The arraignment took five minutes. Joey pleaded not guilty, the judge set bail at fifty thousand, Rabinowitz paid the court clerk, and

Joey walked out of the Federal Building a free man with a May 18 trial date. Nobody cheered when the bail was announced; if Jack Dance was Robin Hood, Joey Machine was Sir Guy.

Forty hours later, around midnight, a green Nash sedan slowed down in front of the Griswold House and an unidentified man in the backseat dumped a bundle into the street that rolled over several times and came to rest against the curb. Then the sedan sped off. The hog-tied corpse was identified as Leo Campania, a suspected leg-breaker, killer, and all-around dogsbody for the Unione Siciliana, which kept its headquarters at the Griswold. Forensic pathologists in the Coroner's Court Building removed a .38-caliber revolver slug from Campania's brain, tested it, and reported that it had been treated with garlic.

Fred Ogilvie took a picture, that Howard decided not to use, of the corpse on the dissecting table—mouth slack, eyeballs glittering crescents, hair matted in back where the bullet went in—and I wondered, looking at it, if this was the same Leo whom Frankie Orr had asked for when it came time to remove Clyde Norman's ensanguinated body from the Griswold's private dining room. What Joey lacked in finesse he made up for in the art of plain speaking. For the time being at least, he had reclaimed his title to the East Side.

As always an investigation was launched, and as always the streets were cleared of lowlifes for a few days, including one George "Stink" Barberra, who was let go after a telephone call to relatives in Philadelphia seemed to confirm he'd been visiting them the night Leo got capped. It was the kind of thing for which Jack Dance got picked up all the time, but he had two of Kozlowski's dicks to vouch for him. The Nash, believed to have been the same car involved in the fire-bombing of Jack's rented house on Howard, was winched out of Lake St. Clair six weeks later. It was registered to a Moses Cleveland whose address on Fort Street turned out to belong to the Presbyterian Church, and who on further investigation was found to have died in infancy in 1903. Long before that, public interest in the case had languished. As the election year of 1932 crept closer, the Democratic drums were beginning to beat a funeral tattoo for the Hoover Administration in the form of a platform based on economic recovery and Repeal. Watching bootleggers killing one another off contained all the drama of a duel between the last two dodos.

But spectacle was always current. In March, Andrea St. Charles got the assignment to cover a wedding at St. Boniface Cathedral downtown, followed by a reception at the Griswold. Salvatore d'Annunzio Bornea, a/k/a Sal Borneo, had the honor to announce a ceremony uniting his daughter, Maria Aletta, to Francis Xavier Oro, formerly of New York City. The bride wore ivory lace brocaded with pearls, a Paris original, with a veil and an eight-foot train borne by her bridesmaids in lavender gowns and picture hats, and the bowers of orchids and white roses in their profusion brought back memories of the Dardanello funeral in 1925, a $100,000 affair complete with bronze casket and the most ostentatious floral display of all bearing a card signed by Joey Machine as neatly as he had wired the bomb that put Phil in the casket to begin with.

No such token from Joey arrived at the wedding, at which if he was invited, he didn't show.

My own absence was less conspicuous. Andrea, whose press invitation allowed her to bring a guest, had asked me to escort her ("seeing as how this is as close as any girl will ever get you to the altar, poor dear"), but I said weddings made me nervous and begged off. The truth is I was yellow. I never set foot in the Griswold from the night Frankie Orr cut Clyde Norman's throat until they tore it down. The spot where it stood still gives me the cold shimmies.

As I said, I wasn't missed. The guest list at the reception included Henry and Clara Ford, who sent their regrets along with a goldware table setting for twelve in a hand-carved rosewood box. Several judges and a state senator attended among the yeggs in their wing collars and the retired professional hostesses in sable and mink. The cake, wheeled out on a special dolly by a sissy chef in a white hat, was six feet tall with angels and bluebirds and a perfect likeness of the bride and groom on top, carved in ivory by an eighty-year-old artisan imported from Palermo for the occasion. Although no cameras were allowed inside the church or at the Griswold afterward, the *Banner* ran a blow-up from a shot taken from across the street of the bride's father, in top hat and cummerbund, scowling at the federal men noting down the license plate numbers of the Cadillacs, Lincolns, LaSalles, and Packards parked at the curb in front of St. Boniface.

It's all there in poor Andrea's column, or most of it, gone the color and texture of last year's leaves, as dead as Andrea herself. At the time it was apparent to everyone but her, caught up in her ruffles and paté, that more than a couple had been wedded that Saturday, and that many happy returns were anticipated from the teeming area that lay between Woodward Avenue and the Detroit River.

They had forgotten about Jack Dance, however. People had a habit of doing that, always to their regret.

Chapter Twenty-One

The Wayne County Building, occupying the block bounded by Randolph, Congress, Brush, and Fort streets, was finished in 1902 at a cost of $1,600,000, a lot of money at that time although not as much as it was in 1931. It's sandstone over granite, a tower with a brass cupola and spire on a horizontal fretwork of Renaissance windows, baroque balconies, bronze quadrigae that are somehow supposed to be carrying Progress in their chariots, and Ionian columns among a thousand other fussy little details, like government itself. The courtroom where Jack Dance's trial took place was faced with translucent white marble from Roman quarries with swirls of English vein, Alps green, Verona blue, Sienna orange, red and yellow Numidian, and domestic gray. The benches were curly birch and sycamore, hand-rubbed to a deep umber gloss, and the judge's bench, which really wasn't a bench at all like the benches in the gallery but a tall counter, was chocolate mahogany with beveled panels and a reproduction of that same chariot-and-four design embossed on a bronze seal the size of a bicycle wheel on the wall behind it, flanked by the Stars and Stripes and the state flag on their American eagle staffs. The air had no smell at all. The atmosphere was antiseptic, like an operating room in a hospital; a place where men and women in gowns and surgical masks extracted justice with forceps in absolute sterility. Sitting there sequestered from the granite, tarry smell of the city, the angry horns in the street and the cries of the newsboys on the sidewalk, you got some idea of how juries arrived at the decisions they made. Justice thrives in a vacuum.

Jack, seated at the defense table beside Nathan Rabinowitz rummaging inside his briefcase, was dressed for the occasion in navy worsted with a quiet sheen and a domino necktie, the black and white halves joined at right angles like squares on a checkerboard. He'd had a haircut, a question mark of shaved skin showing pink around each ear and his curly forelock pomaded and combed back neatly, although as the first day wore on it would loosen and fall into its accustomed place on his forehead. At his elbow sat Bass Springfield in a white shirt and black necktie and his old suitcoat, cleaned and pressed with the cuffs turned. Finding a new one in his size had evidently proven too tall an order even for the great criminal attorney. I'd never had a good look at the big Negro without a hat or his worn cloth cap, and now I stared at the back of his head with its close curls turning gray like steel wool. I wondered about his age for the first time.

Vivian occupied a space behind Jack in a gray tailored dress and pillbox hat with a veil, protection against the photographers who prowled the room before the judge's arrival, aiming their dropfront cameras with salad-bowl flashguns attached at whoever caught their eye. I drew the end of a bench three rows back, reserved for the press, marked off with a white ribbon like a church pew set aside for the family of the bride. For the rest of the spectators it was first come, first served, and some of them had been lined up outside the building since before dawn.

The jurors, looking privileged in their box seats, were all male. You could tell the manual laborers from the office workers by the way they ran a finger under their collars every two minutes and re-settled the knots of their neckties below their Adam's apples. It had taken nearly a week and the entire stock of challenges allowed both attorneys to select a jury of twelve and two alternates who had not read or heard enough about the killing of Mary Margaret Connor to have formed an opinion about the case weeks before.

Judge Steelbarger, his face looking a little less congested this morning, entered, sat down, and threw the trial into gear. Assistant County Prosecutor E. Wharton Clay, a wiry, overwound watchspring of a man who wore rimless spectacles and parted his thin hair in the middle, and defense attorney Rabinowitz, mildly Yiddish with his reading glasses folded in his hand, never on his nose, presented opening remarks. Jack appeared attentive when Clay called him a "swaggering killer" and again when Rabinowitz explained that the county's case was based on hearsay and innuendo, but he was sitting with one arm over the back of his chair and his profile turned toward me and I saw his right nostril distend slightly as he swallowed a yawn. When he wasn't up and moving, even his own fate couldn't hold his interest. Springfield kept his broken hands in his lap and stared down at the table the whole time.

Wharton called his first witness, an assistant medical examiner I didn't know named Werner Kersten, who testified that he'd removed a nine-millimeter slug from the dead girl's cerebellum—specifically, the isthmus rhombencephalon—where it had lodged after entering through her right eye at an angle consistent with the trajectory of a bullet fired from the window of a passing vehicle. The prosecutor spent a good deal of time establishing the angle and none at all on the bullet's caliber. According to my contact in Detroit Ballistics, attempts to match the firing pins of Jack's Lugers to indentations in the ends of ejected shells found at the scene had been inconclusive—they almost always were—and there was no similarity at all between the striations on the slug that had killed Mary Connor and the rifling of the Lugers. It had not occurred to me that Jack would have the calculation to surrender a pair of weapons different from the ones he had used on Sylvester Street, or more likely replace the barrels. That smacked of advice from Lon Camarillo, the experienced Unione killer; in which case he had passed it on sometime before the shooting, as he had been in Canada when it took place and in jail from the time he came back until Jack turned himself in. Whatever the details, the guns were not introduced in evidence.

Rabinowitz didn't cross-examine the pathologist, who was excused to make room for a Mrs. Castellano, three hundred pounds of Sylvester Street housewife in a polka-dot dress with hennaed hair in a page boy cut not unlike the dead girl's, which didn't remind anybody of Colleen Moore in *Lilac Time*. She had been cooking breakfast for her husband when she heard the shots—"Crackle, crackle, just like bacon fryin' "—and looked out the kitchen window in time to see a car speeding down the street. "Blue and yellow it was, big, with wire wheels. One of them fancy-schmancy Doozenburgers."

When Clay finished questioning her, Rabinowitz drew a paper from the stack he had removed from his briefcase, walked up to the witness stand, and held it up in front of her. It was an automobile advertisement torn from a magazine.

She nodded, jiggling her chins. "Yeah, that's it."

The lawyer turned and showed the advertisement to the jury. Then he handed it to the court clerk, who passed it up to the judge. "Let the record show that the witness has identified a nineteen twenty-six Studebaker as the car involved in the shooting."

After lunch Clay tried to repair the damage by calling upon two other witnesses who had seen the car roaring away from the scene. Rabinowitz established during cross-examination that neither had managed to get the license number and seemed satisfied. Court adjourned for the day.

Joey Machine, Dom Polacki, and Aaron Stahl were not on the list of those subpoenaed to testify. All three had sworn in their statements to the police that they had seen neither the car nor the shooter. On the second day the county's star witness, an unemployed hod-carrier named James Liam, took the stand. He was a lean Irishman burned reddish-brown from years of lugging bricks and mortar up steep ladders in the urban sun, with sandy-looking skin and a long face with a thick lower lip that hung down exposing amber teeth. His grizzled hair had been cut at home and his neck and wrists stuck a long way out of his collar and cuffs. He had been standing on the corner, he said, when the Duesenberg drew abreast of the three men walking along the street and the man on the passenger's side fired at them, missing and hitting the girl, who was running past the trio headed in the opposite direction. Liam said he had recognized the man with the gun from his picture in the newspapers.

"Do you see that man in the courtroom?" Clay asked.

Liam pointed a black-nailed finger at Jack.

"Your witness, counselor." The assistant prosecutor had short legs for his body and a banty strut.

Nathan Rabinowitz, who had been polishing the half-lenses of his reading glasses with a handkerchief, put them down and folded his hands. He didn't get up.

"Your name is James Liam?"

The witness nodded, then said yes when the judge told him to speak.

"Then who is Liam Dougherty?"

The witness hesitated. A restlessness rippled through the gallery, like leaves stirring. "Who?"

Rabinowitz ran a finger down the sheet in front of him. "Liam Sullivan, Tom Liam, Timothy Liam, Harold Liam O'Farrell; do you know any of these names, Mr. Liam?"

Clay objected. Judge Steelbarger overruled the objection.

"In fact, Mr. Liam, they're all names you've used in the past, are they not? And every one of these names is accompanied by at least one felony arrest in the Detroit metropolitan area, isn't that right?"

"I ain't been convicted but twice," Liam said.

Steelbarger gaveled back the groundswell. The lawyer consulted his sheet. As far as I could tell he didn't need reading glasses or any other kind. "Grand Theft Auto, two arrests. Three arrests breaking and entering, one conviction. Another conviction, violation of the Volstead Act. Drunk and disorderly, lewd and lascivious conduct—uh-oh, what's this one for perjury?"

"They dropped that."

"Because the man you testified against was convicted on other evidence; otherwise it might have been a different story. Is it possible, Mr. Liam—I'll call you Mr. Liam to avoid delaying these proceedings by reciting all your aliases—that you testified in that trial in return for a promise by the Detroit police not to prosecute you for auto theft the second time? That if you refused and were found guilty, it would have been your third offense and you might have received a sentence of twelve to fifteen years in prison?"

"That ain't—"

"And is it not correct that the most recent complaint against you, for breaking and entering, is still pending and that the police offered to drop the charge if you agreed to testify against my client today? In fact, aren't you what is called a professional witness, someone who will swear to anything under oath in return for proper compensation?"

All of this came over and through the objections of the assistant prosecutor and gavel-banging by the judge to avoid a riot in the gallery. When order returned, Steelbarger sustained Clay's last objection on the grounds of badgering the witness and directed the defense counsel to ask his questions one at a time.

"Thank you, Your Honor. I'm finished with Mr. Whatsizname." Rabinowitz slid his glasses into a stiff leather case and returned to his papers.

Clay appeared unruffled—a sign, based on the theatricality of his opening remarks on the first day, that he had been ruffled thoroughly. His next witness, a motorist who had passed the Duesenberg going the other way in the next block shortly before the shooting, had picked Bass Springfield out of a line-up as its driver, but appeared uncertain about his identification when the defense attorney established that the man couldn't tell Bill Bojangles Robinson from Al Jolson in blackface. With a show of determination, the assistant prosecutor presented a member of the truck convoy hijacked by Lon Camarillo and others of the Dance gang back in June, to establish the existence of the long-standing enmity between Jack and Joey Machine that had led to the attempt on Joey's life the day the Connor girl was killed. He was a gum-chewing youth in a sharkskin suit and fawn-colored spats with a carnation in his buttonhole.

The cross-examination was brief and gentle. "Mr.—Salerno, is it?"

"Yeah, and I ain't got no ali-asses."

The gallery laughed. Steelbarger banged.

"Mr. Salerno, in your expert opinion, was this a well-planned assault?"

"Well, it worked."

"Not just something they made up as they went along? A complex maneuver worked out to the last detail beforehand?"

"Yeah, sure. It must of been."

"Thank you. No more questions."

The witness was allowed to step down. Clay rose to announce that the prosecution was resting its case. Judge Steelbarger, his face redder now than it had been at the beginning, glanced at the clock and adjourned until the following morning.

I was the first witness for the defense on the third day of testimony. The clerk, a tired-looking man with a neck too big for his collar, swore me in on a Bible with its pebbled cover worn smooth where other hands had touched it and I sat down. Immediately, perspectives changed. From the witness stand the room looked bigger and more crowded and I wanted to shake the eyes off my lapels. It was like looking out from inside a bright mirror.

Rabinowitz had changed too. He was neither the soft-spoken rabbi of Jack's arraignment nor the cagy officer of the court I had played intellectual tag with at the House of All Nations. The glasses remained in their case as he came out from behind the defense table holding something that looked like a newspaper clipping pasted to a sheet of looseleaf note paper. His step was light, he seemed years younger and every bit as aggressive as the assistant prosecutor tried to appear.

"You've been a member of the press how long now, Mr. Minor?"

"Ten years this April."

"Your column appears in how many newspapers?"

"At last count, two hundred and fifteen."

"You've come far in ten years. Success like yours must require a talent for observation and a deep regard for the facts."

Clay rose. "Your Honor, is there a point to this or is counsel for the defense recruiting for the tabloids?"

"I'm merely attempting to establish Mr. Minor's qualifications as a witness before this court."

"Objection overruled. Proceed."

I said, "I've got a good eye and I don't write fiction, if that's what you mean."

"In that case I would like to read for the record a column you wrote that appeared in the *Banner* on Sunday, November thirtieth of last year." He held up the sheet. I saw my picture with the ridiculous pipe.

There was another objection and a whispered conference at the bench involving the judge and both attorneys. The upshot was that Rabinowitz received permission to read aloud a portion of the column I had filed in the special Sylvester Street edition, a reflective piece based on Jack's actions in the Belle Isle Bridge ambush about his behavior under fire. Recited in a flat monotone in that sterile room it sounded gushing. I couldn't look at Jack, but I knew he was wearing that barn-door grin. After a minute I realized the lawyer had stopped reading and was addressing me.

". . . still of that opinion, Mr. Minor?"

I straightened in the hard chair. "Which opinion is that?"

The gallery tittered. Rabinowitz smiled tolerantly and returned to the clipping. " 'In the heat of events, Jack Dance is equal parts Buffalo Bill, Annie Oakley, and every matador who ever passed a veronica: Graceful, gimlet-eyed, and as nerveless as a well-placed bullet.' Still true?"

"I never write what I don't believe."

"Then you don't think my client would become rattled in his excitement and forget his marksmanship?"

I saw where he was headed. So did the assistant prosecutor, who interrupted with an objection about speculation.

"Your Honor," said Rabinowitz, "Mr. Minor is by his own testimony a trained observer. That's what I've spent these past five minutes establishing before this court. If he's not in a position to speculate, who is?"

Steelbarger overruled the objection, but warned defense counsel to proceed with caution.

"Shall I repeat the question, Mr. Minor?"

I said, "It wouldn't be like Jack Dance to screw up because he was scared or in a hurry."

The room sighed. But he wasn't through.

"I now remind the jury of comments made in this court yesterday by Nicholas Salerno, a witness for the prosecution, during cross-examination of his account of the hijacking of Joey Machine's beer shipment by members of Jack Dance's gang." He appealed to the court recorder, who took a minute to find it in yesterday's transcript. Finally she read:

" 'Rabinowitz. Mr. Salerno, in your expert opinion, was this a well-planned assault? Salerno. Well, it worked. Rabinowitz. Not just something they made up as they went along? A complex maneuver worked out to the last detail beforehand? Salerno. Yeah, sure. It must have been.' "

He thanked her. "Gentlemen of the jury, I leave it to you to decide whether this Napoleonic strategist, this bullfighting sharpshooter, is the same man who missed three stationary targets not one, but sixteen times, from a distance of less than twelve feet."

E. Wharton Clay let the buzzing die down before he approached me with his hands in his pockets. The light was hitting his glasses at an angle that let me see my face in both lenses.

"Do you fire guns often, Mr. Minor?" He spoke quietly, although not as quietly as his opponent did when he wanted people to hang on his words.

"I fired one once, on the police range," I said. "I wasn't good."

"Not in the service?"

"They rejected me. My blood was too sweet for them. They said I was a borderline diabetic."

"Do you attend shooting matches?"

"No."

He tugged at an earlobe. "I'm puzzled. From where do you derive your knowledge of marksmanship?"

"Common sense. I figure a man who hits what he's aiming at is a better shot than one who aims and misses."

"I see. How many bullfights have you attended?"

"None."

"So in other words you have no way of knowing just what kind of a shot the defendant is, or how cool he is when pressured. You just wrote what your readers wanted to read so more of them would buy papers."

Rabinowitz objected without rising. "Is counsel for the prosecution delivering his summation at this time?"

"Sustained. Phrase it as a question, counselor."

"I withdraw the comment," said Wharton, resuming his seat. "I have nothing more for this witness."

I stepped down in a daze. If he had ever asked, did Jack Dance tell you, late at night in the big empty city room of the *Banner* with only the lamp on the night desk burning, that he had shot the Connor girl, it would all have been over. I learned something about justice then, about how it can walk right by the truth and never know it because of the blindfold.

Vivian Dance, who had been sitting behind her husband in a smart blue suit and veil during my testimony, didn't come back after lunch. Jack kept glancing back toward the double doors. As soon as the afternoon session started, Nathan Rabinowitz stood and called for a directed acquittal. I had covered a couple of trials and it was nothing new. Every defense attorney fired that shot and none of them seemed surprised or disappointed when it was rejected. But Steelbarger fooled everyone, including the man who had made the motion: He granted it. Jack and Springfield were free.

None of the reporters in attendance waited to hear the judge finish chewing out the assistant prosecutor for burdening an already groaning docket and wasting taxpayers' money on a trial for which the county was inadequately prepared. I beat the *News* guy to the only unoccupied telephone booth in the lobby, but I didn't call the *Banner*; I dialed Jack's number in St. Clair Shores to get Vivian's reaction. Jack's brother Tom answered.

Chapter Twenty-Two

The window in my shared office was closed, but I could read the newsboy's lips as he chased pedestrians down the sidewalk on their way to their cars and home. It was on the front page of the *Banner* he was waving: RIPPER FREED! The thick sans-serif letters as black as a mafioso's moustache against the otherwise virginal page, the words stacked one on top of the other and filling the space from just below the masthead to the bottom. This time the kid who had carved the letters got credit under Graphics on the Page Two flag, but no more money than the dime an hour he earned sorting *p*'s and *d*'s into their slots in the typecases and cleaning up, despite having had to provide the FREED in a hurry; he had finished carving GUILTY only a few days earlier. It was a dramatic Page One by any standard, and I don't suppose many of those who saw it dwelled very long, if at all, on the headline's interior fallacy: If he'd been freed, then he was no longer the Ripper. In any case, the distinction is still ignored, and Jack's has joined the long list of parenthetical names that appear in chronicles of the dry time: Al (Scarface) Capone, Fred (Killer) Burke, Charley (Lucky) Luciano, Jack (The Ripper) Dance. Time and legend are tougher than the courts.

My column had consisted of an analysis of E. Wharton Clay's and Nathan Rabinowitz's vastly different courtroom styles, with a passing reference to my special viewpoint from the witness stand. Howard had been surprised and disappointed that I didn't make it more personal—*BANNER* REPORTER GIVES EVIDENCE was to have been the headline when the acquittal changed everything—but I said that Chuck Kobler, the *Banner*'s court reporter, had covered my testimony thoroughly in his story, as did every other scribe in town. In fact it irritated me to be everyone else's beat and I wasn't about to be my own as well.

Standing there at the window, I knew that a woman was on her way through the city room and that it wasn't Andrea. No one was so crass as to whistle—that's for the movies, like the cigar-chomping editor who says, "Why, you," just before he slugs someone—but the chairs stopped squeaking as they never would if the mayor walked in wearing his inaugural top hat and red silk ribbon, and I was aware of a general lifting of the atmosphere, as in a stuffy elevator when a messenger boards carrying a bouquet of flowers.

Vivian tapped the open office door with the back of a gloved hand. She had on a turban with a small feather in it and a fur jacket over a pale yellow silk blouse and a forest-green broadcloth skirt that caught her legs several inches below the knees. I had been mourning the passing of the short flapper skirt before then, but the length accentuated her long slender calves. She was wearing fur half-boots.

I turned from the window. "I thought you'd be out celebrating with Jack."

"I hate parties. I have ever since Southampton. Besides, I'd just slow him down." She took in the office, Jensen's empty desk. "Are you busy?"

"I almost never am."

"I want to talk."

I went over and took my hat and coat off the peg. They'd been covering a cartoon Jensen had bought last fall and tacked up, showing ex-Mayor Bowles and ex-Commissioner Wilcox trapped inside a bottle with three X's on the label and a cork jammed into the neck. Already their faces were getting hard to place. "There's a joint down the street."

"I don't feel like going to a joint. Can we just walk?"

It was a warm evening for late February but damp, with a light fog rolling in from the river. We walked in that direction. The beams of the car headlamps in the street seemed to bend in the mist at right angles, like searchlights trained on the surface of a lake. Walking beside me clutching the collar of her coat, Vivian lifted her face to the moisture. Her profile was her best feature, the high forehead and long straight Mediterranean nose and clean chin.

"I wanted to explain about Tom," she said.

"You don't have to."

"No one has to do anything for you. That's how you work, isn't it?"

I said nothing.

"That sounded wrong," she said. "I didn't like you at first, what you do. It was hard to think of reporters as human after what happened when I was divorcing Gus. Jack told me you did him a favor once. He didn't say what it was."

"It gave me an in."

"I don't think that's why you did it. You like him, don't you?"

"I don't understand him."

"That has something to do with it. I like him too. So does Tom, although he doesn't approve of him." She paused. "We haven't done anything, Tom and I haven't."

"When did he start coming to your house?"

"After Sylvester Street, when Jack was in hiding. He wanted to make sure I wasn't being bothered by police and reporters. He's a solid man. Jack's exciting, but he isn't solid."

"They both used to work for Joey Machine."

"Tom told me. He said that's over."

"It's over when Joey says so. He doesn't acknowledge bad investments. You should know that if you're thinking of leaving Jack for Tom because Tom's solid."

"I'm not thinking anything like that. I don't know what I'm thinking."

We crossed Jefferson with the light and walked along the river, a trough of milky fog with the Windsor skyline crumbling away to stacks of lighted windows on the other side. Dusk was sliding in in long connecting shadows.

"What do you think he'd do?" she asked.

"Kill you both," I said. "Or one of you. Or he won't. He wouldn't know himself until he did it, or didn't. You ought to know that by now."

"He really didn't mean to hurt that little girl. She ran into it."

"He told you about it?"

"I asked him. It's funny, being what he is and doing what he's done, but Jack doesn't understand death. Tom told me that when their mother died, their father wouldn't tell them what happened or where she went. I think Jack's still waiting for her to come back. Down deep he thinks they'll all come back when they get tired of hiding. That's why killing doesn't mean anything to him."

"Maybe he's right."

An icy wind skated the water and roughened our cheeks. We turned our backs to it and started back. "He won't keep on missing, will he?" she asked.

"Who, Jack?"

"Joey Machine."

I let a bull pass us in his long double-breasted uniform coat doing stunts with his nightstick.

"There's a bookie named Arny D'Agostino," I said. "Ex-bookie now; his brother takes care of him. A couple of years back some guys took him out of the smoke shop where he ran his book and strung him up by his wrists from a pipe in the basement of the Healy Building. They roughed him around a little, nothing new. Then they took a strip of gauze and one of the guys who had gonorrhea dripped onto it and they pasted it over Arny's eyes and left him up for three days. By the time they cut him down he was blind for life. Joey figured he'd stolen about thirty thousand dollars from him over a period of eleven months."

After a while she said, "And they're trying to get him for unpaid taxes."

"This is his business, his and Sal Borneo's and Pete Rosenstein's and the rest. They all took the same chances and they're not in business to make it easy for the next guy up." *When you get to hell, chiseler, tell them Sal gets what's his.*

She shuddered and took my arm with an embarrassed little laugh. "I think I'm ready to go to that joint now."

It was a loud little place that had been there since before the ink had dried on the Eighteenth Amendment, full of smoke and the smell of hot grease from the grill behind the bar. We waited ten minutes for a booth to open up and had gin fizzes under a caricature of George M. Cohan bearing his signature. You went there to watch people, to remind yourself you weren't living on some burned-out asteroid in a dead solar system.

We had a drink apiece. During a lull in the din I said, "Do you mind if I ask you something?"

She looked very young in the light of a candle guttering in an orange glass on the table. "I never knew a reporter to ask permission."

"This one's for me. I asked it once before, but we didn't know each other then, and that was for publication."

"What do I see in Jack?"

"Don't tell me again he has ideas," I said. "We're in a depression. Ideas are cheaper than apples."

"I run with winners."

"One courtroom upset doesn't make him a winner."

"I didn't mean that," she said. "I married Gus Woodbine because my father wanted me to and because he looked like he had it all. Only he was destroyed by someone who had more. They said I drove him to suicide, but it wasn't me. The Woodbine was his dream. More than that, it was a good automobile, maybe the best. When Ford and Chrysler and his own friends at General Motors squashed it, he never recovered. Big business made him a loser. So I moved up to big business."

"Jack Dance is big business?"

"None bigger. Obviously you don't know how much the alcohol business took in last year. Nobody does, because bootleggers don't file taxes. It isn't the money, though; it's who's on top. You know that game, scissors cut paper, rock breaks scissors, paper wraps around rock?" She made the accompanying gestures: two fingers, fist, flat hand. "I play that game with my husbands."

"There doesn't seem to be much percentage in it, for the risk."

"Now you're beginning to understand."

I shook my head. "That's Jack's game, not yours."

"Don't let this Southampton accent fool you. As gamblers go I make Jack look like Mary Pickford."

"So if Gus was scissors and Jack's the rock—" I paused. "Well, Tom does work on a paper."

She sobered. "Don't try to be clever, Connie. Not on your feet."

That ended the evening. A few minutes later I put her in a cab out front. I hung on to the door. "I won't say anything."

"I know. It gives you an in." She leaned forward from the shadows in the backseat and pressed her lips to mine for a second. Hers were cool. Then she sat back and looked out the window until the cab drew out of sight, a girl from Southampton in furs and a turban in a place where they blinded you and cut your throat with a steak knife and blew you to pieces and threw you in the river and shot you in the eye because you were late coming home from church. She'd be just fine.

Frankie Orr's wedding came after that, and then Joey Machine's trial in the Federal Building in a wood-paneled courtroom with the United

States seal behind the bench with its hypocritical eagle clutching an olive branch in one set of talons and a fistful of arrows in the other. Nathan Rabinowitz wasn't present, having represented Joey only at his arraignment while his attorney of record, a tax lawyer named Cranston, like The Shadow, freed himself from a similar case in Washington involving a United States Congressman. A totally bald man with a handlebar moustache who looked like a circus barker, he wore a bow tie and suspenders that showed when he hooked his thumbs behind them while addressing the court. The trial made front pages its first week—pictures of Joey and Cranston leaning their heads together at the defense table like lovers, Joey patting back a yawn while an accountant for the Bureau of Internal Revenue reeled off an interminable list of figures from his notebook, the gangster getting out of his famous Chevy while Dom Polacki held the door for him in front of the Federal Building—but without a body count or such ornaments as lunkhead bulls perspiring on the stand and platinum blonde witnesses with fox stoles and red, red lipstick, the story lost momentum in a hurry. The remaining two months of depositions, objections, motions, and private meetings in chambers were pushed to the inside pages by more photogenic, if less far-reaching, daily dramas. Photostats of pages from ledgers don't move as fast on the stands as shots of tramps' corpses found cut in two on the tracks by Union Station.

Not that the tabloids were reduced to such dregs. Frankie Orr, having bailed out of the East Side for the time being after Leo Campania's passing, had assumed the pinball machine concession from Dearborn to Woodward Avenue beginning in March. His skull-busters pushed the nickel games, which repaid a penny a point above a chosen score, into blind pigs, whorehouses, and legitimate establishments until their cartoony sproings, whirrs, buzzes, and flashing lights became a familiar part of the local landscape. Detective Chief Kozlowski parlayed the anti-gambling sentiment at City Hall into a series of raids, smashing the machines to sputtering, snapping bits and confiscating the coins they vomited out. Unione lawyers then dug up a friendly Recorder's Court judge who slapped a ninety-day restraining order enjoining the police from approaching to within forty feet of the machines, but the next day a Sergeant Swoboda, an alumnus of Kozlowski's old Hamtramck neighborhood, led a plainclothes team into a dance hall on West Grand and they blasted away with revolvers and shotguns at four machines bearing labels clearly identifying them as the property of Orr's Motor City Game Owners' Association. Despite an argument that the shots were fired from a distance of forty-one feet, Swoboda was suspended for a month without pay and the judge who had issued the injunction fined Kozlowski five hundred dollars for contempt of court. Meanwhile city attorneys went to appellate and got the injunction reversed. It was a new kind of gang war, conducted entirely in the marble halls of justice where the crack of gavels rang like gunshots.

Lieutenant Hermann Gabriel of the Prohibition Squad, taking advantage of the confusion, tipped over fourteen blind pigs during the month of May. Fred Ogilvie, who with Ernie Swayles was invited along on one of the raids, snapped a picture for the front page of the grim-faced crew in fedoras and rubber raincoats seated under the tarpaulin of the confiscated beer truck they used for cover, armed with short-handled axes and black Thompsons and pump shotguns cut back to the slides.

With all that going on, none of the city papers caught a fire in Oakland County that destroyed a barn and its contents, chief among them a JN-4 "Jenny" biplane that had seen service behind American lines during the war. Sheriff's investigators, combing through the ashes, found the remains of a simple incendiary device involving a can of high-test gasoline and a blasting cap, much like the bomb that had gutted the rented house on Howard Street in Detroit the previous June. The destruction of Jack Dance's one-craft air corps came over the wires as a simple arson and was treated as filler by the Detroit papers that used it at all, the *Banner* among them. It was another message from Joey, subtler than the Campania murder, but an indication that the hundreds of hours in court hadn't slowed him down. Even he wasn't savage enough to order a killing while his case was being tried by an unsequestered jury, but a match job in another county could pass unnoticed by all but those for whom it was intended.

It was a waste of gasoline, however, and with the price having gone up to twelve cents per gallon; because late in May, when the complainant in *The People of the United States of America v. Giuseppe Garibaldi Maccino* had rested and the defendant was preparing to take the stand on his own behalf, Jack hit him hard, and at the very core of his kingdom on the river.

PART FOUR

May 1931–August 1932

The Collingwood Massacre

Nowhere in the world may the trend of the new industrial cycle be perceived more clearly than in Detroit. In this sense it is the most modern city in the world, the city of tomorrow.

—Matthew Josephson,
"Detroit: City of Tomorrow,"
Outlook, February 1929

Don't shoot—I'm not a bootlegger.

—Detroit automobile window
sticker, c. 1930

Chapter Twenty-Three

"You should've seen it."

And as Jack told me about it later in the little apartment on Crystal Street, I did. Not because of any talent he had for description, but because his enthusiasm acted as a kind of conductor to his own mind's eye, like an electric arc. I saw the sawdust-strewn dock at the foot of Riopelle Street in the area the press called Smugglers' Alley; the big black Franklin backed up to the edge of the dock where men in cloth caps and rollneck sweaters loaded wooden crates into the trunk and backseat carefully, to avoid breaking any of the bottles packed in wood straw; the scout car, a gray Chrysler sedan parked crosswise of the Franklin with the four armed men inside, two in front, two in back; and blocking the mouth of the alley, long enough from radiator cap to rear bumper to close Jefferson itself, the Buick Standard Eight, black on tan with a coffin-shaped hood, ironically christened the Empire Saloon Car, its driver standing with one foot on the running board and his Thompson's snout resting on the toe of his other wingtip on the ground. This was what Jack saw through the thick window of a deserted warehouse on the opposite corner from atop a stack of empty packing crates. I smelled the dry rat droppings in the huge room, the dank air from the river. The moon, high and small and broken in half as if someone had tried to pry it out of the sky, shone straight down and made patches of shadow under the figures on the dock.

"The lookout, that's the glamor job," Jack said. "He's got to smile at the folks who wander in, ask them to keep moving, he can't be a lug. I used to do it for Joey. You dress up for it.

"That's the weak part, see; the good-looking ones that can talk, they ain't always hard enough. This night it was Nick Salerno. You remember him from the trial. A creampuff. Hard on the outside but all soft and gooey when you break the crust."

After a little while a Model A coupe passed the alley without stopping on Atwater and blew its horn. That was Jack's signal. Andy Kramm and Lon Camarillo had found no Machine reinforcements in the immediate area. Jack jumped down from the crates, left the warehouse, and rejoined Bass Springfield sitting behind the wheel of the flatbed Dodge half-ton truck they had stolen from the same parking lot where they got the Model A. But he didn't get into the cab. Six empty wooden barrels stood on the flatbed, arranged in a horseshoe. Jack climbed inside it, Springfield started the motor with a ka-*pow* followed by a clatter of lifters, stripped the gears, and cranked the horizontal steering wheel around corners and down narrow back streets with the headlamps off until they came out on Jefferson, where he tugged them on. At Riopelle he swung toward the river, ignoring stop signs, and stood on the brakes convincingly in the last block to avoid piling into the big Buick.

"Shee-*it*!" he whined.

Nick Salerno, who had leaped up onto the Buick's running board to save his knees, hopped down cradling his submachine gun and approached the driver. He had on a light tan topcoat with a dark silk lining and a brown derby tilted like Edward G. Robinson's in *Little Caesar.* "Mister, you better be blind drunk."

"I's sorry, boss. Man tole me delibber thisyer *ce*-ment to one-one-two-six Dubois. This it?"

Here Jack interrupted his own narrative. "*Du*bois, that's how he said it, like noise and toys. He laid on that plantation nigger shit with a trowel. But Nick, he lapped it up."

The discovery that he'd called a colored man mister, snide as he'd said it, turned Salerno nasty. "Four blocks down, buck. Take off the fucking hat when a white man's talking to you."

Springfield removed his cap. Balancing the gun along his right forearm, the lookout slid a black rubber flashlight out of his slash pocket and shone it into the driver's face. Whether he recognized the Negro from court was never determined. He was still looking at him when Jack, who had alighted from the flatbed on the other side, circled behind him and put a serious dent in the derby with the butt of his Luger.

It was a new pistol, acquired to replace the pair he'd surrendered to me, which as unlicensed firearms, the law had refused to return to him after his acquittal. Salerno grunted and sagged into Jack's arms, dropping the Thompson across his buckled knees and from there to the pavement without setting it off or making a racket. Moving quickly, Jack dragged him a few feet away, stripped him of his topcoat, shrugged into it, threw his own hat onto the flatbed, poked the dent out of the derby, and cocked it over one eye. The coat was tight in the shoulders and the hat was too big, but he made it stay in place by tucking one ear inside the crown and picked up the tommy gun. Springfield, meanwhile, had stepped down from the cab to cover Salerno with his .45. He needn't have bothered. The gum-chewing young gangster who had helped Nathan Rabinowitz destroy the case against Jack Dance died several hours later of a fractured skull without regaining consciousness.

The man in the front seat on the passenger's side of the gray Chrysler hailed Jack as he approached in Salerno's coat and hat carrying Salerno's submachine gun. "Nick, if it's bulls, tell 'em to call Joey tomorrow. This one's paid for already."

Jack's answer was to draw back the Thompson's breech and slam a shell into the chamber.

There was a moment, a vacuum in time, during which the men in the car interpreted this action. Then the Chrysler rocked on its springs. Holsters squeaked, shotguns rattled. Meanwhile Andy Kramm and Lon Camarillo, who had parked the Model A on Orleans and cut back to Riopelle on foot between dark empty warehouses, stepped out onto the dock. Andy had his Thompson and he and Jack flanked the Chrysler with the choppers braced against their hips while Lon threw down on the men near the Franklin with his Browning Automatic Rifle. The loaders stood there holding crates of whiskey with their weapons in their pockets.

Jack ordered the gunmen out of the Chrysler. "Touch the clouds, gents. Just like in *Cimarron.*"

As they obeyed, big men all in fedoras and coats too bulky for spring, Jack greeted them. " 'Evening, Jim. Fat, looks like you put on a couple-three pounds. Cheer up, Ricky, you still got that redhead at home?" He sniffed the air. "This's got to be Stink, unless one of you boys shit his pants."

The fourth man out of the car, as big as Jack, with his hat jammed down on top of his ears and his mouth open for purposes of breathing, was Stink Barberra. Shadows pooled inside the pouches under his eyes.

"Drop the hardware now. One at a time, so the dock don't fall down."

The shotguns had been left in the car. They bent and laid their pistols and revolvers gently at their feet. Barberra took longer because he had a handgun in each of his side pockets and another in a shoulder rig under the coat.

"Don't forget that little two-shot in your hat, Stink," Jack said.

He removed his hat with both hands, exposing his white bald head and the black fringe that stopped where the hat began, his tiny eyes, and took out a nickel-plated Colt derringer, and put it on the ground next to the others.

"Now get down on all fours and crawl under the car."

They hesitated, Barberra longer than the others, then did as directed, getting sawdust and grease on their camel's hair and alpaca.

Bass Springfield joined them holding his .45. Jack asked him if he'd left Nick untied.

"He ain't going nowhere."

"Okay, get rid of these heaters, the ones in the car too. Throw 'em in the drink."

While Springfield was doing that, the weapons splashing substantially, Jack told the men with the crates to finish loading the Franklin. When their hands were free he had them toss their guns off the dock. There were two more crates in the speedboat by the piles. Lon covered two of the three loaders from the edge while they went down the rope ladder. When the cargo was in place Jack had Springfield move the Buick out of the way and told the three men in sweaters and caps to lie down on their stomachs. They complied. Andy and Lon got into the Franklin.

"Jerk them wires," Jack shouted as Springfield stepped down from the Buick. He himself flung up the Chrysler's hood on one side, tore loose the spark plug wires, and threw them after the guns. Lon started the Franklin. Jack took a step in that direction, then turned back, raising the Thompson. "Slither out from under there, Stink."

"Mr. Jack," Springfield said. After disabling the Buick he had gone back for Jack's hat and stopped in the alley now with it in one hand and his pistol in the other, down at his side.

"Get in the car with Lon and Andy. Roll down all the windows. Stink's coming along."

"What for?"

Barberra was standing by the Chrysler now with his arms spread slightly and the front of his coat streaked with filth. "You little shit," he wheezed.

Jack fired a chattering burst over his shoulder. A round struck sparks off the Chrysler's roof and whistled off into the night. One of the men under the car yelled.

"Next one goes in your ear," Jack said. "Shake a leg."

Barberra walked ahead of him and climbed into the backseat of the Franklin. There wasn't room in back for three large men and the whiskey *and* the submachine gun, so Jack heaved it. It arced out past the dock, turned two somersaults, struck the water, and bobbed once, kicking up its buttstock, before sliding straight down. Jack made Barberra transfer a crate from the seat to his own lap and he and Springfield squeezed in on both sides. The garlic smell was oppressive with the doors shut. Springfield hadn't had time to open both windows in back, so Jack cranked down his. He threw out the derby and put on his snapbrim. Then he placed the Luger cocked against Barberra's temple. "Don't hit no bumps, Lon. I ain't sure how much pull this trigger takes."

Lon slipped the clutch. "What do we want with him?"

"Joey depends on Stink," Jack said. "Without Stink we'd still have Baldy Hannion and the place on Howard and an aeroplane. Frankie-boy, he'd still be mucking around in Joey's policy business in the Bottom if it wasn't for Stink. What do you think a shooter like Stink is worth to Joey?"

Andy said, "Five thousand. That's five times what we got for Dom."

"I'm thinking fifty."

"*Grand?*"

"Jesus Mary and Joseph," Lon said.

"He won't pay it," said Springfield.

"Then we'll send him fingers till he does. Stink's got ten."

Barberra sat with his big-knuckled hands curled around the edges of the crate in his lap and said nothing.

"Look at this here," Andy said.

At the stop sign on Guoin, a cross street, two uniformed police officers sat in a black-and-white Oldsmobile touring car with mounted spotlights and a gonger on the left side. The car pulled out behind the Franklin and followed it for two blocks, then turned east on Woodbridge. Jack lowered the Luger a couple of inches.

"Fat wasn't fooling when he said they were taken care of," Lon said. "I bet they heard that chopper, too."

Jack shook his head sadly. "I thought they was going to clean up this town."

"Lucky it wasn't that bird, Gabriel," said Andy.

"That lunger, forget him. It's the bulls that won't stay bought you got to watch out for, like Kozlowski." But Jack was distracted. "You know the thing about cops? They can go anywhere, do anything. Nobody stops them, asks where they're going or what they're up to. Not even other cops."

"Bulls got it made in this town," Andy agreed.

"It ain't just this town. It's because they're bulls. They could walk into the ladies' toilet, who's gonna stop them? It's like they're invisible."

"You got a wife. Why would you want to walk into a ladies' toilet?" Andy was puzzled.

"I don't. It's just something I thought of."

Having a hostage complicated matters. They'd planned to stash the whiskey in the disused blockhouse at Fort Wayne like always, but a prisoner needed feeding and guards. After they had driven around aimlessly for half an hour arguing, Jack suggested they drop off the cargo as planned and take Barberra from there to Bass Springfield's apartment on Crystal Street.

"Celestine's there," Springfield said.

Jack wanted to know if she could cook.

"Beans and fatback."

"Stink ain't particular. Are you, Stink?" Jack dug an elbow into his ribs. He'd put away the pistol finally.

Stink said, "You little shit."

"Pick up the needle, Stink. That record's busted."

"What's wrong with St. Clair Shores?" Springfield asked.

"I got neighbors."

"Who, Johnny the Rock and the Fleischer brothers?"

"We got an agreement: No mob stuff in the neighborhood. One more in yours won't be noticed. Pull in here, Lon." He pointed at a little parking lot next to a corner market with a sign in the window that said OPEN 24 HOURS in English and Polish. They were in Hamtramck.

"What for?"

"Didn't the air corps teach you no manners? You don't invite yourself over to somebody's house without bringing something."

Jack and Andy got out to shop while Springfield and Lon watched the hostage. They came back ten minutes later with a box of groceries, which Jack put on top of the whiskey crate on Barberra's lap. "Polack behind the counter wanted to know if we was throwing a party," he said when they were back on the road. "Tell 'em what you said, Andy."

" 'Sons of Italy.' "

Chapter Twenty-Four

"Thanks for coming, Minor. Can Dom get you anything?"

I hesitated, then said no thanks. I wasn't used to good host's manners from Joey Machine. He shook my hand inside the greasy little office behind glass on the ground floor of the garage without rising from the ancient desk chair and waved me into the only other seat in the room, straight hickory with a rung missing. The desk, gray steel, was shoved against the brick wall and a wooden mail case stood on it with its pigeonholes stuffed full of papers. A bulb with a funnel shade hung by a cord from the ceiling, its light pooling through the glass onto the concrete floor outside the office and a row of automobiles in various stages of dismemberment. It was late, the garage was closed. The air smelled of stale exhaust.

Joey was in vest and shirtsleeves with the vest unbuttoned, no necktie, and his cuffs turned back on his hairy wrists. He'd been working; an old-fashioned black adding machine with a big handle stood on the desk, surrounded by curls of tape like empty cocoons whose larvae had left a residue of anonymous figures in martial rows. At midnight it was a fevered kind of clutter, as if he had to work all night to manufacture the evidence that the lawyers for the Bureau of Internal Revenue presented against him during the day. The trial, in its second month now, had taken its toll. His face looked even pastier than usual, he had blue-green smudges under his eyes like thumbprints, and he was smoking a lot. The index and middle fingers of his right hand, between which a Lucky Strike rested, were stained black, a Vesuvius of gnawed butts had erupted over the sides of a cheap tin ashtray on a pile of yellow bills of lading. Big Dom stood outside facing the glass, the reflected light from the bulb accentuating the gorilla cast of his lower features. Insofar as his battered and bitten face was capable of expression, he looked worried.

"Sorry about the dump," Joey said. "I'm having some work done upstairs. Steel plates in the walls, iron mesh over the windows, couple of other improvements I can't talk about. Costing me a fucking fortune. I don't know why the feds are breathing hot air down my ass. I'm building my own little Leavenworth right here."

"Concerned?"

"About who, the feds? No. Hell, no. Taxes, what kind of yellow shit is that to pull? They want to stop me selling beer, why don't they walk up and arrest me for that like men instead of pulling this chickenshit? It's the kikes I'm concerned about, that wild-ass Dance and all his tribe. You know why they call them Purples?"

"I heard it was because they got their start during the cleaners and dyers' war."

"No, it was because one of the first people them pukes robbed, hit him over the head and lifted his wallet—his fucking wallet, for Christ's sake, with maybe two dollars in it and change—he was a butcher, and he told the bulls they was all purple like rotten meat. That's the first true thing that was ever said about them and it still holds. It ain't enough them Washington nancies hung this tax thing around my neck, that asshole Borneo and his pup Frankie Orr, the Pinball Prince, think they can muscle in on me while I'm in fucking court eight hours a day; no, I got to have this crazy Jew gunning for me so I'm stuck in this hole for the next three months while they turn my office into fucking Fort Knox. Now he pulls this."

He lit a fresh Lucky, forgetting the one he'd parked half-smoked and smoldering on top of the pile of butts. "What I could do is send some boys up to St. Clair Shores and snatch that society dame he's hitched to, teach him two can play this kidnap game. But I ain't like that, I don't touch family. I'm not a Hun. I don't kill little girls."

"Who'd he kidnap?"

When Joey Machine called you in the middle of the night, admitted he remembered you, and asked you to come see him, you went without asking why. I figured if he was sore enough at me for whatever reason to give me the river treatment, he'd have sent two guys for me. I'd thought maybe he needed another favor, which meant he had something to trade. I hadn't had a beat in weeks. The column was as bleak as a Wall Street report.

"Fella works for me named George Barberra. You wouldn't know him. Snatched him in the middle of a delivery."

"They took Stink *alive*?"

"Oh, you heard of him. Four ayem this morning, shit, *yesterday* morning, my phone rings in Rochester, it's the kike himself, he says, 'Rise and shine, Joey, I got your boy Stink.' Then he hangs up. Christ, my wife's in the fucking bed next to me. I don't sleep the rest of the night. Five ayem there's a knock on my door, car takes off out front and leaves rubber all down the block. There's a package on the stoop with a pink ribbon tied around it. It's too small for a bomb, so I open it and there's Stink's knucks. I know they're his brass knuckles because there's friction tape wound around the part you hold like he uses to protect his hand, they've both been busted before. On the inside of the wrapping there's a note: 'Call you at the garage. Love, Jack.' *Love*, for Christ's sake. What's he, a nancy? So when I'm not in court getting a blister on my ass sitting on that hard seat, I'm here waiting for the fucking phone to ring. Well, tonight it rang."

I waited. Something momentous was about to happen. It was in the air, like the monoxide that filled the garage. He stooped and slid a leather suitcase out of the kneehole of the desk. It wasn't even a new suitcase; the straps were cracked and the corners were scuffed and shaggy. He laid it down on the concrete floor gently, reverently, and opened it, unbuckled the straps that held the clothes-press in place and flipped it back. Thirty Benjamin Franklins smiled up at me, each on top of a stack as high as the suitcase was deep.

"Fifty grand," he said. "A five and four zeroes. That's the price, and don't think I didn't have to send my best collector to ten different places to get it."

"Barberra's worth that much to you?" My tongue felt like leather. People who say money makes your mouth water have never seen five hundred one-hundred-dollar bills all in one place.

"More, only don't tell the kike. Accountants? I can stand outside any business school you name and buy ten Prestos for half that. Collectors? Drivers? Legs? They stand outside waiting to work for *me*. A shooter like George, that does who you tell him to do when you tell him to do it and nobody else, and draws his pay without holding you up for more than you agreed on—well, you come up with a figure, I'll pay it if I can raise it. Understand, I'm not telling you any of this, you didn't hear it, if you say you did, I'll deny it. I think a man should know why he's carrying someone else's money, assuming his risks. I'm not Sal Borneo, treat you like a junkwagon nag, slap on the blinders and smack you on the ass in heavy traffic."

He covered up the money, closed the suitcase and latched all the latches and buckled all the buckles. Then he stood it back up with its handle on top. He must have done it. I was watching him, and when my brains came back, that was the suitcase's condition.

"I'm carrying it?"

"That's what the call was about. I guess he trusts you. Use one of my people he might get his kike head blown out from under his hat. That's how he thinks, that bughouse killer, that murderer of Catholic schoolgirls."

I stood. "Excuse me, Mr. Machine, but the hell with this. I'm not a messenger."

The telephone on the desk rang, loud in the echoing emptiness of the garage.

"Answer it, it's for you." Joey looked at the clock on the wall, an electric one with a glowing face advertising Fisk tires. "He's ten minutes late. Just like a yid, too cheap to buy a fucking watch."

After two more rings I sat down and lifted the cup off the hook, leaning forward with my elbows planted on the desk. "Hello?"

"Connie?" He sounded out of breath, as he always did when the fever was on him.

"Why me, Jack?"

"I thought you could use the break. I been reading your column."

A dream come true: I had a gangster for a critic. Aloud I said, "Christ, Jack, fifty thousand bucks. If everybody in town who would hit me over the head and run off with it stood in line to do it, you know how long the line would be?"

"As long as you don't tell nobody, you got no better chance of getting hit on the head for carrying fifty grand than fifty cents." I heard riotous music on his end. "It had to be you, Connie, like the song. I'd ask Tom, but it's like I don't know him; he's *Times* now, he don't hang out with no racket boys."

Mention of his brother made me think of Vivian. I asked him if she knew where he was.

"I called her today. I didn't tell her. I couldn't talk long in case Joey had one of his pet bulls put a trace on the line. You going to help me out, Connie?"

"I'm thinking. Where are you?"

"There's a booth in the lobby of the Guardian Building. I'll call you there in ten minutes."

"It'll be closed."

"I know the guard, he's expecting you. Tell him you're from me. Listen, if you don't answer the phone, I'll know you're not interested." The line clicked and buzzed.

Joey watched me hang up. I told him about the telephone booth. The Guardian was right down the street at 500.

"So you going to do it?"

"Who else gets the story?"

When he tried to appear sardonic he looked just like a kewpie. "You kidding? Soon as you leave I'll call Winchell, tell him all about how I got shook down like some snotnose kid in the street."

I rose and hefted the suitcase. It didn't seem heavy enough for what it contained. Money never does, physically.

He turned down his cuffs and buttoned them. Something had been consummated, a commitment had been made.

"I'll call," I said.

He put a hand on the hand holding the suitcase. The little eyes crowding the big nose were murky. "A scribe could live the rest of his life in Mexico on dough like this," he said. "That wouldn't take as long as he'd think."

"I'll call," I repeated.

He withdrew the hand.

Walking down Griswold carrying the case, drawing a straight line through the circles of light under the streetlamps, I thought, the President doesn't walk around with fifty thousand dollars. Babe Ruth doesn't. It wasn't a cozy thought. It filled the black doorways, the right-angled shadows between buildings with thugs—frightening ones, like in the cartoons Jensen bought and sometimes drew for the *Banner*, barrel-chested lower primates in cloth caps and striped pullovers and little black masks, carrying blackjacks.

Nothing like that materialized, although I had a bad moment when an eight-cylinder Packard swept around the corner from Congress, dousing me in blinding light and convincing me that bullets would follow. It grumbled past, and for the five hundredth time I decided I'd make a lousy gangster.

The night man at the Guardian Building was in his fifties, the visor of his uniform cap making shadows in the folds of his face; he had a belly and a revolver with a big cedar handle on his hip. He opened the door the rest of the way when I mentioned Jack and I walked past him and down a corridor lit by white light, my footsteps snapping back at me from the bright Pewabic tiles. Everything—sights, sounds, odors—has sharper edges at night. I could smell the industrial wax the janitors used, like stale gun oil.

There were three booths, framed in yellow oak with their doors folded back and built-in short benches inside upholstered like bus seats in black grainy leather. I stood facing them with the suitcase in my hand like a hunky just off the boat, aware that I was being watched by the guard. When the ringing started it took me a second to react—waiting does that—and another second to locate its source, in the third booth on my right. I took the case in with me and closed the door before answering.

"I knew you'd stick," Jack said. "You got it?"

"I got it."

"No shit, how's it feel?"

"Like a suitcase full of snakes. Where do you want it?"

"Anybody follow you?"

"Not here. I told Joey where I was going."

"They'll be waiting when you come out." The pause on his end was full of thought and frantic music. "Okay, we'll have to get fancy. You got your car?"

"It's parked around the corner."

"I'm at Bass's place, you remember where it is?" I said I did. "Okay, take this route."

I didn't write it down. I wasn't likely to forget it.

When the guard let me out I saw the car, a long low Cord, parked halfway down the block on the other side with its lamps off. The end of a cigarette glowed in the darkness of the front seat, a tiny red eye. I didn't look directly at the car, but turned and walked up the street the way I had come. Behind me I heard gears meshing, tires crunching slowly on asphalt. At Congress I turned the corner. I didn't see the car again until it appeared in my rearview mirror when I pulled away from the curb. Its lamps were on now. The suitcase lay beside me on the seat, a shabby thing worth ten times more than the Viking V-8 it was riding in.

I took Congress to Woodward and turned north. Headlamps turned behind me a block back. We drove at a stately pace up the main stem, as broad as a pasture and gunbarrel-straight, dividing the city straight up the middle like the part in Valentino's hair. It was almost empty at that hour. It gave you the feeling you could drive to the North Pole and back all in one night and never see another soul. Fort, Lafayette, Michigan, State, the cross streets bending in toward the center of the web: Grand Circus Park. The half-circle of grass looked black at night.

I wrenched the wheel hard to the left. The Viking bucked up over the curb, front axle first, then rear, a double jolt that snapped my teeth together, prepared though I was, and pitched the suitcase onto the floor under the dashboard. The wheels plowed twin furrows through the grass, mushed down. For a panicky moment I thought I was stuck. Then I bumped over again, again, and came down on Bagley. I gripped the gearshift knob, round and black like an eight-ball, shoved it forward, accelerated, then yanked it straight back into third while squashing the pedal to the firewall. The gears bawled, the throttle made a noise like a phlegmy old man clearing his throat, the tires spun, caught. The steering wheel jerked my arms straight. The Cord's headlamps flashed in the mirror at a Krazy Kat angle, then dropped out of the corner.

At Grand River I turned northwest, then took Adams east and wound my way toward the Black Bottom and Crystal Street. There was no sign of the Cord behind me. Either I'd lost it or the driver had killed his lamps.

Chapter Twenty-Five

The screen door had new patches to go with the old ones, and new rents that needed patches. The old colored woman who answered my knock was wearing the same tattered housecoat of more than a year before but no hairnet this time, and as thin as her hair was, with startling pink scalp showing through it in streaks, I wondered that she had ever needed one in the first place. She looked at my white man's clothes, hat and necktie with no funeral in the neighborhood or Baptist meeting to justify them, the suitcase, heard what I had to say, and unhooked the screen door. She was a sunken post in a changing tide, that old woman in her house that needed whitewashing; she would look as she did and live as she had regardless of who was mayor and who had killed whom for whatever reason and whether liquor was banned or legal, not out of any conscious sense of determination or pride but because this was where she had landed, this was the condition of the deck. The furniture was the same, the odd floral covers on the sofas faded one step closer to plain white, but clean. Only the worn rug was missing, having evidently grown too thin to contribute and therefore banished. Even the homemade radio set on the painted table, the room's one sad nod toward luxury and leisure, was in the same unfinished state; a loose crystal I had noticed on my first visit lay in the identical spot.

Music was playing behind the door in the dark upstairs hallway, Jack's kind, hot horns and jungle drums. I knocked.

"Yeah?" This was a new male voice, which threw me, there in that place that defied evolution. Eager young barracudas of Jack's stamp had drifted in and out of his association in the past, but since Sylvester Street, it had strictly been the three with whom he'd started minus Baldy Hannion. There was no brewery now to give him a foundation, no collateral of a physical nature to make his standard worth following. Hunches are for the old and established. The young need a sure thing.

"Connie Minor."

The door opened six inches and a boy of nineteen or twenty inserted himself into the rectangle. He was shorter than Jack but nearly as broad, and much softer. He had a ring of fat above his belt under a white shirt with the collar spread, a round face and thick red hair and gray eyes with a watery sheen and a harelip. The gun in his hand was a .38 revolver, the snubnosed kind bulls carried. I had never seen him before.

"Let him in, for Christ's sake, does he look like a torpedo?" Jack, wearing pinstriped trousers and a shoulder holster over a BVD undershirt, shoved him aside and grabbed my free hand. "Get in Connie, how the hell are you, you're letting the flies out."

I let him pull me inside. It was a railroad flat, a series of rooms lined up all in a row so that you had to pass through all of them to get to the back. We were in the kitchen. It had a shade drawn over its only window and bulging yellow plaster on the walls and newspapers taped over the places where there was obviously no plaster at all. The linoleum on the floor was dirt-colored. There were a cot with rumpled bedding on it in a corner, an old Michigan Stove Company woodburner with a warming oven overhead and yellow calcined grease on the black iron and nickel, a cast-iron sink, an icebox dripping into a pan, and an oilcloth-covered table where Andy Kramm and Lon Camarillo sat playing dominoes until I came in with the suitcase, when they got up and came over. In the next room, visible through the open door, a portable phonograph with a daisy-petal horn stood on a chest of drawers playing King Oliver. The place stank pungently of old meals and urine, the way they all did, the way they all still do in that neighborhood. That's how civilization smells under the toothpaste and powder.

"Open it up." Andy was staring at the suitcase.

"That ain't no way to treat a guest." Jack took the suitcase from me, lightening me by more than just pounds, and sat me down at the table. "They followed you, right?"

"I lost them at the park like you figured."

"Joey's chewing their asses out right now, I bet."

Someone knocked at the door: Bang-bang, pause, bang. Jack set down the suitcase and opened it with the Luger in his hand and the soft young man, who had stepped out when I came in, entered. "No sign of anybody outside." The harelip didn't seem to get in the way of his speech.

"Connie, this here's Vern Scalia. Vern's the reason you're here."

We exchanged nods. He stuck his revolver inside his belt. It had several thick rubber bands wound around the grip to keep it from slipping down.

"Vern's the one told us about the shipment. He used to work for Joey. Joey don't know yet he don't no more."

"Just what we need in this outfit," said Andy, building a skyscraper out of dominoes. "Another wop."

Lon gave him his death's-head stare.

I said, "Shipment?"

"You should've seen it." That's when Jack told me about the hijacking.

Bass Springfield came in on the end of the story from one of the rooms in back. He was wearing a blue work shirt and overalls and carrying a Negro baby wrapped in a towel with the name of a hotel stenciled on it. I'd heard a baby crying the moment I'd entered the house, but I'd assumed it was in another apartment. He was feeding it milk from a beer bottle with a nipple on it. His deformed hand held the bottle like a claw.

Jack saw me staring, laughed. "Bet you never guessed Bass was a daddy. We didn't neither till we got here. Celestine tied into him for bringing us, didn't she, Bass?"

"She's asleep," he said, in response to nothing.

"Little Quincy's gonna be a slugger," Jack went on. "You got to see the shoulders on this kid. Knock that ball clean into the white side of town."

"He ain't." Springfield jiggled the child in his arms. "He gonna be mayor, wear a tall hat." It was a tone of voice I'd never heard him use, as close to real laughter as I ever heard him come. He hadn't taken his eyes off the little dusky face since he'd entered.

"That ain't no ambition. If I had a kid I'd want him to be the one *pays* the mayor. Clear that table, boys. It's Christmas."

Andy and Lon swept the dominoes into a deal box and Jack hoisted the case up onto the table and opened it. For a time they all stared at the neat stacks inside, Springfield dividing his attention for the first time. Then Jack started picking up the banded sheafs and checking the bills, pushing them back rapidly with his fingers like a bank teller. He dug down, selecting stacks at random, destroying the symmetry inside the suitcase. While he was doing that, a pretty, short-haired colored girl came in wearing a plaid bathrobe and man's shoes on her feet and took the baby from Springfield; it had begun to cry again. Without paying attention to any of us she set down the bottle, opened her robe, and popped a brown nipple into the child's mouth, jiggling and humming something tuneless, turning away from the table and the fifty thousand dollars in cash she had not looked at once. That's what I remember when I think of Celestine Brown, whom I never heard speak a word: A young woman who made maybe twelve hundred a year working at Ford's, breast-feeding her baby in the presence of a fortune she didn't acknowledge. The boy would be about eight now.

I said, "What about Barberra?"

"Tell Joey he'll be back in the garage tomorrow. It's healthy to sweat a little." Jack stretched a bill between his hands, held it up to the bulb in the ceiling. I guessed he was looking for Series 1921. Joey had experimented with counterfeiting ten years before and given it up as too risky.

"He'll want to hear I saw him."

He put back the bill and dropped the lid. It wouldn't close now so he let it gape. "Lon, take him back."

I followed the former ace through a bedroom that had to be Celestine and Springfield's—the bottom drawer of the bureau had been pulled out and lined with towels to serve as a crib, and a rectangular framed sepia print hung on the wall above the iron bed showing two rows of solemn-looking Negroes in baggy white baseball uniforms, the front row down on one knee leaning on their bats—up to a closed door that he unlocked with a key he took down from atop the doorframe. He pushed it open but didn't go in. I got the impression I shouldn't either.

It had originally been a walk-in closet and had probably served as a storeroom at one time, but not lately because the poor don't have anything to store. It had no windows and only a chain fixture, with the bulb removed so that the only light in the room came through the door. Barberra was sitting up on a folding cot, one of those wood-and-canvas army assembly affairs, in a shirt that needed changing and wrinkled trousers and his white socks, the soles black with dirt, his wrists and ankles bound with wire. In that light he looked balder than Baldy

Hannion, the Oklahoma train robber, whom it was commonly believed Barberra himself had killed, but not as bald as Joey Machine's Washington lawyer, Cranston, who shaved even his fringe; but his scalp was as naked as a skull and just as white. It didn't look as if it had ever had hair. He blinked in the light, he had a two-day carpet of black beard. The little room smelled of dirty socks and a white enamel chamber pot under the cot, which was empty at the moment but would always be tainted no matter how thoroughly it was scrubbed and disinfected. And beneath that, garlic.

Lon closed the door and locked it, replaced the key, and we returned to the kitchen. We passed Celestine in the bedroom, tucking the baby into its makeshift crib and humming, perhaps unconsciously, the "Royal Garden Blues," now playing on the phonograph. Jack or someone had changed the record.

"He doesn't look too happy," I told Jack.

"Stink wouldn't be happy being happy. He thinks you got to be mean all the time to do people. He's healthy, that's what counts, like they say." He was straightening the stacks of bills in the suitcase. Andy was watching him, looking fascinated more by the action than the money, like a dog staring at the hand that's pointing instead of what it's pointing at. Vern Scalia, watching from his post by the door, was definitely interested in the money. I could see the bills reflected in his eyes—blue to go with his red hair, courtesy of some ages-dead Viking visitor to Sicily—the gray tip of his tongue coming out to wet the groove in his cleft lip. I'd disliked him on sight.

Springfield, looking as if he had never held a baby in his life or predicted its future, stood with his hands in the pockets of his overalls, the way he always did when he wasn't using them, scrutinizing one of the newspapers on the wall, as if it weren't his apartment and he didn't see them every day. He was staring at a six-month-old picture of a Coast Guard officer with gold braid on his cap swinging a bottle of nonalcoholic champagne at the bow of a new cutter designed to outrun any bootlegging craft on the river; an obsolescence even before its hull got wet. I knew then that I would never be at home among these men, one of them, honorary or otherwise. They were always waiting for me to leave so they could get on. I don't know why it bothered me, but it did.

The Pious Heart was there, of course, hanging all alone in its gummy devotion in the middle of a patch of plaster with a fresh crack running through it—caused, no doubt, by the nail that supported the picture.

You could track Jack through the city by the nails he left behind to hold up that devout adolescent.

"I'll go," I said.

Jack was still sorting. "Thanks, Connie. Sorry you lost sleep."

"I don't want to do this again."

"Can't blame you. Stink's hard enough to take dressed and barbered."

"You know what I mean. Next time call someone else."

"If that's what you want."

I hesitated. "You're letting him go in a few hours, right?"

"I said I was."

"Your word's not worth shit, Jack. Everybody knows it."

He looked up, a brick of bills in each hand. I felt a flash of the old paralysis. He wasn't subject to rages, but you just never knew what he was going to do. A beat, then he grinned. "Get some sleep, Connie. I ain't so crazy I'd chop down the money tree. Not yet."

Vern Scalia opened the door for me and I went out. When I think of Jack I usually see him the way he looked that night as I was leaving, a boy in a gangster's thick-muscled body with his hair grown back out long and curling, the upright V of his broad shoulders and narrow waist and the inverted V of the shoulder rig over his ribbed undershirt describing a perfect diamond. Fast music playing. The next time I saw him he was dying.

The Black Bottom at half-past one, ante meridiem: Puddles of blue neon and red argon on the sidewalks, as if a Martian had taken a leak on every corner; fat, middle-aged Negroes in belted coats with Chesterfield collars and yellow spats and big Panamas, the uniform of the policy baron, by special arrangement with Hizzoner Joey G. Machine; old colored men in soft caps and holey sweaters drinking from bottles wrapped in paper bags; young shines practicing their steps on corners for their big break at the Graystone Ballroom downtown; small black boys running, threading their way through knots of saloon-hoppers, clutching paper sacks full of policy slips; willowy Negresses in ostrich feathers and monkey-fur collars hanging all over white men in fedoras and peaked lapels, the men grinning lopsidedly with gold-foil-wrapped bottles under their arms, clutching pairs of long-stemmed glasses, taking the party down the street and up the stairs; a friendly place for the next half hour, at the end of which the unwritten curfew kicked in and then it would be everyone to his own side of town and God help the white man whose watch stopped. Night belonged to the Negro; it could be rented by the other side, but not bought.

I parked by a booth on Harper and called the garage. The wind shifted while I was dialing and sticky blue smoke drifted from an alley where three coloreds in red band jackets were smoking muggles. I closed the door.

"You *see* Barberra?" demanded Joey when I told him I'd made the delivery.

"He's okay. Jack says you'll have him back in the morning."

"It's morning now."

"After daylight, then. He looked like they've been treating him well enough."

"Fuck I care how they're treating him? I just want him breathing and in one piece. The kike tell you what he did to Nick Salerno?"

"I don't think he meant to hit him that hard."

"Where they holed up?"

It shouldn't have thrown me. I'd thought my silence on certain things was a given, bestowed on me by right of my trade. But Joey didn't recognize rights, didn't understand givens. I said, "If I told you that, no one in this town would trust me to tell me it's raining."

"Trust, I trust that suitcase I sent you up there with. When you got dough you don't need trust. Who was there?"

"His gang."

"That motherfucker Scalia was there, wasn't he?"

I said he was. It wasn't the first time Jack had underestimated Joey.

"That shitbag, that snake-fucking Sicilian son of a mangy whore. That ass-kissing back-stabber."

There was more of this. I could never tell how much of his famous tantrums was real and how much staged to buy him time to think. The murders carried out in his name were too well orchestrated to have been the product of simple fury.

At length he ran out of vituperatives. His breathing was more phlegmatic than usual. Then the line went dead.

"You're welcome," I told the dial tone.

Chapter Twenty-Six

"Mouse, I'm not going to beg you," I said. "There are stories and stories, and even the ones I *get* are deader than Isadora in twenty-four hours."

"Not this one," he said, jigging in his seat like a kid. On top of being a midget, Mouse was high-strung, and when you managed to get him off his feet he was always drumming his pudgy fingers and bouncing the foot crossed on his knee and jerking his head around as if he suspected someone was gunning for him. He kept his porkpie and oversize coat on indoors and out regardless of the season. I think he thought they made him look bigger, whereas they had the opposite effect, creating the impression that county officials had finally found a way to get rid of the downtown lobbyists by shrinking them. "I ain't sure I should tell it to you, though. I'm thinking of shifting my operation to the Federal Building. I need a lever there."

I signaled a passing waiter for another round. We were sharing a table in the Green Lantern in Ecorse, candles stuck in green prewar wine bottles on red-and-white-checked tablecloths within earshot of the crap tables in back. The waiter, also prewar—black handlebars and a bow tie—brought me a beer and a vodka gimlet for Mouse and left with our empty glasses. When Mouse lifted his glass to sip, I placed a twenty-dollar bill on the ring. He set the glass down on top of it.

"Thank you kindly, Connie. Things are slow at County since they kicked Jack Dance. It's like he took the heart right out of the reform movement."

"Is that why you were in the Federal Building, where you saw whatever it is you saw?"

"I didn't see it. I heard it. A friend of mine saw someone getting into an elevator."

"You don't have any friends, Mouse. Just clients. Who'd he see?"

But he wasn't ready to let go of it just yet. Like all small men, and Danny Moskovitch was the smallest I knew who didn't talk with a sissy accent while Edgar Bergen drank a glass of water, he liked being the center of attention. "What do you know about due process?"

"J. Edgar Hoover calls you a yellow rat and you go to jail for a thousand years. Get to the point."

"What would you say if I told you my friend saw Orville Cranston getting onto an elevator with one of the jurors in the Machine tax evasion case?"

He had me then. His sharp little face bent into a series of happy triangles, he drummed his fingers and bounced his foot. I folded my arms on the table. "What's the friend call himself?"

"I can't tell you that."

I reached and snapped the twenty out from under the glass without spilling it. Big-deal Houdini stuff.

"Hey!"

"I can buy twenty rumors for a buck, Mouse. I need a name. The juror's if not your friend's."

He looked troubled. "He didn't say which juror. I got to clear it with him before I tell his name. It'll cost you another twenty for his cut."

"Take it out of your end."

"That ain't fair, Connie. Ten's what I slip bailiffs to tell me what goes on in the jury room."

"I'm bleeding, Mouse." I sat back folding the bill between my fingers while he turned over his conscience, not exactly a job for a heavy lifter. I'd have paid him fifty if the tip was good, but he didn't need to know that. Evidence that an attorney had established contact, accidental or otherwise, with a member of the jury in a client's case was grounds for a mistrial at least. In this specific situation I suspected that more had passed between the two than just the time of day.

Mouse was about to speak, and I knew what his decision was going to be, when our waiter came back and told me I had a call. The caller wouldn't identify himself. I said shit and got up. "Hold the thought, Mouse."

"It's almost lunchtime. I got to get back to County and earn supper."

"I'll make it quick." I let him see me fold the twenty into my vest pocket.

The telephone was on the wall in the craproom. Eddie Berman the bouncer, a gray lump in a checked jacket, who bore no small resemblance to an iguana and carried an ash cane he used to pry fatmouths off their feet, shuffled away a discreet yard or so while I lifted the earpiece. The first thing I heard after I said hello was a long hawking gurgle, followed by a small explosion and then a rustle of paper tissue. "Minor?"

"What can I do for you, Lieutenant Gabriel?"

"You know the Ferry warehouse?" He didn't seem surprised that I'd guessed who he was.

"Brush and Lafayette," I said.

"Second floor, northwest corner. There's a friend of yours here."

I hung up fifteen seconds after he did and returned to the table to make my excuses. But Mouse had left.

Late June was everywhere. The air was bright with hot concrete, soft tar, cotton dresses, and loud radios in uncovered convertibles. I parked on Brush and walked around to the front door of the warehouse, a city block of brick arches and cement cornices the pigeons loved that looked like the Roman Forum, only more ambitious. A uniformed bull I knew slightly let me in and told me they were waiting for me upstairs.

"They who?"

"Lieutenant Gabriel and the chief."

"Kozlowski?"

"You know another chief?"

A kid in livery, dressed for the offices upstairs, took me up in the elevator. When he opened the cage I stepped out into a wall of sweet grainy odor, the smell of tons of stored seeds and something else, a pleasant, cloying aroma that reminded me of Sunday afternoons after church and roast pork steaming on the table. I got my bearings and headed northwest. Sunlight poured through the tall windows, the shafts smoking with millions of golden seed particles, and lay on the bare floor in rectangular patches as in a cloister walkway.

I recognized the Laurel and Hardy figures of Gabriel and Kozlowski among a group gathered around an object in the corner, a sack of grain or something hanging from the beamed ceiling. A flashbulb flared, the dead bulb was plucked out and tossed to the floor, where it popped like a half-loaded shell in the room's vastness.

"Fuck the sweep," Gabriel was saying, his thin Cracker voice irritated, wobbling in the rafters. "Let's just call Philly and have them grab him when he steps off the train. Isn't that where he goes every time he caps someone, to visit relatives? The guinea's a good family boy. They see a lot of him."

The pork smell grew stronger as I approached, and long before they noticed me I knew what the dangling thing was, who it was, and my stomach did a slow turn.

Kozlowski spotted me. "Normally when we find 'em swinging, the first thing we do is cut them down," he said without greeting, "see can we revive them. We didn't need no medical examiner to tell us we didn't have to bother this time, did we, Doc?"

"No, he's been dead at least twelve hours. Hello, Connie." The examiner, who had climbed a six-foot stepladder to examine the corpse while it was still suspended, was Paul Anderson, the man who had found the unfired Luger cartridge in Lewis Welker's mouth. He was wearing a corduroy sportcoat with elbow patches, like a U of D professor's, and a blue polka-dot necktie that ran out of material above his sternum after the long trip around his linebacker neck. "You can take him down now."

His wrists had been wired to a steel beam that ran the length of the ceiling, after which a blowtorch had burned big oval holes through his clothes and suppurating blue scars on the flesh beneath. Somewhere along the way, either from pain or fear when it was happening—I couldn't believe fear, not of him, not even then—or after the shock finished him, his sphincter and bladder had released, and under the odor of scorched cloth and roasted meat lay the stench of a public toilet. He was wearing his old cap and shabby suitcoat, the one Nathan Rabinowitz had had repaired for his day in court with Jack Dance. His expression wasn't pained, but stoic, as it had always been, as it would always be now, until the worms got him.

Bass Springfield, the best left fielder the Biloxi Bullets had ever had. He had hit safely in thirty-eight consecutive games, his son was going to be mayor someday. In the two years I'd known him he had said maybe twenty words to me total.

While the police photographer, a swarthy slob with filthy nails and a soup stain on his hat, took pictures of the room, a morgue attendant I bribed regularly to steal autopsy reports went up the ladder with bolt cutters while his partner got to stand with his arms around Springfield's hips to catch him when the wires parted. There were several plainclothes detectives standing around, some of them wearing the rubber raincoats and galoshes of the Prohibition Squad, holding useless axes and looking like guests at the wrong party. If Gabriel had brought a raincoat, he had taken it off, but his ubiquitous Panama was wrapped in cellophane. Kozlowski had on a new-looking Palm Beach suit and his old fedora and tiny wingtips. The suit had already begun to conform to his sloppy configuration.

"We got an anonymous call there was a still up here," said Gabriel, I assumed to me, although he was watching the attendants. "Nobody here knew anything, I have it on their authority. Nobody had any business on this floor today. Maybe. My six-year-old nephew goes blind the same way every time his dog shits on my sister's carpet. Anyway, we had to get a forklift to move the stacks of crates so we could get to Springfield. They put them there last night to block the windows, keep the torch flame from showing outside."

Kozlowski thrust a blowtorch at me, unlit. I flinched anyway. "Go ahead, take it," he said. "It's been dusted."

I took it in both hands, the first time I'd ever held one. It was heavier than expected and shaped like a watering can with a jet and a screw valve on top. Cool to the touch. I smelled kerosene.

Kozlowski said, "They left it behind, as who wouldn't, get stopped on the street carrying a torch, ha, with a barbecued stiff upstairs. Smell the handle."

I hesitated, then lifted it, sniffed. I handed it back.

"That stink don't wipe off as easy as prints," he said. "You'd think the son of a bitch would wash his hands once in a while."

Gabriel produced a wad of tissues from a pocket and coughed into it. He made a business of folding and returning it to his pocket, for once without inspecting the results. "I saw that column you wrote a couple of weeks back, about Dance kidnapping Stink. The chief thought maybe you left something out."

The last strand of wire let go with a noise like a guitar string snapping. The attendant on the floor woofed and almost sat down under the corpse's sudden weight. Its arms remained stretched over its head, its knees didn't bend. If its toes weren't pointed downward the attendant could have stood it on the floor like a statue. Kozlowski laughed.

"You boys're going to have to bust him in two to get him in the drawer," he said.

Anderson said, "Not till I'm through with him. Postmortem contusions are hard enough to subtract from the rest without broken bones."

"We know *what* killed him, Doc. All's we need is *when*, exactly."

"Tell me when he had supper and I'll tell you when he died."

I said, "They were holding Barberra in Springfield's apartment. Springfield's wife and baby were there. I don't have to tell you why I didn't write about that." I watched the attendants roll the corpse like a log into the rubber bag they'd unzipped and spread on the floor on top of the canvas stretcher. It was as if Springfield's stiff crippled hands had spread throughout his body.

"They probably blindfolded Stink when they brought him there and when they took him out," Gabriel said. "They didn't have to bother. Stink's got ears and a nose and he can add up to twenty-one if he takes his shoes and socks and pants off. We sent a car for the woman. Maybe she saw something."

"Are you arresting Machine?"

"We'll talk to him." Kozlowski relit his stogie. As often as they smoldered out, I figured he got them at the same place Jensen bought his pipe tobacco. "My guess is he was holed up with his lawyer all last night, or out whoring around in front of fifty witnesses. Sure you didn't see nothing else that night?"

"A new Cord followed me for a while downtown. I lost it at the park."

"Could you identify it?"

"I wouldn't mistake it for a Studebaker in court."

Kozlowski laughed his snorting laugh. "Yeah, ain't them sheeny legals something. Okay, Minor. If you hear from your pal Dance, tell him we want to talk to him. We called his wife, she ain't seen him since yesterday. Maybe he's in the river."

Anderson and the morgue attendants took the body in its rubber cocoon down in the freight elevator in back. The kid in the main elevator looked at me a second time when I got in. "You all right, mister? You look a little green."

"Touch of influenza."

"That's tough. You see the nigger? I bet it was the Klan, them Black Legionnaires."

"Shut up, you little bastard."

"Hey, fuck you."

Jensen was out of the office. I called Jack's house in St. Clair Shores. Vivian answered.

"Did the bulls tell you what happened?" I asked without saying hello.

"No, they just wanted to know where Jack was. Do you want to talk to him?"

"He's there?"

"It's Connie," she said, away from the phone.

"Connie, what's up?"

"Jesus Christ, Jack, Joey's looking for you. What are you doing at home?"

"I just stopped in to show Vivian I'm still kicking. What do the bulls want? I'm clean since May."

There is a compulsion to tell about death. It's still unique after all this time. I told him about Springfield. I didn't leave anything out. There was a long silence on his end, and for once no music. Then something banged in my ear and I thought someone had been shot. More banging then. He was hammering the receiver against something, a wall or something. I shouted his name several times. A copy boy stuck his head inside the door curiously, then withdrew it. After a couple of minutes Jack's voice came back on. There was a humming on the line now, the words were broken up by static. I figured the tin cup must be smashed almost flat. "I'm here, Connie."

"You better get under somewhere," I said. "The others too. Joey and Barberra are on the prod."

"They better be. They better come with cannons and a fucking tank." He thanked me for calling. We said good-bye.

I didn't write about Springfield's death. I let the others have that beat. Howard ran something from the well and when it appeared I was already pixilated. Somehow—I'd been to several places first and I don't know now where it was or how I found it, she was moving every couple of weeks now to stay ahead of Gabriel—I landed at Hattie Long's. I remember how she looked, the expression on her face when she saw me, its heart shape and astonished drawn-on eyebrows and beestung lips, I even remember what she was wearing, a silver lamé shift with a scoop neck and a chain around her waist, sandals with glittery heels, but I don't remember what was said, or if anything was. I woke up with two girls, still drunk, one or both of whom I had seen someone mounting from behind, cowboy fashion, someone who looked a lot like the guy whose picture ran every day in the *Banner* on top of his column sucking a cold pipe. "That's how Greeks fuck, honey," said the other one, the one watching. The guy slapped her, just like a gangster, just like James Cagney. I had a sprained wrist the next day and Hattie charged me twenty dollars extra for dental work. The girl had a loose tooth. Johnston, Hattie's bartender-bouncer-ex-prizefighter, backed the claim. "See if I come back to this dump," I said, paying. I was still drunk. It took me an hour to find my car, by which time I was sober and mean. I rear-ended a Polish welder from Dodge Main on Joseph Campau and took a swing at him. Two bulls, one of them a mounted patrolman with spurs on his boots who smelled like Tom Mix's horse Tony, pulled him off me. I was booked as a disorderly person. Howard Wolfman bailed me two hours later.

Professional detachment, that's my middle name.

Chapter Twenty-Seven

The death of Bass Springfield meant war, after a fashion, and after its fashion nothing happened for a while. Joey Machine himself was under federal surveillance during his tax trial and beyond Jack's reach unless Jack was screwy enough to knock him down in front of the most reliable witnesses this side of the Entente Cordiale. He wasn't that screwy and he did nothing. The news business became downright dismal. When an eleven-month-old Inkster girl was rescued from a drain tile on Michigan Avenue where she had managed to get stuck for a couple of hours, the *Banner* gave the story front-page play for a week in spite of the fact that she was a Negress. The Black Legion, a particularly rabid local outlet of the Ku Klux Klan, wrote letters. Howard was desperate enough for copy to print two of them.

Aside from prostitution, journalism is the only work I know that's hardest when business is on the bum. I used up my store of ideas a week into the Great Calm and wound up dead in the water. One morning, when twenty minutes of staring failed to produce a column from the wall opposite my desk, I went motoring. I sought, if not a murder, at least a couple of tangled fenders and a fistfight, or some other demonstration of human nature of the sort that kept Will Rogers's typewriter smoking. Anything to prevent an L-shaped hole from appearing under my picture on Page Three.

On that morning, angels walked the land. Drivers indicated the correct turns a third of a block up the street. Pedestrians used the crosswalks on the green. Motorists stopped politely to let other motorists pull out of parking spaces, signaling early their intention to stop. The spectre that haunts the reporter's nights is the fear that the entire human race will decide in a body to start over fresh and broadcast the spirit of the Good Samaritan from Barbary to Burma. I could write a column about a day when nothing happened, but what if it happened again tomorrow? Other writers stocked their wells: Not me. The work is a dead enough lift on an immediate deadline without borrowing others.

I was nursing a fantasy about plowing through a group of nuns and reporting the event—nothing but nuns would do, and I'm not half-sure I wasn't lucky no nuns appeared just then, to say nothing of the nuns' luck—when I turned off Seven Mile onto Littlefield and passed a gray frame house with a wooden sign swinging from the porch roof. WATCHES SOLD AND REPAIRED. Antique letters with looping serifs. *J. Danzig, Prop.*

Come clean, Connie. I was going to lie and say I went looking for the secret of Jack Dance's past the day I visited his father in his shop; but when you fudge on the small things you gnaw a little off the foundation under the big things. I stumbled onto it, pure and simple.

I parked down the street and walked back. It was a Jewish neighborhood on the crawl northward, lined with bakeries and pushcarts and shapeless old women walking with their beautiful black-eyed daughters and old men sweating in their stiff collars and black wool suits. An orange cat that must have gone twenty pounds watched me from its hollow in a split and bloated cushion on the porch swing as I mounted the steps.

Whatever the condition of the old man's eyes may have been, there was nothing wrong with his hearing. He was holding the screen door open for me when I came over the last step, smiling his trampled-looking smile and blinking behind his nearly opaque lenses. He wasn't wearing a coat, but his dusty black vest was buttoned up all the way, with a knitted fob hanging out of the watch pocket like a tongue. His curly white hair made his shirt look yellow, and his bow tie, slightly off plumb and red everywhere but the pale ovals where he placed his thumbs, seemed to have bled all the color from his face. The thick old-fashioned wedding band on the hand holding the door had slipped an eighth of an inch around, showing the end of a wad of white tape inside. He was thin with the emaciation of some progressive disease. His wrists reminded me of stemware and as I went in past him I caught a sweetish sickroom smell of medicine and decay. I stood on a rubber mat just inside the door and took off my hat. He let the spring pull the door shut.

"Is it a watch you want?" His teeth barely touched his lip on the *w*'s, softening the *v* sound of his Yiddish pronunciation. He had worked long and hard to rid himself of the accent and he had come as close to success as he ever would.

We were in a narrow foyer with buff paper on the walls that had turned the color of tarnished gold. The room beyond had been a parlor before someone had carried out the furniture and carried in two thick glass cases with nutwood frames, set at right angles with a bronze rococo cash register holding down one end. The shelves were lined with green plush. Upon them gleamed circles of gold and silver scrolled all over—antique pocket watches, thick as teething rings, with stems the size of marbles. Tapestry curtains over the front windows put the room in twilight. The place smelled of brass polish and yellow oil and the odor of genteel rot that I was coming to associate with its owner.

My resolve shriveled. I felt like a gate-crasher at a funeral.

I held up my left wrist with the Timex strapped to it. "It loses five minutes a day."

He had me take it off and held it up to his ear. "Clocks, they are the only things that tell you what is wrong with them. But you must know their language. This one is saying, 'I have a gear with a broken tooth.' I can fix. You come back tomorrow."

"I'm Connie Minor," I said. "We met at your son's wedding."

He nodded. "This I know. You write about John in the paper."

"I didn't think you'd remember me."

"My eyes are bad. My head is fine. My ears too." He stood stroking the watch.

"I'd like to ask you some questions about Jack."

"For the paper? You will mention the shop?"

"If you like."

"Sometimes John is reading to me what you write. It doesn't sound like John. Maybe I won't sound like me."

I didn't know what to say to that.

"Business is bad. No one wants to spend time with old men and watches on a nice day." He closed the main door and locked it and flipped the OPEN sign so that it read CLOSED through the window.

He turned and went around the glass case with the cash register on it, his heels scuffing a little, and then through a door at the back. After a moment I followed.

I don't know what I expected from my first glimpse of the rest of the house. A stale Victorian room, probably, with a horsehair sofa and mismatched wingback chairs—the house my father died in. The room Jerome Danzig led me into contained a pair of chromium-and-leather director's chairs and a davenport of the same material, assembled from four pieces like an erector set. A glass table with a shiny frame sneered at the homely upright telephone it was supporting. I wouldn't see anything like it until I visited the Chicago World's Fair two years later. The House of Tomorrow went like hell in that room with its tarnished-gold wallpaper and dust-motes spinning in a shaft coming through a window with flouncy faded curtains. It would have been a dining room before the parlor was moved there from the storefront.

"John bought the furniture." Danzig opened a drawer that hung suspended by some mystical device under the top of the telephone table. "He said the old room looked like Madame Glyn lived in it. I said I don't care, I live in the shop. Ah." He swept something off the top of a thick album bound in dirty blue cloth and carried it to the sofa. The weight of it bent him over. It would run about a pound.

"Does Jack—John—give you money?"

"I don't take it. Later, always, I find it in the cash drawer. I open up a bank account, I don't touch. He might need it. This is John and Tom's mother. She died."

I joined him on the davenport. The woman in the wedding picture, mounted on stiff yellow cardboard with the name of the studio engraved in extravagant script on the border, was grave and large-boned in a gown of ivory lace. The bridegroom was Danzig, without glasses and with dark hair and a razor collar. Tom had his father's eyes, thoughtful and brooding. Jack had his mother's jaw and build and his eyes were his own. He had inherited his curly hair from his father and nothing else, and in such an obvious way that he seemed to have rejected it deliberately. Mr. and Mrs. Danzig made a solemn-looking couple, even for the time when the picture was taken.

A putty-colored hand, scarred and calloused at the fingertips from decades of handling cogs and wheels and jewelers' implements, turned the brittle black pages. Picture postcards tinted by hand. Snapshots with serrated edges. Brown newspaper clippings that disintegrated before the eyes. The old man provided commentary. Tom at ten, holding up a medal for penmanship. John at six, posing with a stick and hoop, one black stocking drooping below his knickers. Danzig standing in the doorway of his first shop on Kercheval with his thumbs in his vest pockets. Uncle So-and-So with one foot on the running board of his new Edison electric. A flood in someone's basement. The Littlefield house with a horse and phaeton parked in front of it. Grainy, fading, poorly composed pictures taken looking down through the viewfinders of Kodaks, Brownies, Arguses. Step back. A little to the right. No, left. There.

"I don't see any other photos of Mrs. Danzig."

"She passed away in nineteen twelve. This is Tom at his graduation. He made a speech."

No graduation shot of Jack. I would have been surprised to see one. If any were taken, it would have been about the time I met him at Hattie's place on Vernor. I couldn't picture a photographer getting him into the gown and mortarboard even if he'd earned them.

In his carefully de-ethnicized tones, the old man recounted family history. His father had been a watchmaker with a five-syllable surname in Danzig. After his parents were killed in a pogrom, relatives pooled their money and sent Jerome to America. An exhausted civil servant at Ellis Island, unable to spell his name or misunderstanding his English, had rechristened him after his home city, and it was as Jerome Danzig that he became a citizen in 1910, by which time he had married and come to Detroit with his pregnant wife and small son Tom. Anna Danzig never fully recovered from her second pregnancy and died when John was two.

I knew then, with a sickly sinking sensation, why I'd put off coming there so long. It was all so suffocatingly ordinary, and nothing in it explained Jack Dance.

Danzig turned pages as he spoke. At one point, more to interrupt his drone than to feed my curiosity, I asked him to go back one. It was a picture of the boys in trunks and swimtops on a beach. John, two inches shorter than his towheaded brother and chubby, was resting his hand on the shoulder of a girl of twelve or thirteen with a big bow in her dark blonde hair, wearing one of the ridiculous puff-sleeved swimming dresses that were hardly ever worn anymore outside of Mack Sennett comedies. She was squinting into the sun behind the photographer, distorting her features, but she looked familiar. Something nudged me and I looked out the window. I asked Danzig who she was.

"That's Emily, the boys' cousin. That was taken on Belle Isle, summer of nineteen twenty-four. John spent a lot of time with her then. He was going to marry her when he turned sixteen, but I told him he couldn't. She was Mrs. Danzig's niece and his first cousin. It was the law."

"Was it serious?"

"No. Well, I caught him throwing his suitcase out of his window one night; he was going to meet her and take the train to Toledo and get married there. I took away the suitcase and locked him in. Emily went to Muskegon and married a man in the cement business. She had a girl last year."

"Eloping sounds serious."

"They were children. He said if he couldn't marry Emily he wouldn't marry anyone. You were at his wedding."

I let it go then, reluctantly. I'd had a headline—JACK THE RIPPER'S FIRST LOVE—but it evaporated. Burnt-out passion never sold a newspaper. The story told me something, however. If I was any judge of proportions, the chunky kid in the photograph could have broken his diminutive father in two without putting down his suitcase. Yet he'd meekly allowed the old man to lock him in his room. Whatever had swept him off the path of church and community, it hadn't been permissiveness.

"You said John had a room?"

"He shared with Tom. I changed nothing. In case one of them wants to stay. So far . . ." He shrugged.

"Could I see it?"

"Wait, there are more pictures."

So I sat through the rest of the album. Tom's first bylined article for the *Times*, Jack and Vivian cutting their wedding cake, photographed at a different angle from the similar shot that had run in the *Banner*, Andrea St. Charles's account of the reception. A lot of strangers in long skirts and mail-order suits, identified as Aunt Inez and Uncle Ignatz, or names to that effect. A blurred clipping from the legals of the old *Evening News* announcing a list of new citizens, with *Jerome Danzig* underlined in faded brown ink. Anna's obituary, sparsely worded; each "beloved" would have cost extra. There was no chronology to the order in which the items appeared, as if they had been pasted on whatever page happened to present itself when the book was opened. Unusual for a watchmaker. Or perhaps not. He was the first watchmaker I had ever spent any time with.

At last he put the book down and I followed him up a narrow enclosed staircase without a runner or paint on the plaster walls to the second story. A small metal cylinder of the type that usually contained a *mezuzah* was attached to the hallway wall at the top. It was the only religious artifact I saw on the premises. In most Jewish households it was nailed to the front doorframe for luck. Maybe Danzig thought he needed more luck upstairs.

At first glance, the room told me more about the parent than it did about the sons. It didn't look like a place where boys had lived. There were no pictures of Babe Ruth or Red Grange on the walls, no litter of baseballs and pocket knives and movie theater ticket stubs on the bureaus; just a Spartan neatness about the two single beds and steel-point engravings hung in plain wood frames of the signing of the Declaration of Independence and Lord Cornwallis's surrender and George Washington's farewell to his troops. I knew without looking that no copies of the *Police Gazette* lay hidden under the mattress Danzig had pointed out to me as John's. The future bootlegger would have found a better way to smuggle his impure thoughts past his father. For all the old man's air of shriveled depletion, unless he had lied about not changing anything in the room, his authority had reached from the barren storefront on the ground floor to his sons' most private corner. Inside those quiet walls I saw emerge a family tyrant on the European order.

The nightstand on Tom's side of the room had two shelves containing schoolbooks. There were books on the small table on John's side, too, but these were of the Tom Swift variety and probably hadn't been opened in many years. A picture in a standing frame on John's bureau was turned toward a corner. I had to step between the bed and the bureau to look at it.

It was another shot of John in his middle teens with his cousin Emily. Both were fully dressed, he in a suit that might have been the same one he was wearing when I met him, she in a dark sailor dress with white piping. She had the big bow in her hair and was looking up at John, who was grinning at the camera and hugging her tightly with one arm.

I knew then why she'd seemed familiar. I had seen that rapt, upward-tilted profile, dripping with devotion, in every place Jack

Dance had lived since his honeymoon. The artist might have used Emily as his model had he not died when she was still a little girl. From the hair bow to the slightly plump cheeks to her worshipful expression, she was the girl in *The Pious Heart.*

A married man couldn't carry around a picture of a strange girl without raising too many questions, but a painting that reminded him of her could pass as just another of his many idiosyncracies. And he would go on breaking laws as long as he continued to remember the law that had taken away the girl he had chosen.

I thanked Danzig for the tour through things past and left. I found something else to write about that day, and the next and the next. The *Banner* wasn't right for Jack's story. Neither was any other paper, and I haven't told it to anyone before this.

I never went back for my watch, either. Six months later Jerome Danzig was dead, and for all I know, they buried it with him. At that, he outlived Jack by three months.

Chapter Twenty-Eight

Meanwhile the Machine tax evasion trial ground on and on. Joey's gross earnings for the seven-year period covered by the indictment, however much of their impression was lost by the dry adding-machine tone in which the government's accountants read the figures into the record, were staggering: Liquor, $224,000,000; gambling, $175,000,000; prostitution, $53,000,000; protection, a paltry $14,000,000, but coming up fast in the stretch. Henry Ford, running a poor second to such enterprise, had no comment for the reporters who reached him, but was said to have remarked in private that even the Jews could learn a thing or two from that man Machine. But they were just meaningless strings of zeroes to Detroiters who had to scratch to come up with two pennies to read them. Public interest in the proceedings didn't pick up until the defendant took the stand on his own behalf. The *Banner*, thanks to court reporter Chuck Kobler's business-school shorthand, maintained a faithful transcript, a portion of which I provide here, from United States Prosecutor Melvin I. Chouser's cross-examination:

CHOUSER: You admit that you willfully refused to pay any income tax for the years 1924 to 1930 inclusive?

MACHINE: Not willfully, no. It was a mistake.

CHOUSER: You forgot to file a return seven years in a row?

MACHINE: No sir. I was told I didn't have to.

CHOUSER: Told by whom?

MACHINE: A lawyer I talked to once. He said I didn't have to pay taxes on illegal earnings under my Fifth Amendment rights against self-incrimination.

CHOUSER: When did you find out this advice was incorrect?

MACHINE: When I was arrested four months ago.

CHOUSER: Who is the attorney who told you you didn't have to pay taxes on illegal earnings?

MACHINE: I didn't catch his name. He was someone I met in a blind pig a long time ago.

CHOUSER: Do you expect this court to believe you risked a fine of fifty thousand dollars and a lengthy prison sentence on the word of someone you spoke to in a saloon?

MACHINE: What, you never gave nobody free legal advice?

CHOUSER: Will Your Honor please instruct the defendant to answer the question prosecution has put to him?

MACHINE: Keep your shirt on, counselor. Yes, the man was introduced to me as a capable attorney and I felt he had no reason to lie under those circumstances. When I found out about this action I consulted my own attorneys and when they told me I owed the taxes I naturally wanted to make good, Joey Machine don't welsh. When I offered to pay the forty-six thousand they said I owed, the government turned me down.

On July 2, six weeks and two days after the trial began, the defense rested and Judge Wilson Abernathy adjourned court until after the Independence Day break. The prosecution spent all of July 7 on its summation, recapping the dramatic figures and driving home the point that when a major abuser of the tax system failed to do his duty, his burden was placed on the shoulders of every taxpaying citizen; appealing to the jurors' pocketbooks, if not their sense of justice. Cranston, speaking a fraction of that time the following day, chose the same tack, explaining that if the government had accepted the defendant's offer to settle his debt, it would be richer by the sum of $46,000 plus the cost of a lengthy trial and that it was in the jury's power to prevent similar raids on its wallets in the future by returning a verdict of not guilty. They were both convincing arguments based on a strong premise with a dollar sign in front of it, and I speculated in my column how different the lawyers' strategies might have been had the trial taken place two years earlier, when the stock market was cresting the wave and Detroit rang with the "mighty din" of pneumatic hammers, not the "sad sibilant shuffling" of cardboard soles on concrete in front of the Department of Public Welfare.

The jury deliberated for thirteen hours that day and seven hours the next. At four P.M. they filed back into the courtroom, their expressions as unreadable as a first date's. The foreman, a well-known local funeral director in blue serge and a cinerary black toupee, rose and read the verdict from a sheet of government stationery.

"Of the charge of evasion of federal income taxes for the year nineteen twenty-four, we the jury find the defendant not guilty.

"Of the charge of evasion of federal income taxes for the year nineteen twenty-five, we the jury find the defendant not guilty.

"Of the charge of evasion of federal income taxes for the year nineteen twenty-six, we the jury find the defendant not guilty. . . ."

By the third "not guilty," the groundswell had started, and the declaration that the defendant was innocent of willful nonpayment of taxes for the years 1927, 1928, 1929, and 1930 was lost in the jabbering and hooting and cracking of palms on backs and of the judge's gavel. Joey, beaming like a new citizen, shook Orville Cranston's hand, gripping the attorney's wrist with his left like the President. The picture made the front page of the *Banner*, with the text of Joey's surprisingly eloquent off-the-cuff justice-is-served remarks, delivered in the lobby of the Federal Building after adjournment, appearing on Page Two opposite another boxed item containing the U.S. prosecutor's grim prophecy about a hostage America, and a Jensen cartoon between showing a senile Uncle Sam chucking a thug in a baby bonnet and five o'clock shadow under the chin. A wire story from Chicago, where Al Capone was preparing to face charges of tax evasion, reported that United States Attorney George E. Q. Johnson was troubled by the decision in Detroit. Outrage got a real workout in the press that week. Meanwhile Joey's blind pigs on the East Side ran out of booze satisfying the thirsts of customers who packed the joints celebrating the verdict or hoping to catch a glimpse of the former defendant toasting the system. They were disappointed. He was back in the Acme Garage with the three accountants he had hired to replace the phenomenal Presto, toting up six weeks' worth of losses and brainstorming plans to recoup.

As soon as my column was finished for the trial extra, I went to the County Building and dragged Mouse out from between pillars.

"You win," I said. "Twenty for you, twenty for your friend. Who's the juror he saw Cranston getting into the elevator with?"

"Scram, Connie. I'm meeting a guy."

"Yeah, me. You ran out from under a double sawbuck in the Green Lantern, Mouse. That's not like you."

"My friend made a mistake. It was two other guys."

All the county courts had just let out. I realized I was shaking a midget by his lapels in a crowd. I let go. He adjusted his clothes, the suit with Felix the Cat on the label. "If the jury bought Joey's sob story, it's the draw," I said. "It happens. If Joey bought the jury, it's news. How much?"

"C'mon, Connie. Nobody fixes the feds."

"In nineteen twenty, Arnold Rothstein bribed the Coast Guard on Long Island to help him unload twenty thousand cases of Scotch smuggled from Europe. Everybody fixes everybody, Mouse."

"My friend made a mistake, what can I tell you? Seen my card?"

I took it from his hand. It was engraved in shiny black ink on heavy gray stock and read:

DANIEL MOSKOVITCH

ARRANGEMENTS

There was a telephone number in the lower right-hand corner.

"When did you get a phone?"

"It's in a booth in the Federal Building. See you there sometime, Connie." And with a broken-field maneuver Knute Rockne would have appreciated, he ducked around me and took off at a rattling clip down the marble hall, holding down his hat.

So Mouse had found his lever.

I gave it the college try. I tracked Orville Cranston to his base of operations in the Book-Cadillac Hotel, Jack Dance's old stamping ground, but the desk clerk said he'd checked out. Information gave me the number of his firm in Washington, D.C., and I left a dozen messages with a receptionist who sounded like Old Virginny, but he never returned the calls. With the help of the city directory and a Michigan Bell employee who sometimes sold me unlisted numbers, I established contact with four of the jurors. Two hung up on me when they guessed what I was after, I took a secretary to dinner who put on her glasses to read the menu and squinted at me the rest of the time and finally admitted she'd changed her verdict at the last minute so she could be home in time to hear "Amos 'n' Andy," and I was talking on the telephone to the fourth party on my list and not making any progress, when a twenty-four-year-old lawyer with a firm that specialized in class action suits walked into the office and snapped open an injunction under my nose ordering me to cease harassing his twelve clients. Since the *Banner* and the Continental News Syndicate were included in the order and subject to the same penalties for refusal to comply, Howard Wolfman invited me into his office and asked me in his mild albino way to find something else to write about.

While all this was happening, Joey Machine, having whipped the United States Government, had turned his attention to winning back the East Side. Within ten days of his acquittal, two stores in the Black Bottom with policy rooms in back were firebombed, a barbershop that specialized in hair-straighteners and the book on the Windsor racetracks was invaded and its clientele clubbed bloody with pistol barrels and baseball bats, and two men walked into the bedroom of a palatial apartment over a rib joint on Harper and fired seventeen bullets into a colored numbers boss named Big Nabob and his companion, a blonde who had formerly taught home economics at the Merrill-Palmer Institute. He died instantly, she expired at Detroit Receiving Hospital an hour later without regaining consciousness.

Big Nabob, born John Thomas, had enjoyed a loud reputation for a Negro underworld figure, renowned for his wide-brimmed white felt hats, gold front tooth, and the rose and pink and lavender silk suits with which he draped his six-foot-six-inch, four-hundred-pound frame, as well as for his custom cream-colored Cadillac with stone marten seats and solid gold fittings. He had gotten his start as a bouncer in a pool hall on Hastings, served a two-year bit in Jackson for manslaughter after belly-walloping a belligerent Negro customer through a plate-glass window and down two stories to his death, then became a policy collector. From that position he furnished statements of earnings and other useful information to Joey Machine, who had just begun to take an interest in numbers. As a reward for meritorious service, Big Nabob was given the management of the lucrative Hastings Street franchise by Joey after the Machine mob muscled in, along with a junior partnership in the policy business for the entire Black Bottom for continuing to protect the interests of the Mechanic, as the owner of the Acme Garage was known to the Negro population. The gold tooth and custom Cadillac followed, and wherever Big Nabob went he was surrounded by colored bodyguards nearly as large as he.

Joey's trouble with the government changed things. The rumor in the Bottom ran that the Mechanic was going to prison; war threatened among the dispossessed black policy bosses for the territory that had been snatched from them when the whites moved in. Another rumor had Big Nabob meeting with representatives of Frankie Orr to request the support of the Unione Siciliana in maintaining his hold on Hastings. The giant Negro was seen dining in his back booth in the rib place with three Mediterranean-looking men, among them Leo Campania, the Unione torpedo whose corpse was later dumped like a bundle of newspapers on the doorstep of the Griswold House. And now Big Nabob himself was riding in the backseat of the bus to Paradise, his bodyguards having made themselves as scarce as five big men in striped suits and sunburst ties can get.

Detroit hadn't heard the last of him, however. Three days later, while police were still half-heartedly questioning witnesses and suspects in the homicide, Big Nabob's funeral procession rolled east on Monroe from the Second Baptist Church to Gratiot and south on Mt. Elliott to the cemetery, led by a white Packard hearse containing the king-size casket, bronze with platinum handles under a mound of red and white roses, with the Cadillac behind it carrying his widow Esther and three hulking brothers—his former collectors—trailing a string of Lincolns, LaSalles, and sixteen-cylinder Auburns that held up traffic for nineteen blocks. The graveside ceremony, performed by the Reverend Otis R. R. Idaho, pastor of Second Baptist and a flamboyant figure in his own right in robes of yellow and purple satin, invoked Christ's mercy for the soul of the departed while placing an order for hellfire on the heads of his slayers and included rollicking renditions of "What a Friend We Have in Jesus" and "Praise God, From Whom All Blessings Flow," led by a white-robed female choir and accompanied by a Dixieland band in derbies and frogged coats. Rumors that the Black Legion planned to disrupt the proceedings proved false, but Big Nabob's brothers carried sawed-off shotguns to the graveside, in case they didn't. If the obsequies didn't cost quite as much as the Dardanello send-off of 1925, it outdid that Catholic service in flash and volume. Even the police, normally quick to put down anything that looked like a show of force among the Negro netherworld, maintained its distance.

It was news, and although the dead man's color kept it on an inside page, the *Banner* sent a reporter. I turned down the assignment. I had already attended one funeral more than I cared to, when Bass Springfield was buried at the end of June.

The movies prefer rain when someone is put under, black umbrellas and sodden flowers. In life, funerals are saddest under bright sunshine, when everywhere you look you're reminded of the day the dead missed. Of the seventeen people who attended the graveside service, one was the minister, an assistant of Reverend Idaho's, one was the funeral director, six were professional pallbearers, and two were gravediggers. The mourners included Celestine Brown, her baby, Vivian Dance, Tom Danzig, and me. Jack wasn't there because two other men were, parked in a gunmetal Cord on Mt. Elliott across from the cemetery; it was the same car that had followed me from the Guardian Building the night I delivered Joey Machine's fifty thousand dollars to Springfield's apartment until I lost it at Grand Circus Park.

Celestine, wearing a plain black dress and hat without a veil, held the baby wrapped in a blanket on her lap in a folding chair and looked straight at the minister as he read from St. John:

" 'A woman when she is in travail hath sorrow, because her hour is come; but as soon as she is delivered of the child, she remembereth no more the anguish, for joy that a man is born into the world.' "

I had brought Celestine there. As we turned away from the casket, eight hundred dollars' worth of simple black oak, paid for by Jack along with the rest of the funeral, Vivian asked if she and Tom could take her back to Crystal Street. I looked at Celestine, who nodded. They started toward the LaSalle with the baby. Tom and I followed more slowly. He was wearing a tan felt fedora and blue serge double-breasted. His face had aged, pulled tight to the bone; his sandy hair had begun to glitter at the temples. He couldn't have been more than thirty.

"How many does this make?" he asked as we walked.

"Killings? I'd have to check. City Hall isn't providing a tally this year."

"Now he's killing his own."

"Jack didn't do this," I said.

"Didn't he?"

"Springfield knew his chances. He wasn't stupid. He wasn't Jack's slave."

"We're all his slaves. What are you?"

"A journalist."

"Bullshit. You're Jack's satellite, just like the rest of us. We think we're going our own way when all we're doing is turning in his orbit. You dropped everything to deliver that ransom."

"I got a story out of it."

"You'd still have done it if Joey hadn't let you write about it at all. You justify your part in all this because you think you're a nonparticipating observer, when the truth is you'd do anything Jack asked you to."

"What about you?"

"I'm a satellite too. I said that."

We had reached the LaSalle. My Viking was parked behind it, its new front fenders and radiator gleaming a little brighter than the rest of the car; the accident with the Dodge Main worker had set me back two hundred dollars. Tom opened the doors on the passenger's side of the LaSalle for the women. After shutting them in he said, "Sometimes he doesn't even *have* to ask. Like what you did for him when he killed Lew Welker."

"You know about that?"

"I was there when he killed him. I'm the one who suggested he put that cartridge in Lew's mouth and sew his lips shut, as a message. Remember, we were both still working for Joey then."

He looked for my reaction. His eyes were like Jack's and yet not, darker and less open, as if the things Jack did that had no effect on him were reflected in his brother's eyes: Pictures in the attic to Jack's Dorian Gray. "See, we'll all do handstands to earn a pat on the head from Jack. We will for as long as he lives."

The moment went, as they will. When it did we shook hands and got into our cars. The gray Cord remained at the curb a few seconds after the cars pulled away, as if in indecision, then moved out behind the LaSalle.

Chapter Twenty-Nine

One night last week my telephone rang at eleven o'clock and I awoke convinced it was Jack, dead these eight years. It turned out to be a drunk looking for someone named Angie and the conversation was over in fifteen seconds, but I sat up and smoked and listened to the radio for half an hour before I was ready to go back to sleep.

I can count on one thumb the occasions when a call that had anything to do with Jack Dance came in any other time than between 11:00 P.M. and 2:00 A.M. They were his optimum hours, during which his considerable energy glowed brightest, as if he were one of those tropical flowering plants that bloom by moonlight, closing their petals at the first rays of the sun, although Jack never closed his until the end. He rarely apologized for the hour even though it always meant getting up and dressing and going out to do something illegal for him in some unlikely place; the implication was that I was somehow at fault for not being ready to go and waiting for his summons. This was the Jack Dance egocentric theory of the universe and its laws were inviolate.

As it happened, I was awake, and dressed after a fashion, when he called me the last time. It was a sweaty night toward the end of August, too hot to sleep, too thick to get up and do anything, and I was lying in the dark, the thought of the heat of the sixty-watt bulb in the lamp on the nightstand unbearable, in my pants and undershirt and bare feet, handling a Chesterfield between thumb and forefinger like Peter Lorre, to keep it from getting too greasy to burn and trying not to touch flesh to flesh. The jangling of the bell was a welcome interruption and a cool sound, like chimes stirred by a breeze you could neither hear nor feel. The metal of the earpiece and standard felt cool for a few seconds.

"Hot enough for you, Connie?"

"That's beneath you, Jack."

"You ought to take a drive, crank down the windows and move some air."

"As for instance where?"

"The Griswold House."

That cooled me off. "Nix," I said. "Count me out."

"You ain't heard what I got."

"Doesn't matter. We had this conversation, remember? Just before Springfield got it. Besides, I don't go near the Griswold. The Griswold isn't in my world anymore."

"You mean on account of what happened to Clyde Norman there? Hell, that wasn't nothing. Did I ever tell you what Joey did to Arny D'Agostino?"

"It's too hot to swap stories. Get somebody else."

"I don't trust nobody else."

"Call your brother."

"This don't involve Joey. It's something on the side. Case dough. That fifty grand had wings, it's gone. Now I got to buy—"

"I don't want to hear it."

Long pause. Music. Glen Gray. The Casa Loma Stomp. "Okay, Connie. I won't bother you again."

The next day a messenger came to the *Banner* and handed me a package wrapped in brown paper the size of a pack of cigarettes. Jensen, stuck for an idea at his drawing board, watched me undo the string and pluck a brass-jacketed pistol cartridge out of a box stuffed with cotton. "Advice from a fan?" he asked.

"More like a mortgage-burning." I looked at it for a while and put it in a pocket.

It was Andy Kramm, a year later when he was in the Wayne County Jail awaiting transportation to Jackson to begin an eighteen-month sentence for armed robbery, who told me about Jack's big thing, the one I'd turned down.

"I'd do anything for dough, that's what everybody thinks," Andy said. "That's how come the jury was only out forty-five minutes on this piece of shit. But I didn't want the best part of that one. I took a vacation, went up to Seney to do a little fishing. Didn't catch nothing unless you count saving my own life, which I do. I guess you could say I quit. Jack said no sweat and got Vern Scalia. That's how come it was the harelip and not me in that apartment later with Jack and Lon. You remember that kid Frankie Orr had with Sal Borneo's daughter, what did they name him, Pasquale?"

"Sure." The baby had been born in August after a five-month pregnancy and weighed less than two pounds. I'd consumed larger steaks.

"They had him in an incubator at St. Mary's with about a fifty-fifty chance to live, a hunnert to one against without the incubator. Funny, ain't it, the way they give odds at hospitals? I bet the East Side book was hot on that one. Anyway, Jack's idea was to call up Frankie and remind him how someone could accidentally kick out the plug on one of them incubators. A new father'd pay fifty grand for information like that, he figured."

"That's dirty even for Jack."

"You don't believe me?"

"I'd believe anything of Jack."

"You knew him better than most, then. Let me ask you something. Why do you figure we liked that guy so much?"

"You tell me."

"It was something Jack told me himself. When he and Vivian was honeymooning in Atlantic City, they bought tickets on a ride called the Hammer. It was shaped like that, with the handle attached to this forty-foot tower and they strapped you inside the head part, then twirled it up and around, faster and faster each time. Jack said you could feel your face flatten out as you swung up to the top, then hung there a second, then tipped forward and down, wham! like somebody swinging a hammer. He said it scared the shit out of you, you couldn't wait till it was over, but after it was over you wanted to go again. How'd you feel when you found out he was dead?"

"First I was relieved. Then I was sorry."

"Me too. I been thinking on it a lot lately, and I think that's what Jack was doing, taking that ride for us over and over, scaring the shit out of us but making us want him to take it again so we didn't have to. We was glad it was over, but that didn't last."

It didn't satisfy me at first. Two summers later, when Dillinger was haring across the Midwest, knocking down banks and hick police department arsenals and getting more press than FDR, I decided there was some truth in Andy's theory. But by then Andy was dead too.

"Why'd he hold up Frankie?" I asked. "What happened to the fifty thousand Joey paid him for Barberra?"

"He didn't tell you?"

"He just said it was gone."

"Jack gave every penny of it to Vivian. She was the one paid Rabinowitz to spring him from that Connor rap. He never took nothing from her he didn't pay back, you can say that much about Jack. He killed little girls and threatened little babies but he wasn't no pimp."

"Did Frankie pay?"

"Let me tell you something about having kids. This comes from somebody that never had one so you're talking to an expert. They cut your balls off. I know that don't make sense, you got to have balls to make a kid. But after you make one you might as well hang them over his crib to play with for all the good they do you. If you snatched the old Frankie, the Conductor, the guy that iced Vinnie Cool on the train in New York, if you snatched him and stuck a knife in his belly and offered to let out three yards of gut if he didn't give you ten bucks, he'd spit in your face, and if you went ahead and did it, he'd use the gut to strangle you with. But this wasn't the Conductor Jack was dealing with, it was Papa Orr, whose kid Pasquale was his ticket to the twenty-first century. Did he pay? You bet he paid, and with a Unione guard ringed three deep around the incubator. That's why them Sicilians never kill family. They don't want to set a precedent."

"Would Jack have pulled the plug?"

"Search me. Search him too. That's why I never played cards with Jack. He wouldn't know if he was bluffing."

"How much of this is guesswork and how much do you know? I mean about Frankie paying the ransom."

"You was in that apartment, you saw what was there. You know why he needed the money?"

"I know," I said.

It was Hattie who told me, that night in September, almost three weeks after my last telephone conversation with Jack. She was waiting for me in the lobby of the Parker Block, in a light summer dress and a patch of a hat pinned to the side of her head and one of those mysteries of engineering, a pair of shoes held on by only a strap across the back of the heel; the first time in years I'd seen her in street clothes. She had asked the doorman to call up for me.

"Why didn't you come up?" I asked.

"Sure. 'Fallen Dove Visits *Banner.*' Your boss did me up good the last time I had anything to do with this rag. I got closed down for three weeks."

"Before my time. Listen, I'm sorry about that thing in your place that night. I had a shock."

"We're there to be made love to and kicked around. But you have to pay for the privilege." She was minding her language in the doorman's presence.

"Who's watching the store?" It was past dark out. Hours after the evening edition hit the streets, I'd been upstairs tinkering with the column I'd started months earlier, about the Black Bottom. The new version started with a comparison between the funerals of John "Big Nabob" Thomas and Bass Springfield.

"Johnston is. I'm not here to be social, Connie. Where can we talk?"

I led her back into the elevator and closed the cage. The building was almost deserted at that hour. Her makeup looked blotchy in the light of the yellow overhead bulb. It would have looked blotchy anyway. I wondered if she was sick.

"Jack's going to get himself killed," she said.

"Do you know what a chase is?" I asked.

"What?"

"I don't mean two guys running after each other. It's a kind of frame you screw together to lock the type in place when you're going to print something. We've had one ready to go for months, a headline. It's upstairs, I can show it to you. It says 'Jack Dance Dead.' All we need is the details."

"I mean he's going to get himself killed tonight. He and Lon Camarillo and that harelip are going to hit the Acme Garage."

"Did he tell you that?"

"What's it matter who told me? Men always think they can talk in front of whores, like we're priests or doctors or something and won't pass it on. It isn't true."

"What do you want me to do?"

"Stop him. He'll listen to you. You're the most levelheaded guy he knows. He told me that once."

"I'm not sure we're still speaking to each other."

I don't know why I was doing that to Hattie. No, that's a lie, I did too. In that way I was worse than Jack, who as bad as he got never did anything out of malice. Levelheaded guy, my ass. I was all jacked up—

Jacked up, yeah—because a whore I thought I knew had slept with someone I liked, just because of that, like some kid. She knew it, too. A sheet of contempt came down behind her made-up face. She slipped a hand between my thighs.

"Please, Connie."

I took her wrist and shoved it back at her. I tasted bile, as if I'd just caught a whiff of myself. "What makes you think he'll be killed?"

"Because if I know, Joey knows. I'll tell you who told me. It was that harelip Vern Scalia. He's got a fat mouth for a kid. They've got a police car and uniforms and they're going to go in like it's a raid, like Capone's boys did in Chicago. Only they're not going to kill Joey, they're going to take him and ransom him back to his mob just like Stink Barberra. Jack told Scalia it's better that way, make him look like a sap in front of the whole town. Worse than killing him. Connie, it's nuts. It must be all over the East Side by now."

"Take it easy. Where is Jack?"

"The Collingwood Apartments. It's at Collingwood and Twelfth. I don't know what room. Scalia didn't say."

"When did he say they're doing it?"

"I don't know. Any time now. Connie, the apartments are too far. Can you head them off at the garage?"

"What with, my press card?"

"Call the bulls. If he sees them, he'll back off."

"Joey's expecting them to come dressed like bulls. I cover bloodbaths, I don't start them. I'll swing by the garage, see if there's any activity. If it doesn't look like they're expecting the Kaiser I'll call the bulls."

"Thanks, Connie." She kissed me. Not exactly like an aunt, but not like someone who'd proposed to me either, a thousand years ago.

"If I get anywhere, you know it's just a stay of execution," I said. "Can you see Jack as an old man? Hell, can you see him thirty?"

"It's just the knowing. I wish Scalia hadn't said anything. I wish I hadn't heard him. Hurry, Connie." She pulled open the cage.

"Go back to your place. Jack can add. If he sees you, he might do something wild even for him."

We'd had some rain. The streets were shiny and reflected the buildings with their lighted windows to an incredible depth, so that the Viking seemed to be cruising along ten stories in the air. Approaching Griswold from Congress, I killed my lamps in the last block, glided over to the curb, switched off the ignition, and coasted to a stop so the brake lights wouldn't come on. I could see part of the garage from there, the big sliding doors and yellow ACME flaking off the bricks above them. It seemed quiet. I didn't know how a gang stronghold under siege looked.

After a minute or so I got out and walked around the corner, my hat on the back of my head and my hands in plain sight, but I hoped swinging naturally; I was trying hard to look the exact opposite of what I imagined a street soldier looked like on his way to do something nasty. Sometime later when I was telling the story to Doug Keenan in the House of All Nations, he asked me to demonstrate. When I did, turning around at the end of the aisle to the men's room and walking back, he shook his head and bought me a drink and said if I ever walked into the *Free Press* Building looking like that, the security guard would have plugged me on sight.

Nobody plugged me that night, and I went on to the next corner where there was a telephone booth and dropped in a nickel and dialed the number of the police department. From there I had a full view of the front of the garage when the big door opened, pushed by a man in a hat and unseasonable topcoat. The long gray Cord rolled out and stopped, blocking the sidewalk, while the man slid the door back the other way on its track and got in on the passenger's side in front. Then the car turned right and headed north on Griswold with a gargle of exhaust.

I saw a lot in that thirty seconds. When the garage was open I saw Joey at the desk in the glassed-in office he was using while his headquarters upstairs was being bulletproofed, and the man who was sitting in there with him; and when the car door opened and the overhead domelight winked on I saw the driver's face under the curled brim of his hat, his pouchy eyes and the exploded veins in his cheeks and the sagging mouth, and because senses have memories I smelled garlic. There were two more men seated in back.

"Police."

I hung up. A Checker cab came up the street with its light on just as I left the booth and I hailed it. The two-minute walk to my car would have cost me five blocks.

"Collingwood and Twelfth," I told the driver, climbing in. "Show me what this thing will do."

Chapter Thirty

All the way up Twelfth I thought, *so Joey doesn't know.*

Because if he had the word Jack Dance was coming, he wouldn't be sending the troops away from him, taking the chance the two carloads of shooters would pass each other on the street and leave him open in the garage. Because the cheap son of a bitch wouldn't spend the gas if he knew all he had to do was wait and they would come to him. A whore knew, but Joey didn't. There was some significant higher meaning in that, something cosmic, but whatever it might have been was shunted aside by another thought, more basic: *You stupid shit, why didn't you talk to the police when you had them on the phone*?

Another easy one. For the same reason a friend I once had, forced to use the fire escape in just his shorts when his apartment caught fire, remembered he'd left his wallet in his pants and climbed back up and found the pants on the floor under the smoke and took his wallet out of the pocket and then tossed the pants back into the flames. When you're running on instinct there is no room in your head for more than one thought at a time.

The apartment building was typical of Northwest Detroit, neat, placid-looking, and built of brick and wrought iron. When pictures of it appeared in the papers the next day it would look sinister with all those arrows and dotted lines and a big black Maltese cross on the window of the room where it happened, but when I first saw it, it was just another building on a quiet street scores of blocks and a world away from Smugglers' Alley, Robbers' Roost, and the unsavory things that happened there. The Cord was nowhere in sight. Well, the hurry for them wouldn't be on the way *there.* I paid the driver and went inside.

In the small neat foyer, lit by an overhead fixture, I felt the icy wave that usually preceded paralysis. I didn't want to be in the building when the others came. The cab had passed a telephone booth two blocks back; if I could find out the number of the apartment I could go back and call the manager's office and be put through. There was a bank of brass mailboxes in the wall to the right of the door. I skimmed the nameplates. The name I wanted, which would be fictitious, would have been added recently, written on a piece of paper and taped in place. Jack would do that even though he wouldn't be getting mail, to avoid making the neighbors suspicious.

I don't remember what the name was. I had just come to it when I heard the first shot. When it's a shot, you always know it from a backfire or a heavy book dropped on a bare floor; it fills your head and rings afterward. There were two, spaced a half-second apart and very loud inside the walls, then a short silence, then a cluster of them, *bammity-bam-bam*, then another pause, then one more, final, isolated in a deliberate void like the slam of a door.

I forgot about being paralyzed and started up the stairs. The light was out over the stairwell. I had just time to think that lights don't stay out in nice buildings, that someone must have loosened the bulb deliberately, when suddenly I was no longer alone. He thundered down straight at me, filling the well with thumping footsteps and rustling clothes. Something struck my left shoulder hard, an open hand, and I spun, half-voluntarily, back-first to the wall, eyes shut tight. *This is it*, I thought. *Your last second.* Then he brushed past, breathing hoarsely and smelling of mothballs and adrenaline-sweat and something else, something burned, and down to the bottom of the stairs and around to the back of the building. A door slammed for real. More slams outside that could have been mistaken for gunshots any other time, then a motor roared and gears farted and tires chirped. The engine sound faded as it changed pitch to second and third. Then silence, bottomless and profound.

The tenants were starting to gather in the upstairs hallway, blinking, tying robes. A door stood open halfway down, leaking out light and blue fog. When I got to it, the stench of charred sulphur and cordite parched my nostrils, a hundred times stronger than it had smelled coming off the man on the stairs. The air was hazy.

It was an unfinished room, smelling of paint, with newspapers spread on the floor and a five-gallon bucket trailing threads of medium blue down its sides into a congealed puddle at its base, half-covering a picture of the *Graf Zeppelin.* The furniture was draped in sheets. Lon Camarillo sprawled across a covered overstuffed chair with a blue hole in the center of his forehead and his chin pointed at the ceiling. Both his hands twitched in his lap. Vern Scalia lay half on his stomach on the floor just inside the door, the back of his white shirt pierced in three places and caked; exit wounds, the coroner declared later. His right arm was extended within a foot of Lon's Browning Automatic Rifle leaning in the corner by the door, which was as close as he had gotten when someone whose shoeprint showed clearly in the blood on Scalia's shirt planted a foot between his shoulderblades and fired point-blank at the back of his head. Of the two, Lon being the experienced killer, trained in France by the army and at home by the Mafia, only the harelip had gone out fighting.

Jack wasn't there.

There was an angry patch of blood on one of the newspapers on the floor an equal distance from Scalia and Lon, whose hands had stopped twitching. I stepped into the room for a closer look. I saw a partial palmprint. From it a trail of spatters led crookedly to a door on the far side of the room, smeared in two places where the bleeder had fallen, then pushed himself back up. I went that way, laid my hand on the door. It opened to my touch. A long way off I heard sirens and the first police gonger.

The room was dark. I groped for the wall switch, pressed it. It was a small bedroom with twin beds, unmade, separated by a wooden nightstand, its only window directly above the stand. I saw my reflection in it. The light was coming from a lamp that had occupied the stand until it had been knocked over onto one of the beds, its shade tipped so that the bulb was shining directly into my eyes. The trail led between the beds.

I moved out of instinct. I know I didn't have time to put it together. As the Ballistics crew worked it out later, the bullet missed my head by two inches, splintering the doorframe and burying itself in the plaster wall on the other side of the room I had just left. I don't even remember hearing the shot, although my ears rang most of the next day. I banged my elbow throwing myself sideways to the floor, and that bothered me more and longer.

"That you, Stink?"

He sounded raw. The bed on the right was between us. I couldn't see him.

"Jack, it's me, Connie."

Nothing. The sirens were still many blocks away. I could hear the alarm clock ticking on the nightstand.

After a long time—probably no more than two minutes—I dragged myself toward the bed. "Connie Minor, Jack. Remember?"

When more time had passed I got my knees under me and peered over the mattress. He was down between the beds out of sight. I heard something else now besides the clock and the sirens: A sawing, as of breath dragging in and out and bubbling slightly on the intake.

I stood up.

He lay on his side almost under the other bed. He was wearing his vest and shirtsleeves and what I thought was a dark red tie until the light caught it as he inhaled and I saw blood bubbling out of a hole in his chest. His right arm was stretched out with his Luger at the end of it. It was cocked and pointing at my groin.

"Jack, it's Connie."

He didn't hear me. I saw his grin, saw his finger whiten on the trigger. Then it relaxed. "Connie?"

"Lie still, Jack. Help's coming."

"Connie?" he said.

"Yeah, Jack."

"Shit, Connie."

"Yeah, Jack."

He let his hand fall with the pistol in it. I knelt beside him and got a hand under his head. He'd been hit in the stomach too, and once in each leg. He started to say something a couple of minutes later, then coughed up a cup of blood. He didn't try again and by the time the first of the uniforms came into the apartment he had died.

The room seemed larger without him in it. I lowered his head to the floor and got up. On the wall opposite the beds, where the light would strike it when the sun came up in the morning, hung the painting of the girl praying beneath the crucifix.

Something was different. I didn't think the change would be that sudden, and it took me a while to figure out what it was. The apartment was quiet, there was no music. Later when the bulls drew the sheet off a cabinet radio in the living room they found that a bullet had smashed a tube. Up to then it had been tuned to Kay Kyser's Kollege of Musical

Knowledge on NBC. The loud music had drowned out the killers' approach.

They found other things as well. In addition to Lon Camarillo's B.A.R. and Jack's Luger, the arsenal in the apartment included a Thompson submachine gun believed to have been Andy Kramm's with two extra fifty-round magazines, fully loaded; Bass Springfield's heavy Colt automatic pistol without a trigger guard; two Smith & Wesson revolvers; and a sawed-off Remington pump shotgun, all cleaned and loaded and lined up on the counter in the little kitchen off the living room. The shotgun's discarded barrels and a hacksaw turned up in a trash can behind the building, wrapped in newspaper. The search also uncovered three unissued Detroit police uniforms hanging in a closet and, in the drawer of the nightstand, a pink slip made out to a J. Danzig for a 1930 Oldsmobile touring car like the ones the police used. The car itself was eventually discovered, complete with a new black-and-white paint job and a growler on the running board, in a garage on Woodrow Wilson that had gone out of business in March.

I had just come out of the bedroom when the uniforms entered with guns drawn. I let them throw me up against the wall and pat me down. When Chief Kozlowski showed up, they had heard enough from the neighbors to turn their backs on me. The chief's Palm Beach suit had continued to conform to his frame in the three months since I'd seen him and had grown as wrinkled and discolored as his hat. He looked at me sitting on the sheet-covered sofa and scratched the mole between his eyes. "How come whenever a stiff turns up, you're there too?"

"Jack called me tonight and invited me over for an interview. This is what I found."

"Horseshit. Your timing ain't that good. Try again."

"Okay, a dame told me. You can take me to the basement at Thirteen Hundred and the only name you'll get out of me is mine. You can sell her to the papers as the Mystery Woman."

"Quit fucking me over, Minor. I like the interview story better."

"Looky here, Chief." A swarthy plainclothesman I remembered from the Ferry warehouse had been poking around inside the paint bucket with the stir stick and lifted it out with a .32 revolver dangling from its trigger guard on the end, blue paint dripping in threads off the barrel.

"Smart. These sonsabitches don't take chances getting nailed with the tools. Keep fishing." He reached down, grabbed a handful of Vern Scalia's fair hair, and lifted up his face. "Hello, Harelip. Finally sold yourself out, did you?" He hung on for a moment as if waiting for an answer, then let the face drop and stepped over the body to examine Lon. "Nice shot. He's looking a little healthier these days."

"In there's the rest of it." I jerked my thumb over my shoulder.

Kozlowski went into the bedroom and came out a few minutes later. "Shit. What're we going to do for fun around here now?"

"That's just what Jack said."

"What'd he say?"

"Shit."

"He say anything else?"

"He took a shot at me and asked me if I was Stink."

"Deathbed statement," he told the other plainclothesman, who nodded and went on with his task. He had fished a second gun out of the bucket and laid it on one of the newspapers next to the first. Kozlowski looked back at me. "Neighbors said one of 'em ran the wrong way, down the front stairs. See him?"

"Not his face."

"Big man?"

"They're all big."

"Not by my ruler. Smell him, maybe?"

"It wasn't Barberra."

More detectives had arrived. One of them opened the closet and whistled at the three uniforms hanging inside. Kozlowski, who had gone into the kitchen to check out the guns, came out and looked in the closet.

"Looks like they had something in the hopper," he said to me. "Looks like it was tonight. It don't look like they was fixing to give no interviews."

"I told you it was a mystery woman."

He mangled his stogie a moment. "You scribes all think you're shockproof and water-proof. What if we book you as an accessory?"

"Then you lose your deathbed statement."

"Listen here, you butt-fucking Greek." He leaned his face inches from mine, the hot tip of his cigar aimed at my right eye. "Didn't think I knew about that, did you, Broncho Billy? I got more whores owe me favors than Joey Machine's got whores. I took heat before for playing hard hockey, I can take more. Maybe they junk me back down to lieutenant, put me back with the Prohibition Squad or in charge of nigger killings, but you'll be the one pissing blood."

My eyes were starting to water. I sat back.

"You're looking for a gray Cord." I gave him the license number. "Barberra was driving. He had three men with him."

"Got that?" he asked the swarthy plainclothesman, who nodded again. He had salvaged the last of three revolvers from the paint bucket. "Get it out to the state police. I want uniforms at every train station too. He ain't going to be in Philly for this one." When the man went out, Kozlowski straightened. "You got something under your hat besides your ass, Minor. I was worried about you for a while."

"Fuck you."

"Scribes. Climb our asses when you think we ain't doing our job and then when we do, you say fuck you. I wasn't the one made that sack of shit Dance look like Jesus. You done that."

"If you did your job more often, maybe I wouldn't have had to. Maybe you'd be Jesus."

"I get it. You're clean. It's the rest of the town that's shitty."

When I looked down I could see the outline of the Luger cartridge in my pants pocket. I carried it every day now. "I'm not clean," I said. "The difference is I know it."

"I'd sure as hell hate to have to live on the difference."

The lab crew came next to dust the doorknobs and sweep the floor, and after them came the press to take pictures of the guns on the counter and on the floor bleeding paint on the newspapers and of the bodies being rolled out the door and to ask Kozlowski if he thought the Dance gang would counter-attack.

"You're looking at the Dance gang," he said. "All except Kramm, and he ain't got the balls."

At the morgue they took the sheet down to Jack's waist so the photographers could snap him with his scrubbed wounds showing and his hair plastered back the way it never was in life and the tag on his toe identifying him as the 77th corpse that had been logged in that year and the bulls standing around the table with their hats shoved back and their hands on their hips displaying their bellies and the butts of their revolvers, like big game hunters posing with the skin and claws of the tiger they'd killed. None of them realized it wasn't Jack Dance on the table, just the package he came in; the 180-pound body that his crackling energy walked around in to avoid blinding us all. Wherever that energy had gone when the body became useless, it was probably grinning.

Chapter Thirty-One

Late last summer—August 5, 1939, if that's specific enough for these proceedings—a Mrs. Janet McDonald, divorcee, pulled her car into her garage, closed the door, ran a hose from the tailpipe through a hole in a window into the car, and went to sleep with her daughter Pearl, aged eleven, beside her on the front seat. Within two days of the murder-suicide, copies of a letter bearing Mrs. McDonald's signature were delivered to all the Detroit newspapers and to authorities at the city, state, and federal levels. It read:

> On this night, a girl has ended her life because of the mental cruelty caused by Racketeer William McBride, ex-Great Lakes Numbers House operator. McBride is the go-between man for Lieut. John McCarthy.
>
> He arranges the fix between our dutiful Lieut. and the Racketeers.
>
> Should you care to learn more of this story, get in touch with McBride through Ryan's bookie, 222 Lafayette Street West; Phone Clifford 1572.
>
> He glories in telling lies, so don't believe everything he tells you, as I did.
>
> Janet McDonald

The sob sisters got a lot of play out of the tragic plight of this woman scorned, who evidently held that her daughter had been wronged as deeply, hence the decision to take her along; I can only imagine what a pro like Andrea St. Charles would have done with it if she'd lived to write about it. Meanwhile there was the expected public outcry, the expected raids on bookie parlors citywide, the expected interrogations, and the expected exoneration of McCarthy, head of the Detroit Rackets Squad, by his superiors. But the newspapers pressed for deeper action, and within three weeks of Janet McDonald's suicide, a one-man grand jury was appointed to probe accusations of widespread corruption in the police department. Despite the almost exclusively Irish nature of this alleged conspiracy—McCarthy had begun his career in law enforcement under the political patronage of Big Jim Dolan, the Irish Pope, dead in 1937 of a cerebral hemorrhage—its slow uncovering during testimony led to a panic of resignations throughout the department, among them that of Deputy Commissioner, formerly Chief of Detectives, Valery Kozlowski. He is now presumably caring for his crippled wife and using his rubber truncheon to train stallions on his ranch near Kalamazoo. I miss him in the way you miss the enemy you know, whose dangers and weaknesses are predictably familiar. Perversely, I don't miss the reasonably honest Hermann Gabriel, who took a disability pension and moved to Arizona when the Prohibition Squad was disbanded.

The resignations rocked gangland. Having established prices and a payoff system comfortable to all parties, the vice lords were now forced to begin negotiations all over again with the reform people. Breaking in new partners is always frustrating.

It's no problem of Joey Machine's, however. In 1932, Detroit, having beaten the rest of the nation to the punch by drafting its own law against the manufacture and sale of alcoholic beverages a year before the ratification of the Volstead Act, repeated its boldness by lifting the ban locally twelve months ahead of Repeal. But by then, Joey's monopoly of the policy business on the East Side had cushioned the blow, and in the fall of 1935 he was conducting an aggressive campaign of defense against a brand new charge of federal income tax evasion, this time for the years 1931 through 1934, from his newly bulletproofed headquarters above the Acme Garage when he fell victim to his unvarying weekly routine, the only truly tidy element in his messy, haphazard, miserly life. Monday through Friday found him putting in his daily twelve hours at his desk, taking all his meals in as he counted receipts and kept tabs on the betting with his collectors by telephone; Saturdays he rested at home with his wife in Rochester; Sundays he paid a visit to the house on Sylvester, where the books were kept, to tally the weekend take, always heavy after the Friday payday. The raid by the Treasury Department in 1931 had forced him to install an early-warning system there, and he no longer offered an easy target to boulevard shooters by walking to the corner, using his car instead for errands of twenty blocks to a hundred yards, but every Sunday between 1:00 and 1:10 P.M. he and Dom Polacki and one or more of his accountants drove around the corner to a little walk-up restaurant where he enjoyed his usual plate of pasta and clam sauce washed down with red wine before returning to the books at 2:30.

At 2:24 P.M. Sunday, October 20, Joey was walking down the narrow staircase from the restaurant to the ground floor with Dom and a bookkeeper named Anthony Napolitano when a man standing at the bottom swung a Thompson submachine gun out from under his coat and sprayed thirty-seven bullets up the stairwell. Dom, a fast shooter for his size but not known for his accuracy, got off two shots from the .32 revolver he carried under his right arm without hitting the assailant, who made his escape in a late-model Auburn driven by another man.

Dom Polacki, born Casimir Mischiewicz, was killed instantly when a .45 slug tore through his heart. Napolitano was pronounced dead at Detroit Receiving Hospital with a bullet in his brain. Joey Machine was hit in the chest and stomach but lived for another three hours, babbling deliriously, while a police stenographer sat by his bed at Receiving jotting down his ravings. During the last hour he lapsed into unconsciousness. In one of those ironical twists the press loved, the coroner declared that the shot that actually killed Joey was fired from Dom Polacki's gun—a ricochet.

The transcript of his rambling last comments appeared in all the newspapers the next day. About the only thing in it that made sense was the recurring plea: "Get the kike off my a—."

The killer and his driver were never identified, although both had been seen clearly by several witnesses. It was decided that they had been shipped in from out of town for the job. No arrests were made, but it's widely assumed that Frankie Orr put Joey on the spot, with or without the approval of Sal Borneo, who by then was in semi-retirement after a disabling stroke. Currently, Borneo's attorneys are fighting his indictment on charges of income tax evasion and labor racketeering on grounds that he's too ill to stand trial. The rumor is he's dying, which, if true, will make him the first member of Detroit's organized underworld to expire from natural causes. Meanwhile Frankie—Mr. Oro now, a family man with a slightly undersize eight-year-old boy and a wife who only comes out at weddings and funerals—has been elected unanimously to head the Unione Siciliana. He hasn't garroted or used a steak knife on anyone in a long time, which I count an improvement forced upon him by his new executive status. He pays taxes, has his suits made at the same place that dresses most of the General Motors board of directors, and surrounds himself with bodyguards with college degrees who know how to tie a formal bow and look no more menacing in evening dress than the Detroit Lions at a polio benefit.

Back to 1931. Despite the fact that the serial numbers of the revolvers used in the Collingwood Massacre had been filed off by an expert, the three killers and the man who drove the car away afterward were identified in record time. Inspector Frank Fraley of the Canfield Street station told Kozlowski that eyewitness descriptions at the scene fit two of the three men he had ordered out of the nearby Orlando Hotel the previous night on complaints that they were using their adjoining rooms as an office. He knew them because they had all been guests of the station at one time or another: Irving Milberg, Harry Fleischer, and Henry Keywell. All three were known Purple Gang killers who hired out to all sides in the gutter wars; Fleischer and Keywell were commonly believed to have been among the shooters who carried out the St. Valentine's Day Massacre for Capone. In the early confusion, some of the papers reported that the slaughter was the result of an altercation with members of the Little Jewish Navy, the Purples' archenemy of the moment. The *Banner* got it right from the start, thanks to Walter DiVirgilio's ability to bring coherence to my late-night call to the rewrite desk. The *Times* got it right, too, for reasons I'll go into later.

The warning the state police broadcast over its new radio band said that the suspects in the massacre were "desperate men who would rather shoot it out than submit to arrest." They must not have heard it, because within two days of the event all four, Barberra included, surrendered without resistance when police raided the apartment where they'd been hiding less than twenty blocks from the Collingwood; a neighboring tenant had grown suspicious and tipped off the bulls. The four were relieved of nine pistols and revolvers, several boxes of ammunition, and ten thousand dollars in cash.

The evidence when they came to trial was convincing. Inspector Fraley's claim of having ousted them from the Orlando Hotel suggested that they'd been using it as a base of operations while they cased the Collingwood. Upstairs apartment dwellers who had witnessed the flight of two of the killers down the back stairs picked Stink Barberra and Henry Keywell out of a lineup at headquarters. Under heavy interrogation in the Beaubien basement, Irving Milberg, believed to have been the wheel man, identified Harry Fleischer as the third shooter, the one who had brushed past me on the front stairs. Add to that Jack Dance's dying reference to Barberra, related on the stand by Chief Kozlowski as if he'd been present when it was made, and the traces of garlic the police lab found on all four of the bullets removed from Jack's body, and Wayne County Prosecutor E. Wharton Clay had the strongest case he'd had against anyone since the Sylvester Street shooting, with happier results for justice in the absence of a Nathan Rabinowitz to speak for the defense. (The word in the back rooms was that a grateful Joey Machine, who had not been named by the defendants in interrogation, had tried to enlist Rabinowitz's services in their cause, only to learn that the famed criminal attorney had retired from practice.) After a brief deliberation, the four were convicted of murder and conspiracy to commit murder and sentenced to life imprisonment, a major blow to the Purple Gang's reputation for invincibility and an indication of how thoroughly a public beset by the Depression had grown weary of flashy gangster residue from the dead twenties. The convictions held in appeal.

Of the four, Irving Milberg and Harry Fleischer are serving their terms in the Southern Michigan Penitentiary at Jackson, and Henry Keywell, branded an incorrigible, has been removed to the prison's tougher branch in Marquette in Michigan's rocky Upper Peninsula. George Barberra, after several unsuccessful escape attempts, was transported to Alcatraz in 1936, where last January he and Arthur "Dock" Barker, late of Ma Barker's celebrated family of outlaws, were shot and fatally wounded by guards while preparing to swim to the mainland and freedom. Barker died later in the prison infirmary, but Barberra was dead when they pulled him out of the water.

Vivian Dance, formerly Mrs. Gus Woodbine, née Vivian Louise Deering, married Tom Danzig a year or so after Jack's death, but the marriage didn't take and she went back to Southampton, a divorcée two times over and quasi-notorious gangster's widow—social pariah, thrice married, a woman whose photograph had appeared in newspapers outside the society pages. I lost track of her after that. I hadn't seen her since the night she kissed me getting into a cab in front of a blind pig after Jack's acquittal in the Sylvester Street trial. Maybe she's looking for a pair of scissors to cut Tom's paper. She attended Jack's funeral, of course, but I didn't, although I sent flowers. (A geranium plant, actually, earth-smelling and tough of leaf, which I thought he'd have appreciated.) It would have been like watching them bury an empty can.

The *Banner*, like its fellow Detroit tabloids the *Daily* and the *Mirror*, did not survive Prohibition. It folded at the end of 1933 after a period during which it became a grotesque parody of itself at its lurid peak, as when it offered cash prizes to readers for locating missing parts of a corpse some psychotic had deposited in trunks throughout the city, treating it like a contest. As circulation fell off, I entertained the fantasy that my position as a syndicated columnist would prevent me from going down with it; hadn't I placed first in the 1931 Continental News Syndicate's Excellence in Journalism competition with my five-part series on the Black Bottom? The framed certificate was on the wall next to my desk, I had made a down payment on a new Marmon roadster with the $150 check. But I had failed to take note of the trend when editors began canceling my column, until by the end of my three-year contract with CNS it was appearing in less than a hundred newspapers, with the number going down weekly. Lloyd Bundle bought me lunch at the Statler and informed me that as of August 1, I was free to begin negotiations with other parties. "Very sorry, Minor, but it seems you're associated in the public mind with bootleggers and hijackings and midnight massacres, all that rat-a-tat stuff, and nobody's interested anymore, not even Hollywood. Musicals, that's what they're making now. You might consider moving out there, I hear they need writers. Your stuff would sound great in Dick Powell's mouth." I thanked him for the advice and didn't hit him even once.

On New Year's Eve, 1933, I attended a party in the *Banner* offices to celebrate a fresh deck, Repeal, and the short loud life of a newspaper whose final issue had hit the streets six hours before. Nearing midnight, Howard Wolfman invited me into his office, popped the cork on a bottle of champagne, and filled two glasses. "I bought this just today," he said, setting down the bottle. "My first illegal act, if you don't count libel." He looked buttoned-down as always in his thick sparkling eyeglasses and snug necktie and navy cashmere jacket despite the heat of a malfunctioning radiator; in the city room the female file clerks, inhibitions seriously damaged, had already begun taking off sweaters and shoes and stockings, with more to follow. The scene was being replayed in offices and private homes and restaurants across the city, across the country. The Big Thirst was being slaked after thirteen years, fourteen in Detroit.

I picked up my glass. "I don't think we'll be raided tonight."

"I hope not. I'd have to get out an extra, and I can't pay for the ink." He raised his. "To anything. To truth in journalism, honesty in government, and—what?"

"Absent friends."

"They're all absent." We clicked glasses and drank. It was the first and only time I ever saw him imbibe. Readers and detractors of the *Banner* alike would have been surprised by the neat quiet man behind the splashy headlines, the grainy pictures of corpses in puddles with their eyes blown out.

"What are you going to do?" I asked him.

"A fellow I cubbed with on the Chicago *Daily Journal* is getting up a picture magazine in San Francisco. He wants me to edit it. I'm not sure just how one goes about editing pictures, but I'm broke enough to give it a try."

"He wouldn't by any chance be looking for writers?"

"No one wants writers anymore, Connie. They want photographers and cartoonists. Jensen signed a contract with the *Saturday Evening Post* last week."

"I hope they throw in a year's supply of matches."

"Do you need money? I can get an advance from my friend in San Francisco and arrange a loan."

"Thanks. I've got an interview Tuesday morning with Roberts and Gorman."

"Ad copy?"

"People will always need to sell things."

"We can't all be tabloid writers." He took one more sip and poured the rest of his glass into a potted plant. "I never did understand what people see in this stuff. It wasn't worth a revolution."

"Everything's worth a revolution," I said. "Even revolution."

"See, that's what was wrong with your stuff. You always had to educate people." He stuck out his white hand. "Take care, Connie."

I took it. "Good luck in Frisco."

"I won't need it. It isn't a real town, like Detroit."

I never saw Howard again. I never saw the magazine either. It folded after one issue.

There isn't much left to tell about Jack Dance, the dry time in Detroit, and me. I heard Hattie Long got out of the life after Joey was killed and bought into a legitimate beergarden in Royal Oak; but I said that. I haven't seen her since the night she came to tell me about Jack's insane plan to kidnap Joey Machine right out of the Acme Garage.

That last conversation with Andy Kramm I mentioned took place in the visitor's room at the Wayne County Jail. A boyish-looking thirty-three in denims, with his fair hair combed forward over a thinning widow's peak, his bright blue eyes and thousand-candlepower grin—the one mannerism, I always thought, that Jack borrowed from anyone—he chain-smoked Chesterfields he bummed from me but seemed resigned to his year-and-a-half sentence, if not to the penny-ante nature of the crime of which he'd been convicted, the armed robbery of a service station in Romulus.

"Fifteen bucks and change, that's all there was in the till," he said. "Not even a buck a month for how long I'll be away. That's as many bullets as them bums fired in that room at the Collingwood."

"Why'd you stick it up?"

"Tapped out. There's no money in legging no more, now that they're fixed to make it legal."

"I never thought I'd see the day when a bootlegger would be standing in a breadline."

"You won't, neither. We're crooks, not tramps. Nor Communists," he added quickly. "I'd like to see this bum Stalin try to muscle in on the East Side. There'd be caviar shit all down Mt. Elliott." But his own mention of the Collingwood affair had started him thinking in another direction. "I didn't see you at Jack's funeral last year."

"Would've been spooky if you did. I wasn't there."

"Too bad. It was okay. They kept out the pukes and the press, it was private. First time I had on a yarmulke since my cousin Ray's bar mitzvah. I bet I know why you didn't show up."

I told him my reasons.

"That ain't it," he said. "Not all of it. I bet it was because Tom was there."

"Tom's doing okay. I hear they're going to make him assistant city editor at the *Times*." I was changing the subject.

"He's marrying Vivian, did you hear that?"

"I heard. The town's not that big."

"The bulls thought it was Scalia tipped Joey where they was hid out;

Scalia didn't move fast enough to stay out of the way or Joey double-crossed him, took him out too for turning on Joey in the first place. If he turned on him he'd turn on Jack, that's the way the bulls seen it."

"Kozlowski said he finally sold himself out."

"Kozlowski always was full of shit. They was all full of shit. I know who tipped Joey, and it wasn't Scalia. You do too, I guess."

I said nothing for a moment. The way the police had it figured, Barberra and the others had been using the Orlando Hotel for a jumping-off point until the word came down to hit the Collingwood, only to be interrupted when Inspector Fraley ordered them off the premises, delaying the event twenty-four hours; but I had seen the killers leaving the Acme Garage that night and knew that they had been using the hotel while they scouted the neighborhood, probably on some smoky tip that Jack Dance or one of the others had been seen in that area. They didn't have the specific location until the night of the killing, a location provided by the man I had glimpsed sitting in the fishbowl garage office with Joey Machine. I knew, all right, but I wasn't sure how Andy knew. I asked him. "Who did Jack use to pick up and deliver the ransom for Frankie Orr's baby?"

"His brother, who else you think? Tom fucking Danzig. He brought the fifty grand to the apartment in the Collingwood. He was the only one who knew where Jack was besides Lon and Scalia, because Jack told him. And he was the one who called Joey and told him where he could send his shooters."

"He didn't call," I said. "He went in person. I saw him at the garage that night."

"It explains a lot," Andy said after a moment.

"Yeah, like how the *Times* beat every other paper in town to the street with the story on the massacre. They had the headline all set to go while it was still happening. All they needed was the details."

"The son of a bitch."

"The son of a bitch," I agreed. *We'll all do handstands to earn a pat on the head from Jack,* he had told me as we were leaving Bass Springfield's grave. *We will for as long as he lives.* That's how he'd justify it. I wondered if he thought it covered scooping the rest of Detroit while he was at it on the hottest story of the year, his brother's murder.

I've already reported the rest of what Andy Kramm told me during that visit. From there he was taken to Jackson, where he was released in February 1934 after serving his full term. In April of that year he was reported among the bandits who escaped from the Little Bohemia Lodge in northern Wisconsin with John Dillinger when federal agents opened fire on the building. One month later, exiting a bank in Greencastle, Indiana with two companions and a sack containing eleven thousand dollars in stolen bills and securities, Andy walked into a wall of shotgun, rifle, and pistol fire from a posse made up of local police officers and storekeepers. He was dead before he hit the sidewalk.

For me, like Jack and Springfield and Lon and Joey and Kozlowski and Gabriel and Frankie Orr and Hattie and Vivian and Howard and all the rest of them, all that fading cartoon cast, he's alive somewhere, waving brightly to someone as he did to me while the guard turned him back toward his cell. I stood there smiling faintly back and fingering the object in my pocket, the thing I was never without, worn smoother than any emery wheel could get it and probably too small now to fit snugly in the chamber of any pistol, my rosary, the essential lie of my life, the thing that had sent the stool pigeon Lewis Welker to Purgatory with the taste of brass on his tongue and his killer unpunished. I still have the cartridge, and unless it falls through a hole in my pocket someday or winds up at the cleaners or is just plain misplaced, someone will take it off my body too. It is my own personal exclusive portable drip-dry wash-and-wear no-assembly-required Mark of the Beast.

That's the story, end of column, thirty; and if you think it's been too long in the telling then I've made a bum job of it, because it should seem no more than a brazen moment in time. To feel what we felt, those of us who were there, you had to have been there too, and to have been like us, when the river that glittered on the border between the United States and Canada seemed to match the honey glow of the liquid gold that flowed across it when we were all too young and stupid and full of piss and rotgut to believe for one second that it would ever stop flowing.

Jack had a phrase that covered it:

You should've seen it.

The third day: September 27, 1939

For a moment after he finished, the courtroom hung in time, suspended by the humming of the fan and the little exhalations the shorthand machine made as the recorder palpated the keys. The special prosecutor, looking less like Old Man Prohibition now and more like a young lawyer insulated by marble and mahogany from the street outside, stirred himself from behind his table.

"You've revealed an appalling number of unreported crimes," he said. "Were you afraid of reprisals if you told what you knew?"

"Only if they involved clamming up whenever I entered a room, or not letting me into the room at all. I had to work in this town."

"I don't agree that your rights under the First Amendment regarding a free press include withholding evidence in a murder. Even if I did, I'd have to ask what stopped you from going to the authorities after you left newspapers, when keeping silent was no longer a professional consideration."

"I didn't leave newspapers, counselor; newspapers left me. When Prohibition ended I became a relic, like slave bracelets and F. Scott Fitzgerald. A few years ago, Steele Gilmore at the *News* offered me a Sunday column, one of those old-fart retrospectives: 'On this day in nineteen twenty-five, Clara Bow was appearing in person at the Oriole Terrace, prime rib was eleven cents a pound, and Fat Freddie Gunsberg was discovered floating facedown under a dock in Wyandotte.' I turned him down. I may just be selling toothbrushes and toilet paper now, but at least they're *new* toothbrushes and toilet paper."

"Answer the question, please," said the judge, twitching his eyebrow-feelers.

"What was the point? Jack was dead, Joey was about to be, and Frankie Orr was beyond reach even if I had a corroborating witness to the Norman murder, which I didn't. There was nothing to be gained."

"If that's the way you feel why are you talking now?"

"You're not a journalist. I'm not sure I can explain it so you'll understand."

"Please try."

He leaned forward, folding his hands between his knees and staring at the floor, where curls of varnish had collected at the base of the railing.

"When you know something that nobody else knows, it belongs to you. It's all yours. When you tell it to someone, you take him in as a partner and lose half of it. When he tells somebody, you and he each lose half of the half, and so on, until everybody has a piece and you've got nothing. Then you start to forget."

"From what you've told this grand jury I'd say it's better forgotten," said the special prosecutor. "That will be all for now, Mr. Minor. Please remain available in case it becomes necessary to recall you for further testimony. You should also be aware that a transcript of these proceedings will be handed over to the local authorities after the grand jury has adjourned. It will be up to them whether to pursue criminal indictments against you for withholding evidence and accessory after the fact of murder. You're excused."

"I told you you wouldn't understand," he said.

The air in the hallway smelled different, which is to say it *had* smell; the static institutional odors of waxed linoleum and people waiting on benches. He didn't recognize the other witnesses waiting to be called, but he felt he should have, even if they never raised their eyes except to see who had come out. Well, he'd changed too. At forty-five he was as old as Howard Wolfman had been at the time of the *Banner* wake, older than Joey Machine lived to be. The only suit whose pants he hadn't outgrown was the one he was wearing, the gray worsted he'd bought for meeting advertising clients. He'd been skinny in the old days, a jack-rabbit among rhinos. Funny how you could be lean when times were fat and fat when times were lean. *You need exercise, Connie*, Jack would say. *Get your hat, we'll hop across the river.*

The reporters were on him then, a couple of vaguely familiar faces in the crowd but mostly youngsters, hotshots with their press cards in their hatbands like Pat O'Brien in *The Front Page*, some of whom had probably read his column with a flashlight under the covers, the *Banner* being a parental exile from respectable homes; reading about midnight runs across the ice and gilded flappers in shimmy skirts and young sheiks in tight chinchilla coats and gray fedoras, Fatimas smoking between their lips. "Connie *Minor*? I read him when I was that high to a sock garter. He must be a hundred years old."

"What'd you tell 'em, Connie?"

"They ask you who killed Joey Machine?"

"Turn this way, Connie."

"You tell 'em what you did with Jack the Ripper's Lugers?"

"Who's your tailor, Connie? You look like shit."

No comment, you sons of bitches. Read about it tomorrow. Hear them in the *News* cafeteria later: ". . . so then he says, 'Now that I'm a white man I can't stand you niggers.' That's Minor. Bastard's got the shortest memory this side of Neville Chamberlain."

He almost passed her in the crowd, thin woman, not a sob sister, red-dyed hair in marcels under a cloche hat that emphasized the lines in her face, the skin shrunken to the bone. Harsh makeup, raccoon eyes with big eyebrows that looked as if she traced them on around Mason lids. "Hattie?"

She took his arm, a talon's grip, and they walked around the wainscoted corner. That section of hallway was deserted, paved with toilets and supply closets. Her calves were okay below the below-the-knee skirt; they'd been the least bit thick before and now they were just right. She let go of him, making a reluctant production of it, turned to face him. "You put on some," she said. "It suits you. You always were kind of puny."

"Lanky," he corrected. "Like Bobby Jones. Are you testifying?"

"Next week. I heard they were cutting you loose today."

"Same old Hattie. The prosecutor didn't know that this morning."

"Don't say 'same old' to a hag. They tell me you sell soap."

It was like being told he masturbated. He got away from it. "You're still tending bar, I heard. Out in Royal Oak."

"Roseville. I married my partner. He's a good man. Dumb as a cork."

"The best kind, I'm told. Hell," he said. "How are you, Hattie?"

"I've got cancer. Three doctors told me it's terminal. Three kings wins the hand."

He said hell again. She smiled and took his hand. Hers was cold, as if it had spread that far. He missed the beestung lips when she smiled. "I should've been repealed with Prohibition anyway," she said. "I'm as ready as I'll ever get. You're the one I'm worried about. I always did, you know. When I found out you went out on the ice with Jack I wanted to go out after you and drag you back."

"I never knew."

"You weren't supposed to. When you threw me over later I went after everything in pants. I wanted to catch a disease and die right then. It's kind of too bad I didn't. I bet it's one way no one else has tried."

"I didn't throw you over. You threw me."

She let go of his hand and slapped it. "You didn't call."

"I tried."

"When it was too late. You don't put off calling a girl to propose marriage. How did you think that made me feel?"

"I thought maybe you were too busy sleeping with Jack to feel anything but Jack. He told me all about lying low at your place so nobody knew he was in town to kill Jerry Buckley."

She got angry then for real. "That's why you didn't call? I was a whore, nitwit. You broke dates to be a newspaperman. I had a career too. Maybe not the most respectable one in town, but I was good at it. It's what I did."

"He paid you?"

"You think I was in love with him?"

"Most women were."

"Yeah, and they'd have been damn disappointed, because he was one rotten lay. He did everything on the gallop, Connie. Everything."

"I'll be damned."

"There's a scoop."

"Hattie, I blew it."

"We both did." After a pause, she smiled again. "You look good, Connie. I had to see you. Not many of the old gang left."

"There's none of them left."

She kissed him. Her lips were cold, but not as cold as her hands. And then she left, her heels echoing off the linoleum and marble.

The bar where he kept his office in Hamtramck was almost empty at that time of day. He held up a palm to Oscar polishing the tables, in greeting and to tell him he wasn't drinking, and started toward the corner booth and his portable Underwood permanently parked there.

"Second, Connie," Oscar said. "Letter came for you."

He waited while the bartender, a thickset twenty-two-year-old with bouncer's biceps, the owner's nephew, stretched across the bar and rummaged on the shelf below. The plate-glass window looked out on part of the Dodge Main plant across Joseph Campau.

"They used to sell it out of their trunks right out there in front," he said. "The big Polacks would come out between shifts and drink it standing up."

"That's what Uncle John says." Oscar extended the envelope. "It's a letter, not a package this time."

He hefted it, glanced at the New York return address, ran his thumb under the flap.

Dear Mr. Minor:

Thank you for the look at your proposal, which I'm returning to you under separate cover.

I have no doubt that your experiences as a reporter would make a compelling book. Unfortunately, the market at present is saturated with Prohibition stories.

I wish you good luck in placing it elsewhere.

Sincerely,
(signed) Burton Weems
Senior Editor

He shook his head. Oscar's bright face clouded. "Sorry, Connie."

"Nothing I'm not used to. On second thought, I'll have a whiskey sour."

In the booth he read the letter again, then crumpled it one-handed and bonged it into the wastebasket beside the table. He took the cartridge out of his pocket, glanced at it, and stood it up on the table beside the typewriter. Then he skimmed the top sheet off the typewritten stack next to the wall and without reading it selected the sharpest of the pencils standing erasers-down in a chipped dusty schooner, licked the tip, and marked an X across the entire page. From another stack he drew a fresh sheet and cranked it into the Underwood. For a moment he sat there, hands hovering over the keys. Then he began typing.

I saw Jack Dance the first time in Hattie Long's place on Vernor the night the bulls tipped it over. . . .